By AUGUST LI

ARCANA IMPERII
Incubus Honeymoon

BLESSED EPOCH
Ash and Echoes
Ice and Embers
Iron and Ether
Cairn and Covenant
Calling and Cull

Published by DSP PUBLICATIONS
www.dsppublications.com

INCUBUS HONEYMOON

AUGUST LI

DSP PUBLICATIONS

Published by

DSP PUBLICATIONS

5032 Capital Circle SW, Suite 2, PMB# 279, Tallahassee, FL 32305-7886 USA
www.dsppublications.com

Trade Paperback ISBN: 978-1-64080-745-7
Digital ISBN: 978-1-64080-744-0
Library of Congress Control Number: 2018934249
Trade Paperback published July 2018
v. 1.0

Printed in the United States of America

This paper meets the requirements of
ANSI/NISO Z39.48-1992 (Permanence of Paper).

For the lovers who know when it's time to fight.

Acknowledgments

My gratitude to Ann Attwood and Rebecca Cohen for hunting down plot holes, polishing up the British dialogue, and encouraging me to stay true to my vision.

While working on this book, I lost one of the best friends I've ever had, Merlin, who was by my side for over eighteen years. Anyone who has ever had a cat knows that the love he gave me when I was less than my best, and in spite of my many flaws, cannot be exaggerated. Though he won't know and it won't bring him back, I'd like to memorialize him here. He's left a void in my life and my heart that will never be filled.

And not to leave out two other fine cats, Charles, the inspiration for Charlene, and Spooky Mulder, a good man if ever there was one.

~Gus

INCUBUS HONEYMOON

AUGUST LI

DSP PUBLICATIONS

CHAPTER ONE

I AM quite literally the stuff dreams are made of.

As swellheaded as that might sound, it's a simple fact—I am everyone's dream come true, no matter who they are and no matter what they dream. It's how I survive: discovering someone's deepest desires and fulfilling them beyond their expectations. It's a process I relish, and one I can say with absolute modesty that I have become damned skilled at over the years. I'm no good at confrontation, and I don't like conflict. Fighting of any kind goes against my nature.

But this hunk of knob-snot was starting to chafe my tenders, and not in a good way.

"I'm sorry, sir, but the shop is closed for the day." The big bald guy in a black T-shirt that stretched almost translucent over his chest graced me with a smile so saccharine it made my teeth wiggle.

He might be bigger, but I wasn't going to let him intimidate me. Probably he knew the deal here, but he had no power of his own beyond those veiny biceps he was so obviously flexing. It had to be a bugger to understand the real power that moved the world but not be able to take part in it. Like a guy who couldn't get laid watching porn. Thinking life fucking owed him something. My judgment might seem harsh, but he was fucking with me for no discernable cause. Besides, I could tell. It was easy to sense what he wanted, but it wasn't anything I could offer.

My powers are impressive, but they fall short of curing someone of being a muppet.

"The shop's always closed," I said. "Because there is no bloody shop. Look, mate. I've been here before. Don't give me a ration of shite."

Hecht's Engine Repair and Machine Shop sits on a run-down corner of North Philly's Strawberry Mansion neighborhood. Sounds pretty, yeah? Fields and fruit and flowers. Beautiful three-story manors—old brick Colonials with white Doric columns—with window boxes and garden paths.

It's not.

Sure, it was at one time, and some of the Victorian mansions near the park still stand, though they probably won't for much longer. Here, farther to the east, the urban decay crept in quicker.

There was a KFC across the street, and the rancid grease mingled with the more appealing smells of a Chinese place a couple blocks over and the persistent stench of garbage. Even in the face-numbing cold, when piss and puke froze as soon as they hit the asphalt, the eggy odor of refuse remained. I was tempted to pull my black wool scarf over my nose.

"Come on, mate." I pushed my shoulders toward my ears so my secondhand peacoat would cover my neck. "It's fucking freezing, and neither one of us wants to stand out here. I just want to go in for a drink."

The man looked at the Pennsylvania Dutch hex symbols screwed into the cinder block wall. "I'm afraid you're mistaken, sir. This is an engine repair shop, and we're closed."

The rows of dusty half-assembled lawnmowers, the couple of dirt bikes, and the shelves of metal parts with their patinas of grease might've convinced the casual shopper. But then, Strawberry Mansion didn't get a lot of casual shoppers. Anybody who did business here did it because they couldn't get anywhere better—or, like me, they had another objective.

"Sorry I couldn't be more helpful. If you'll come back tomorrow, we can discuss your small-engine needs." Even as he said it, a couple of guys in those puffy parkas with the iridescent shells moved past, with no more than a nod from the doorman. One of them pushed a button, and the garage door set in the back wall rattled and screeched its way open. Before it closed again, honey-colored light and a few bars of music spilled into the chilly gray shop.

Even I'm not immune to the cold, and shoving my hands in my pockets wasn't returning much sensation to my numb fingers. I never hung out at mage bars. Too dangerous, too much drama, too many pretentious twats to suffer. But tonight something pulled me in, a scent on the wind that had me salivating, like when someone's having a barbeque in the neighborhood and the smell sets your stomach complaining.

You can't rest until you sink your teeth into a plate of ribs, not after that smell has put the idea in your head. You don't even have to be hungry to start with.

Except this was more a spicy, vegetal smell—red clover and white peppercorns. Now I have a way of finding what I need, a sort of instinct that pulls me in the direction of somebody who might find an association… mutually beneficial. I couldn't say this felt quite the same. Maybe it was more curiosity, a sort of compulsion, but for whatever reason, I couldn't let it go.

Felt like I'd be shortchanging myself if I walked away now.

I turned to the man again, deciding to give it one more try. I knew my limitations, and I've never had much of an attention span. "Look, brother. I just want to sit down someplace warm and have a quiet drink. What's it going to take?"

His brown eyes moved slowly from my face to my scuffed Chuck Taylors and back up, but I couldn't sense even a flicker of what I usually look for in humans in his expression. He was just bored, wishing he was somewhere else, and being a petty tyrant was giving him the only hard-on he was going to get. "I *am* sorry, sir."

"Wanker," I muttered as I turned to leave. In the doorway, I bumped shoulders with a guy heading in. He mumbled an apology even though it was my fault, and when I lifted my head, our eyes met. His were soft, teddy-bear beige with a burst of gold around the irises, like sunflowers. A few strands of auburn hair, glimmering with frost, fell across the left one and over his cold-pinched pink cheek.

"Leaving?" His voice was a crackling fire when you've just come in from the cold, shaking the snow from your hair and grinning because you've just cut down the perfect Christmas tree. Hot cocoa, and not the kind from a packet.

"Seems like," I said. "The fine gentleman tells me the *machine shop* is closed."

He patted me on the arm just above my elbow, and his energy soaked into me. Pumpkin spice. A strong hint of cinnamon. He was the prairie, endless fields of buttery corn growing so fast you could almost see it. But he hid it behind high walls, walls topped with razor wire. He didn't want to share, possibly didn't know how, which meant he held nothing useful to me. Except maybe a ticket inside.

If I could convince him to help me out. Wouldn't be as easy as usual, given he didn't seem to want what I had to offer. Or was he deliberately shutting me out? Could these mages do that?

I shook off my distraction and met his eyes. "I'm not looking for trouble here, mate. I'm a decent bloke what just needs a drink. I can't say what's got this guy's knickers in a twist. Doesn't seem fair."

Something told me this kid might be swayed by a lack of equity, sympathy for an underdog. He had the look of somebody who'd never walk away from a stray puppy. I tried my best puppy dog eyes as I waited to see if I'd read him right.

"It's bloody cold," I pressed.

The young man turned to the doorkeeper. "Really, Maurice?"

The big guy shrugged, grinning like a kid who'd broken his mother's favorite vase but thought he was cute enough to get away with it. "The regulars don't like new faces in here, Em. Makes 'em jumpy."

"Well I'm a regular, and I'm bringing him in as my guest. Do you have a problem with that?"

"No! No, sir. Go right ahead." Maurice hurried to press the button, and I could almost see his dick shrivel. If he'd been a dog, we'd be wading through a puddle of piss that marked his submission. Without wasting another second on the impotent prick, I followed my benefactor through the rusty metal door.

We entered a narrow hall paneled in warm cherry. The young man shook his head. "I don't like bullies. Just don't make me regret this."

I held up my hands in surrender. "Wouldn't dream of it."

He regarded me, looked a little harder this time. "So… incubus?"

"I don't like that term," I told him, stopping before we reached the archway into the bar and trying to get a better sense of him. As always, it was easiest for me to read his… not desires, exactly, but yearnings, wants, and they were beautiful: sharing a handmade quilt in a window seat with an upholstered mat, watching the snow fall… tea: English Breakfast with lemon and lavender… the smell of books… mornings when the woodstove has burned down and it was freezing everywhere except under the blankets so you resisted getting out of bed… pancakes….

Em nodded. "But I'm close enough?"

"I guess." We went inside and took seats at the bar.

When most people imagine a mage bar, it isn't Hecht's—Hex—whatever. No black lights here, no fishnet-clad girls dancing in cages, no patrons milling about in leather corsets and too much eyeliner. No whips and chains—at least not in the main area. If memory served, they had some rooms downstairs….

Behind the bar, an older woman in a Flyers sweatshirt smiled at Em and pulled a Yuengling from the tap.

"Glenlivet," I said when she turned to me.

While she went to pour my drink, I focused on him. Rogue mage—I'd bet my life on it. Despite his homey charm, he had sharp edges, a defiant streak and the ability to back it up. His power crackled between us, leaving an ozone taste on my teeth. Plus he'd done that blocking thing, only letting me see the surface ripples of his wants, and I'd never encountered that. As we watched each other, I unbuttoned my coat and he unbuttoned his.

"But you are one," he said, swirling his hex-marked glass between his hands. "I've read about creatures like you, but I've never met one. Is it true you can sense what I desire?"

I closed my eyes. I had to concentrate to get at it, and I wasn't used to putting in effort for shite. "A house in the country, miles from anyone. Worn fabric… quilts fraying around the edges and hot pads with burn marks…. Cats. A pantry full of meals in mason jars that you can put in the Crock-Pot. To… to be left alone?"

With a slow blink, he took a gulp of his beer and licked the foam from his lips. "I guess it's true."

"There's more." I felt it, hidden away behind his barbed wire fences.

"Don't trespass, incubus."

"I'm not what you think," I told him as our bartender put my scotch down on a napkin.

"Then what? Explain it to me." Em lifted his beer in a mock toast. "Price of admission?"

"Tell me your name first," I asked him.

"Emrys Rathburn."

I hadn't heard of him. I looked down at my hands, but weirdly, they weren't any different than when I'd come in. He had no desires that could affect me. I moved my attention up his homemade-looking striped scarf and to his eyes. They still danced with that cheery glow, but fire was only comforting until you got too close. He arched a brow to remind me he was waiting.

I decided to try, though I'd never been asked to explain my existence before. Who was? "The ancient storytellers had it all wrong. They liked to paint me as some sort of predator, finding a human host and sucking him—or occasionally her—dry.

"Well, I guess they didn't completely miss the point. I like to leave my lovers sucked dry, but not in the way the old bards and minstrels imagined. They claimed I ensnared mortals with my charms and drained their life force. They thought I needed that energy to sustain myself. But what they don't understand is that I feed off fascination. The heat and imagination that sparks to life when a mortal looks at me and imagines the possibilities… that's what keeps me going. And the more creative the fantasies, the more satiated I am."

"So you prefer the kinky stuff?" Emrys asked, leaning a little bit back from me. "The, uh, downstairs kind of thing?"

"That's not what I mean by creative." I sipped my scotch and rubbed my eyes with my thumb and forefinger. It was hard to explain, and his lack of physical desire threw me out of my element. "I mean, the more a human is inspired, the more he gains from our time together, the more energy he produces for me.

"But I give as good as I get. It isn't easy inspiring the kind of dreams that taste like delicacies on my tongue. Those I touch usually lead brilliant lives of prolific creation."

"Right." Emrys looked bored. "So how do you benefit, exactly?"

"In exchange, I get to bask in the adoration. That energy… damn. It's hard to describe if you've never felt it. Champagne bubbles in your nose and a bump of coke… but better. Fireworks. The sky exploding in color."

"Hmm."

"Hasn't anyone ever looked at you like you're the whole universe?" I asked him. "Like just your touch would be enough for them to die happy? Wanted you so much you could feel it rolling off them like heat?"

"Sorry, but that sounds ridiculous. And like much more trouble than it would be worth." He picked up his beer and carefully wiped the condensation from the outside of the glass with his napkin. Then he stood. "It was nice to meet you, but I should be going. I need to meet someone."

"All right, then." What else could I say? Contrary to the mythology, I'm not in the habit of inflicting my presence where it's not wanted; I don't have to. I watched him weave through the sparse crowd, toward the pool tables and jukebox at the back of the building, and I felt sad for Emrys, and not at all because he didn't want sex. Some people don't. But twenty-whatever and incapable of being fascinated? That was bollocks. Still, I sensed he wasn't for me. I've been around a long time, and I can tell. But it didn't stop me from hoping something would happen for him, something that would envelop him so totally that he forgot his own name, forgot he even existed outside the awe of it. Just so he could know how it tasted.

Then I caught that grass-cayenne-lily scent again, and I stood to follow it.

Chapter Two

Hex was like a warren. Unsurprisingly given the age of the building, the rooms were kept small so they were easier to heat. Cozy, private, and mismatched. I wandered down the narrow hall, pushing past a few patrons who leaned against the crumbling plaster and brick walls. To my left, salvaged tables and chairs filled some small rooms, empty cups and napkins littering the scuffed wooden floor the only indication they'd held patrons earlier in the evening. I finished my drink and left my glass on a shelf beneath a calendar, something with Romanian priests. It hung from a single thumbtack.

Finally I reached the open area at the back of the building, where half a dozen round tables surrounded the jukebox and a pair of pool tables. Some absolute bastard had queued up a string of Justin Bieber and Taylor Swift songs, and I winced. I thought the goddamn sadists hung out below. Manufactured crap with about as much substance as cheese dip in a fucking jar. I would've kicked the machine, but it was one of those digital jobs, and it wouldn't have done shite.

As I shook my head, the music stopped and blocky letters proclaimed "Unable to Complete Request." I looked over my shoulder at a pretty Asian in a black sweatshirt, a few streaks of cobalt in their hair. "Thanks."

They nodded. They were striking—a gummy candy shark with a meaty sweetness beneath the sour, citric crust—studded with sugar crystals like goddamned diamonds. I wondered why they were sitting alone, twirling the stem of a wine flute between their thumb and finger. "You got it, man," they said, winking an eye lined sparkly blue. "I can't stand that crap."

They pulled a device—maybe it was a phone? Who the hell knew with tech-mages?—from a pocket, and I was forgotten. I touched the pillowy squares on the screen in front of me to pick out some songs: David Bowie, Queen, the Eagles, Blondie, Darude…. "Sandstorm" was one of my guilty pleasures—one of many.

"Starman" played as I looked around. Apart from the tech-mage, who was engrossed in their phone or whatever, I was alone. I looked apprehensively at the narrow door off to the right. The newly-mown-lawn-drizzled-in-Tabasco scent was coming from the stairs beyond it, so I went down.

Underneath, it was darker and more open, the low ceiling supported by thick concrete pillars. There was a second bar here, a U-shaped beacon in the darkness thanks to blinking red Christmas lights strung beneath the counter, and I ordered another drink to bolster my courage. Fuzzy spray-painted glyphs adorned the walls—magic to hide what happened down here from the eyes and ears of others. I shivered at the twisted desires assailing me from the few people milling about. It tasted salty and sick—like what you puked up after too much tequila and too many chimichangas, but without the innocent fun that implies. Here I felt the desire for pain, the longing to see others degraded, broken. Abusing fellow mages and magical beings was a pastime of a certain set of the community, one I'd heard about but never seen up close… or felt. I wanted to run.

I had to be careful around things like that.

As I stood near the bar, cradling my scotch like a flame that would keep me from freezing in this desolation, a group—two men and a woman—moved past me dragging a seraphim by the collar around its neck. It was naked but for a gauzy loincloth, and it looked at me with pleading silver eyes… and I had to turn away. I tasted blood and agony in that glance, coppery, rotten… but I could do fuck all to help. Sure, I could sense what it longed for—freedom, clouds, and to not be hurt anymore—but I had no way of fulfilling its wishes. As far as what the human mages considered magical beings, I was low on the totem pole. My skills were specific, and they could inspire amazing things, but they were no good in a fight, and right now, that sucked a whole hill of dirty arse. I downed the rest of my drink, but it couldn't stopper the shit feeling spewing up like a clogged loo.

Fucking mage bars. This was why I couldn't stand them.

One of the reasons, anyway.

I stood and walked beneath another arch into a wide-open space, cold, loam-smelling, the walls crumbling stone, the floor dirt. In the center, two men were battling with creatures summoned from mystical planes. A shimmering blue narwhal drove its horn toward a fiery fox, which leapt out of the way just in time, a puff of piney smoke in its wake. Great. Real-life fucking Pokémon matches. Mages or not, people are pretty much the same. Most of them revel in fantasy and distraction.

But there…. There in the corner, sitting on the edge of a folding plastic chair, the blue and orange warring across the planes of his face…. There he fucking was.

I didn't even have words. I mean, I'd heard about the fey, about their beauty, but… I couldn't describe it. He was a ray of sunlight penetrating this hellhole, a shaft of brilliance tearing through the clouds to light on a single perfect blossom. The kind of shit that makes you question your whole damn existence, your place in the cosmos, existentially fucking you silly.

All I could think was how glad I was to be alive in this moment.

I tasted rain and honeysuckle and ginger, and I wanted to cry. How could these mages, volleying their creations of water and flame, not feel what was in their presence? Must've been some kind of a spell, a ward or a glamour. Best I could guess was I could see him—really see—because I was closer to what he was than the humans around us. He was a waterfall of sparkles, so bright I had to squint as I sat down across from him, straddling the cheap plastic chair and resting my elbows on the back. I didn't know what to say, and I gaped. My mouth was probably open, and I might have been drooling. But….

"No one has seen one of your people in a thousand years. What are you doing here?" Here, in this basement reeking of mold, where the elite practitioners of magic demonstrated their strength by raping angelic beings. "Why now?"

"You think I have chosen this?" His corn-silk hair, almost white, spilled in waves over his shoulders. His skin was like marble, marred by no pores, but tinged slightly blue, especially around his eyes. It looked like makeup, intentional. Maybe it was. He crossed his arms over his chest and looked around with opalescent eyes that changed hue depending on the light. "The humans don't smell any better than they used to."

For all his bluster, he was scared. I could taste it, like bile on ice. I saw it in the way he wrapped his long fingers around his shoulders, his crossed arms protecting his heart.

Mostly I could feel it: his wish to be away from this place, his longing for open spaces and the meadow-scent of plants.

"Go home, then," I said. "Back to your merry green fields and softly swelling hills."

"I would, but I have been summoned. Invoked. I find the ways back closed to me, demon."

"I am not a demon," I said. "At least no more than you. If you want to judge us by human standards, we're both dangerous creatures. Both of us possess powers they cannot control… though mine are usually seen as innocuous. It's why I'm safe in a place like this. I don't have much the mages can use. But you… you…. You're a fey?"

"Have you really never seen one of my people before?" Instead of looking at me, his eyes followed the streams of light zipping back and forth.

"Are you kidding?" I was getting nervous, and I looked around to make sure we hadn't drawn any attention. He was a hundred-dollar bill dropped on the ground, and I wanted to snatch him up before someone else noticed. Don't ask me why. Maybe just out of selfishness. "We should talk. In fact, we should really get out of here."

"Why?"

I couldn't sense much of his desires; usually desires are the first thing I notice about a person, whether it's an aching to be chained to a bed and tickled with a feather duster or just a craving for a late-night taco. The void was unnerving and eerie, like looking at a person with no facial features, blank where there'd always been something before. Still, his pride and defiance showed in the lift of his pointed chin. Telling him he was in danger wouldn't work. I wished I'd listened more when mages talked about dealing with fey. There were a thousand and one rules that no one really knew or agreed on—kind of like that lame joke about the book on understanding women. Not that I'd ever had a problem in that department….

He was staring at me now, his face a perfect equilateral triangle from the points of his long ears to the sharp end of his chin. I hadn't noticed the ears before. Was I the only one who could see through his glamour? Fuck, I hoped so.

Still, it seemed to be wearing thin.

"Why do you wish for me to accompany you?" He drummed his long, sharp nails on the sticky table carved with insults. "Can you provide some distraction better than this one?"

"I'd be willing to try?" Was that what he wanted, a spectacle? Something resembling the decadent faerie balls I'd heard about? Well, I could take him to a club… but I didn't want to. There were a lot of mages in Philadelphia; it was easier for them to hide out here than in nearby New York, especially in neighborhoods like this, the ones the chamber of commerce liked to pretend didn't exist. The mages liked places like that, forgotten and ignored places, because people here knew how to mind their fucking business, so the mages didn't have to be as careful. If they realized he was here, in the city, he wouldn't be safe anywhere. They'd chase his skinny alabaster arse all the way to Mexico if he tried to run. And why did I care? It wasn't my nature to be a protector. I was a selfish creature, and a lazy, opportunistic one. I'd come to terms with it long ago. It had never bothered me before, but then I'd felt out of sorts since I decided to come in here. I wanted to leave, go someplace with way fewer fucking mages. None at all would probably be safest. "I'd just really appreciate it if we could go somewhere else."

"So you desire my company? Well, a favor for a favor, then, perhaps."

I was tiptoeing toward a minefield. "What favor?"

"I come with you, and you help me find whatever mortal charlatan pulled me into this…." He looked around the dingy basement and shook his head. "Ugh."

"And force them to release you, I assume?"

"Oh no," he said, low and dangerous and hungry. "No, I'll take care of that on my own."

"Still a little one-sided, don't you think?"

He lifted one shoulder, and it jangled an earring I hadn't noticed—little cloisonné leaves hanging from chains. "Then I suppose I'll have to amuse myself."

This wasn't fun. It wasn't flirting. Flirting was an amuse-bouche; even when it was tangy, it made me curious to sample the next thing. Even when it straight up tasted like shit, I wondered if I could change the flavor. This was a cup of poison, and I was about ready to say fuck it and go on my way—I'd come looking to feed, after all, hoping to satisfy my curiosity, and I'd done that—but just then I noticed a silhouette, backlit from the lights of the bar, coming our way. I recognized her, or rather, I recognized that aching yearning to see someone broken and begging, to have their pain or salvation in her hands. It was the woman who'd been tormenting the seraphim.

I almost panicked. I didn't know if this fey motherfucker could fight, and that evil bitch was a mage. Probably powerful too—a seraphim was no cheap plastic trinket. How would we get past her? Fucking hell. I avoided people with her kind of desires for a reason: I didn't want to fulfill them, and I didn't want to reach the point where I wanted to want to.

Pancakes and tea…. A book you could read six times and still notice things you'd missed…. Heirloom tomatoes….

Motorcycles with neon lights, a computer virus that would erase all student loan debt, and a blonde in a red dress with big tits, tattoos, and a nine-inch cock…. For a fucking Square Enix game to come out on time, for once…. Two blondes….

Emrys and the tech-mage. They intercepted the woman, and Emrys put his hand on her shoulder, gently guiding her behind one of the concrete pillars and away from us. The tech-mage shone some kind of bluish light on whatever Emrys took from his pocket—whatever it was, the woman wanted it. I could feel her hunger.

"Now," I said to the fey. "We have to go now."

"Then you agree to my bargain?"

"Fine. Whatever."

"Ah, good. Then let's just seal our agreement." He stood and placed a long-fingered hand on my belly.

I felt like something crawled up my spine on the inside and bumped against the base of my skull. For a second everything blurred into a smear. "What did you take?"

"Don't worry. I'll give it back when our arrangement is concluded."

I tried to push it to the back of my mind as I grabbed his elbow and tugged him toward the steps, hopefully before the woman's attention wandered back our way.

CHAPTER THREE

HE CHOSE the chicken place over the Chinese. I should've argued, but I didn't. We sat in a booth by the window, a bucket of Original Recipe and an assortment of sides between us. I ate. There was nothing else to do, and I was hungry. Plus, fuck it. This shit was good. Cheap and filthy. I could appreciate that now and again.

He crossed his arms over his chest and looked around. The restaurant was empty except for a couple of teenagers in the back and an old guy cradling his small coffee like it was the Holy Grail.

"So this is where you wished to bring me? Am I supposed to be impressed?"

I washed a bite of mac and cheese down with a swig of Dr Pepper and glanced at my reflection in the dirty plexiglass. With no one's desires to shape me, I was nondescript: fairly handsome, average face, short hair. Forgettable. I didn't like that. Of course, overlaid on that image was the real me, and I liked that appearance—though it would make every mortal in this place soak their trousers. But I found no one to draw on, except maybe the pimply kid behind the register, and I didn't really want to be a cigarette or Bugs Bunny in Viking drag. I wondered what my companion saw. Could he perceive the pale skin, the pink eyes, and the long silver hair? The horns? Humans who could see me as I really was were one in a hundred million. After all, that only happened when their greatest desire was the truth.

And most mortals ran from the truth like it was a big angry bastard with a flamethrower and a hard-on.

"You're supposed to be safe." Manners dictated I look at him before taking the last biscuit, but he wasn't interested in the food. Hadn't touched it.

"Aren't you gallant. I'm to assume I'm safer here than at the other human tavern? Why?"

I muffled a belch with my sleeve. "You ask a lot of questions. Eat some coleslaw and let me think."

"I fear if I did that we would be here for a decade's worth of mortal time."

"Ha-fucking-ha, arsehole."

The fey swept his perfect hair off his shoulder. "You're vulgar."

I knew it was true. The only filter I ever had was that lent to me by the whims of others. If someone wanted prim and proper, I could be a fucking vicar. But without that shaping influence, I tended towards straightforward. Blunt. Besides....

"And your people are paragons of virtue?"

He blinked twice. Even his eyelashes were white. They were enchanting, like fine lace. "I don't have to explain my people to you. You're my servant now."

"Is that what you want?" I asked him. "Someone obedient? Docile?" The shapers of the world, those with true power, tended to prefer equals, a challenge, but I could do submissive. Some direction would be nice. It could already feel the lack of it affecting me, pulling my thoughts all over the place, making me more distractible than usual.

"You can't tell?"

I used my pinky to push the dark chicken bones on my paper plate. "No. Not with you. It's not a comfortable sensation for me. I feel a bit out of my element."

He stared at me awhile before he spoke. "Why were you so adamant about leaving that human gathering?"

"You don't know? No, you wouldn't. When was the last time you were here?" I waved my hand to indicate the mortal world.

He gave me a pitying look, his eyes wide and his little rosebud mouth puckered. I liked his lips—pale pink at the center but lined in that muted blue. "Time passes differently in this realm than it does in my own."

"Do you remember Rome?"

"Rome." His changeable eyes glazed as he looked out the grease-streaked window. "The dancing. They threw such lovely little soirees. And the noblewomen snuck out to the forests to court our favor." The fey wiggled his long, pale fingers in front of his face. "Burned dead animals and such."

"Well, that's been about two thousand years. Most of the mages now agree that something happened around that time, some kind of schism. Human magic users went underground. Your kind started to disappear. You know anything about that?"

"What is there to know?" He looked around pointedly. "Very little has changed. The mortals still huddle in their crumbling abodes, eating spoilt carcasses. Burning things that smell bad to stave off the cold. It's distressingly dull."

"Actually, a great many things have changed." I took a sip of my drink. "I've been around, and I've watched it happen. I'll give you a brief summary, if you want."

"What else have I got to amuse myself with?"

"I'd hate to bore you."

"Then don't," he said.

I don't get irritated easily. It's my nature to sense people's quirks and avoid what they dislike, but this arrogant son of a bitch…. And the second one in as many hours.

Tonight was not shaping up to be my night. Seemed like everyone was determined to be as much fun as a tick latched on to my bollocks.

I took a breath, closed my eyes for a few seconds. "Okay. Octavian declared himself Caesar, called himself Augustus. Lots of things happened as a result, but the ones that are important to me and you are these: the magic users started to retreat. They bowed out of government, sort of snuck off the scene. No more priestesses and augurs advising emperors, no wizards on the battlefield. Then Christianity took root—it was this little cult out of a Roman province, but it gathered a lot of power. Its followers weren't big fans of those who had dominance over nature, and things only went in the shitter with time. The nymphs disappeared from the oceans; the dryads abandoned their springs. As the years passed, things got worse and worse for the humans. Many only lived two or three decades before they died.

"But in the meantime, the magic users broke off into sects. They bided their time, and by staying hidden, many of them survived some very bad stretches, times when they would've been killed if they'd practiced openly. Some of them only wanted to preserve knowledge, but others gathered some real power, and they used it to influence things from behind the scenes. Some of them are still doing just that, unbeknownst to the population at large."

He blew a puff of air out his aquiline nose, his nostrils flaring. "Mortal politics. Dull and ridiculous as it gets. I've never understood why they expend so much effort to garner influence when they'll be dead before they get a chance to enjoy the fruits of their labors. So they're still at it? Poking each other with pointy sticks over petty disagreements?"

Nice attitude. "You see, weaponry has changed a bit since you were here last. But the interesting thing is the timing. Most of the guilds think we're due for some sort of an upset—it's been two thousand years since the last big wave hit the magical world, and a lot of them seem to think that's some special number. They cite prophecies, things like that. Apparently they've found a lot of clues hidden in poetry and art."

"What do they think is going to happen?" He tilted his head to one side and his eyes glittered in an unnerving way. Almost like he gave a damn.

I dragged my plastic fork through my mashed potatoes, carving furrows through congealing brown gravy. "They don't know, or they disagree. I never paid it a lot of mind. It's weird, though."

"What is?"

"You're here, and that could mean something. See, your kind are so legendary, so coveted…. The mages have been trying to summon faeries for… I don't know, since back when the magic first broke, or whatever it did. None of them have been able to accomplish it. I understand it was easy once."

He bared his teeth a little between his pale lips; his canines were long and sharp. "It was never *easy*, demon. We are not servants to be ordered around, and we go where we like, when we like. It is true that occasionally we might be tempted by the company of a mortal who was especially beautiful or talented or interesting."

"But you weren't tempted this time, were you? You were forced here." I couldn't resist taking the shot at his ego, giving his rosy little tit a subtle twist. "And I understand it's happened before."

He turned toward the window with his long nose in the air.

"Something must've changed," I pressed. "The guilds have been watching for it. Waiting for a sign that the—the whatever—is beginning."

"What is this foolishness to do with me? What do I care what the humans think or do?"

"I thought you wanted to find the person who summoned you."

At that, he smiled madly and ran his tongue along the edge of his sharp upper teeth.

"Oh, I do want to find them. I'm going to curse them." The way he said it, he might've been describing his weekend plans to drive down to the beach and spend a couple days sipping daiquiris. "I haven't decided how yet, though. Maybe I'll make them dream of their worst moment every night while they sleep. Or make them see how all their loved ones are going to die. Make all their food taste like curdled milk. What do you think?"

"I kind of think you suck," I muttered. "I don't understand taking pleasure in watching people suffer."

He curled his fingers in front of his chin and examined his long pearly nails. "It's not a matter of pleasure; it is satisfaction for a slight against me. So, tell me of these human guilds. Likely one of them is responsible for this irritation."

"I don't think so. I don't know if you understand what a prize you'd be. If a guild mage managed to drag you here, he or she'd snap you up. I can't convey to you the influence one of them would gain by accomplishing it. But there was no one waiting, was there? Where did you first… appear?"

He fluttered his fingers. "Some filthy corridor not far from here. I sensed magic nearby, and I followed it to that ghastly little tavern, thinking to make short work of the one who dared to interfere with me. But they were not present."

Around two hundred years ago, back in Leeds, I'd seen a group of mages try to call a faerie servant. Dozens of them got together, all pooling their magic. They'd consulted the stars and planets to choose the optimal time to perform the ritual, and they'd prepared for weeks. The rite went on for days, full of chanting and drawing mystical symbols. Sacrifices. At the end of it, a little fissure of lavender light crackled at the center of their circle, but it disappeared almost as soon as it formed, and the group still counted their efforts a great success. No way somebody summoned this fucker and just missed him. "There wasn't anyone about?"

"No one of any significance," he said.

I bristled a little; all humans had significance. All humans were fascinating, their experiences and desires so unique and varied, not one the same as another. To me they were diamonds with wonderful facets and full of brilliant light. But I'd already seen the futility of arguing with him. And as I have already explained, I'm just too fucking lazy.

"Why were you so adamant on us leaving that other establishment?" he asked again. "You haven't answered to my satisfaction."

"Don't you see? It's dangerous for you. Any mage that gets the chance—any one of them—will bind you, and you'll be a slave."

He snorted. "Please. You honestly think that's within their ability?"

"You don't get it, do you? You're here, and you can't get back. You don't know anything about this world. Some of these people are very powerful, and some of them are not nice. Did you know there's a guild of mages who specialize in flesh manipulation? The things they can do to a body would give even you nightmares. And they're killers for hire; even the Sekhet-Aaru are terrified of them."

"What is the Sekhet-Aaru? The word sounds familiar. Egyptian?"

"They like to pretend so, but I think their ties are loose at best. Egypt was already a corpse picked over by the Romans before their guild formed. If anyone has any knowledge of that magic, it'll be the Antiquarians, and they don't like to share. But Sekhet-Aaru has power. They control many important corporations, and they have a lot of influence over international politics. I've heard they manufacture wars when they're worried the general public might be getting too complacent, when they might have the leisure to start noticing them."

"Then these people, the best and strongest amongst them, are surely the ones who called me here!"

"Fuck me, I hope not."

Arching a shimmery white brow, he said, "Scared, demon?"

"Fuck yes," I said, "and if you're not, you've got your head up your arse."

"Delightful."

Just then, the group of young guys in the back of the restaurant got up to leave. As they passed by our table one of them focused on me. I felt myself melding into what he wanted: a muscular man with dark skin, a little older. A mentor, someone to show him the ropes. A conspirator, someone to share secret passions. He wanted to explore, to run his hands over firm planes and discover hidden gardens of dark hair. His desires were strong—masculine aromas, the taste of sweat, sweet but vulgar pleas grunted out…. In the window, I saw the me he wanted: square jaw dusted with stubble, tendons in the neck prominent, close-cropped curly hair…. He would be inebriated, spilling fascinated energy I could feed off for weeks before it even began to fade into the expected….

"Ugh. Close your mouth before you begin drooling, incubus." The faerie's voice snapped my attention away from the young man, and he followed his friends out into the chilly night. "I'm afraid you're going to have to wait to indulge your baser proclivities. You need to accomplish the task you've been enlisted for first." He stood and smoothed the lapels of his snug gray-green blazer.

I curled my fists. I could still taste the sizzling energy that young man would've radiated as I fulfilled his deepest desires. Now I'd lost him, and I snapped at the faerie. "There's nothing base about what I do, and besides, you don't even have an idea where to start looking for the boring mortal who has enough power to ensnare you."

I could almost hear his teeth grinding. "Well, they are obviously not in here."

He turned on his heel and strutted out the door, and I followed, off to try to find a fucking needle in a whole city full of fucking needles.

Chapter Four

My demon servant muttered under his breath as we traversed the snowy walkways of the decrepit human settlement. What an annoying creature; I should have chosen someone better to assist me, but now I'd saddled myself with this dour being whose only motivation involved inserting his member into some mortal and imagining it was a profound act. If he needed to sate himself, I couldn't understand why he didn't just pick someone and get it over with. As if there was any difference between them. As if one hole in a piece of meat was superior to another.

He mumbled curses and threw me nasty looks over his shoulder as he led me along. The buildings around us blended into each other, as uniform and unremarkable as the humans inhabiting them. "Do you have a destination in mind, or is this merely a leisurely stroll?"

"Look—What's your name, anyway?"

I stopped in the courtyard of a large shop, an apothecary, I would guess, now closed for the evening. Its name seemed to be Drive-Thru Pharmacy. My name, obviously, was much more significant, and it would take a far cleverer ruse to trick me into revealing it. "Wouldn't you like to know."

His breath froze around him as he sighed and shoved his hands into the pockets of his tatty coat. "There's no reason for you to be such a twat. We're stuck together for at least a while, and I need something to call you. Just tell me what, yeah?"

Watching his frustration amused me slightly. "No."

"Fine then, fucker. It's Blossom. I'm calling you Blossom."

I expect he thought his choice would displease me, but it hardly mattered. Soon both he and this hideous place would be a distant memory. "Very well, then. I shall call you Inky."

"I hate that goddamn— No, forget it. Let's just get this done."

"A sound plan." I nodded. We had been walking for a little while, and in the distance to the south, I could see some imposing structures, tall and seemingly made of crystal or glass. Though they appeared very far away, I felt sure if anyone had the gall and talent to call me to this world, it must've been one of the powerful sorcerers the demon mentioned. And they likely made their homes in those grand buildings. I pointed. "Let us go that way."

He stopped and swore in the ancient mortal tongue the Romans spoke. Latin is good for cursing—it can be quite vulgar—and his use was creative. After a few moments of ranting, he exhaled loudly and curled his shoulders forward. "You're out of your mind. We can't walk all the way to Center City."

"Why not?" I answered him in Latin; it was as good a language as any the humans used, and I doubted he would understand the subtle beauty of mine. "I find it highly unlikely that you have anywhere more pressing to be."

"You are such a prick." He switched back to the language of the locals, some variant of Germanic, I thought. "You don't know anything about this world! It'd take hours to walk all that way, and it's fucking freezing, and it's bloody dangerous! And not just because of the mages who are almost certainly looking for you!"

"You speak as though you have a better destination in mind. Please, don't keep me in suspense."

"Do you, like, sense something?" he asked. "Like a tug toward the one who summoned you?"

I had little to lose, so I listened. The few stunted trees here were silent, sleeping out the winter, dreaming in drawn-out, melancholy notes of remembered springs. The wind was cruelly playful, offering staccato whispers of nipping flesh red and hardening the short grass to tiny daggers. To the west, I sensed a large green area, and beyond it, a river, the water sluggish and dirty, sad and resigned to the loss of its former splendor. To the east, close, was poetry—human music and words that were almost a spell, an unusual, Orphean magic, that of the best mortal storytellers. It could be dangerous—in the most skilled hands, it could enthrall even my kind—but I sensed nothing else, and so I began walking in that direction, down a broad lane labeled Diamond, an irony if ever there was one. The demon hurried to follow me.

We'd only proceeded a short distance when he began complaining, muttering about the cold through clacking teeth. His big body spasmed and shook, and when it started to vex me, I requested a small favor of the wind. It complied happily, glad to see one of my people, and did not ask for anything in return aside from the pleasure of raking its chilled fingers through my hair. The temperate air encircling the demon thankfully silenced his complaints, and he even grunted out a few words of gratitude.

I waved my hand. "I did it only to spare myself from being subjected to your mewling."

"Arsehole," he said, but he lowered the shoulders he'd bunched around his ears.

Before long we reached some sort of a complex comprised of large square buildings, mostly redbrick and glass. They sat on broad lawns, and wide, tiled walkways wound between them. "This place is almost pleasant." I stopped and looked over my shoulder at Inky. "What is it?"

"A school. Temple University. We're near the Tyler School of Art." He opened his mouth and tasted the air like a serpent. "There are so many desires here, so much *want*...."

"You can fornicate later," I told him, "after we've found the one who summoned me. Do they teach magic at this school?"

My question seemed to surprise him, and he stopped walking. "What? Hell no. There aren't schools that teach magic. It's only done in secret. But there could be mages here.... Unless you get in with Sekhet-Aaru or maybe the ESM, magic doesn't exactly pay anything. Most rogue mages need day jobs. Still, I doubt one of them could have the skill to pull you over. But then nothing about this clusterfuck makes much sense to me."

"You are ever so helpful." I turned away from him. If he hadn't been mildly entertaining, I'd have dismissed him as more trouble than he was worth. But it seemed the brunt of finding this human conjurer would fall to me. I followed the anemic veins of magic. It was like trying to track a filament through thick brambles, but eventually we reached a hall, and light came from within. From the window, I saw a group of young people gathered inside, holding sheaves of paper and standing in a lopsided ring. I stood listening as they seemed to rehearse some kind of performance. The acting was lackluster, barely mediocre, but the words held power that I hadn't yet felt in this realm.

A gangly boy with greasy yellow hair and an overbite read from his script. "I'll rhyme you so eight years together, dinners and suppers and sleeping hours excepted. It is the right butter-women's rank to market."

The girl who responded had a faint glow to her and she was nice to look at, with round hips and a glorious mane of curls standing out from her face like rays of light. I thought she might make a nice addition to one of my estates, where she could wear a dress made of buttercup petals and dance for me. "Out, fool."

As the boy fumbled to find his place, flipping pages, I felt Inky's warmth at my back. "This is delightful," I told him.

"It's just an old play. We should leave. We're not getting anywhere here."

"No. I want to keep watching." Ignoring his protests, I turned my attention back to the group as the boy recited his next lines.

"For a taste: If a hart do lack a hind, let him seek out Rosalind. If the cat will after kind, so, be sure, will Rosalind."

I laughed. "Clever."

"It's all about sex, you know," Inky said. "He's comparing Rosalind to an animal looking to mate."

"Oh hush. I want to hear more of this."

"We're getting real fucking far finding the person who summoned you here."

"Just be quiet, demon." I rubbed the glass to clear away some of the rime and watched the boy, waiting for him to continue. His mouth hung open, and if I didn't know better, I'd say he was staring right at me. But that was impossible; he wouldn't see me unless I wanted him to. Cut off from my lands and hampered by the summoning, my powers weren't as strong, but I could certainly manage to shield myself from the gaze of these clueless mortals. And this young actor had neither the beauty nor the talent to entice me to show myself.

"If the cat will after kind… the cat.…" He stammered and raked his sweaty fringe off his face. "The cat will… the cat. Cat. Cat, cat, cat. The cat will after…. Rosalind…. Cat."

A redheaded girl stepped forward and smacked the lad on the shoulder. "What the hell, Dave? It's written right there!" She gestured angrily toward the pages clutched in his shaking hand. "Can't you read what's right in front of you?"

I bit my lip in anticipation, hoping they would fight. If that happened, I predicted the girl would emerge victorious.

He scratched at his limp hair. "I feel…. The cat will after…. Rosalind…. The cat. Cat. I… I feel kind of sick."

"Fuck, Dave," said the redhead. "You begged for this fucking role. Put a little effort into it."

A dark-skinned young man came to stand between them. "Look, it's late, and all of us are tired. Let's meet back up tomorrow after class."

The girl shook her head but eventually acquiesced. The people in the room gathered their packs and filled them with their possessions before shutting off the lights and filing out. I pressed my hand to the window. "I wanted to hear the rest of the story. We should follow them and persuade them to continue. You know the mortals of this time. What will serve us better: bribery or threats? Maybe a small enchantment to make them want to continue. It might do wonders for their performances. I wonder if we could find a suitable arena to stage the show, somewhere comfortable to sit."

"Easily distracted much?" Inky asked. "Liked it, did you?"

"It was tolerable," I told him, and he seemed to soften at my words. He even smiled as he gripped my elbow to lead me away.

"There's a lot to like about this world if you give it a chance, Blossom. That was Shakespeare. He wrote plays. There's actually one all about faeries."

"Indeed? What does he have to say about us?"

The demon smiled, flashing sharp teeth. "Mostly that you're a bunch of arrogant, self-absorbed twats who use people to get what you want. It's almost like he's met you."

"You should leave the witty poesy to him," I said. "I would like to attend one of these performances… that performance."

"You can do whatever the fuck you like once you cut me loose, mate. Besides, what's got you so interested?"

Something about the words echoed through me. "If the cat will after kind…."

"It's about sex."

"Likely you think everything is about sex, demon. I sense there's something more here."

Inky huffed. "Oh, and why does a cat seek out another cat, genius? For intellectual conversation?"

"There was a thread of magic. I felt it."

"Well, you wouldn't be the first to say that about Shakespeare. So… maybe the mortals aren't so boring and insignificant after all."

I looked around. Behind the rows of little square windows waited little dull lives. All essentially the same, only one in a million with anything novel to offer. "They're specks of dust floating on the air. Occasionally one catches the sunlight. That's all."

He shook his head. "They're more like grains of sand on a beach. And if you look closely at a grain of sand under a microscope, every one of them is unique, a jewel. You can spend an eternity on their facets if you're willing to look."

I pulled away from his grasp. "Well I'm not willing. I don't want to. You can scratch around in the soil to your heart's content when I am gone, looking for gems in the mire. I only want one—that one grain of sand that can get me out of this place. It'll probably be as easy to find as that makes it sound, so if you have anything useful to offer, please don't hold back."

"I thought you could sense magic," he shot back.

I had thought so too. I had been sure I'd felt a spell working, the tiny threads of enchantment coming together to form… something… but: "All I sense here is mediocre acting. It's pitiful, really. I'm glad I didn't compel them to finish their show. It would have surely been a disappointment."

I started walking, eager to be out from beneath the suffocating shadows thrown by the humans' massive structures, eager for open sky, for air free of the choking odor of some kind of burnt chemicals, eager to be among things familiar to me, in a place where I had agency. There was nothing more disagreeable to me than the tightening of that unseen manacle. I had never thought to feel it again, and I wanted to make someone hurt for reminding me it had ever happened at all. Inky followed me, big feet and heavy boots carving troughs through the dirty snow, a petulant scowl on his face.

Curiosity finally got the best of me. "What is wrong now?"

Inky stopped when I turned to face him. He jammed his hands into his pockets and tilted his face toward the jaundiced stars fighting to burn through the fetid haze hanging over the human city. When he spoke, his breath came out in puffy clouds, tinted a sickly ochre by the streetlamps. "Their desires were so, so pure. Distilled, almost. Like an expensive vodka. All the nastiness filtered out. You could drink and drink, get so pissed and happy you'd fall on your face, and never even have a sore head the next day."

His pinkish eyes were glazed, and he stared off like a mortal hearing faerie music. I huffed out a sigh and hoped his fugue wouldn't last. As much as I hated to admit it, this world was strange to me, and I would accomplish my goal faster with him than without. I waited while he continued.

"The boy. The boy playing the part of the clown. His yearning lay over top of everything, like a thin handkerchief. It covered everything he did. There was a girl when he was at school, maybe in the tenth grade—Jennifer. It hurt that she was kind to him, felt like pity. He wants to make a name for himself, be someone, all so she'll see him as worthwhile. He doesn't even want to sleep with her; he just wants to see it in her eyes: the recognition. All the work he's doing, all the nights without sleep, are so that she'll look at him and see a valuable person. He wants her to be proud to say she is his friend."

That sounded pathetic, incomprehensible. How sad it must be for the mortals, who couldn't just take those who interested them and keep them in one of their castles to look at whenever they liked. "And so what? You'll fuck him and make him all better?"

"No. I can't help him. Can't fulfill that desire. Doesn't mean I don't feel it, appreciate the beauty of it."

"How's that?" I asked.

"I don't know if I can explain it to you, Blossom. It's kind of like walking past a restaurant, smelling food you can't eat. You still imagine how it might taste."

"Well that's stupid." I turned the corner and walked toward a row of shorter, squatter buildings with a few skeletal trees between them. "I can eat what I want, though I certainly don't dwell on the flavor. There's always the next thing to sample, even if after a while there's nothing new."

"That's true," Inky said. "But some of them are so good you don't ever forget. If I had time, I could be that for that boy… the person who looked at him like he was the sun and stars… special. In time, I could've made him believe it, made him believe in himself. And he would have adored me for it."

His talk was making me feel practically ill with ennui, and I sped up, moving toward a little tickle I sensed at the base of my body. "Well, when you have repaid your obligation to me, you can go back and fuck him until he's seeing stars."

"It's not the sex. Not completely."

I didn't care, didn't care how his kind justified whatever they did with, and took from, the mortals. I only wanted to be somewhere I didn't feel vulnerable. I found it a profoundly irritating sensation, one that obnoxiously demanded I focus on it. I wouldn't tell the demon so, but this felt very different from the last time I'd been across the veil. I quickened my pace toward the vibrations I felt, and after several moments of my silence, Inky seemed to get the point.

It must've been too cold for the mortals, because we encountered few of them on the street. The taste of magic—a metallic tang at the back of my throat—increased as we moved east along another street deceptively called Emerald. I wondered if the human lanes named Excrement and Sewer shined with jewels in this world. Finally I noticed a solitary figure standing on a corner, and the arcane power swirled around him like hundreds of tiny comets with prismatic tails.

An unexpected turn of events, but whether for good or ill, I could not yet be sure.

CHAPTER FIVE

THE GUY was Greek, if I had to guess. He looked like he'd just crawled out of bed wearing an Eagles hoodie over fleece pajama bottoms printed with Tasmanian Devils, poor bastard. A black knit beanie covered his head, but corkscrew curls sprung out around his neck and jaw. Dark stubble covered a round chin that advertised a healthy appetite, something I could respect. People who took pleasure in a good meal tended to be simple and decent. All this sorry son of a bitch wanted was his bed, his memory foam pillow, and the soft body of his girlfriend wrapped around him—her ample tits and belly pressed against his back. He wanted the space heater they plugged in near the foot of the bed and the way it blew warm air under the blankets. But there was a need—more than a need, a *compulsion*—to stand out here. It shoved his other desires to the side.

He came up to us with a folded paper clutched in his shaking hand. He thrust it at Blossom. "I, I need you to have this. It's… we're opening a deli. This is the menu. I need you to take it. We… we have mutton."

"Give it to someone else." The faerie flinched, and the kid stood, hand still extended and shivering in the cold.

"No! No. You. It has to be you." The guy's eyes widened and he gulped for air, his free hand clutching his chest. With my fondness for artists and sensitive souls, I had learned to recognize the onset of a panic attack.

"Take it, fucker," I urged when Blossom stepped back. Reluctantly the faerie held out his pale hand, even muttered a few words of thanks. The kid just stood staring, mouth hanging open, skin slick with sweat despite the cold. "Now tell him he can go, for fuck's sake. Let him go."

Blossom grimaced, but he waved his spindly little fingers and said, "You're dismissed."

The weird chicken-wire barrier holding him prisoner dropped away, and the kid's want smelt like lavender fabric softener and his girlfriend's strawberry shampoo. His head snapped back like somebody had hit him, and he looked around, cursed, and stumbled in the opposite direction, slippered feet tripping over chunks of dirty snow.

I reached for the menu, tugging it out of Blossom's grasp. There was a picture of a sheep's head at the top, above the words RAM Deli, with a list of sandwiches and salads featuring sheep meat underneath. Poor bastard would've done better in Center City or somewhere people would pay more just for weird than here, where people gladly tucked into dollar cheeseburgers and a steak sandwich was the ultimate luxury. No way would they pay $13.95 for a fucking sheep-meat sandwich when a cheeseburger was a dollar.

"What a bizarre person," Blossom mumbled. "And so terribly dull. Sheep, honestly. Why would he think I would want that? Disgusting."

I knew my chin must have been hitting my chest, my shock flashing through the chilly gloom like a sign advertising Live Nude Girls. As opposed to the dead ones. But shit, one couldn't make generalizations where mages were concerned. I forced myself to focus on something besides the sparkling naked bodies in my poor, neglected imagination. "Are you fucking kidding me here, Blossom?"

He turned to me, his eyes almost neon. Glowworm green. "No, I'm not kidding. My people don't eat carcasses or rotten things."

He was daft, had to be. Either that or he had one fucked-up sense of humor. I spoke slowly. "And you don't think there was anything unusual about that exchange? Like, oh, I don't know, that he was clearly ensorcelled somehow?"

"Ensorcelled to tempt me to eat a dead sheep? Who would do such a thing? We're here sifting through this refuse, digging around in trash not even fit for swine, when our jewels are clearly somewhere else." He looked toward the distant glow of the downtown skyscrapers.

"What do you base that on?" I asked.

"Who else would be worthy of summoning me here? Certainly not some slinger of sliced sheep."

I wondered what he'd taken from me, whether I could live without it. I didn't feel any different, and I sure as fuck didn't need this. "And you really don't think it's worth having a look at this deli? Not even worth walking past? It's only a few blocks away."

"I suppose if it will silence your prattling, it is worth a short stroll. I doubt anything interesting will occur, but I suppose I can only live in hope."

What a twat. Still, I accepted the concession and walked toward the address printed on the flyer. It was to the northeast, towards Kensington and the Badlands, which was far more dangerous than Strawberry Mansion, and a part of town I'd usually avoid. I just wanted to get this fucker out of my hair so I could find a receptive mortal to fuck the snot out of and feed off for at least a weekend, though after this, a solid month would be nice. I didn't like feeling vague, and I needed someone's desire to define me. Preferably someone who enjoyed getting oral sex until their legs felt like jelly, but I was quickly approaching the point where I couldn't be choosy. I needed some positive energy to sustain me, and I sure as fuck wouldn't be getting it off Blossom.

Though his ass in those snug gray trousers…. Would he taste like he smelt: cherry blossoms smashed in your fist and sprinkled with curry powder?

I stopped in the street and dug my fingernails into my palm, focusing on the sting. No, hell no. Bad idea, that. Worst idea of the century. Pissing on a live wire bad.

The address listed on the deli's menu led us to an octagonal building on a corner lot. Its plywood exterior was painted puce, the roof shingles canary yellow. Apparently it had once been a hair salon called Curl Up and Dye. If the bleached piece of copy paper taped in its window advertising "Summer Highlighting Special! Five Foils for $25" hadn't alerted us to how long the business had been abandoned, the frozen dog piss staining the snow around the realtor's sign couldn't be missed. Some Picasso had also used orange spray paint to tell the world "Jenny eat a$$ real gud." Predictably, Blossom shot me a smirk. "Want to paint a picture, Inky? Remember all the idyllic details of this— Wait."

At a subdued squeak, I pressed past the faerie towards the back of the building, where a pair of dumpsters sat, their lids encased in filthy ice. I bent down when I heard the soft mewl again, resting my elbows on my knees, making myself small and unthreatening. Waiting. A pair of eyes like chartreuse marbles caught the light, followed by that small voice. The sweet little voice. My heart soared, and I felt like my grin would split my skull. "Oh, that's right. Come on, then." I clucked my tongue.

The little tuxedo cat approached me cautiously. I met her eyes and blinked twice, very slowly, and then I held out my hand, rubbing my fingertips together. For all her shyness, she bounced up on her hind legs to butt her head against my palm when she got close enough. She had four white feet, a white teardrop over her nose, and a strip of white across her muzzle that looked like a handlebar mustache. Soon she placed her front paws on my thigh, purring. She was skin and bones, probably a year old or less. When I thought I wouldn't scare her, I scooped her up and situated her inside my jacket so she could get warm, all the while waiting for the faerie twat to say something disparaging. Well, he could fuck right off.

I stood with the kitten securely inside my coat. Movement caught my eye—something big coming from the alley behind us. This fellow was brown with black stripes and a thick coat, maybe a Maine coon or a Norwegian Forest cat, and a scrappy old bastard, judging by his shredded ears. He came within a foot of me, sat on his haunches, and yowled.

Others followed: a black tom missing an eye, a big tabby wearing a collar with a bell, a little white Persian like a cotton ball with blue eyes. A calico with a bobbed tail. A famished grimalkin followed by a litter of babies. One that looked like a cross between a Siamese and a fucking bobcat. Two little blondies with orange eyes traveling together. Blossom came to stand next to me as the cats kept coming, appearing from alleys and behind buildings, from underneath bushes and bins. It was like the shadows were spawning them, and in no time, a sea of glowing eyes surrounded us—thirty cats or more, all of them sitting on their haunches and staring up at us like they expected some kind of fucking show.

I would've been a daft tit not to remember the students back at Temple and the boy muttering "Cat, cat, cat." No way was this a coincidence.

When it seemed they had our attention, the cats got to their feet in unison, turned, and walked to the front of the garish little building. When we didn't follow right away, they sat down and focused their shiny, unblinking eyes back on us. I looked at Blossom and shrugged. Cats didn't act like this; I liked them a lot and knew a bit about them. I respected their resistance to submission, their individuality. They were fuzzy little anarchists, and they made their own way. But this lot sure looked like they had a goal in mind, one they'd work together to achieve.

As soon as I started walking, the clowder turned as one and made its way onto the street. They gathered in the middle, waiting until we caught up. I was still expecting some snide remark from Blossom, but when he passed me, his green eyes were bright. He might have even been smiling. I hung back for a minute just to watch the spectacle, shaking my head. Only a fucking faerie would prance up the street behind an army of alley cats. All he needed was a fucking flute to complete the picture.

Or maybe I was remembering that old tale in reverse. Whatever. I was happy; being around cats, with their big shiny eyes, soft fur, and little bean toes, made me happy. Blossom seemed happy around them, too, and that made me hate Blossom less, which also made me happy. I didn't enjoy conflict; I liked warm squishy feelings. Sweet, wet, sticky emotions like strawberry jam. Something you could lick and let the sugar dissolve in your mouth. I leaned down to nuzzle my face against the black-and-white kitten sleeping happily in my coat. "I'm going to look out for you," I told her. "You and me, yeah?"

She mewed in response, and I looked at the bizarre parade moving up the street. Hell, at least we were getting somewhere. This couldn't be accidental, and all I could do was see where it led us.

At least there was no one about to make a lame pussy joke.

Chapter Six

Animals were more trustworthy than humans. At least they didn't have an inflated sense of self-importance. Besides, I liked cats. Of all the creatures, they managed to take advantage of the mortals while resisting their yoke. In a way, they played with them the same as my people did. The big striped tom rubbed against my leg and looked up at me. When our eyes met, he closed his very slowly. *Come on. Come, faerie. We're almost there.*

Where are we going?

I do not know, answered a skeletal gray female with a white tummy. *But we need to take you there.*

Do you know why?

We only know it's important, said a plump tabby in a collar.

Cats shouldn't be collared. I waved my fingers and the strip of sparkly pink cloth fell to the ground.

Why do you want to do this? I asked them. *Are you trying to help me?*

We want to hunt, said a soot-colored adolescent cat. *We want to eat warm flesh and to mate.*

You are not cat, said a sleek white one, *but you are more cat than the others.*

Your blood smells familiar. Something we have forgotten but recognize now that we scent it. We will guide you.

But where? I asked.

Here. Here. Here! In this place. In this location is where you need to be. Your hunt begins here.

Why?

We do not know. We wanted to bring you here. We were made to want this.

We are here now. We have done this thing. We can go on to our hunts, to our shadowy secret places. This is your hunt. It begins here.

The cats stopped in front of a dilapidated building, forming a crescent around the path that led to its door.

A facade that I assumed was supposed to mimic bricks or stone but didn't look like anything close covered the front; metal planks—also gray—covered the sides. Aluminum awnings spread over the narrow windows, flecked with snow and black, crusty soot. The ground floor was dark, but flickering golden light pulsed weakly behind some of the second-floor windows.

The cats looked up at those windows and serenaded them with a discordant chorus just as the demon came huffing up behind me, practically colliding with my back before he skidded to a halt on the slippery path.

"Can you feel it?" I asked.

His breath plumed from his purplish lips, but he nodded. "Magic, garish magic, with no attempt to hide it. Like spray paint right in the eye: so obvious and irrefutable it fucking stings. We should go up."

As much as I wanted to disagree, I could find no logical reason. I turned to my feline friends. *Thank you. Go hunt. May warm flesh quiver between your teeth and hot blood flow down your throats. If I can ever return this favor you have done, think my name and I will come.*

A few of them dipped their heads and others murmured or yowled before they ran off, their light little feet silent on the humans' cold and dirty thoroughfare. Soon I was left alone with Inky, staring up at the small windows of the pitiful dwelling.

"We should go up," he said again. "It can't be a coincidence, the cats and everything, but…."

"But what? I am weary of this dull and dirty realm, so if you have something to say, spit it out!"

His eyes flashed. I didn't know if his kind could feel anger or affront, but his offense was plain in the way he raised himself to his full height and pushed his shoulders back. It was interesting. "I'm weary of you, you daft, annoying, arrogant, self-righteous son of a fucking cunt. I can't wait to tell you to fuck off and forget I ever saw your pointy little face. But only a fucking imbecile wouldn't even consider this could be some kind of trap. But you're so goddamned smart and so fucking precious, you can't imagine anyone would dare."

I… couldn't. What mortal conjurer could equal my abilities? What mortal conjurer with the ability wouldn't understand the danger? My people had tutored a few prodigies, but magic came hard to the mortals. For them it was like painting when they had to break through three stone walls before they reached the canvas. Few of them could breach those boundaries to consider the colors on the palette. It wasn't something close to their fingers, something easy for them to smear and swirl into magnificent creations. Those who knew the canvas existed at all were considered grand masters among their people. For us, crafting those masterworks was as simple as extending our arms. Inky had known mages, so he must've realized the same thing. But there was something I didn't understand. "Why are you so angry?"

The demon canted his head toward the sky. Smothered as they were, the stars lit the planes of his face, silvered the ridges of his horns in a way worthy of a statue. He was magnificent in that fleeting moment, all energy waiting to be given form, waiting for the bargain to be struck, gorgeous raw material like virgin marble. When he turned to me, his eyes radiated a rose color to rival the sunrise. But he was incensed, and I still didn't understand.

"You're a cunt!" he growled. "I avoid the mages because they're so damned arrogant it makes me puke, but you're worse. You want my help, you fucking indenture me, and when I offer anything, all you can do is argue! Offer some fucking insult you think is clever. I don't like it. I don't like it because there are real people, real lives involved in this. People who can get hurt. People who don't deserve to get hurt to fucking entertain you." He kicked a chunk of ice into the street, where it shattered. "I was only trying to be decent. Those mages back at Hex would have strapped you down and peeled you open like a fucking banana. I never thought I'd regret saving someone from that, but I can't stand you. All I want is you gone, but you're too daft to even see the way to your own redemption."

"Well, don't let common civility get in the way of you speaking your mind."

"You fucking asked, fucker!" He looked from side to side, probably for something else to stomp. "What does it matter? I don't like you; you don't like me. You're so bloody sure you know exactly what to do, you might as well let me go."

"No, it doesn't work that way," I told Inky. "A bargain was struck, and it must be followed through."

"For fuck's sake, why?"

"Everything is a bargain, a trade. It's the foundation of existence. Starlight and soil traded for plants. Plant life traded for flesh. Flesh traded for soil. Soil and starlight traded for plants once again. It's the basis of all magic. Energy traded for matter. Matter for energy. The bargain is the only true rule. It's always something for something. Nothing can come from nothing; there is only exchange. Even my kind cannot circumvent that one rule." I doubted he would grasp the concept, basic though it was, but he surprised me by nodding.

"Right, right. Like if I want to get laid on a regular basis, I have to give up playing the Xbox so much."

"Ugh. You profane a beautiful concept by comparing it to rubbing genitals and playing with your box."

He laughed, and though I didn't understand the source of his mirth, it seemed to relax him. A small, broken squeak sounded, and his face softened even more. A little white snout poked up between his lapels, and I took a step closer.

Inky crossed his arms over the little black-and-white cat. "I don't care what you say. I'm going to keep her, and I'm calling her Charlene."

"Charlene." I felt it a suitable name as I stretched a finger toward the kitten's nose. Her rough pink tongue dragged over my skin. "It's good to have a cat along. The cats told me my hunt started here. I have always found cats to be wise and perceptive."

"They told you…? You can speak with them?"

I tilted my head. "Of course."

Inky's eyes grew wide and glossy. "Whoa. That must be so cool."

"It can be insightful," I said. "They did say this was the start, so I guess we should go up."

"Been saying that for five minutes now," he muttered.

It was easy enough to shift the mechanism in the door—a trade of occupied space for empty space was a fair bargain. Inside was a foyer, I suppose, though it was worse than poor. The printed chemical sheet beneath my feet—patterned in hideous shades of yellow and brown— was caked with gritty mud. The walls were crumbling and eaten through with mold; the bright terra-cotta paint couldn't mask it. Inky went to a row of black metal slots and examined them. After a few moments he waved me over.

"Look at this." He pointed to a strip of paper above one compartment, which read: SM/DAM/RAM. "Yeah? R-A-M. RAM. RAM Deli. Bet that's not a coincidence." He traced his finger across to a label proclaiming 2C.

"2C is a location?" I doubted anything would come of this; I was still sure I had been summoned by a powerful wizard in one of those towering glass buildings. However…. "Can you take me there?"

Inky motioned toward a narrow staircase, and I followed him up it into an equally narrow hall dotted with several flimsy doors. After observing them all, the demon stopped in front of one with a lacy paper heart pinned to it and turned to me. "Do we knock, or—"

I pushed between him and the door. "Of course we do. We're not savages."

I rapped my knuckles against the paper-thin wood. A light came on, casting a grainy golden glow under the door. A moment later the door opened and a metal tube poked out.

Inky grabbed my waist and pulled me across the hall, shoving me against the wall and shielding me behind his body. He raised his palms up next to his head and spread his fingers, saying, "Hey, relax, mate. We only want to talk. Put down the gun."

CHAPTER SEVEN

THE FIRST thing I saw was the Colt Defender 45 ACP poking out between the door and the frame. Nice gun. Expensive. The next thing I saw was the hand holding it: long fingers, elegant, practiced. Moving my gaze upward, I found the gunman's face, and whoa…. Damn. A real stunner. Skin like wild honey, almond-shaped obsidian eyes—fucking gems, those eyes—lips the color of raw clay, swollen as if they'd been hit… or kissed into oblivion…. But no desires. Nothing on his mind beyond defending his home. Though surprising, his yearnings were strong: a place to eat dinner at a table, clean bedclothes, report cards signed and assignments completed, metallic star stickers on paper with large text….

"Fuck off," the gun's owner said, his one visible eye reflecting the yellowed light from the hall.

"We just want to talk to you." I held up my hands, hoping he would see I wasn't a threat.

"It's the middle of the fucking night," he responded. "Get the hell out of here."

As I was thinking of words to reassure him, Blossom pushed past me and stood in front of the splinter in the door. Blossom leaned in close to the young man's face. "I have… valuable items." The faerie extended his hand, and it filled with gold coins. "Yes, you like the look of those. They're all yours if you only agree to speak with us for a few moments."

The door closed, and then it reopened without the chain. The young man still held his gun, held it naturally next to his hip. That told me he knew how to handle it, that it wasn't just for show. He stepped into the hall and leaned against the wall, his eyes flitting between us and the door that still stood open an inch. Now I could see that he wore tight dark jeans, a decent pair of boots, and a worn black hoodie. Common enough clothes, but everything about this kid screamed thug—everything but a penny-sized photo suspended in glittering resin that he wore like a locket. It rested in the divot between his collarbones. "You've got thirty seconds to tell me what the hell you want."

"I think you know why we're here," Blossom said in a reedy hiss.

"If you're looking to score, Blaker's not here. Neither is my mom. Go somewhere else." The kid raised the gun by his hip a couple of inches, but it was enough to make his point.

At least to me.

"I will not go anywhere until my questions are answered." Though melodic, Blossom's voice held an echo of thunder, like a storm rolling in fast, making the grass bow down and the leaves shudder. "I offered you a fair trade for the information, but if I must resort to force—"

The kid raised his voice and got up in the faerie's face. "I offered you thirty seconds to tell me what you wanted, and they're up. Fuck. Off."

Down the hall, a door cracked open, then another, strips of light intersecting on the dingy linoleum.

I pushed between Blossom and the kid, smiling, groping desperately for some hint of what motivated him here, something I could use. I saw an image of a birthday cake, a little pink dress in a store window, spaghetti and meatballs served on a folding table, Christmas snowflakes cut from copy paper....

"Look, this is your home," I told him. "I understand. I understand that all you're trying to do is make a home here, and I appreciate that. We don't want to threaten your home, and we don't want to threaten you. Can we come in? Before somebody calls the cops?"

He laughed. "Like the cops are going to come out here."

"Still," I continued. "You don't need to attract attention. The truth is, we need your help, mate. Rather badly. And we're willing to pay for it. You could use the money, couldn't you?"

He narrowed his eyes, but his shoulders relaxed ever so slightly. "What kind of help are we talking about?"

"We just want to talk," I said. "I swear that's all we want. Just to ask a few questions."

The kid's eyes darted to the handful of coins Blossom held; he probably saw a roll of fifty-dollar bills. I could see the internal battle he fought. He didn't trust us—who would?—but he needed that money. In the end, he needed it enough to heave out a sigh and push the door open with his elbow. He used the .45 to usher us in, used it to point to a dilapidated sofa. When we sat, he came around to stand in front of us, between the scuffed coffee table and a TV playing some late-night variety show. His shadow was stark against the screen. "What the fuck do you want here? Make it quick."

Now that we were here, I didn't even know where to begin. I looked around the tiny flat: a single room barely big enough for the couch and TV, separated from the kitchen by a bar with two stools, the stuffing poking out from their blue plastic seats. Across from it was a closed door with a creased poster taped to it: a unicorn standing in front of a waterfall. A lot of books covered the cheap pressboard shelves, sat in piles on the green shag carpet, and filled some cardboard boxes. The place was worse than a dump—amoeba-shaped brown stains covered the ceiling tiles where the roof leaked—but somebody was trying hard to make it a home.

I realized if I didn't say something, Blossom would, and nothing good could come of that. Manners, I told myself. Filter. "What's your name?"

"Why?"

"Because I'd like to know?"

He raked his long fringe out of his eyes. "Dante."

I shot him the brightest smile I could muster. I wished he had some desires to shape me, to make me pleasing, the thing he most wanted to see. It would've been easier to gain his trust, but he just didn't give a fuck. "Nice to meet you, Dante. I'm called Inky, and this is Blossom."

He rolled his eyes. "Fucking tweakers."

Blossom leaned forward and rested his elbows on his knees. "Do you know much about magic, Dante? Have you ever seen it done? Have you seen it done by anyone around here?"

His words had the predictable result. "All right. Time to go. Leave the money on the table. A deal is a deal."

Blossom's eyes went wide with surprise. "I always honor my bargains."

Dante scooped up the wad of cash and shoved it in his pants pocket without ever taking his eyes off us. "Got any more?"

Silly boob that he was, Blossom didn't recognize the threat. He smiled. "Plenty. As much as you want. I can shower you in treasure if you help me find the one who cast the spell on me. I'm sure it must've been someone in this building. You see, the cats led us here."

"You're crazy," Dante said. "I don't want you junkie assholes coming to my house, and you can tell my mom and Blaker I said so. I'm not putting up with this anymore. Now get the fuck out of here."

I put my hand on Blossom's knee. "We might as well go. There's nothing here."

"But there has to be!" the faerie insisted. "The cats! Besides, I can feel the enchantment catching against my skin like spider's silk. And…. What is your surname?"

"Mayfield," Dante said slowly.

"And your middle? Your middle name?" Blossom practically buzzed with manic energy.

"Ambrose. Why?"

Blossom ticked off the letters on his fingers. "D-A-M."

"Congratulations," Dante said. "Now leave. This is the last time I'll ask nicely."

As I stood, I grabbed Blossom by the wrist. I'd drag him out of here if I had to. Not only did I not want to find out what would happen if he got shot, this kid didn't deserve our shite. It was plain as the stain on the rug he hadn't summoned the faerie.

The door opposite the kitchen opened with a creak, and a small round face peeked out, backlit by a warm golden glow. "Dante? I heard people shouting. I'm scared." The little girl clutched a stuffed pink pony with a yellow mane and tail tight to her chest. I could see the resemblance between her and Dante in the shape of their cheeks and chins, but her eyes were bigger, her lips fuller, her complexion darker. Where Dante's hair was straight and black, hers was golden-brown and curly, held back in little braids tipped with bright plastic flowers.

Dante shoved his gun down the back of his pants as he hurried to cross the space. Kneeling, he placed his hand on the little girl's shoulder. "Don't be scared, Rosalind. My, uh, friends were just leaving. Go back to bed, baby."

"Is Momma here?"

"She—" His voice cracked. "She isn't back yet."

Just then, Charlene stirred inside my coat, poked her head out, and yawned out a mewl. Rosalind's eyes widened. "Is that a kitty?"

"Yeah," I answered.

"Is it yours?"

"She is," I said proudly.

"Can I pet her?"

I looked to Dante, and when he nodded once in permission, I crouched down and opened my coat a little farther. Rosalind touched my cat on the head like she was touching the crown jewels, and she asked, "What's her name?"

"Charlene."

"Charlene." Holding up the stuffed horse, Rosalind said, "Charlene, this is Touchstone. He's my pony." She pushed the horse's plush hoof against Charlene's paw like they were shaking hands. "He thinks you're very beautiful."

Behind me, I could hear Blossom whispering to Dante. "Rosalind. Rosalind Mayfield. And what is her middle name?"

"None of your business."

"*A*." Blossom continued as if Dante hadn't spoken. "An *A* name. R-A-M. Like the sheep meat."

Dante pushed past Blossom and knelt back down, touching his sister's cheek. "It's time for Charlene to go home, baby. And you need to go back to bed."

The girl shook Charlene's paw again. "Bye, Charlene. I'll say a prayer for you before I go to sleep. I'll ask God to send two angels. One to watch over me and one to watch over you."

"Okay, baby," Dante urged. "Back into your room."

"Dante, can I have a glass of water?"

"Yeah. I'll bring you one. Go back into your room."

As soon as the girl left and the door to the hall clicked shut, Dante was back in Blossom's face. Blossom was still whispering to himself, his eyes wide and his lips peeled back in a way that made him look completely off his trolley. "We were meant to come here. R-A-M and the cats! The cats will after Rosalind."

Dante pushed the barrel of the gun into Blossom's cheek, denting his flesh. "Get your pasty ass out of here, and if I ever see you again, you're fucking dead. Got it?"

"But—"

"Come on, Blossom." After steadying Charlene, I grabbed him by the shoulder and pulled him out of the flat, then down the stairs and back out into the chilly night. As soon as we hit the sidewalk, he broke free and faced me with a snarl.

"What are you thinking, demon? The cats were right! The cats came after Rosalind. We need to go back inside. I'm going back to make them tell me what I need to know."

"The hell you are."

He crossed his arms over his chest. "Why not?"

Above us, the blinds were cleaved open a hair, and I knew Dante was watching. A block away, a dark figure with a hood up leaned against a lamppost. Also watching. "We need to get off the street. Now."

"Why?"

"What are you, five? Come on. We're being followed. Probably by the person who lured us here. We need to shake them."

"But that doesn't make any sense!" he protested.

I turned in the opposite direction of that dark figure and walked as fast as I could, tugging Blossom like a mule on a rope. When I glanced back over my shoulder, the person had moved—keeping their distance, but definitely following. Something seemed almost familiar in the way they held themselves, their posture. But that had to be paranoia. It'd been a weird fucking night, and I was off-kilter and acute.

"Do you honestly think they'll be a match for me?" Blossom continued.

"Look, arsehole." I leaned close and spat the words into his pointy ear. "Magic will attract attention—attract more mages. Mages who likely tricked us into coming to this place and waited for us here. Who knows how many of them could be around? Can't you like… do something to hide us?"

"Oh. Of course I can." He reached his long fingers above his head, moved them in circles. In less time than it took me to look back down, snow and wind pelted us, coming so fast and thick that I could barely see him even though he stood inches from my face. The snow was almost a solid wall, just coming at us horizontal.

"This isn't what I had in mind!" I shouted over the howl of the wind. "We've got to get out of this—find a place to go!"

"I have an idea," the faerie said, and he clasped my hand, seemingly oblivious to the snow that smacked me in the face like frozen rocks. He sprinted cheerily up the sidewalk, and I let myself be pulled along like a toy on a string. It was either that or stand there and fucking freeze to death.

Chapter Eight

The person who resided in the blue square dwelling was one who saw shadows and dreams, one who could look past the mundane world into other realities. Since Inky and I were shadows and dreams, this was as good a place for us as any. I knocked on the cold metal door, disturbing a little grapevine wreath with a faux wren perched on one side.

It was early morning, a time when most mortals slept, but the lights in the little domicile came on, and soon after, the door opened to reveal a tiny woman in a floral nightdress covered by a pilled yellow sweater. Her wispy white hair was pulled back in a severe knot, and her face was as lined as a dry riverbed. But when she saw us standing there, snow thick on our heads and shoulders, she broke into a wide, toothless grin. She reached up and closed her small fists around two locks of my hair, pulling me down to smack loud, wet kisses on both of my cheeks. "Ramon! It's so good to see you. You don't visit your poor old mama as often as you should. Come in, come in. Get out of the cold. And your brother is here too! Raphael, come inside. You're letting out all of my heat. I don't work for the electric company, you know."

There was very little heat to speak of in the tiny room we entered—some sort of seating area similar to the one in Dante and Rosalind's residence: a battered settee; stacks of paper tied up with twine; thin glossy books arranged in piles; and hundreds of little statues, animals and things—arranged on every available table and lined up in formation on much of the floor. The old woman had created careful trails between them, and she traveled along one to reach the small kitchen visible through a large open square. She turned on a light above a table piled with more paper and knickknacks, announcing, "You boys must be hungry. You look so thin. I'll make us a proper breakfast, and we can sit and talk. How does that sound?"

"Good, good," I said, bending down to pick up a little squirrel holding an acorn. I dusted off his back with the cuff of my jacket and carried him to a windowsill, where I set him next to an owl with wide eyes and an elfish little man in a furry red suit. There was also a stack of corks and a half of a potato sprouting in a metal dish. A bronze-finished birdcage hung from the ceiling, stuffed full of more little creatures like the wren on the wreath outside. It also held some faux pears covered in glitter, and they caught the sun when I shifted the old plaid curtains. "What an interesting and delightful place."

"Oh, Blossom." Inky laid a hand on my shoulder and shook his head. Charlene wailed mournfully as a clicking sounded in the kitchen, followed by the whoosh of a flame and the clatter of pots and pans.

"What's wrong now?"

"This poor old woman."

I looked around at the little statues and some crystal moons and stars hanging in front of another window. A large jar held a beautiful variety of small colored orbs that I couldn't wait to get my hands on and examine closer. And artwork covered the walls—realistic black-and-white depictions of a number of people, alongside pictures of bottles of perfume and sumptuous meals. The wall itself was quite lovely as well: painted roses in vertical lines with satiny green strips between them. I was confounded. "Poor? This woman seems to have a great many valuable possessions. Some truly wonderful items."

"No, that's… I mean, I think she must have Alzheimer's."

"Have what?" The woman was smiling and humming as she hunched over her frying pan, steam rising in a veil around her.

"Dementia," Inky said. "She doesn't know what is really going on around her."

"Of course not," I answered. "She sees other realities, visions. That's why I chose this place. Do you have a problem with it?"

"It's just sad, that's all."

"Sad? Tell me, what are her desires?"

Inky turned his head toward the kitchen, and Charlene butted him beneath the chin. "She doesn't really have any. She thinks everything she loves and values is already here."

"Another reason I chose to come here. The last thing I want to watch is you fulfilling someone's desires. This woman already has everything she could possibly want."

He picked up a metal canister of beans with a spoon sticking out of it. "She only thinks she does."

"Well, it's the same thing. Come now. We were invited to have breakfast, and it would be rude to be tardy. I'm sure Charlene is hungry as well."

The table held more wonders: fronds of fabric leaves edged in glittering gold, spools of thread in every color of the rainbow, and a veritable army of salt and pepper shakers, delightful pairings of one black and one white cat, samurai and geisha, vegetables with smiling faces, eager to season their people for consumption. I couldn't help laughing with delight. A pair of plump pigs with curly tails and wide, innocent eyes stood next to a pineapple and a palm tree. Fascinating! It must have been truly wondrous to possess such items, to be able to pick them up and inspect them anytime. I could see how that bestowed happiness on this woman.

Our host insisted upon putting our coats in a small cupboard with some mops and brooms, and then we took our places and accepted our repast on thick plates in primary colors. We ate sautéed plantains with sweet red onions, fried cheese cut in triangles, and I gave the eggs and thick, spicy sausage to Charlene, who then curled up in a basket full of skeins of yarn, underripe mangoes, and packets of sunflower seeds. The coffee was delicious, strong and sweet.

The conversation was even more entertaining. Mrs. Guzman saw me and Inky as her sons, Ramon and Raphael. Her perceptions were not limited by the linear confines of most mortals. She saw, all at once, past, present, and possibility. So when she asked me about my wife, I declared she was a Spanish princess, and the old woman cheered. When she asked again moments later and I explained my wife was an English student, a prodigy studying starlight and the nature of perception, she responded with equal enthusiasm. For her, the possibilities existed simultaneously.

Inky was good at the game. I imagine he honed in on her aspirations for her sons and spun the tales she most wanted to hear. Her fondness for her children shaped him as well; as they talked, his skin became a dark shade of olive, his hair mahogany and straight, his eyebrows thick above his expressive brown eyes. Watching him spin tales of his children, all geniuses, about to enter university, amused me almost as much as Mrs. Guzman's gleeful reaction. Then he spoke of his daughter, a makeup artist on movie sets in Hollywood, and the old woman clutched her chest. I hoped she wouldn't die; it would make staying here more difficult, and I liked it here.

After our meal, Mrs. Guzman announced, "You boys are tired. Such hard workers, both of you! You'll get a good sleep now that your bellies are full. Come on. I kept your room just the way you left it."

She ushered us into a tiny chamber with a narrow bed hugging each wall. In her eyes, we were children again, and she said, "I'll clean up. You boys take a nice nap, and maybe later we'll go to the park."

The door closed with a soft click, and Inky dropped onto one bed, folding his arms behind his head and staring at the water-stained ceiling. "I doubt we're going to the park or anywhere else in this fucking storm you called up."

It was clear there was no pleasing this one. "You wanted to make sure we wouldn't be followed, and now we won't be."

"But now we're stuck in here, and this place makes me sad. There's so much loss here, and it's tearing at me."

I went to the chest of drawers pushed against the wall a few feet opposite the beds. A lacy mandala covered the top, but the wondrous little statues were absent. Instead, a yellow metal vehicle with big segmented wheels and an overstuffed leather glove sat on the surface. Two pictures hung on the green-and-yellow striped wall above it: a man with short-cut hair and a wide smile, wearing what I assumed was a military uniform, and a younger fellow with shaggy fringe and a pensive expression, his shoulders curled forward and his long fingers wrapped around his arms. "Huh. These must be Mrs. Guzman's sons. A brash, idealistic hero and a calculating schemer. I wonder if the younger boy is a mage. He has the look."

"This isn't some fucking story, Blossom."

I looked over my shoulder at Inky, who'd propped himself up on his elbows on the bed. "Of course it is. Everything is a story. Just because we're partaking of this one doesn't change its nature. What is a story when all is said and done? It's merely a series of things happening."

"But this poor old woman sees things that aren't really here."

"She sees into other realities." I picked up the padded leather glove and slipped my fingers inside, wondering what it could be for. "There is always a bargain, demon. The more she perceives of other worlds, the less she is able to see of this one."

"But this is what actually exists."

"Does it?" I asked him. "Does it exist if you don't perceive it on any level? Aren't things you can see and touch and hear and feel the ones that exist? And how can you be sure the things you perceive are the same ones perceived by others?"

"I...." Inky shook his head. "You're hurting my fucking brain. Besides, we should figure out what's going on here."

"Agreed." I sat on the bed across from him, and he rose up to face me, raking his long silver hair away from his eyes. "I'm sure you have an opinion on what that might be."

Inky dragged his hand down his face and covered his eyes with his fingers. "That's just it. I fucking don't. I don't get this at all. From what I can tell, someone, some mage or group of mages, succeeded in summoning a faerie here. That's you. So they did that, and all I can suppose is you didn't pop out where they expected. So they lured us… planted these clues to bring us here…. But fuck me, why? Why would they make it a challenge for us to find them? That doesn't make a damned lick of sense."

I steepled my fingers and tapped the tips of my thumbs against my lower lip, thinking, trying to imagine what it would entail to weave magic like that. "No. It's impossible. To craft an enchantment like that, they would have had to either know exactly which mortals we would encounter and bewitch them, or… or the spell would have to be crafted to react to our presence, to influence anyone we might come in contact with. And even that doesn't account for the sheep-meat fellow. He was looking for us. Only a spell that affected this entire area, screwing its tendrils into everyone and everything on the chance we might interact with them…. But no. There were steps in it, cause and effect. The players speaking of the cats, and then the cats appearing. The caster would either have had to influence those actors to put on that play—probably months ago—or they would've had to know of it, known to use it. That… that kind of magic is impossible. It would take the skill of one of my kind and the calculation of a human. It would take years to construct something like this. Even then, there are so many variables to take into account. So many minutiae that could throw the whole thing off."

Inky's eyes scrunched to slits, and his pinkish irises darted back and forth, not that the changes he'd undergone for Mrs. Guzman's benefit seemed to fade without her presence. "Some of the guilds have years. Sekhet-Aaru does. They could've put this in place. They think long-term, orchestrating political movements among the mortals that won't yield anything in their lifetimes. I understand they went to great lengths to fuel the animosity between Islam and Christianity, with the ultimate goal of destroying both religions. Leaving a hole for magic to fill when the mortals need something to guide them. But they know it's going to take three, four generations. Maybe more. Hell. Some say they've been at it since the Crusades. They can wait. I've also heard rumors they're allowing global warming, positioning themselves to save humanity when things start getting rough. They're playing the long game, trying to get things just right so people will accept mages as their rulers again."

He had no knowledge of the way magic ebbed and flowed, leaving empty caverns behind to swell into other spaces. The balance escaped him. "It can't be done, Inky. It would mean everyone… everything was mobilized toward bringing us to this point. It would mean a spell that changes and adapts on its own, magic given a will, for lack of a better explanation. Something that lives independent of the caster. It's impossible."

"Then what?"

When I stretched out on the small bed, my booted feet hung over the scalloped wood at the foot. I didn't know how to answer him. No one and nothing I knew of had the power to assemble a spell like this—I couldn't have done it myself, and that made me… uncomfortable.

"Then what, Blossom?"

"I… I don't know who could've done this, or how. I…."

There was another scuffed blue chest in the corner of the room with three drawers. Pale wood peeked out from deep gouges in the facade. On it sat a doll's head atop a conical base covered in shimmering silver brocade. The thing had teardrop-shaped eyes and a mournful little mouth, wings with feathers congealed by metallic paint. I stood and picked it up, holding it on flattened palms a few inches from my chin. What if…?

"What if it is wild magic, raw magic directed by someone who doesn't even know they're directing it?"

The bedsprings creaked, and I felt Inky's warmth at my back. "What are you thinking, Blossom?"

"The girl," I said. "The girl who prayed every night for an angel to save her. If she—" The idea that this little peasant had manipulated me was horrifying, wrong in every way, but I could think of nothing else. "What if the magic answered her call? What if it brought me here, made everything happen in just such a way so that I would come to her?"

"That's…." Inky put his chin on my shoulder and stared at the shoddily constructed thing I held, its tangled yellow hair coated in dust, its rosy cheeks bisected by scratches. "Do you really think? Wait, though. Most mages have a sort of glow about them. Colored light. I didn't see anything like that."

I threw the grotesque doll to the ground and crushed it beneath my boot, flattening its hollow head and making the candle fly from its chunky hands. "Some of them can hide such things. In the young especially, the power can ebb and flow: strong and bright at times, nonexistent at others. We have to know. If it is true, that little urchin is the greatest mage in a millennium. This is…. We have to know. We have to go back to that house."

"And do what?" he asked.

"And get her to release me."

"And if she can't?"

"If she can't," I said, "then I will do what I need to do. The spell is broken upon the caster's demise."

"You can't be serious."

"Why not?"

"What the— What? Kill a little girl? What the fuck is wrong with you?"

I turned to face him, catching and holding his gaze with my own. "Of course I'll attempt to reach a bargain first. But I refuse to remain trapped here. Mortals die every day, demon. Do you think you can stop me?"

He opened his mouth, revealing thick, sharp fangs between his purplish lips. "You son of a fucking bitch. You piece of shite. No, I can't stop you, but I sure as hell won't help you. You know what? I hope you fuck up and end up strapped to some mage's table while they prod at your insides. Fuck you. I'm off."

"You won't ever regain what I took from you," I told him.

"I don't fucking care. Being in the same room with you's making me sick." He left the tiny bedroom, slamming the door behind him.

I kicked the pieces of clumsy angel into the corner and then returned to lie on the bed. I'd rest a few hours, and then I'd go back to the girl and her brother. I liked the boy; maybe I'd take him home with me, make him into my champion. If nothing else, he would be pretty to look at during my parties and balls. I didn't need that stubborn, stupid demon. Now that I knew what to do, I would be home in no time. I would just rest until my storm subsided. It might take some time; I'd perhaps been overzealous. But that was all right. There was no hurry now.

Chapter Nine

My TracFone buzzed again, bouncing across the coffee table. I knew I couldn't keep ignoring it, as much as I wanted to stay at home with Ros after those fucking tweakers had been here. But Raf's text message flashed in all capital letters:

NOW, MAYFIELD. CAR'S OUTSIDE. NO TIME TO DALLY.

I replied *OMW* and locked Ros's door from the outside with the padlock only I had a key for. She'd be scared if she couldn't get out when she woke up, but it was better than the alternative. I wished I could just decline this fucking job, but Ros needed new clothes for spring. I didn't want her getting made fun of because her shit didn't fit right, and I didn't want to let down Raf—he'd been pretty good to me. I'd do this and be back by the time she had to get ready for school.

I could even pick up some of those cinnamon rolls she liked. She'd understand.

My .45 was still on the table, and I shoved it down the back of my pants. I kept my .38 snub-nose in the freezer, behind the brussels sprouts no one in this house fucking ate, and the leather holster was cold when I stuck it down the front of my jeans, in easy reach of my left hand. Being ambidextrous had its advantages, but that chill made my dick shrink and my balls curl up close to my body. I was sick of being cold, and it would still be a long time until spring.

Ignoring the shitty weather, I jogged down the steps and slid into the cab of an old pickup truck with the words Carl the Junkman scrolled across the side in chipping paint. Powdery snow fanned from the back tires as the driver pulled onto the street, and I gripped the edge of the seat to brace myself as I slanted my eyes toward the old man sharing the car with me. In his thermal shirt and denim overalls, with his wild gray curls tucked beneath a beat-up 76ers cap, Carl looked like he should be puttering around in a vegetable garden.

"Dante, my man." Carl nodded at me, and I returned it. He fiddled with the dial on his radio, and soon Miles Davis's voice filled the cab as we drove down the abandoned streets toward the highway, both of us bitching about the weather.

We soon pulled up to a warehouse close to the Schuylkill River, north of the city. A tractor trailer was waiting, the back doors hanging open, exhaust fumes coming out in a black stream. Carl went to stand by the ramp leading out of the truck, where wooden boxes moved down the conveyor belt. It looked like this truck carried mostly restaurant equipment from what I could see printed on the boxes hiding our merchandise. A big guy in a heavy blue jacket flicked his cigarette into the snow and stood to retrieve our cargo, hauling out smaller wooden boxes labeled with things like *cooking oil* and *table linens*.

As they rolled down the metal conveyor, Carl loaded the boxes into the bed of his own truck. He was fast and neat, making a Jenga of the narrow crates, packing them tight. I felt shitty not helping him, but that wasn't why I was here. All I had to do was make sure everything went smoothly, and then I'd get paid and I could buy some new clothes for my sister. We didn't usually have any problems picking up Raf's shipments. Not many people knew about them, and those who did knew better than to fuck with us.

With me.

I'd built a decent reputation for myself since coming to work for Raf.

I was thinking about the cute little outfits on display at the Gymboree at the mall when two assholes came around the corner of the building holding assault rifles, black ski masks covering their faces like something out of a bad movie. I yelled for Carl to get down, and he ducked around the side of the truck and crouched by the wheel. For all he looked like somebody's sweet grandfather, he'd done this before, and he was old for a reason. It got quiet after that, weird and still. I could distinctly hear Louis Armstrong singing "What A Wonderful World" from Carl's radio as snow seemed to drift down in slow motion. Skidding through the powder, I threw my back against the side of the truck and pulled my Colt from my pants just as the *pop-pop-pop* of their weapons broke through the eerie quiet, like a can opener piercing the metal of the semi. One of the tractor trailer drivers dropped to his knees, arms wrapped around his middle to try to hold in the blood shooting between his fingers. He fell on his face in the snow just as I got one of the assholes in my sights. I squeezed the trigger and his head exploded like a poppy, blood and brains splashing the warehouse's aluminum siding, the red bright against the rippled metal and the spatter almost perfectly round. The other guy was crouched around the side of the long, low building, and I kept my eye on him, waiting. His frozen breath showed me every move the dumb shithead made. These motherfuckers were messing up my plans, and it pissed me the hell off. Anger makes some people sloppy. It gives me an edge, a boost to my speed and perception. I felt like I knew everything that was happening around me. As the white cloud got thicker and closer, I knew the dick who thought he was so clever was coming my way, and I got ready. He peeked around the corner, firing a few shots that pinged off the fender of the truck. I kept my head down and watched. Raf had taught me early that one good shot was worth ten minutes of carpeting everything in sight. It took time, but eventually the asshole stepped out from the edge of the building, waving his fancy gun back and forth like he'd seen too many stupid action flicks.

I positioned the .45, held my breath, and popped that asshole right between the eyes. Some nasty shit flew out of the back of his head before he fell, a red stain expanding around him. I scanned the area, and seeing no one else, I left my cover to check on Carl, running in a crouch to where he knelt.

Finding him unhurt, I said, "I'm going to take a look around, make sure that was all of them."

"Be careful, Dante." Carl put his revolver back into the front pocket of his overalls.

I went around the side of the warehouse where the two assholes had come from. Their tracks stood out clearly in the snow, and around the back of the building, I found a little blue hatchback. How the hell did they think they were going to get Raf's merchandise in that shitbox, anyway? The keys were in the ignition, and there was nothing in the glove box, the back seat, or the trunk. I pocketed the keys and did a sweep of the nearby buildings. Most of the warehouses stood abandoned, but enough were in use that it wouldn't look suspicious for a truck to head down this way. One good thing about the snow: it was hard to hide movement, and when I didn't find any more footprints or tire tracks, I headed back.

Carl had finished loading the crates into his truck, and the driver had dragged his associate into the trailer. It was none of my business what he did with him. As for the other two....

"Guess we better take care of these jokers," Carl said, clapping a hand on my shoulder.

"Yeah." I went over to the closest one, knelt down, and pulled back his mask. White guy with a buzz cut. He had some prison ink on his face and neck, including a big swastika next to his left eye and an iron cross on the middle of his throat. His buddy was a pudgy fucker with bad skin and a thick red beard. Neither of them had any ID, but the big bastard had a phone in his pants pocket, and I turned it off and shoved it into my coat with my own. "Assholes," I muttered. My anger was still humming through my veins, and I resisted the urge to kick the body closest to me.

Using some stones and gravel from around the lot, we filled their pockets to the brim before we hoisted their sorry asses into the back of the truck and covered them with the tarp. A quick detour to the river's edge would take care of them.

"Gimme your gun." Carl held out his gloved hand.

"What?"

"Your gun. You can't keep it, not after this. We'll put it on one of these guys, make it look like an inside job—if they're ever found."

I pulled out the .45 and looked at it. He was right, and I'd lost weapons before, but still. "Damn, man. I love this gun."

One side of Carl's mouth quirked up as he shook his head. "Boy, you work for an arms dealer. Now give it up. Ain't worth the risk."

With a sigh I knew made me sound like a baby, I handed it over. Carl scrubbed it down with a disposable wipe before wedging it under the tarp. "And now we should get out of here."

"You'll get no argument from me." I followed him to the truck and got inside.

He pulled a cigarette from the pocket of his shirt and lit up, exhaling smoke like it was some kind of gift from God. When he held the pack out to me, I took one. It wasn't the first time I'd popped a guy, but I was jittery, my hands shaking, and I hoped it would help. Maybe it would at least take the edge off my need to fucking pound somebody. Carl looked me over as he held out his plastic lighter. "You got any blood on you?"

"No, got 'em from a distance."

"Good. Let's get rid of these clowns and get this shipment to Raf and then hit up the Denny's. What do you say, man? All-you-can-eat pancakes. You like pancakes, right?"

"I don't dislike them," I said. "But if it's all the same to you, I'd rather get home. I have to help my little sister get ready for school. She's smart, you know? I bet she'll be a scientist or an engineer. But I gotta make sure her attendance is good. I think she can really get somewhere, as long as I do that."

"That's great to hear, man." Carl lifted his hand, and I slapped it. "I'll drop you off. Just as soon as we pay a visit to the scenic banks of the Schuylkill."

"Thanks. Hey, could we stop by a Wawa or a Kangaroo Express? My sister likes donuts. I'll get you a cup of coffee."

"Sure, man. I like donuts too." After we did what we needed to do, Carl maneuvered the truck into the parking lot of a convenience store. We went inside, and I made a beeline to the men's room to scrub my hands and arms down. There wasn't anything visible on me, but I'd had to touch those bodies, and I would think about it every time I rubbed my face if I didn't wash up. It probably would've sounded stupid, but I didn't want to touch my sister or make her breakfast after having my hands on those pieces of shit, even if I had been wearing a pair of old work gloves Carl kept behind the truck seat. After I left the bathroom, I filled a cardboard box with a dozen assorted donuts while he poured himself a coffee and heated a sausage-and-egg biscuit in the store's microwave. When it beeped, we met at the register, and I pulled a twenty from my pants pocket to pay.

"Raf's gonna need to know what happened, brother," Carl said as he situated himself in the driver's seat, donut crumbs clinging to his chin and the wiry gray hairs around his lips.

"Yeah, I know. Look, can you fill him in? I gotta get home. Help my little sister get dressed and shit. She's there by herself."

"Sure, man." Carl pulled the truck onto the road. "I understand, and Raf will too. You did good work today, Dante. You're one hell of a shot. Glad I had you along."

I nodded. "Can you drop me off?"

Carl grunted out an affirmative response, but we'd only made it a few blocks before the storm started, pelting snow so thick the truck's wipers couldn't keep up.

"Good Lord Almighty. I might have to pull over." Carl shifted the truck into Park and put his four-ways on. "I can't see a foot in front of me. We'll have to wait until this settles down."

I couldn't wait. "Tell Raf what happened, okay? Tell him to give me a call. I'll be at home." I opened the door and dropped out of the cab, hitting snow that already reached past my ankles. I didn't wait for Carl's response; I had fourteen blocks to go before I made it home. I pulled my hood over my head and did my best to cover my face with my sleeve. Even for Philadelphia, this was a motherfucker of a snowstorm. I'd never seen anything like it. Ros's school would probably be cancelled, and that was all the more reason for me to make it back as fast as I could. I trudged through the drifts, trying to ignore the stinging pieces of ice hitting me in the face.

My skin was numb by the time I made it to our building, my pant legs were soaked, and another six inches of snow had come down. The door to our apartment was still locked, and it was quiet, though not a whole lot warmer than it was outside. After unlocking Ros's door, I went into my room and stripped off my wet clothes, tucking the contents of my pockets into a dresser drawer. I slipped on some sweats and a long-sleeved T-shirt and went to make some hot chocolate for my sister and more coffee for myself. I'd been up all night, and I was going to need it, especially now that the adrenaline and anger were burning off and all I wanted to do was sleep.

After breakfast, I got the Wii from the safe by my bed, where I kept it so my mom couldn't trade it for glass, and we spent the rest of the day playing *Mario Kart*.

I was at the stove making grilled cheese sandwiches and tomato soup for dinner when my phone rang—Raf. I hurried to turn the stove off, went into the bathroom, and turned the faucet on so Ros wouldn't hear what I was saying. Sitting down on the edge of the tub, I answered the call.

"Carl tells me you had some trouble picking up today's shipment," Raf said.

"Not too much. Just two guys. They're taken care of."

"I heard you performed admirably. I should give you a raise. But first, we need to talk, and we shouldn't do it over the phone. I'll send a car to pick you up."

"Ah… is that absolutely necessary?"

"I think you know it is," Raf answered. "Is there a problem?"

I raked my hair out of my eyes and rested my forehead against my palm. "Just… my mom's been out for two days now. She's gotta be running low on cash, and that means she'll be dragging herself back here. Probably that piece of shit Blaker too. I'd rather not leave Ros alone with them."

"I respect that you want to take care of your family, Dante. But I have to protect my interests, for the benefit of all of us. We can't let something like this go—not even for a night. We have to decide what needs to be done, and I'd like to have you here for that."

Shit. He was depending on me, and I didn't want him to lose his faith in me or start thinking I was a deadbeat. I couldn't let that happen. I'd busted my ass—fucking risked it more than once too—to get where I was, and I needed this job. Needed it to take care of Ros. "I'll be there."

"An Uber's on its way." Raf hung up.

Steam had filled our closet of a bathroom by now, fogging the chipped mirror. I turned the water off and braced my hands on the edge of the sink. I could do this, make it work. I had to.

In the kitchen, I put a sandwich and a bowl of soup on a plastic TV tray. "How about if you have dinner in your room tonight?" I said to Ros.

She stuck out her lower lip. "But I want to watch TV."

"Come on, now. We've been watching all day. It's time to go into your room."

Ros narrowed her eyes but got off the couch and picked up Touchstone. "Where will you be?"

"I have to go into work for a little bit," I said as I went into her room and turned on the lamp beside the bed. I set the food down and patted the yellow quilt with the pink flowers, and Ros sat where I'd indicated.

"I don't like being here by myself."

Those words and the scared and abandoned look in her big eyes hit me like a punch to the gut. She shouldn't have to be scared… shouldn't have to be locked in here to stay safe…. I was doing the best I could, but she wouldn't understand. She shouldn't have to. I forced a smile and waved toward the dolls on her desk, positioned around the children's sewing machine I'd bought her for Christmas. Since then, I'd been picking up scraps of fabric from the remnant bins at craft stores. I lifted up one of the plastic dolls. "Hey, it looks like Mustardseed has a new dress." The little figure wore puffy yellow pants beneath a skirt that looked made from cut leaves, with a little leaf crown to match. Damn, my sister was talented. When I was her age, I still put my underwear on backwards half the time.

She frowned at me. "That one's Ariel, silly. He's a boy. Can you bring him to me?"

Her room was so small I didn't even have to take a step to set the doll on the pillow next to her.

"Can you bring me Oberon and Robin Goodfellow too?"

I surveyed the dolls, not wanting to pick up the wrong ones. Most of them were off-brand knockoffs from Chinatown, but Ros was always changing their clothes and hair. I chose a boy in a silver vest and an androgynous figure with a mop of frizzy white hair and a patchwork tunic. Her smile told me I'd scored.

"I need you to keep these guys safe while I'm away," I told her, sitting down and running my hand over her springy curls. "These guys are pretty small, so I'm going to lock the door. Don't open it, okay? Even if you hear Mom come in. Especially if you hear her. You know she's… sick, right? She'll need to get her rest."

"I know, Dante," she whispered, looking down and plucking at the little leaves on Ariel's head. "She's always sick."

"Sorry." I didn't know what else to say, how to explain to my sister that our mother couldn't take care of her. I kissed her on the forehead. "I'll tell you what. You be good and stay in here until I get back, and this weekend we'll go shopping and get some new clothes for you. Maybe even another doll."

She smiled wide. "Could we get me a deer? I really need one of those. A hart."

"Sure, if we can find one."

"I love you, Dante." She wrapped her skinny little arms around my neck, and I couldn't breathe, could hardly see past the tears stinging my eyes. It took a few minutes before I could tell her I loved her too. Then I hurried to leave, securing the padlock on the outside of her door when I reached the hall.

Pressing my palm against the cheap wood that was nowhere near enough to protect her, I called out, "And remember to say your prayers."

"You remember to say yours too!" she answered.

I did. I prayed hard while I stood on the street waiting for my ride, my breath freezing in clouds around me. *Please let her be okay. Please keep her safe. Please, please, please.*

Chapter Ten

I'D BEEN to Raf's place up in East Falls a few times, and it always sort of kicked me in the nuts, because it was exactly the kind of place where Ros deserved to grow up: big old trees, parks, bike trails. Good schools and coffee shops and Indian restaurants. No ridiculous mansions, just neat little row houses painted different colors. No marble floors or ballrooms, just cute, cozy places with rosebushes out front and little yards with barbecues and swing sets. Looking at them, imagining having one for my sister, with a pink bedroom on the second floor, made me feel something sharp in my diaphragm. I guess maybe it was longing.

Raf lived in one of them, a corner house he'd been renovating since I met him even though he could've paid someone to have the work done. Hell, if he wanted to, he could've lived in one of those ridiculous mansions that took up a whole city block, hired a bunch of maids and a butler. But on paper, Raf was just a humble man, working from home translating novels and textbooks into Spanish, tutoring occasionally. He drove a Jeep Cherokee and volunteered at the library. He was a pillar of the community. He was also a smart man, and I respected him.

I got out of the SUV and went up the neatly shoveled walk to the porch. The snow around me reached to my thighs, and it was still coming down steadily, though without the blinding, biting intensity it had that morning.

I rang the bell and Raf answered the door, wiping his hands on a tea towel. He looked just like somebody would expect a guy who translated books to look: tall, brown hair cut neatly, some gray at his temples. Dark olive skin, clean-shaven, in good shape but not a bodybuilder. He wore khaki pants and a fitted V-neck sweater in a rust color that brought out the reddish brown of his eyes. "Dante! I finally installed that espresso machine I was telling you about. Can I offer you something?"

"Sure. That sounds great." I stepped into the foyer and knelt down to take off my boots. Raf was very proud of his original hardwood floors. I shrugged off my jacket and left it on a hook by the door, and then I followed him through the living room and into the big, modern kitchen with its terra-cotta tiles, granite countertops, and handblown red glass accents. I took a seat on one of the stools at the island while he fiddled with the massive stainless steel contraption. It clanked and guzzled and puffed out steam. He filled a doll-sized cup with thick black liquid and handed it to me. Smiling, I accepted it and took a sip. Actually, I didn't like it much—too strong and bitter. I preferred the creamy french vanilla stuff that came out of the machine at the Wawa. Guess I wasn't very refined.

"Why don't we go into the study?" Raf indicated the hall on the opposite side of the kitchen, and I let him lead even though I knew the way.

When we got there, Raf went behind his old-fashioned desk and set his own drink on a coaster. Behind him, the snow collected in little crescents on the panes of the big bay window, like something off a Christmas card, all sparkly. The lights in there were set into the ceiling, and it gave the room a fuzzy yellow glow, making the floor-to-ceiling wooden bookshelves gleam. The gas fireplace set into a stone column in the corner added to the effect.

I took a seat next to Carl on the leather sofa. I didn't know he would be here—but then I wouldn't have seen his truck on the street. Raf was too careful for that. Opposite him was a big guy with a shaved head who just went by Devereux. I didn't know if it was a first or a last name. He was some relation of Carl's—a second cousin or something—from Louisiana. In an armchair next to Devereux was his friend Louie, a good-looking guy with long dreadlocks tied in a ponytail. He was wearing a leather jacket tonight, but I knew he had the most kickass sleeve on his right arm—tropical flowers so lifelike you could see the dewdrops on the petals. If I could ever afford to get some ink done, I was gonna find out who his artist was, get something like that for myself.

"Gentlemen," Raf said. He nodded to a small woman with pixie-cut dark hair perched on a velvet ottoman next to the fire, her long, thin legs crossed at the ankles. She had big gray-green eyes, and her snug leggings and satin tank top left little of her slim, muscular body to the imagination. Her bone-china complexion might've looked sickly except for the deep rose that swept across her prominent cheekbones. "Lady." Everyone was always saying how hot she was, but Moirin scared the shit out of me. She got pissed off at the tiniest thing and would want to fight—if she wasn't joking. I could never tell the difference. She liked baiting people, seeing if she could sucker them in, backing them into a corner until nothing they did or said was right. I tried to stay away from her. I wasn't interested in games that ended with me getting my ass kicked—or grudge-fucking her. Not that she hadn't tried… both, actually.

"We have a problem," Raf continued. "Dante, why don't you tell the others what happened this morning."

I took a sip of the nasty coffee to buy myself a couple of seconds, convincing myself there was no reason to be nervous. All I needed to do was tell them what went down. So I did. "Me and Carl went to pick up the shipment. Weren't expecting any trouble, but then out of nowhere these two assholes showed up, trying to jack the goods, I guess."

"Where are they now?" Moirin asked accusingly, her eyes narrowed.

"The fucking river," I answered a little testily, and was surprised at her nod and expression of respect.

"Describe these men," Raf prompted.

"Skinheads," I said. "A younger one with some Nazi shit tattooed on his face, and a fat one with a beard."

Raf steepled his fingers, pursed his lips into a thin line, and nodded. "This retaliation isn't completely unexpected. These white supremacists have been trying to gain a foothold in the area. The… current political climate has encouraged them to be bold, made many of them feel validated in beliefs that no doubt all of us find despicable. Now, you know how I do business. I am a supplier of quality items, and I don't discriminate. I have been asked to, upon many occasions and by many organizations, all of whom would stand to benefit if their competition didn't have access to my products. I've stood by my position, however, and I've gained the respect of the various factions in this city: the Black Mafia, the Dominicans, the Puerto Ricans, the Triads, the Poles, the Irish… even the Italian families here and in New Jersey and New York. I'm Dominican myself, but even that hasn't swayed me toward favoritism. Remaining neutral has served me quite well."

"Nobody's had the bollocks to try and steal from us before." Moirin shook her head.

"I made an exception to my policy when I was approached by this gang," Raf said, looking at each of us in turn, meeting our eyes. "They call themselves the White Liberation Front, and until now they've been a rural movement, operating out of central Pennsylvania and upstate New York. These… individuals are known mostly for human trafficking, specifically the abduction and sale of boys and girls of color—often the children of illegal immigrants—for purposes I don't think I need to describe. They make no secret of the opinion that certain people belong in the servitude of others. I declined to do business with them, and they weren't happy."

Moirin got to her feet, made a fist, and smacked it against her other hand as she paced in front of the fire. "No. No fucking way. The Irish won't stand for this. Kids? Hell no. There's just some things you don't fucking do."

Devereux nodded and leaned back. His face was in shadow, but the firelight glinted off his eyes. I wouldn't have fucked with him on a dare just then. "Tell me where to find them and I'll take a crew and wipe them off the face of the planet, you can be sure."

I was feeling a little sick, the espresso rising like lava up my throat. All I could picture was Ros's scared face, kids like her, kids who didn't matter because their families didn't have money…. "Fuck. I'm glad I killed those assholes."

"You did good work, Dante," Raf said.

Carl nodded and patted me on the back. "Clowns never knew what hit 'em. This boy right here like Jesse James, and I ain't playing."

That reminded me. "My gun. The Colt. I had to get rid of it. I need another one."

"I don't work out of my home," Raf said.

"I need another one!" What if these jerk-offs came looking for us, for my sister? What if I had put her in danger? "Raf, I need one."

"We'll. Talk. Later." His tone invited no argument, so I nodded and tried to take another sip of the coffee. My hands were shaking so bad, the rim of the cup knocked me in the teeth. I set it on the floor and folded my hands in my lap, hoping nobody had noticed. I couldn't afford for them to see me as a liability. As long as I kept this job, I could take care of Ros and keep putting some money back so she could go to college someday. I was a high school dropout—I wouldn't get another job that would even pay enough to keep us fed. I tried to let the tension out of my neck and shoulders while I waited for the conversation to continue.

"I don't intend to retaliate," Raf said.

"You're shitting me!" Moirin's eyes widened until I thought they'd drop out of her head.

"No, ma'am, I am not. I won't seek retribution, but know this: I will keep these pieces of filth out of my city, away from the children who live here. I will do what it takes to ensure they don't gain a single block of territory, not a single inch. Now, I am owed a lot of favors by a lot of people, but I would prefer to handle this internally."

"Well, it goes without saying that if these bastards show their faces in any black neighborhood, they won't be leaving again," Louie said. "I'll spread the word. See to it."

"Same goes for the Irish," Moirin said. "I'll make sure of it."

"It ain't the black and Irish kids we need to be worrying about," Carl said. "We need to get the word out to the neighborhoods where people might not have papers, where they can't go to the police if a kid turns up missing." He smiled. "I'm just an old junkman, and I talk to a lot of people. Just an old man shootin' the breeze. That's me."

"Excellent," Raf said. "If we can bring people together, make them forget their differences for a common cause, we can drive these scumbags out of Philadelphia. I don't expect a lasting peace, only a united front until we achieve our goals."

"I'll see that I make that plain to 'em, boss," Carl said.

"Let the Haitians and the Pakistani communities know they might see some of our crew from time to time," Devereux said in his leisurely accent. "Tell them we are there to hunt us some Nazis. We won't sell on their turf or interfere with any business they're running."

I wanted to help, and then I remembered: "I took a cell phone off one of the bodies. A set of car keys too." I pulled them from my pocket.

"Well done, boyo!" Moirin said, clapping. "Give them here. I have a friend who'll see what we can find out from these."

I tossed them, and she caught the phone in her right hand and the keys in her left.

"It's late," Raf said. "All of us should get some rest. Thank you for coming. There's no need to drag this out, but as soon as the weather breaks, let's start spreading the word. Few people in this city will want to make enemies of us, but if they are dealing with these people, that's what they'll do. Conversely, let them know their aid in this matter won't be forgotten."

Everyone got up to leave, and I followed them, even though I wasn't sure who would be giving me a ride home. I felt like I was in a nightmare, and there was some security in knowing I could still get up and walk away, that I still had control of my body if nothing else.

"Dante." Moirin stopped short, causing me to bump into her back. She looked over her shoulder at me and winked. "You look like you could stand to take your mind off your worries, boyo."

"I'm fine. Thanks."

"You mean to say you wouldn't like a pretty girl to distract you for a bit?"

I gritted my teeth and held my temper. I wasn't in the mood for this shit. "I appreciate it, Moirin, but I just need to get home."

"Ha! You thought I was offering?"

Dammit, I'd fallen into her trap again. "Of course I didn't think you meant you would—"

She turned to face me, hands on her hips, and now her nipples grazed my chest. Great. "Oh, am I not pretty enough for you, then?"

"You're very pretty."

"Well, well. If you like what you see, why not do something about it?"

Raf intervened to save me, thank Christ. "I need a word with Dante."

I turned back toward Raf's desk. "Yeah?"

Moirin giggled. "I'm only taking the piss out of the lad, Raf. No need to defend him. Trying to get him to laugh was all I was doing." She patted me on the shoulder. "I'll be on my way."

"How about if I give you a ride home?" Raf stood and pushed his desk chair in.

"Yes! I mean, that would be great."

By the door, I got into my boots and coat. Another few inches of snow had fallen while we talked in the study, and it crunched beneath my feet as I followed Raf to the Jeep. I got inside while he cleared the windshield with a brush.

"What a storm!" Raf said as he started the engine.

"Sure is. Came out of nowhere too."

"Listen, Dante. You've been with me for a few years now, and you've always been dependable and loyal. I'd like it if you would let me move you and Rosalind somewhere safer. I know you worry when you have to leave her behind, and I don't like asking you to do it. I have a nice little apartment south of here, on Cherry Street, not too far from Franklin Square and Chinatown. It's a nice area, and I think it would be good for the two of you. It won't be hard for me to make it look like you're paying rent. In fact, it'll help me launder some of my money. That was the reason I bought it in the first place. What do you think? The schools are good, and there are parks and museums close by. Lots of nice places to eat. Plenty of history."

The snow streaked past the windows as he drove, making me feel like we were going down a tunnel. Like I was still at home playing *Mario Kart* with my sister, things blurring past in my peripheral vision, little more than smudges. I swallowed hard. This was what I wanted for Ros, and it would be stupid not to say yes. But then what would happen to my mom? She wouldn't pay the electric bill, and the place would be freezing. She wouldn't pay the rent, and she'd end up out on the street. Fuck. No matter how I looked at it, Mom would die without me there to make sure things got paid. To keep food in the house and remind her to eat once in a while.

But she was an adult, and she'd had her chance. Ros deserved a chance. She shouldn't have every opportunity taken away from her because she was unlucky enough to be born into our family. She had as much right to a life as someone who'd been born into a rich family, and I couldn't make sure that happened, not on my own.

"Dante? What do you think? I'd love to have you and your sister live there, and I wouldn't take it out of your pay. Call it a bonus."

"I… shit. That's so generous of you, Raf. I'll think about it, okay?" Somewhere, not even buried too deep, I knew I'd say yes. Shit, I had to—even if it meant not being around to make sure Mom stayed alive.

We pulled up in front of my building, and the place looked sadder than ever, lopsided and ready to collapse under the weight of the snow. I didn't imagine anyone would care enough to dig it out. It sure as shit wouldn't be the only condemned building in this area that people were content to ignore while it slowly crumbled. I reached for the door handle, but Raf caught my arm, stopping me. He reached into his pocket and pressed a wad of cash into my hand. "You've earned this."

I clutched the money to my chest, my cheeks hot. I was ashamed of my need, of my desperation. Ashamed that I couldn't provide for my family. But I was in no position to turn it down. "Thanks, Raf."

He looked out the windshield, where the snow grew thicker and thicker on the glass. "Those guns today, they came all the way from Russia. Smuggled into Alaska, down the West Coast, around South America, and all the way up to Maine where they were hidden underneath lobsters to get to me."

"Thought I noticed a funny smell," I said, forcing a smile that I doubted fooled Raf.

He was still holding my arm, and he stared into my eyes with an expression I couldn't quite identify. "This was an important shipment, one I put a lot of work and planning into, and one I needed. You made sure it got to me. This isn't charity, Dante. I… I value you. I want to keep you."

"I'm not going anywhere," I said. "Except to bed. I've been awake close to forty-eight hours, and my ass is kicked."

"I understand. Please consider my offer."

"I will. Thanks again."

I got out of the Jeep, but Raf didn't pull away until I closed the door to our building. I trudged up the stairs, my feet feeling like cinder blocks. After I got Ros off to school in the morning, I could spend the whole fucking day facedown in my pillows, and I couldn't wait.

The door to our place was cracked open. Instantly alert, I pulled the snub-nose from my pants and shouldered into the apartment. Dark. Quiet. An infomercial played on the TV—hairspray with no alcohol.

Ros's door leaned against the wall, torn from the hinges, my padlock on the floor, the doorframe splintered. The dolls were scattered across the floor, and one of my mom's old college books lay open at the foot of the bed. I flung open the closet door and pushed aside the dresses and sweaters. Her shoes stood in a neat row.

"Ros? Ros!" In the bathroom, I looked behind the shower curtain and in the little alcove where we kept the washing machine. Sometimes she climbed into my bed when she got scared, but she wasn't there tonight.

She wasn't anywhere.

No, dear God, no. The fucking Nazis. I ran out onto the street and looked up and down, as if that would do a damned thing. What the fuck had I done? I turned my face toward the sky and screamed my throat raw, and then I fell to my knees in the snowbank, sobbing and choking. I puked up the cup of espresso, staining and melting the snow, and then I reached into my pocket with a shaking hand and touched Raf's name on my contact list.

"Dante?"

At first all I could do was cry and sputter. And scream. Then I heaved in a few deep breaths. "Come back."

"Dante, you're scaring me. What—?"

"Just come back! Raf! Come back! I need you. I—" I gagged again, though my stomach was empty.

"Okay, okay," he said. "I'm turning around. Just keep calm. We'll figure this out."

I looked up at the stars and screamed again. I didn't have words for this, for the fear, the rage. I prayed he was right. What would I do if he wasn't?

Chapter Eleven

Bless the Pennsylvania Department of Transportation. Those hardworking and dedicated bastards kept the buses running until the snow was asshole deep—enough for me and Charlene to make our way to a club on 13th Street. I was fucking horny—hungry—and I needed something.

The place was kind of pretentious, touristy, but I was too desperate for activism. I made sure the doorman saw what he wanted and the bartender saw someone worthy of getting a drink. Sipping my watered-down scotch, I looked around. It was early, and with the storm, the place was pretty empty. But a guy sat at a table in the corner. He looked nervous—out-of-town type—and I went over and sat down across from him. He was cute if average—dirty-blond hair and blue eyes, a striped polo shirt over stiff, new jeans—but he seemed receptive, greeting me with a smile and a lift of whatever purplish red shite he was drinking.

"First time?" I asked.

"What? Oh, in here? Yeah. What about you?"

"Not my first time." I ran the tip of my tongue along the rim of my glass, holding his shocked eyes the entire time. "So what do you think?"

"About what?"

The way he blushed and trembled was adorable, intriguing. Even better was his desire washing over me, shaping me into his fantasy. It not only made me big—tall and muscular—it told me how to interact with him to fulfill his needs. I set my drink aside and leaned my elbows on the table, forcing my way into his space. "What do you think about me taking you into the bathroom and pounding your ass?"

"I… I don't know."

"Yes, you do. You'd love for me to fuck you until you can't stand. There's nothing wrong with admitting it." I tipped my cup and downed the rest of my drink. "I'll be in the men's room—for five minutes."

Without waiting for his response, I turned and left, my cat tucked under my arm. When I got to the gents, I took off my jacket and made a nest for Charlene in the corner of a stall. I dropped a kiss between her sleek little ears and whispered for her to wait for me. She lay down and curled up against the lining of my coat, and I went to stand by the sinks.

My shy lad crept around the door less than two minutes later. He smiled at me, and I smiled back. "Where are you from?"

"M-Missouri," he said.

"Hmm. Married?"

"Does it matter?"

"No." I grasped him by the shirt, spun him around, and pushed his chest against the counter. I smacked his ass, then his inner thigh. "Spread your legs."

Even as he complied, he looked over his shoulder at me with wide eyes. Sweat glimmered across his forehead and above his lip. "What? Here? What if someone sees?"

"Then they'll see me giving it to you good," I answered with another slap to his flank. He wanted a bit of rough, and I could do that. "Do you have a problem with that?"

"No, I-I want this. I don't care if someone watches."

I pulled his pants down and scraped my nails over his round, lightly furred cheeks. In the mirror, I saw his eyes roll back and his face turn bright red, the flush creeping all the way down. He needed this, and I was going to provide. I could already see in his scrunched-up expression how much he adored me, and I knew how to coax him even further toward that forbidden edge he'd always dreamt of stepping over. "Yeah? You'd like that? You'd like an audience of men in here watching while I tear you apart? Maybe jerking off, getting so turned on by watching what I do to you?"

"Ugh. Oh God."

I moved my hand to the flap in his underpants. "What, baby? You want some guys in here to watch you? I can make that happen for you."

"You… you can?" His eyes were like the sky when the clouds shifted and the blue poked out, his desire decadent summer, ice cream dripping on asphalt, chewing gum liquid in the heat, pineapple juice with too much cheapass gin. Jolly Ranchers stuck to their wrappers, making your cheeks suck in when the tart flavor hit your tongue. All melty and sticky and so sweet my mouth watered. I couldn't wait to feast on that pulpy sunshine pouring out of him. I was going to make this perfect—better than he imagined while he jerked off when his wife was out shopping with her sister.

"I'm going to take such good care of you, you sweet little thing." I smiled, and a minute later two men came into the restroom: an older gentleman with close-cropped gray hair and a stout, burly bloke with a thick brown beard to match the wavy mop on his head. My particular skills might not have many practical applications, but when I needed them, they delivered. "We have an audience, my sweet. Are you ready?"

Before he could answer, I pushed two fingers into his mouth, rubbing them against his tongue. "Get them wet," I whispered, leaning down next to his ear and flicking my tongue along the edge.

He sucked sloppily on my fingers until they were coated in his saliva. He grunted, and the bearded man groaned and unzipped his fly. "See that, baby? He's so hot, watching what I'm doing to you. Look at what you're doing to these men. It's just like you always wanted. You're driving them crazy."

He dropped his head to the edge of the counter and sobbed, but it was the good kind of crying, the breaking of that wall of guilt and judgment so the golden light could pour out. "Oh God. Fuck me. Now, please. There's… there's things in my pocket…."

He rooted around and came up with a handful of condoms and packets of lube. I couldn't infect him, but telling him so would intrude on his dream—what he wanted was another man, a human man, and so that was what I became. Looking in the mirror, I saw my tan skin and square jaw, receding dark hair cut short. I slid the condom on and tore open the lube with my teeth. It was watermelon. Appropriate. Perfect. Summer. Perfect fucking summer, warm and sweet and so juicy it dripped down your chin. I squeezed the packet and let the clear gel drizzle over him. He shivered pleasantly and arched his back, tilting his hips into the air.

His skin was so red it looked sunburnt, lips shiny with spit, hands shaking where he gripped the edge of the counter. Behind us, the two guys were kissing, rubbing and squeezing each other. My lad's eyes flitted to them now and then, but mostly he watched me, watched me like I was some deity descended from heaven. I'd hoped to get a snack to keep my strength up, but I'd happened on a feast fit for a king.

Except I wasn't feeling his energy seep into me, wasn't satiated at all.

"What are you waiting for?" he rasped. "You… you haven't changed your mind?"

This guy whose name I didn't know, who probably worked selling office supplies or some kind of insurance, he needed me. He'd shaped me into exactly what he had always wanted, and I might be his only chance. I bent over him and sucked at his neck, pulling the salty skin up between my lips and teeth. "No, I've always wanted to do this, fuck somebody like you. You're perfect, baby, and I'm gonna make you come so hard." I fucked him for all I was worth, fucked him like he was the only man I'd ever touched, the only one I'd ever touch.

He'd given me a tattoo, an anchor and a rope on the side of my neck, and I slipped completely into his fantasy, doing just what he needed without having to think about it. "You like this?" I panted as I pulled his collar aside to nip at his shoulders.

"Yeah."

"Tell me. I want to hear it."

"God… I-I love this." He soon lost the ability to form words, nothing coming from his swollen lips but long, low moans mixed with choking cries of pleasure.

I watched him break apart, all his cells or molecules or whatever the fuck we're made of spinning free, dancing about in the negative space, and slowly coalescing until he came with a ragged scream—a newborn cry of transformation. And that's only a flowery metaphor to anyone who hasn't been with me.

After I finished into the condom and we separated, the guy stood and looked at me with wide eyes, wobbling like a baby horse. But I could see it in his face—he knew his legs would hold him, and he was ready to run. With a smile, he brushed his lips over my stubbled cheek. "Thank you. This… all of this has made me think."

Against the wall, the hipster with the beard grunted into the older guy's neck. They weren't really concerned with us anymore.

"'Bout what?" I asked.

He grinned, showing slightly crooked teeth. "I… I don't know. Maybe about staying in Philadelphia, looking for work. I… I was always too scared to…. I'm not so scared, though. I think maybe I could do it. Ha. Probably just endorphins or whatever. Afterglow. It's probably stupid to consider changing your whole life just because of a fuck in a bar bathroom."

Sensing he needed it, I reached out and pulled him to my chest, wrapping him in my arms and stroking his damp hair. "The reason's not important. Your life needs changing or you wouldn't be thinking about it at all."

He nodded against my thick pecs covered in dark hair. I was liking this role he'd written for me, starting to see myself slipping easily into it—I could do worse than a bloke who liked a bit of rough, urgent sex and dirty talk but sweet cuddles after. Being there next to me made him feel safe, and I understood the anchor tattoo. That's what he wanted, what I was to him: something to keep him in place while the chaos surged and swelled all around. I rather liked that idea. Sure, in time, months or a year or two from now, someone else would catch his eye and I wouldn't be the pinnacle of perfection anymore—he'd start noticing that I snored and left crisp crumbs in the bed, that another boy had better calves—but I could soak up the honeymoon energy until it waned, feed on it for however long it lasted.

Except I couldn't. I could see the gilded glow spilling from his every pore, taste it on the air like fresh-cut lawns and barbeque smoke, but that's all it was. Meals I couldn't eat. It was awful, like starving while watching a fucking cooking show—enough to entice but impossible to get my hands on. I started to get scared. This had never happened to me before.

"What's wrong?" my companion asked.

I shook my head. "I've got to get going."

He chuckled. "Me too. Company meeting at the hotel tonight. Will I see you again?"

"I don't think so."

He nodded and stepped away from me. "Well, this was good."

"It was." I reached out, scraping and clawing, desperate to close my fingers around even a crumb I could lick off my hand. But I couldn't. "You'll do well here, if you decide to stay."

"Yeah. It's the one good thing about being an insurance adjuster, I guess. You can find work anywhere."

"Yeah."

He turned away, and I didn't want to let him go. I was so hungry, so desperate I wanted to clutch him to me, get a taste of that satisfied essence he was spilling. But I couldn't, and it wasn't his fault. "You know, I think you're going to have an inspired life."

"That's a heck of a thing to say."

"I can just tell. You just have to chase it. Don't settle. If you remember today, remember that." Fuck, what was I? A football coach? A bloody motivational speaker? I usually had more time to be subtle, but I needed to leave him better for the experience. That was the whole point of me.

Despite his sweaty hair and the bruises on his neck, he looked formidable when he straightened his back. His blue eyes were clear, determined. "I will. Thanks again."

He left the room, and I was alone. The other two had slipped out without my noticing and were probably fucking each other senseless somewhere nearby. In the mirror, I began to change back to nondescript and unmemorable, with the real me just behind the veneer the mortals saw. If I squinted at my reflection, I could see my horns, the softness to my face and lips. I'd liked being a big bastard, the kind of bloke who might wear a knitted beanie and watch boxing. Being abstract again, having no identity so soon, was unnerving, but not as unnerving as not being able to absorb the honeymoon energy. Fuck. I turned on the faucet and splashed some cold water on my plain, forgettable face.

As if she sensed my distress, Charlene crept out of the stall and wound her little body around my ankles. She would be getting hungry too. I'd go back into the bar and order some chicken or something. No reason we both had to starve.

I picked my jacket up off the floor and put it on. Thank fuck this place was clean—at least at this hour of the morning. After tucking Charlene in close to my chest, I took a last look at the room. I knew what I needed to do, because I knew what that pale pointy-eared bastard had taken from me. I'm a lover, not a fighter, but the thought of his face made me wish I'd meet a lad who got turned on by ninja serial killers and blood spatter.

Charlene mewled and butted against my chin. I nuzzled my cheek against her head. "I know, mate. First you eat, and then we go deal with the delicate faerie flower."

Chapter Twelve

I WAS having a lovely party with Mrs. Guzman, drinking Mama Juana—the very excellent home brew she used as cough syrup or kept for when getting inebriated was an absolute necessity—and enjoying the dancing of her little figurines as music wafted into the kitchen from the living room. I enchanted a trio of little men in ponchos with curled mustaches to accompany the tune on the stringed instruments they held, and stuffed rabbits pranced in a line while glass birds fluttered around the light over the table.

Mrs. Guzman—Corazón—made a delightful dance partner. As soon as I was free of this realm, I would take her to one of my houses and weave flowers into her hair. I would conjure a terrace beside a waterfall where she could dance and dance… and I would find some mortal musicians to play the spicy, sensuous music she seemed to favor. I'd construct columns wrapped in ivy and hibiscus to surround the tiled floor. It was nice to have that decided and to have something to look forward to when I returned to my lands, something to occupy myself. Making things and perfecting their every detail until I tired of them was a favorite pastime of mine.

Of course, that dour demon had to interrupt our merriment sometime well after dark. He pounded on the door until we let him inside, snow sloughing off his body as if he was one of my people, of the variety who favored frost and ice. Mrs. Guzman patted his cheeks and took his rumpled jacket to the closet. Inky indulged her with a smile but narrowed his pink eyes at me. "You pig-fucking son of a bastard whore."

"Language, Raphael," Mrs. Guzman said in her lilting voice as she spun and took a sip from her dainty chalice. She went to put a new disk into her machine while Inky backed me against the living room wall.

I heard a soft mew, followed by *He's very angry, fey-friend. He wanted to mate, but it wasn't successful.*

"Ah, the incomparable Charlene. Good evening, my love." I smiled and bowed to the black-and-white cat, and she swatted me in the mouth with a paw, leaving a small cut on my lower lip.

"Don't you try sucking up to my cat, cunt." Inky shoved his fist into my shoulder, but I pushed past him as another jaunty tune began.

I held my hand out to Mrs. Guzman. "My lady."

"Ah, Ramon. You are so handsome. My beautiful soldier boy. Such a hero." We began to dance, the figurines on the floor scurrying out of the way of our feet. "Where is your lovely wife tonight?"

"Well, she commands a large portion of your ruler's forces," I said. "Training them takes more of her time than she would like. But no one is better equipped for the job, because they cannot match her intimate knowledge of warfare. Alas, keeping this realm safe remains her priority, though I am sure she would prefer to be here. Duty to one's people is a heavy burden."

"An admirable young woman," Mrs. Guzman said. "Her hands are probably full with all the terrorists. Isis and Al-Qaeda."

"Exactly," I answered, dipping her. "And on top of that, being such a legendary beauty that artists are lining up to commit her image to paintings and statuary. And we mustn't forget her enthralling singing voice."

"A movie star and a general," Mrs. Guzman muttered dreamily. "Does that mean I will have to wait for grandchildren?"

"Hardly! My wife is already pregnant with twins! A boy and a girl. She insists our daughter must have your name."

"Isn't that wonderful! Oh, I can hardly wait to get my hands on the little *angelitos*. You will have to forgive me if I spoil them rotten."

There was a high-pitched, scratchy screech, and then the music stopped. Poor Mrs. Guzman looked positively crestfallen as she drained her little goblet and stumbled to sit on the lurid sofa, her head lolling back against the cushions.

"Enough, asshole," Inky hissed through his teeth. "You took something of mine, and I want it back."

I crossed my arms over my chest. "Then fulfill the bargain you agreed to, demon."

Charlene became agitated, and Inky released her from his coat. She went to swipe at the rabbits dancing in a line, batting at their white whiskers as their bulky hind legs thumped up and down.

"You fucking prick," Inky said. "I only wanted to keep you safe because nobody deserves to get tortured. At least that was what I thought. I'll be amending my opinion after meeting you. You don't want me and you don't need me, so fucking let me go. Let me live and get what I need from the mortals."

Obtuse, that's what he was. I had tried to explain this, but it seemed I would need to repeat myself. "There are rules. The deal is struck, and it needs to be fulfilled. You need to complete the task you agreed to do for me."

"I only agreed because I didn't want you to die!"

Mrs. Guzman snorted, having succumbed to her potent liquor, and the Mama Juana in her cup spilled onto the carpet. I made a chicken wearing a blue bandana around her neck remove the glass, the stem in her ceramic beak. "The reason is not important, Inky. What's important is that you agreed. That is an oath you cannot break."

His ridged horns almost scraped the ceiling when he threw his head back, growling. "Fine! Let's go back to the little girl's house, then. But I'll say this, you little cunt: I won't let you hurt her. If it comes down to it, I'll stop you. I won't let a kid get hurt. Don't fucking test me. I just want you gone and myself back to normal, but there's just shit you don't do. Understand?"

"Yes, yes." I waved my hand. "You're very chivalrous. Everyone take note. Quickly, someone erect a statue showing how absolutely heroic you are. The song of your deeds will ring from the hills."

"Fuck you. Let's just get this over with."

"If it means I have access to my home and my estates, then lead the way, demon."

With a grunt, he turned back toward the door. He clucked his tongue, and Charlene came running. As he bent to pick her up, I said, "She will be safer and more comfortable if we leave her here."

"Yeah, I guess." He gave her a scratch behind the ears, and together we walked the short distance to the building where Rosalind Mayfield shared rooms with her brother. The sun was just coming up when we arrived, and it washed the conical heaps of snow lining the walkways with diluted yellow and soft rose.

Inky was tense as we climbed the stairs, his fists furled tight. Even though he knew he would lose, he had every intention of fighting me for the safety of the child. Pitiful as it was, it also struck me as somehow endearing. Anyway, I felt sure it wouldn't come to that. The chance that this girl had woven so complex an enchantment was as slim as a wisp of dandelion fuzz. I just needed to be sure, so I knocked on the flimsy door.

It opened much faster than it had before, and the pretty boy grabbed me by my lapels, dragged me inside, and slammed my back against the wall. Pink tainted the whites of his eyes, and his lips pulled back to reveal clenched teeth as he pressed his weapon against my face. The metal produced a dull ache along my jawbone.

"Where's my sister, you son of a bitch?"

"What? Is Rosalind—"

"I'm asking the questions, you piece of shit. Where is she?"

"I would also like to know," I told him. "The entire reason for our visit this morning is to speak with her."

Dante drew back and, with the hand holding his small weapon, hit me in the face. It hurt, and though my skin did not break, a fuzzy pain bloomed behind my eyes, and for a moment darkness spilled in at the periphery of my vision. This had all been quite interesting, but enough was enough. I waved my fingers and he flew back, shattering the little table in front of his sofa when he struck it. Faster than I expected, he was on his feet again, a cut across his cheek dripping blood and his weapon pointed at me. "You're fucking dead!"

"Wait!" Inky stepped in front of me, his arms stretched out. My, he *had* developed a protective streak. It almost seemed he'd grown in stature as well. "Dante, please listen."

"Why? Why shouldn't I just shoot both your sorry asses? Give me one reason."

"Because if we do know anything about your sister, you won't find out if we're dead." Inky took a cautious step forward, as if he approached a wounded beast. "Not that we do. We don't even know what happened here."

"Then what the fuck are you doing here?" The boy's hand dropped just a hair.

"We wanted to talk to your sister. We need her help, actually."

Dante's eyes narrowed. "With what?"

"I'm… I'm afraid that's going to take some explaining." Inky blew out a breath and shook his head. "I don't know how I'm ever going to convince you to believe any of it either."

"I'll see to that." As I stepped around Inky, I licked the first two fingers of my right hand. When I reached the boy, I made him stand still. Oh, he wanted to kill me, wrap his hands around my throat and squeeze until I was dead, but it was easy enough to prevent. I swiped my wet fingers across his left eye, and then I stepped back. His reaction was sure to be… unpredictable.

For a few moments the boy thrashed his head and cursed my existence and my ancestry with an impressive array of colorful phrases. He quite literally swore at me until he ran out of breath to continue.

Then, chest and shoulders heaving, he slowly lifted his head and focused on me—on both of us. His eyes widened, and then he scrunched them shut. He kept them closed a long while before he opened them again.

"What the fuck did you do to me?"

"I simply washed away the gauze in front of your eye," I told him. "I have allowed you to truly see. It's quite a gift, and to imagine, I granted it with no thought of recompense."

"You gave me something! What was it? What did you give me?" The boy was trembling, breathing as if he'd run up the side of a mountain, the color leeching out of his skin.

Inky pushed past me and put a hand on Dante's shoulder. A few broken cries escaped Dante, and he clearly wanted to flinch away, but I thought it best to keep him immobilized a bit longer.

"Dante, look at me," Inky said in a firm but gentle tone.

"N-no."

"Yes. Look at me." Inky took Dante's chin between his thumb and finger and tipped his head up. "Good start. Now take a nice deep breath. Slowly. Breathe, or you're going to pass out."

It took many moments before the boy composed himself enough to ask, "What are you?"

"I'm just a different kind of person to you," Inky said, stroking his cheek. "I'm…. The people who know about my kind call us magical creatures. There are a fair few of us in the world still."

"Bullshit," Dante said. His hand twitched like he wanted to reach for Inky.

I thought that might actually help, move things along so we could get on with the important part. "I'm going to give you back the use of your hand, so long as you agree to drop that funny little weapon as soon as I do. Do we have a bargain?"

He nodded, and the piece of metal fell with a soft thud. Slowly, Dante reached up and held his fingers a few inches from Inky's face. Inky smiled, and it was disarming, that smile. Dante returned it, though his lower lip still quivered, and he pinched a strand of Inky's silvery hair. Then he stretched his quaking fingers out and closed his hand around one of Inky's horns, tugging at it as if he could dislodge the thing. "H-holy shit. What are… what the hell are you?"

Inky made a sound like a growl and a hiss. "That's the word in our language. Your people, some of them call us demons, though that's a misleading word. Makes us sound like cunts."

"But you're not?"

"Cunts? Some of us are, some aren't. Same as your kind. I try not to be one, but nobody's perfect."

Dante turned to me. "And… and him?"

"Cunt of the highest order, I'm afraid. But to answer what I think you're asking… fey," Inky said.

"Like a faerie?"

"Yeah."

The boy tilted his head. "My sister believes in faeries. When she was little, she always wanted me to read from *A Midsummer Night's Dream* and *The Tempest*. Anything in my mom's old college books about faeries. I imagined they'd be… different. And you say there are more?"

"More like me. Some, anyway. Not like Blossom. Not for a long time."

"How come I've never seen one before?"

"You couldn't see," I said. "I've fixed your eyes now, though."

"I don't…." His little mortal mind was breaking, filled with more than it could hold. "Look, can you let me go? I need some coffee. Something."

Inky shot me a foul look, and I rolled my eyes. It wasn't like the boy could harm me anyway.

Dante stretched his arms and trudged into the kitchen to pick up a glass carafe. He tried to pour the contents into a cup, but his hands shook, he dropped it, and it shattered. He stood staring at the mess and then sank to the floor, wrapped his arms around his knees, buried his face, and wept softly.

Inky hurried over and crouched down next to him, rubbing circles on the back of his neck. "Hey, now. It's a lot to take in, I know that, but you'll be all right."

"My sister's gone…."

"You got anything stronger to drink in here than coffee?" Inky asked.

Dante sniffled and then laughed. "I'm not old enough to drink."

"Bollocks. Blossom?"

"What?"

Inky shook his head. "For fuck's sake, make yourself useful. Conjure us up some rose-petal wine or something."

"Oh." I wanted to refuse, just because he had been so uncouth about it, but I found a pitcher and filled it. It seemed to calm the boy down a little bit.

"It's really good," he said, looking up at me with his big, wet eyes.

I crossed my arms over my chest and turned away. "Of course it is. It is also strong, so don't gulp it down like a camel."

"Okay." His hands shook less as he set the pitcher aside, took in a long breath, and released it in a segmented sigh. "You said you wanted to talk to my sister. Why?"

"I believe there is a small chance she summoned me here, and I would like her to release me."

"Blossom means to say Rosalind might've accidentally used magic to call him here from his world, and he can't go back unless she lets him."

"Thank you for repeating exactly what I said, Inky," I told him. "Did I accidentally speak the wrong language?"

Dante tapped his fingers on the ugly tiled floor. "So you think my little sister conjured up—"

I held up a hand. "Summoned."

"You think Ros summoned a faerie? How? Why?"

"Some people have magic and don't realize they have it," Inky said softly. "We don't think she meant to do it. But sometimes if a mage wishes hard enough for something, it can happen."

"Why would she wish for the two of you?" Dante asked.

"Anyone would want me as an ally," I told him. "According to Inky, all of the mages do."

"Your sister likely just wanted… something. She thought she was praying, but she was casting a spell. She asked for an angel, and she got, well…." Inky curled his lip up at me.

I huffed. I'd endured about as many of his insults as a reasonable man could be expected to take. "I have more magic in a hangnail than an angel. Angels are dull, they have absolutely no imagination, and most of them are quite nasty on top of it." Both of them stared at me. "Besides, it's unlikely any mortal could weave so complex an enchantment. Once I determine that your sister did not do it, we'll leave here and never trouble you again."

"So you really didn't have anything to do with her going missing?" Dante asked.

"You think I want to be saddled with a mewling infant to attend?"

Inky glowered. "Just shut the fuck up, you twat. Dante, we didn't, I swear we didn't. We really did just want to see if she had magic, if maybe she'd brought Mr. Delightful there over, and if she could get the hell rid of him."

"She's not here. I-I left last night, had to do some work. I locked her door." The boy's breath was hitching again, and Inky put the wine pitcher into his hands. "I was only gone maybe two hours, and when I came back, she…."

"Who would've done it?" I asked.

"I thought it was you. I… almost hoped it was. Better a couple of tweakers than…."

"Than who?" Inky urged.

Before Dante could answer, a sort of shrill song sounded in the sitting room. Clutching the edge of the counter, Dante pulled himself to his feet. He waded through the debris and rooted in the sofa's cushions until he located a small device. I followed, stepping over a gaunt woman covered by a blanket who muttered, "Keep it down, Dante. I told you my sinuses are bothering me."

"Whatever, Mom." He held the shiny little rectangle to his ear. "Raf?"

"Dante. Did your mother come home?" asked a voice.

Dante looked at the heap of bones and scabs topped with snarled yellow hair. "Yeah. I couldn't get much out of her. She's coming down off glass and has at least half a bottle of vodka in her. She doesn't even seem to know or care that Ros is gone. I don't think she had anything to do with it."

"I'm not sure if that's good news," said the other man, Raf. "What about her boyfriend?"

"I don't know. He didn't show up. I might've finally scared his sorry ass off."

"Moirin got some information from that phone you found."

"That was quick," Dante said, hopeful or scared. I couldn't tell.

"Through it, we were able to locate what we think is the WLF's headquarters in the area. She took a crew to stake it out, and as far as she could tell, no children. Ros isn't there."

"Where is it?" Dante asked, bending to pick up his weapon.

"It doesn't matter," Raf answered. "They don't have her."

"You don't know that! Tell me where it is!"

"That wouldn't be a good idea, Dante. I'm doing everything I can—"

"Fucking tell me, Raf!"

"You're not thinking clearly. I don't want you putting yourself in danger."

"That's my decision!" Dante shouted. His mother belched, grumbled, and pulled the blanket over her head. It was clear to see Dante had gotten most of his appearance from his father, as he didn't share her coloring at all. Rosalind's father must have been a completely different man.

"And giving you information is mine."

"Please, Raf. I'm begging you here. I'll do anything."

"And what would you do if you had that information?"

"I'd go there and make those motherfuckers tell me what they did with my sister!"

"You'd be dead as soon as you walked in the door."

"Raf!"

I was growing bored of this conversation, and I did not see it yielding fruit anytime soon. If this man Raf had information that could lead to the girl, I needed to know it. "Dante, give that thing to me."

"Fuck off," he mouthed.

I snatched the device from his hand and pressed it to my face. "Greetings, Raf. I wish to know the location of the girl, Rosalind."

"I don't know where she is."

"Then where is the location Dante wishes to go?"

Raf hesitated. His will must have been quite strong.

"Tell me now."

"It's about an hour away, just north of Pottstown, near a place called Ironstone Creek. It's God's country up there."

Interesting. "Which god?"

"Dante?"

"Tell me more," I instructed. "Tell me exactly how to find this place."

"It's an old cabin," Raf said. He rattled off some numerals that meant nothing to me. Dante scavenged through the remains of the table, located a pencil, and scrawled them across the top of a yellow envelope.

"That will be all, mortal. Goodbye." I handed the device back to Dante, and our eyes met.

"Thank you," he said. "I don't know what you did, but thank you. I need to go there, but…. Fuck. That's at least a two-hour drive. Do either of you have a car?"

"We should think this through," Inky said. "It sounds dangerous, and can you even imagine what the roads will be like up there? It might be impassable."

"Do you have a car?" Dante asked again.

"No," Inky said.

He turned to me. "What about you?"

"I will acquire whatever is necessary," I told him. "I need your sister."

"That's right." Dante nodded and ran his fingers along the sparse black fuzz on his chin. "You've got money. We can get a car. I can get one, no questions asked. How much do you have?"

"As much as you need."

"Good. Hang here for a minute. I'm gonna get some more ammo, and then we'll go. I hope you assholes are worth something in a fight. We might be in for one."

Chapter Thirteen

I sat wedged between Dante and Blossom in a beat-up Dodge truck the kid had procured from a bloke by the name of Earl Howie, and I was pretty sure he meant the earl as a title, judging by the sequin-bedecked crown he wore on a chain around his neck. Blossom had paid with a handful of pine needles, which was going to be bad for Dante when the earl figured it out. 'Course, a lot of this was going to be bad for him—and for us.

At least the truck was warm, and it ran well enough I didn't worry we'd be stuck out in God-knew-where. It had Jersey plates, a fiberglass cap over the bed, and had probably belonged to a plumber or a builder of some kind. There was still a tool chest full of wrenches and shite behind the back seat. I decided not to dwell on what had become of the former owner as I stared out at the abandoned streets.

It took us a bloody hour to get out of the city. In that time, I'd pried some information out of Dante, and none of it was good. Apparently he worked for the biggest gunrunner—what he insisted on calling an arms dealer—in the tristate area. Turns out he pissed off some neo-Nazi fucks, pieces of shite what liked to kidnap kids and sell them into slavery—what they felt was the "rightful place" of anybody who wasn't lily-white. They had a hideout somewhere out in the Pennsylvania woods, and that was where we were going. The three of us. To a house out in the middle of nowhere, full of probably the evilest pricks on the good earth, all of what were likely heavily armed.

Blossom acted like we were on our way to a garden party. Fucking faerie cunt. "So, these enemies of yours," the fey said to Dante in a cheery voice, "how are we planning to kill them?"

"Fast," Dante said.

"But that isn't any fun! And the possibilities are so numerous. Why, once I went to war with one of my enemies. I defeated him and claimed his lands and estates. Then I made the walls of his own castle melt and swallow him and his people up to their necks. When I held balls in his former great hall, my guests and I would throw things at them: rocks, spears, lit candles, arrows…. Ah, those were the loveliest parties."

Dante's hands were white on the steering wheel. "That's fucked-up, Blossom. It's impressive, I guess, if you can really do things like that. Fuck, I feel like I'm in a nightmare. Like I'm going to wake up in the hospital and find out I got hit on the head. It would be a relief too. But, but if you can do that shit, does that mean you'll have my back in there?"

He wouldn't. I knew he wouldn't. He didn't give a fuck what happened to Dante or Ros. If the little girl died, he'd get what he wanted. I couldn't let Dante walk into this mess thinking otherwise. "Make him swear to it, Dante. Make him make you a bargain. And be careful how you phrase it, mate."

"Oh, Inky." The faerie shook his shiny hair around, making the truck's musty cab smell like fresh-cut grass. "I thought we were friends."

"You thought wrong. I think you're the worst cunt I've ever met. Now make the kid a deal. Promise him he'll walk out of this alive. And Ros too."

Blossom leaned forward, eyes glittering behind his squinted lids. I didn't need my skills to see his desire, his avarice. He was nearly slobbering with it. "And what do I get in return?"

"Anything you want if my sister is safe," Dante said without looking away from the road.

"Very well." Blossom started to reach across me for the kid, but I caught his wrist and squeezed the lissome bones. He could turn me to stone or into a fucking toad or whatever, but I wasn't going to let him do to Dante what he'd done to me.

"No. No way, you devious knobhead," I said. "You fucking specify. You tell him that him and his sister will live to a ripe old age, and you tell him exactly what he'll be giving in return."

The faerie was flustered. There was even a stripe of pale pink across his marble-white face. "Maybe I'll just forget the whole thing. It hardly matters to me."

"Got your knickers in a twist 'cause I outsmarted you?" I pushed. I knew it was dangerous, making him mad, but I wanted him thinking about his pride above all else.

"You did not! I'm just not interested in playing this game. It's an awful bore."

"Please," Dante said softly. "Just tell me what you want."

Blossom lifted his chin. "Very well. I swear you and your sister will live a hundred years from this day so long as it is within my power to ensure it, and you will agree to go on a quest for me. This deal will be void if I am killed or incapacitated, of course."

Yes! I wanted to shout and punch the air.

"What quest?" Dante asked.

"Well I don't know!" Blossom spat. "I won't know until one comes up, will I?"

"It's all right," Dante said. "I'll do it. Do we have to shake or something?"

"No," Blossom said. "The bargain is struck."

I could finally gloat, and you bet your plump peachy arse I was going to. "Nice to know little Rosalind will have nothing to fear—even if she summoned you but is unable to dismiss you."

I expected anger, but he just laughed. "Yes, and nice to know you can rut until the stars drop out of the sky to no avail, demon. Since your bargain involves me returning home."

Blossom's storm apparently hadn't extended much beyond the city, because when we left it, the roads were clear, snow only a few inches deep beside them. I stared out at the woods, thinking. What would happen to me if I couldn't feed? I didn't think I would die; I'd just always be hungry, never sated, and that was scarier. I'd also never been crafty, never been one to play games like the one I'd just played. My mind didn't lean toward tricks or manipulation. I certainly didn't get off on outfoxing people, fucking them over with bendy words—at least I never had before. Fuck me, what if I was becoming what he desired? With no one else to influence me, I might be twisting to what he found appealing, and it was plain to see what he found appealing was himself. No. I didn't want to be someone who amused himself by burying people in fucking walls and throwing things at them. I had to get away from this wanker, and fast. My only chance was to find the little girl and hope with everything I had that she could send him packing.

I SAT in my study, staring at my phone. I swore I had been talking to Dante Mayfield, but it felt like that had been days ago. I felt like I had when I'd been a much younger man and had too much to drink, waking up sometime later with no idea whether hours or days had passed. The first time it had happened, my brother had found our mother's bottle of rum, and we'd finished it while watching *Saturday Night Live* in our tiny living room. But it had been over a decade since I'd had more than a few glasses of wine in the evening. The hangover wasn't worth it at my age. A cup of espresso sat on the desk near my elbow, and when I picked it up and took a sip, it was still hot enough to burn my mouth. That meant I had made it recently, so I had probably spoken to Dante recently too. For some reason I couldn't remember what we had discussed, and my memory was normally very good.

Dante had been so upset last night, collapsed in the snow outside his home. He'd sobbed against my chest, and I'd held him, the snow covering us. I'd promised him I would make everything all right, because I couldn't stand watching his pain and fear tearing him apart. I wanted so much for that young man to be happy, to be safe…. I wanted to make sure no one would hurt him….

I pulled up my recent calls and saw that I'd spoken to Dante just over twenty minutes ago. I tried to call him back three times, but each time my call went to voicemail. That was unlike him. He'd always been flawlessly dependable. Only his sister's welfare would cause him to even think about refusing anything I asked….

His sister. He would do anything for her, and….

Oh no.

I picked up the letter opener from my desk, ran up the stairs to my bedroom, and threw my back against the antique Spanish four-poster bed, grunting and heaving with my thighs until I managed to reveal the hidden panel in the floor. Using the letter opener, I pried up the boards. Few knew it, but I'd had good reason for doing the renovations to this house myself—beyond the fact that I liked the work and trusted few others to do things to my standards. I entered my code into the electronic safe, and then I waited the required ten minutes and entered it again. Though I didn't do business out of my home—or even out of my neighborhood—I was not enough of a fool to leave myself empty-handed should an emergency arise.

The safe contained a few hundred thousand dollars in cash, a military-grade Kevlar vest; a Tavor TAR-21 assault rifle with a few of my own custom modifications, including a Nikon scope; dozens of magazines worth of ammunition; a .300 Win Mag sniper rifle with a Nightforce scope; and two 9mm Beretta combat pistols. As I picked one of them up, I remembered Dante begging me to replace his gun. I could've given him one of these. Looking back, I wished I had. I wouldn't have even cared if he'd learned about my emergency safe, because I knew I could trust him. He had no ambition to take my place, and he certainly wouldn't steal from me. But now was not the time to analyze the intricacies of Dante Mayfield. I spent too much time thinking about him already.

I stripped down, put my vest on over my undershirt, and then slid a plain long-sleeve polo and a pair of jeans over the top, followed by my shoulder holsters for the pistols. Hopefully an extra wool sock over the brace on my right ankle would keep the metal from growing too frigid against my skin. I put the two rifles in a gym bag and made sure to replace everything. No matter the sick feeling eating holes in my stomach, I couldn't afford to be hasty or sloppy. Being fastidious and methodical had earned me everything I currently had.

I walked slowly as I left my home, even stopping to check the mailbox. It wouldn't do to arouse suspicion. When I reached my Jeep, I set the duffel bag carefully in the back seat. I didn't exceed the speed limit on my way to Dante's house, even though I wanted to.

It was quiet on Dante's street, and in this neighborhood, I had little to fear from the authorities. The greater danger was my car being broken into, so I hurried into the building and up the stairs. I opened the door with the key I'd had made, and I couldn't believe the mess: the coffee table in splinters, broken glass in the kitchen. Dante's mother snored happily nearby; she'd likely slept through whatever had happened. Ignoring her, I checked Ros's bedroom, which Dante had tried to imbue with as much normalcy and cheer as he could in a place like this. I shook my head. If only I'd offered Dante the Center City apartment sooner. In his room, I found the bed unmade and the safe I'd given him open—empty of ammunition. I ran my hand along the cool cloth of his blue checkered pillow, wondering when he had last slept. Once again I tried to reach his phone, unsuccessfully.

I knew he was going after the skinheads. Hazily I remembered telling him about the hideout Moirin had discovered. It wasn't something I would have ever done, but with an icy shiver moving down my back, I knew I had. I also knew, beyond any doubt, that he wouldn't survive. Even if he'd been rested, even if he'd been armed with more than his little .38, he didn't have a chance. Neither did I. My only hope was to intercept him before he reached the Nazis, and that would take a miracle.

And I still had to take precautions.

I drove to a storage garage in a nicer part of Germantown where I kept two alternate vehicles, ones that I switched out frequently and wouldn't be tied to me. Given the conditions after the storm, I chose the Nissan Rogue. It was a dependable car and not expensive enough to draw attention. I transferred my bag to its back seat and wished for the phenomenal luck I would need to save Dante's life and avoid further involvement with the filth calling themselves the White Liberation Front. My mother would have certainly told me to pray, maybe to appeal to Saint Rose of Lima.

But I'd ceased wasting my time with such nonsense long ago, back when I'd learned virtue not only went unrewarded but often tempted tragedy. No, I would depend on myself as I had been doing for many years.

Chapter Fourteen

A LITTLE dirt road, not even cleared of snow, dead-ended about a half a mile into the woods. I left the truck there and told my—I didn't even know what to fucking call the faerie and the guy with the horns. Crew?—we'd be walking the rest of the way to the compound.

"Look, mate, I'm not especially adept at the forestry gig," Inky said.

I stopped and turned around to look at him, and once again, my mind rejected what my eyes were telling it. He had the lightest skin I'd ever seen, almost as white as the snow out here in the country, untouched by dirty boots and exhaust fumes. It had a pearly shimmer, sort of like the powder girls used on their faces, and the shadows held a purplish tint. His perfect lips, full but still with a distinct bow shape, looked almost artificial, and the lavender color added to it. His eyes, big and round, gave him a trustworthy quality even with the weird color. And the horns. I didn't even want to think about them. The long silvery hair I could handle, but every time I looked at him, I prayed the horns would be gone.

"Aw, afraid of getting your feet wet, demon?" Blossom's voice was like music, and every time he spoke, I smiled even though he scared the piss out of me. Looking at him freaked me out worse than looking at Inky, which sucked because he liked to lean in close to my face when he talked to me. His hair was a wild tangle of white-gold, and his lips were pouty but narrow, like a little heart. His eyes were almond-shaped like mine but bigger, slanted more drastically, and the kind of green I hadn't known existed until I saw them. Right then, he was walking on top of the snow without even breaking through the crust. I shoved the heels of my hands into my eye sockets because… just *fuck*.

"Fuck you, you twat," Inky hissed. "Not everybody likes dancing around in the woods. And look! You've forgotten your little pan flute anyway."

I rubbed my eyes as they continued to argue. God, I was tired, tired like I'd never been in my life, like I could've laid down right there in the snow and slept for a week. Every step took an effort. I was dizzy, and my vision blurred. Maybe I was hallucinating all this bullshit. Maybe I could sit down for a minute, close my eyes. And maybe when I opened them all this would be gone.

But then I thought about my sister, and as soon as I pictured her face, I pictured everything that could be happening to her while I stood around being a pussy. Considering where I had grown up, I could picture it only too fucking well. Every minute, every damn second, mattered. I turned back to Inky and Blossom. "Come with me or don't, but at least shut the fuck up. We don't want these assholes to know we're coming."

Surprisingly, they listened to me and followed in silence until we reached a slope overlooking the cabin. I crouched down behind some hemlock trees to watch and hopefully get an idea what we'd be dealing with. The place was nothing special—long, single-story, built from a combination of gray blocks and washed-out wooden siding. A porch ran the length of the front, and some vehicles—an old station wagon, an SUV, and a pickup truck—sat in the gravel patch near the steps leading up. Some smaller buildings stood out back, storage sheds most likely. It was quiet—no signs of life.

"Well what are we waiting for?" Blossom hissed. "Let's go inside."

"We can't just walk in," I told him. "We'd be dead as soon as we opened the door."

"Not if they don't see us," he said.

"You can do that?"

"Of course!" He stood and sort of glided down the hill, feet barely seeming to skim the surface of the snow. When he reached the flat patch at the bottom, he went up the porch steps, opened the door, and walked right inside.

I expected to hear shouts, gunfire, but everything stayed quiet. I wished I had binoculars or something so I might've seen more than shadow beyond the door Blossom had left hanging open. I turned to Inky. "Do you trust him?"

"Hell no," he said softly. "But he is very powerful."

I took a deep breath, held it a few seconds. "Okay. I'm going down. You don't have to come with me. I understand if you would rather stay here."

He put a hand on my shoulder. "The truth is, I'm worth fuck all in a fight, but I'm not letting you go in there alone."

I nodded. It was hard to imagine why he would care what happened to me—experience told me he probably wanted something—but it still felt kind of good to have somebody watching my back, so I decided not to look too hard at it.

Trying to utilize the cover of the trees and then the vehicles as much as I could, I made my way to the porch steps. It was still quiet in the house. All I could make out were some subdued voices, probably a radio or TV. No footsteps. I hurried up the three steps, pressed my back to side of the building, and peeked around the edge of the door. It was dark inside, gloomy due to the heavy curtains covering the few small windows. The place seemed like one big room—wood floors, some bunks against the walls, an old woodstove with a beat-up couch and some folding chairs around it, what passed for a kitchen off to the left. I could smell the smoke from the fire, BO, and mustiness, like the place had been closed up for a while before these jerk-offs moved in. In the center, Blossom stood looking around, a sort of soft glow coming off his hair and skin. As I took a shaky step inside, I noticed a couple of guys sitting at a table, some empty beer bottles, papers, and boxes of ammo between them. Their attention was focused on a small TV that was playing an old Stallone movie—*Rocky* or *Rambo* or some shit. Their backs were to me, but I froze, ready to shoot. I could probably get both of them—Raf always said I was fast—but the noise would bring everybody else in this hole out. With three cars, I was willing to bet there were more than two guys here.

Blossom walked over and stood between the guys and the TV, cocking his head to the side and crossing his arms. "Well, they're certainly ugly, and they smell terrible, but they don't strike me as especially dangerous."

Holy shit. I stuck the .38 in my pants. "They really can't see us?"

Blossom rolled his eyes. "Few of your kind can see much of anything."

"I'm going to look around."

"I'll help," Inky offered.

It didn't take us long to realize there wasn't much to see. A big mountain of a bastard slept on the couch by the stove, a couple others in the beds. They had cases of beer stacked against the walls, some liquor on a shelf, and about a dozen hunting rifles leaning in some of the corners. An old blanket concealed a shitter and sink, along with more boxes of shells. If it wasn't for the Nazi flag thumbtacked to the wall, anyone would've thought these six assholes came out here to spend a week getting drunk.

There was no sign of Ros.

"Dante." Inky motioned me over to where he crouched by the couch. He pulled a laptop from underneath it and looked up at me with his rose-colored eyes.

It was weird to sit on the floor and lean my back against the sofa where the big fucker with the bare hairy chest snored, snuffled, and farted out cabbagey clouds, but I did. The computer wasn't password protected, and as soon as it booted up, I saw something that looked like a messenger conversation, except weird and outdated—squarish green letters on a black background.

SS Man: male, 9-10, black. Female, 7, poss. Puerto Rican. Female, 14, Syrian.
    UncJohn47: Can poss move. Will make inquiries.
    SS Man: Want at least 10 for females, 5 for male
    UncJohn47: No way 10 f0r 14 yr bitch. 7 if lucky
    UncJohn47: Send pics

I scrolled down, staring in horror at the grainy photographs of the little boy and girls. The older girl covered her bare chest with her hands, and she had a black eye and some other bruises and scrapes. Even with the crappy quality, I could see the boy's face was wet with tears. I thought I was going to puke, and I had to look away for a while before I checked the laptop for anything else. I didn't find anything, but then I was no expert. I'd take it and see if Moirin's friend might have some luck.

"Fuck me," Inky whispered. "Somebody should do something…. I never…. Fuck."

"I have a contact who can see this gets to the cops, at least," I said. I knew I was a prick for thinking it, but I couldn't help being glad I hadn't seen Ros's picture. But that didn't mean they didn't have her. "I have to know for sure. I have to talk to one of these bastards."

I hadn't heard Blossom come up, but he leaned over the arm of the couch and poked the big bearded guy in the cheek with his long finger. The guy blinked a few times, sat up, and scratched at one of his saggy tits.

"Why, good morning," Blossom said. "On your feet. Follow me."

I slid out of the way as the big fucker stood and followed Blossom out onto the porch in nothing but some camouflage pants. His bare feet turned red as soon as they hit the snow, but he trudged after the faerie like he didn't even notice.

Inky shook his head. "I guess this is what we're doing. Nice to be consulted, innit?"

"Let's go," I said, sticking the computer inside my coat. Some fresh flurries fell as we made our way back up the hill, into the trees, and deeper into the woods.

THE TRUCK I found about a mile from the WLF hideout had to belong to Dante. That meant he was already here, but with any luck, he hadn't made his move yet. I selected the sniper rifle and left the Rogue a few hundred yards from the truck, easily following the tracks left by what looked like two men—Dante and somebody else, a full-grown man as indicated by the size and depth of the tracks. Though many of our associates were quite fond of the young man, I wondered who he'd found to assist him on such short notice.

They'd been smart enough to stick to the cover of the trees, but when the cabin came into view, the prints led down the hillside and right to the door, which stood open. Either nothing had happened yet or I was too late. Concealing myself behind some mountain laurel that still had its glossy green leaves, I stretched out on my stomach and used my scope to get a better view, trying to ignore the wet and cold seeping through my clothing. Ten minutes passed before a man exited the building. He was hardly what I had been expecting, with his longish blond hair and what looked like a slim-fitting three-piece suit. A behemoth of a man followed him, bare-chested and in his bare feet, clearly one of the skinheads. He seemed almost docile as he walked out into the snow, and I noticed no trace of a weapon compelling him. Soon after, Dante and another man, a plain one with no real distinguishing features, left the house, and the four of them headed back up the hill and into the forest.

I pulled my knees up beneath me when they passed about a dozen feet to my right. Whatever Dante planned to do, it was best not to have it connected with me or my organization. If he made it out of here—if we made it—remaining anonymous would give me the best chance of protecting him.

When they got a few hundred yards in front of me, I trailed them, easily following the rutted path they left between the trees.

The blond man eventually stopped in a small clearing flanked by old-growth oak trees and a scattering of evergreens. A fallen tree, covered in snow, near the edge of the glade offered me plenty of cover, and I knelt down, my gun hanging from my back by its strap.

"Sit there." The blond pointed to a swell of ground near the base of a large tree. Though I still saw no weapons trained on the big skinhead—

even by Dante—the man acquiesced without argument. "Ask your questions, Dante."

Dante stepped forward as the two men stepped back. One look at his face answered my questions about whether he had slept. He was waxen and pale beneath his golden-brown skin, and dark circles lined his eyes. He appeared ready to fall over, but he drew himself up to his full height, made a fist, and hit the skinhead hard in the mouth, making a spray of blood stain the snow. "Where's my sister, you son of a bitch?"

The man spat more blood. "If I had to guess by looking at you, *boy*, I'd say a whorehouse in China."

Dante hit him again, two backhanded blows that swelled his left eye and cheek. "I want to know if you and your piece-of-shit friends kidnapped a little girl in North Philly last night, and where you took her."

"Well I don't remember," the man said. "Them little brown kids all look the same to me."

"Fucker!" Dante pulled his pistol and pressed the barrel to the man's forehead. "This is the last time I'll ask."

"What? You gonna shoot me, pretty boy?" The man spat again, drooling down his front and into the thick hair covering his chest. "I don't think you've got the balls."

"Yeah? Why don't you ask the two fucks you sent to jack our last shipment? You'll have to go for a swim to find them, though."

Bad move. An inexperienced play. While the WLF would certainly surmise it had been my people responsible for the loss of theirs, they wouldn't have known Dante was responsible or where to find the bodies. That admission could mean trouble for him—for me. Still, it got the man's attention.

"So you work for that taco-eating prick who's too good to sell us guns? He's gonna be in for a surprise when the rest of our crew gets here. He made a big fucking mistake thinking we're small potatoes. A bigger fucking mistake than he knows."

"That's good information to have, but not the information I want," Dante said. "I want to know if you assholes took my sister. Think hard, motherfucker. She's nine years old. Her name is Rosalind Mayfield."

"Suck my dick, boy. Then maybe I'll tell you if you do it better than your chink sister. Or maybe she's a ni—"

I couldn't understand why the man didn't fight back or even try to cover himself as Dante kicked him viciously in the ribs. Through it all, his arms hung limp at his sides, his legs stretched out in front of him until Dante stopped to catch his breath.

"You even think about saying that word, and I'll tear your nuts off with my bare hands," Dante panted.

"Mayfield is a lovely name." The blond man stepped forward, and something about him made my blood run cold. Perhaps it was the amused tone of his voice. Dante was doing what he felt needed to be done, but the spectacle entertained this man. "What is more beautiful than a field in May?"

The skinhead looked up at him, as bewildered as I was.

"That was not a rhetorical question. I'm expecting an answer," the blond continued. "What is the most beautiful thing you can imagine?"

"Your mother's tits, faggot."

"No. That is incorrect, I'm afraid. The most beautiful thing in the universe is exchange, the way one thing is given for something else. Transformation. Because of that principle, nothing is ever lost, and everything is eternal. It is this very principle that ensures trees and flowers spring from putrid flesh. However, the alteration can… hurt." The blond man crossed his arms over his chest, his smile revealing long white teeth.

"What the fuck? What are you—" The skinhead's words degenerated into hoarse cries, and he thrashed as if against invisible bonds. What was going on? I didn't understand, and I neither liked nor felt accustomed to being at a disadvantage.

As I watched, the man's bare feet stiffened, the skin chapped scarlet by the cold darkening to a nut-brown. Frostbite was inevitable, but this was something else. The skin raised up in strips, thick and rough, like… like bark. It couldn't be anything else. From his big toe, a small branch sprouted, complete with miniature golden oak leaves. The man's eyes bulged, and he screamed until his voice was gone. Dante knelt down and poked at the sole of one wooden foot.

"Trees are noble beings, don't you agree?" the blond man asked, arching one fair eyebrow.

The skinhead stared at his feet, his massive chest heaving with his pants, blood-tinged spittle dripping from his chin.

The blond prodded him in the ribs with the pointed toe of an expensive-looking dress shoe. "You're a slow study. Not a rhetorical question. You're only tree to your knees right now. If you want to continue to live as a man, that's still possible." He waved his hand. "You can cut off the wooden parts, or something. However, try to use your limited imagination to envision what will occur if your internal organs turn to wood. I'll be sure to stop before it reaches your chest, so you can still take in air while your wooden guts fail to process food, excrete waste, cleanse your blood of impurities… I'm not sure which of them will kill you first, but it will be interesting to see! Can you feel the change moving up your thighs? I bet it's painful."

"Stop! Please stop!" the skinhead choked out. "We didn't take the boy's sister! I swear. We haven't picked up any product in almost two weeks! We didn't do it, I swear!"

Furry little roots broke through the fabric of the man's pants and wriggled their way into the frozen ground. They swelled and grew, braiding and twisting together, tethering him to the forest floor. Another tore the skin of his ample belly, exposing red meat, though the liquid that spilled around it wasn't blood but something thick and brown. He screamed, his voice cracking, as the fissure widened and the fronds grew thicker. A loud crack sounded; I wasn't sure if it was the ribs or the spine. It took mere moments before the tear reached from the man's throat to his base, where his flesh had already become wood. Within minutes he was no longer recognizable as human from the thighs down. A coating of moss even began to stretch across what was now a tangled mass of roots and thick wood, something that looked like it had been in the clearing for a century. It took a lot to disturb me at this point in my life, but I struggled to breathe in enough to fill my lungs, and it was making me light-headed. My first instinct was to get up and run, but my legs felt like jelly, my right ankle and foot throbbing in the cold. For the first time in my life, I doubted whether I'd be able to use my weapon if I had to.

"I think it's safe to say he's telling the truth," the plain man said, staring in horror at the twisted network of wood that had been a man's legs. I couldn't seem to look away either, though I wanted to.

Dante heaved out a breath and raked his hair out of his face. His whole body trembled, and I had never seen him so pallid. "I-I guess it's good these assholes didn't take Ros…. Not them, and not the two of you. What the fuck? We're… I'm running out of time. She could be out of the state by now, out of the country. What…? Jesus. What the fuck am I going to do?"

The plain man put a hand on Dante's shoulder. "Don't fall apart. We'll keep trying. We'll find her." He turned to the blond and waved his other hand toward the skinhead, who twisted at the waist as he sobbed and gurgled, fresh green branches growing from his chest and abdomen. "What about him?"

The blond shrugged. "What about him?"

"We can't leave him like this."

"Why?" The blond man looked genuinely confused. "He'll be dead in… I don't know. A week at most, probably."

That made the skinhead start screaming again, his face swollen, the skin splitting over the wounds Dante had caused.

"Look, Blossom, I tried to tell you we can't draw attention to ourselves like this. What do you think will happen if someone finds him? It'll lead back to us."

"I don't give a fuck about any of this," Dante said, his voice cracking. "I need to get back to the city… try to…."

The blond sighed theatrically, looking very put upon. "Oh, very well." He wiggled his fingers, and in minutes, a misshapen tree with a round bulge on its trunk sat where the skinhead had been. The twigs and branches sprouting from it soon obscured his appearance, as did the moss and ivy spreading over the surface. Soon his open mouth, frozen in his final scream, looked like nothing more than a knothole, his eyes protruding whorls in the wood. The suggestion of a face was still there, and someone hunting or hiking in these woods might spend a few moments considering it the way one does shapes in the clouds. It was strangely beautiful, and that was perhaps the most terrifying part.

On my hands and knees, I backed away from the most bizarre and horrific thing I had ever seen. Dante and the others stood looking down, and I watched them recede as I put space between us as quickly as I could without making noise. As soon as it was safe to do so, I stood and ran, pushing myself through the nausea and dizziness, feeling like I struggled through something denser than the cold mountain air. I didn't stop until I reached the Rogue, threw the door open, and turned on the engine. My hands shook so hard I couldn't grip the steering wheel at first, and with the strain I'd put on my foot and leg, I didn't know if I'd be able to depress the gas and brake pedals. The pain radiated into my knee, but staying here was not an option. I had never wanted to be away from a place so desperately. As I'd been trained to do long ago, I focused on the task at hand and banished everything else from my thoughts. It allowed me to put the vehicle in Reverse and pull out with a fan of snow.

For probably an hour, I drove in no particular direction, just taking turns on a whim. I concentrated on the act of driving, on the road, the signs, and the scenery around me—blocking the internal turmoil by focusing on the concrete. When a gas station and convenience store came into view, I pulled over and rolled the window down, craving fresh air, hoping it would clear my head.

Already, my mind was trying to convince me none of it had been real, and it was hard to resist the argument that there must be some other explanation. It would've been easy to block it out, but it would also have been irresponsible. I would be creating a weak spot in my business by not acknowledging the threat these… people represented. And they were already associated with me through Dante.

Dante. His involvement was the most difficult aspect for me to comprehend. How had he come into contact with these people? How long had he been hiding it from me? I shook my head. Silly, perhaps, but I'd always imagined my relationship with him surpassed the employer/employee arrangement. I suppose I had hoped we were friends, and I had always endeavored to be someone he could trust, because he had few if any others to turn to.

But my feelings for him could not be allowed to cloud my judgment. I had worked too hard, sacrificed too much, to build what I had. I rolled up my window and started the car, relieved after having come to a decision and formulated at least a loose course of action. I had to find out what I had just seen, how it had been possible. There was still a chance Dante would tell me the truth if I asked him outright. If I determined his activities posed a threat to me, the threat had to be eliminated.

But the power I had witnessed would be an advantage to anyone who controlled it, and if I could orchestrate a way for it to benefit me, I would be a fool not to exploit it, albeit carefully.

I did not get where I was by being a fool.

CHAPTER FIFTEEN

Bloody hell, I didn't know how the kid made it back to the truck. I didn't know how I made it back, and no matter what I liked to label myself, I was a supernatural creature. Of course, Blossom looked as buoyant and sprightly as ever, the knob.

Dante stood in front of the truck, key ring dangling from a finger, eyes glazed. "I don't think I can drive. I can't keep my eyes open. I know people use that expression, but… I don't know if it would be safe, me driving. Can either one of you do it?"

"I can." I took the keys from his hand and got behind the wheel. In a few minutes we were back on one of the winding state roads, and Dante was fast asleep, his head back and his mouth hanging open. He slumped against Blossom's shoulder, and the faerie snorted.

"This is hardly the time for him to be taking a nap."

I shook my head; I was too damned tired to engage in a debate with this twat, especially since I couldn't replenish my energy by feeding. "He's a human being, for fuck's sake. The human body can only take so much, so just let him rest. There's nothing he can do right now anyway."

To my surprise, Blossom adjusted his arm so Dante could rest underneath it, against his chest. He even spread his fingers over Dante's pale cheek. "They're very single-minded, these mortals."

"He loves his little sister, and he's scared. And he hasn't experienced magic until now. I think he's taking it pretty well."

"He's an appealing young man," Blossom said softly.

Yeah, I'd noticed. The faerie's observation only made me imagine what was under that grungy sweatshirt, the tight jeans…. But: "He doesn't have any sexual desire."

"Is that possible for mortals?"

"It's rare," I said. "But not unheard of. He simply isn't interested. Some of them aren't."

"Well," Blossom said. "I suppose that allows him to focus on our mission. What do you think we should do next?"

I couldn't help smiling. "What, you want my opinion?"

"Is there someone else here, demon?"

"I just thought you were all-knowing, your faerie-ness."

"Now you're being a… what's that word you favor? A cunt?"

I laughed. "Nice to be on the other end of it for once. But anyway, all we can do is take him home. He needs to sleep. We're fucked six ways till Sunday if he drops dead from exhaustion. We'll never find the girl without his guidance."

With a grunt, Blossom pointed to the radio. "Instruct this machine to produce some pleasant music."

I rolled my eyes but didn't waste the effort arguing as I scrolled through the stations. When I stopped on "Africa"—good song—he muttered, "Something else."

He finally settled on some public-access channel playing *The Magic Flute*. We didn't talk much for the rest of the drive.

Back in Philadelphia, I dragged Dante up the steps and into his flat. Poor bloke was dead to the world, and I deposited him on the couch, propped his head on the arm, and covered him with the flowery quilt from Ros's bed. Say what you want, but I was glad his mum was gone when we got back. Old minger made me uncomfortable. Her cravings for the crystal were just too strong, and they almost made me feel like I wanted the shite. Like I would do anything for it. Like I could justify anything.

But we were alone, only the TV lighting the sad little place. It was cold, and the walls shook when the wind blew too hard. Which it did too fucking often. I yawned and sprawled out on the small sofa, resting my head on Dante's hip. It was bony, but I was too tired to care. I was even too tired to care what Blossom was up to, sitting cross-legged on the floor and sifting around in the broken bits of the coffee table. I missed Charlene, and I hoped she was okay, not scared, not wondering where I'd gone.…

I awoke to darkness. We'd slept all day and into the night. As I blinked the room into focus, I saw Blossom perched on the edge of the couch by Dante's knees. The faerie held a paper plate with some miniature carrots, raisins, and strips of mozzarella cheese arranged in a sunburst pattern. I was so famished I could smell the concentrated sweetness of the raisins.

"Aren't you a sweetheart." I picked up a thumb-sized carrot.

His gossamer hair glowed in the violet light from the TV. "Anything to expedite this endeavor. You cannot imagine how bored I was while the two of you snuggled up and slavered onto your bedclothes."

Dante rubbed his eyes with his fists, and then he bolted up. "Ros! How long was I asleep? Why did you let me do that?"

"You needed it," I told him, taking the plate and offering it to him. "Eat something."

"Coffee," he grumbled and staggered to his feet. The light came on in the kitchen, and the divine smell wafted over to where I sat. Soon Dante pressed a cup into my hand, and I reveled in both the warmth and the biting, bracing taste. I swore I could feel vitality flowing out from the warm pool in my gut, invigorating my limbs. With my alertness came the hunger, so strong even Blossom looked good.

"Do you drink coffee?" Dante's tone said he was afraid of the faerie. I couldn't blame him.

"Cream and sugar," Blossom replied.

After all of us hunched over our steaming mugs, Dante settled back into the corner of the couch and draped the quilt over his shoulders. "I was sure those Nazi fucks had her. All I did was waste time. It's been almost two days now—I heard somewhere if a missing kid isn't found in forty-eight hours...."

"Shh." I rubbed his knee, trying to banish the erotic visions conjured by the feel of his muscle and bone. The kid was thin and supple.... "We have to think about it logically. Who else could've taken her?"

"There's only...." Dante stood up so fast his foot sent remnants of the coffee table sailing across the room. "Son of a bitch. Blaker."

"Who's that?" Blossom asked.

"My mom's boyfriend. Fucking tweaker. He could've had something to do with this. He'd give Satan a rim job for a few hits of glass."

I reached up and put my hand on Dante's arm, slowly and softly, so I wouldn't spook him in his acute state. "There's something else we have to consider, mate. As much as we might not want to."

Dante's dark eyes reflected the cerulean squares of the television screen when he looked down at me. "What?"

I measured the words in my head before I spoke them. The kid was teetering on the edge of a complete breakdown, and saying the wrong thing could shove him right over. For a fleeting second I wanted to hold him, smooth down the spikes of hair sticking up all over, but I pushed it aside because I couldn't be sure if he wanted it or if I was so starved for contact that I was imagining things. I wanted to ease some of his tension, relieve some of the pressure pushing him into the ground if I could, so I tried to do it through my tone.

"So… there's me and Blossom, right? Magical creatures. Well, there's also humans what have magic. Mages, sorcerers, wizards, whatever you want to call them."

Dante squeezed his eyes shut and shook his head. "Yeah, right."

When I rubbed his shoulder, the globe of muscle felt like a rubber band ball. "Is it really harder to swallow than us?"

"I…. Fuck. So there're assholes running around Philly casting spells and waving wands like fucking Gandalf? Harry Potter and shit?"

"Yes, well, no, not exactly. They're not so open about it. But some of them are powerful, and they're dangerous. There are renegades, but most of them belong to a faction or a guild. It's how they've survived over the centuries."

"What the hell would they want with my sister?"

"Isn't it obvious?" Blossom asked. "If she is indeed skilled enough to summon me here, she would be a great asset to any one of these organizations."

I nodded. "I'm afraid it's true. Not all of the guilds are on the friendliest terms, so it benefits them to recruit. Bolster their ranks. Especially now."

"Why especially now?" Dante asked.

"There's…. They think something's going to happen. Something big. They're trying to prepare."

"The center cannot hold." Blossom's voice was thready and ominous.

I rolled my eyes. "Couldn't you be any more original? That's the most cribbed line in all of human poetry."

"There's a mortal poem that contains those words?"

I was about to explain when Dante interrupted us. "What's going to happen?"

"That's just it." I kneaded the base of my skull, starting to regret the way I'd slept. "Nobody knows. Some of the guilds have theories, but none of them agree. It's been right around two thousand years since magic was driven underground, since the split between the mages and everyone else. They seem to believe this shite comes round in cycles. There are prophecies, that kind of nonsense."

"Do you think it's all bullshit?"

I wanted to say yes, nothing to it, the rantings of some pompous twats to make themselves feel even more important, but…. "It's hard to ignore Blossom popping up. No mage has been able to summon a faerie in centuries, and not for lack of trying. And then if your sister is some kind of prodigy, well, that's a lot to call a coincidence."

Dante took a sip of his coffee and swallowed audibly. "Uh, so, if that's true, if these people, these mages, took Ros, how will we find her? How will we fight them?"

"They're mortal," Blossom said. "They can be killed the same as the rest of their kind."

"But they are dangerous," I repeated. The faerie just didn't get it. "Some more than others. You can't kill them if they kill you first, and some of them aren't generous enough to kill you right away." I regretted what I said as soon as it left my mouth. The last thing I wanted to do was scare the kid worse.

"Nonsense," Blossom said with that mad, scary smile full of teeth. "I'm here. I can kill them."

There was no more sense in arguing with him, and I was too fucking tired. Bloody hell, I needed a shag. At this point I needed a damned orgy that lasted a weekend to fuel me up. Cocks and fannies everywhere I looked. Fields of skin glistening with sweat and dotted with pink like meadows of dewy flowers. I caught myself running my tongue along the edge of my teeth while I looked at the glare on Blossom's long bicuspid. I imagined it breaking my skin, my blood on his pale lips. Was that what he was into? I could oblige. In fact, I was starting to really like the idea, and I didn't want to like it.

I snapped my mouth shut and focused on Dante instead, but there was nothing there. Nothing but the compulsion to find his sister and sheer, undiluted rage. He was single-minded, had been for as long as he could remember. He'd pushed every desire, every aspect of his personality aside to take care of Ros. Somewhere, far beyond the edges of that goal, there was something gray and sludgy, like the dirty crust that formed on top of the snow… gritty and sharp but thick… despair, exhaustion, the hope that one day Ros would be okay and he could stop trying, give in… not have to keep going for her.

Bloody hell.

Dante stood up and brushed his fringe back with the heel of his hand. "Okay. We'll try Blaker first, and I guess, I guess we'll pray he did it. I…. Fuck. Let's just go." He went down the hall and came back with the stuffed horse, blushing when he noticed me watching him pet its knotted mane. "In case we find her."

"Good idea." I still had the truck keys in my pocket. "I'll drive."

Dante directed me to a part of North Philly even worse than his neighborhood—the kind of place those who hadn't lived it would think only existed in movies. We parked in front of a cinderblock building that might've once been a house, its windows boarded up and graffiti covering the pitted brick facade. The wooden second story had all but collapsed, and bits of siding and wet plaster clung to the exposed wooden studs like rotting flesh to bone. A single bulb in a broken glass fixture cast a sclerotic light on the green steel door.

"Wait here." Dante reached for the lock.

Blossom stretched his spidery white fingers over Dante's hand. "I want to come. I haven't had anything interesting to do in forever."

As much as I hated to agree with Blossom, it couldn't be helped. "He's right. You shouldn't go in alone. At least choose one of us. For backup." I felt very official, saying that.

"Choose one of us?" Blossom tossed his head back and laughed, high-pitched and piercing, pebbles on glass. "What choice is there? What will you do if there's a fight? You don't even like fighting. You're no good at it."

"I might like it now," I said, and it was true. The idea of people cowering in front of me gave me a weird thrill. It disgusted me less than it should have, less than I wanted it to.

"Okay," Dante said. "You can come if you want, Inky. But I really don't need you. These sorry assholes aren't dangerous. Half of them will probably shit their pants as soon as I walk in the door. They're just tweaker scum. Addicts. Not even real fucking criminals—unless you count sucking dicks for a couple of hits."

Without waiting to see if I'd follow, he got out of the truck and pushed his shoulders up against the light but bitter wind. I followed because it was better than listening to Blossom whine about not being chosen.

Inside was as cold as outside, and it fucking stank—puke and piss and stale cigarette smoke. It would've strangled us if it'd been a few degrees warmer. A couple broken-down sofas slouched against the wall, and plastic chairs surrounded an old TV in the corner. People sat playing dice and cards at some folding tables, or leaned against the bare wooden supports, or, in a couple instances, lay on the cement floor. There were a lot of people, thirty or maybe forty, but the low light and thick smoke made it hard to distinguish between the shadowed faces. Their desires battered against my perceptions—methamphetamine, crack, heroin—until my skin felt too tight and my stomach crawled up my throat with a searing taste of copper and vinegar. I reached out for Dante and put my hand on his elbow because I couldn't let these feelings define me; his obsession was better, and I let it infuse me: *Ros. Find her. Hurt people to find her. Hurt people who hurt her. It's all fucking unfair and blaming it on somebody helps it make sense.*

The junkies scrambled out of Dante's way. Some of them must've recognized the kid, and they were scared. He took a little satisfaction from that, wanted more of it. I could get on board, and as we waded through the crowd, I found myself glowering at the skeletal faces just to watch them dart away from my gaze like cockroaches when a light flicked on. The fear in their bloodshot eyes produced a buoyancy in my chest, even a little bit of a swell in my trousers. Here, I mattered. I had some control, and that felt damn good.

A man sat slumped in a corner clutching a little glass pipe. His fingertips were stained, dirt and tar ground into the creases and lines of his skin. A sweatshirt that might've once been white hung from his bony shoulders, exposing a long neck covered in sagging flesh. The crown of his head was bald, but stringy hair stuck out like a fan around the base of his head, his dirty face framed by loose folds of skin that hung from his jaw. He looked to me like a camel's fanny. Ugliest cunt I'd ever seen.

When the man first saw us, he smiled, but then Dante scowled, grasped the front of his sweatshirt, and hauled him to his feet. Dante leaned in, even though the bloke smelt like a cartload of sweaty crotches and like he'd quite possibly shit himself at some point in the past week. "We're going to go outside and talk, motherfucker."

"Hey, all right, Dante," Blaker slurred. "Okay, cool. All right, buddy."

Nobody stopped us or stood in our way as Dante pulled Blaker to the door and shoved him out, where he landed on his knees in the fouled snow. He reminded me of an overcooked piece of spaghetti, the way he twisted onto his arse to face us. "Hey, Dante. How's your pretty mama?"

"Shut the fuck up." Shoving both hands in his coat pockets, Dante used the toe of his boot to kick Blaker in the diaphragm. The man fell on his side, wrapped his arms around his middle, and gagged, gasping for air. Dante stood motionless until he recovered.

"What the hell, man?" Blaker whimpered, the side of his face melting a skull-shaped impression into the rime.

"Where's my sister, you piece of shit?"

"I-I don't know what you mean, Dante."

The heel of Dante's boot connected with Blaker's chin, and his head snapped back as a jet of blood shot from his mouth. He lifted his hands to cradle his swollen mouth as he sputtered and choked.

"I'll ask one more time." The squeak of the snow was loud beneath Dante's foot as he took a single step toward the man. "Tell me something useful or I'll put a cap in your fucking head. No one will miss you. Now where's Ros?"

"I-I had to do it, Dante. The guy was real rich, nice black suit. Gave me five hundred dollars. I-I had to, man. I been looking for work, but you know how it is. It's hard out here, man."

Dante's expression remained cold, but his hands curled into fists. I felt his desire to drive those hands into the man's melting skin until his bones cracked and caved in, to smash them to powder. It would feel so, so good, but not as good as seeing Ros safe, eating a pizza from Tony's and watching *The Last Unicorn*.... Her smile, the smell of her hair, the way she fell asleep with her little hand holding the hem of his shirt.... Glittery pink fingernails.... Breath scented with bubblegum toothpaste.

"Where?"

"At that funny building that used to be a hair salon. I-I waited for you to leave the other night, and then I went in. I told her we were going to meet your mom for pancakes. She waited with me until the next morning, and then I took her there. He picked her up and gave me the money."

"Name."

"I don't know, man! I didn't ask."

Dante pulled his pistol and pressed the barrel to the papery skin of Blaker's forehead. "I should kill you." He moved the gun down until it was buried between Blaker's legs. "But not too quick. You deserve to feel every fucking second of it, you son of a bitch."

"No, Dante! No, please! Please!"

Fuck me, but I wanted it, wanted to watch his nuts explode and the blood pool underneath him. I wanted to see the desperation in his eyes and then the despair, and I wanted him to know it was me who put it there.... But that wouldn't save the little girl, so I stretched out my arm and pried Dante away from Blaker. I looked down at his face, at the skin draped off the bone, the greasy sweat coating the pocked flesh. "What kind of car was he driving?"

"A-an expensive one? Black. A Mercedes. Four-door."

I swore I could hear Dante's teeth grinding. His rage was seismic, rumbling through him—through us—until I thought he'd shatter. The gun in his hand shook, and it took all my strength to maintain my barrier between him and the sorry bloke on the ground. "Look, Dante, I know you'd like to kill him. Can't say he doesn't fucking deserve it either. But all it'll do is draw attention we don't need. We should get out of here. Talk. All right?"

He stood for a couple of minutes, every fiber in his being stretched to its absolute limit, years of anger and disgust pooling in his guts until he trembled with the effort to keep it from breaking the surface. Couple that with his ambivalence about his own survival, and I was starting to get worried. I could see Blossom watching us from the truck, his pale profile like a half-moon reflected in the window. I didn't know if he could do anything to calm Dante down, and I had no way to ask. And no fucking time either.

"Dante?" I put my hand on the small of his back, but he drove his elbow into my arm to push me away. Then he grabbed Blaker by his collar again, hauled him up, and slammed his back against the metal door.

"You better pray I find Ros, you asshole. Because if I don't, I'm coming for you. I'll make sure it's the last thing I do in this world to see you dead." When Dante released the man, he crumpled to the ground like an old rag, whimpering and covering his head with his arms. Dante turned on the ball of his foot, shoved his gun into his coat pocket, and walked back to the truck.

I got behind the wheel. Blossom's smell inundated the cab. I could taste dewy maple leaves in the back of my throat, feel the tingle of spice in my sinuses. He was close enough that his hair brushed my cheek, and I wanted to grab a handful of it and pull his head back to expose his neck, clamp my lips down, and suck that rosewater and ginger flavor out of his skin....

I squeezed my eyes shut and concentrated on the cool plastic of the steering wheel against my palms. I was getting desperate, reaching the point where I almost didn't care what the faerie would make me into. Almost. But no. Fuck that. I wasn't like those pitiful bastards in that crumbling building. I was more than what I needed. "Do you know anybody who drives a black Mercedes, Dante?"

"What do you think?"

I'd expected that. "Right. Well, we're going to have to consider the possibility of mage involvement. Gonna have to look into the network, see if anybody knows anything. And to do that, we're going to need help, I'm afraid."

I FELT like puking after what Inky said about needing help. With a couple of exceptions like Raf, Devereux, and Moirin, most of the people I'd depended on had let me down. I mean, I didn't have to look much further than my fucking mother to see counting on someone to have my back was going to lead to disappointment. And I'd figured it out before I left elementary school.

I was so wrapped up in my head that I wasn't paying much attention to my surroundings, but in this neighborhood, where people driving was something of a rarity, it was impossible not to notice someone following us.

"Yo, I think we got a tail," I said to Inky. "Hang a left and go around the block."

Sure enough, the lights of what was probably a van or an older-model SUV stayed with us, following a couple car lengths behind. Shit. What if it was some of these jerk-off mages that had everybody pissing themselves? We couldn't lead them back to my apartment—Mom might be a tweaker piece of shit, but I wasn't going to leave her to the mercy of people with… Jesus. Fucking magical powers. Actually, that possibility got me thinking. If it was those assholes, they might know something about my sister. I don't know if I was stupid or just pissed off, but I'd take my chances beating it out of them. In fact, I liked that idea.

I looked around until I saw a twenty-four-hour coin laundry place. A couple kids hung around in the parking lot, probably selling dime bags. I pointed. "Pull in there."

Inky pulled the truck up beside the narrow slab of cement running underneath the place's grimy windows. I got out and turned to the guys, who were probably only thirteen or fourteen. "Get lost."

One of them held up his hands. "Hey, man, what the hell? We ain't bothering you."

Since I didn't have time or energy to debate, I pulled the snub-nose and pointed it at the kid. "I said fuck off. I won't ask again."

They took off running down the alley around the corner just as the car that had been tailing us—one of those long white vans contractors tend to use—pulled in behind the truck and shut off its headlights.

I took a deep breath and got ready. I had no idea what I was in for if I had to fight a person who could use magic, but I still had my weapon, and in my experience, you put enough holes in a fucker and he'll go down, pixie dust or not. Still, I didn't know how many shots I'd get in, so I focused on letting my anger carry me to that sharp, clear place where everything but me seemed to move in slow motion. I slipped the .38 into my coat pocket. A lot of people have a misconception that letting someone see you have a gun will act as a deterrent or some bullshit—scare them away. But I'd learned that it was a hell of a lot better if they didn't know until it was too late.

I waited, the exhaust from our truck puffing around my legs, as the van's door opened. I was almost disappointed when a big bastard with a bald head, a blond beard, a black jacket, and jackboots stepped out. Unless I was seriously mistaken, this jackass was no mage. "What the fuck do you want?" I asked. "Why are you following me?"

"You're Dante Mayfield." The guy's breath froze in clouds when he spoke.

I spat on the ground. And waited. His hands were empty, but that didn't mean he didn't have a weapon on him somewhere. And it didn't mean there weren't more guys in that van.

"I believe you have something that belongs to us," he continued. "A computer."

No way was he getting that machine. I was going to get it to somebody who could take it apart and find anything hidden on it that might help me, Raf, or those poor kids they'd kidnapped. Then I would turn it over to the FBI, and I was betting Moirin's friend who did all the tech stuff for Raf could help with both. But this prick didn't need to know any of that. "I got no idea what you're talking about."

He took a step toward me. Only about fifteen feet separated us. From this distance I could put a bullet between his eyes in my sleep, and if he knew who I was, he probably knew that—which meant somebody in that van almost certainly had my head in their crosshairs. All I could do was stand there and hear what he had to say. "I think you do. We know who you are, and we know who you work for. We know it was you who broke into our cabin and stole the laptop. We would also like to know what happened to the man who disappeared."

I had to resist rolling my eyes. He wouldn't believe it even if I told him. Not that I was going to. "You must be even stupider that you look, you Nazi asshole. I never heard of any cabin or any computer. Why the hell do you think I know anything about this?"

He smiled as he closed the distance between us, only stopping when I could've reached out and wrapped my hands around his throat. God knows I fucking wanted to. "You smug little mongrel piece of shit. Your time's done, boy, and you don't even know it. All of your kind have worn out their welcome. You, your bean-shitting boss, those coons and chinks you sell guns to… your time has come. The power's back where it belongs now, boy. The big kids are back at the table."

God, I wanted to pop this asshole if only so he'd stop talking. "Yeah, I heard your tired shit before. You and the rest of the stupid motherfuckers who think that idiot in power is going to do anything for you."

He laughed. "I'm not talking about politics, Jackie Chan. I'm talking about real power. You got no idea what we've got in our corner. Now I want that computer, and I want to know what happened to my man. You tell me and you get to live long enough to go back to Juan Valdez and tell him he might want to reconsider supplying us. We're going to come out on top either way, and if you help us out, you might not end up in the ground. We need to keep somebody around to polish our boots."

"I'll be sure and let him know, but don't get your hopes up, Adolf. And since you're obviously an idiot, I'll say it again: I don't know jack shit about any cabin, any computer, or any missing Stormtroopers. So, we done here?"

"If that's how you wanna play it, I guess we are." He looked over his shoulder and nodded at the van.

When the back panel slid open and the barrel of an assault rifle poked out, I'd been expecting it. Before its owner got a shot off, I dove for the asshole in front of me and caught him in the gut with my left shoulder. He hit the ground hard, the breath knocked from his lungs with a *whoosh* and a spray of spit. I flipped the heavy bastard on top of me. At this range, I didn't have a snowball's chance in hell of getting away without getting hit at least once, and this fucker was the only cover available.

I could only pray the guy with the rifle cared enough about his friend not to go through him to get to me.

Just as the gunfire started and then stopped, the guy on top of me shook off enough of his shock to get a beefy fist around my windpipe. When the gray started to pour in at the edges of my vision, I knew I didn't have any choice—it was either get shot or lie here and get fucking strangled. I pulled the .38 from my pocket. I would've shot him in the head, but my arm was trapped between us. The best I could manage was to twist my wrist enough to shove the nose into his ribs. I was just about to black out when I managed to pull the trigger, the powder burning my hand and belly and the recoil knocking me in the gut.

The guy heaved up a glob of blood that struck the side of my face, and then he flopped to his back and pressed both hands to the wound—not that it did much to stop the blood.

I sucked in air just as the guy with the rifle lined up his next shot. I had about three seconds, and I used them to slide on my ass until I was up by the other guy's head—anything to make his buddy think twice about hitting him to get at me. It would last maybe long enough for me to look over my shoulder and decide what to do next. When I did, I saw the truck's passenger door open, just like I'd left it, along with the driver's side door. At least Inky and Blossom had the good sense to stay put—even if Blossom was supposed to be keeping me alive. I was no expert, but I didn't have to be one to know his little bargains came with addendums and shit. Maybe this was one. Nobody was coming to help me. Whatever. I was on my own, and I was used to that.

But I was still fucked. Even though it was only a few feet, I couldn't run for the truck. My back would make too good a target. And even if I made it, this asshole could lay down enough fire before Inky started the engine to hit at least one of us. Shooting him in the kneecaps and then running was an option. I didn't like the odds that he could squeeze off a few rounds before he went down, but I was running out of alternatives—with every step he took toward me. In no time, he'd be close enough to remove any danger of hitting his Nazi friend when he put a cap in my ass.

I had to try. He was looking at my face and not my hand. If I could lift the .38 and squeeze one off before he saw what I was doing…. It was a long shot, but it was the only one I had.

In that second, I decided it was no bigger risk to go for his head than his kneecaps. Whatever happened to me, a world with one less Nazi flesh peddler was a good thing. Might save at least one kid from something so disgraceful I couldn't even imagine it.

Just as I lifted my arm, something silver flashed behind the guy, followed by a hollow thud. He fell on his face, and Inky stood behind him, brandishing a bigass pipe wrench, probably from the tool kit in the truck. The way he looked from it to the asshole in the snow, it was like he didn't understand the connection between the two.

For a second I wondered if he'd done it because I'd wanted him to. But other than questioning how fast he could turn the key in the truck's ignition, I hadn't been thinking about him at all. I'd worry about it later. Didn't much matter anyhow: asshole was unconscious, maybe dead, and his buddy's wet grunts were getting less frequent.

"We should get the hell out of here." I took the hand Inky offered and got to my feet.

"Let's not be too hasty," a voice said, followed by some very familiar clicks.

Inky turned just as a group of men came around the back of the van—seemed the kids selling in front of this place had gone to get their older brothers after I ran them off. And their cousins and their second cousins. At least a dozen big guys had handguns trained on us.

I squinted as they got closer, thinking I recognized one of them—a small-time dealer, sold mostly prescription shit his girlfriend boosted from the pharmacy where she worked. Ran a gang named after one of the streets nearby… I couldn't remember which one. But I knew he bought off us—piecemeal, a few items here and there—and I searched my brain for his name. "Georgie?"

"Dante? That you?" He lowered his weapon. Thank Christ. "We got word of somebody edging in on our territory. Now why would you do that, my man?"

"I wouldn't." I tilted my head toward the Nazis by my feet. "I was just here for these jerk-offs—white supremacist gang trying to get a foothold in the city. Sick fucks who kidnap and whore out kids."

Georgie nodded as he put away his 9mm. "Heard something about that. This is them, huh?"

"Yeah. Look, I didn't want your people getting hurt…."

"Say no more. You and me? We're good. Me and these bastards?" He looked at the two men. "Not so much. Why don't you let us take care of them? This is our street, our turf they're on. It's only right we be the ones to gives their asses a proper welcome."

I was more than happy to put my gun away and shake the hand Georgie offered. Hell, I could've kissed him, because all I wanted to do was get away from here and somewhere I could think of what I needed to do next. "They're all yours, man. Yo, you wanna take your time with 'em? It won't upset me or the boss."

He smiled. "I heard that."

I tapped Inky on the elbow. "Let's go. I guess we're going to have to pursue… other avenues."

"Fucking hell," he said as he followed me to the truck.

Chapter Sixteen

I HATED everything about this. I'd hated that Inky and Blossom insisted we wait to talk to these mages they knew, and I hated that they wouldn't let me go home. They were afraid someone could be watching my place, though they seemed a lot more concerned about Blossom's safety than mine. They dragged me to an old lady's house, and it looked like something out of an episode of *Hoarders*. At least Corazón was okay. She was convinced I was her cousin's grandson, and she told me I was beautiful and kissed me on both cheeks. It was nice, even though she smelled of thrift-store clothes. Then she gave me a bowl of hearty stew full of spicy sausage and big chunks of chicken. I couldn't remember the last time someone had cooked for me, and after a few prompts, Corazón even called me by my name. She said it was a good name, that it suited me.

For a night and a day, she was more of a mother to me than my own had been for ten years.

But now it was evening, and Inky wanted to go to some bar where mages hung out—and he said I couldn't take my gun. Said they'd know, wouldn't let me in with it. I hated that in my bones. I didn't like being defenseless in a place I was picturing as a scene out of Harry Potter—a bunch of freaks and lunatics, probably.

My phone hummed with another text from Raf, but I wasn't ready to deal with him… not unless he had something I could use. If he did, he'd tell me and not just instruct me to call. I knew him at least that well, and I had all this other shit on my plate at the moment.

"You're not planning to wear that, are you?" Blossom sat on the couch next to Corazón, Charlene purring in his lap.

I looked down at my dark jeans, boots, black sweatshirt, and the leather jacket I would never have been able to afford, but it had been a Christmas present from Raf. It wasn't one of those biker-style jackets with the pointy collars and spikes either. Raf was too classy for that. It was simple and fitted, and I liked it because it was warm and buttery soft. "What am I supposed to wear? A cape and a pointy hat? No."

Blossom laughed. "No, of course not. But would it be so terrible to dress for the occasion? Play up your assets?"

"I just want to get this done," I told him. "I don't give a fuck about anything but finding my sister."

"It's a shame," Corazón said. "You're such a handsome young man. You should put on a suit and a nice tie. The young ladies would be sure to notice." She winked.

Blossom threw up his hands, startling the cat. "Exactly. And you might think twice about taking me along. Really. Which of us do you suppose knows how to have a good time, me or Inky?"

"Just shut the fu—" Inky bit back the curse when Corazón scowled. "Just be quiet, you knob. I've told you a thousand times it's too dangerous for you to go to Hex. If one of those mages gets ahold of you, it's all over. You'll be a slave."

Corazón patted Blossom's knee. "Ramon is such a handsome boy, but you must not be jealous, Raphael. I have noticed the girls looking your way too. You're just too quiet for your own good. Always thinking too much."

Blossom smirked as if he'd won some kind of victory, and I had to close my eyes. It was surreal, and I couldn't wrap my head around this shit. I still felt like I was going to wake up from the worst fucking dream ever. Ever since I'd come back from Raf's and found Ros gone, I'd felt like I was in a nightmare, so close to just losing it and screaming that it took all I had to hold myself together. This shit was tearing me up, and I wanted it over. "Can we please just go?"

Inky nodded and patted me on the shoulder. He liked touching me, and it didn't creep me out as much as it should have. I couldn't say the same for the way I caught him looking at me sometimes. But what the hell. These two freaks were the only allies I had, and that was what I hated the most. They didn't give a shit about me, didn't give a shit about Ros except to get her to send Blossom home. But I had to trust them because I didn't have anybody else. It sucked.

It was a good walk to wherever Inky was taking me, and it was fucking cold, but at least it had stopped snowing. I couldn't complain—it'd been my idea to leave the truck in an alley so it wouldn't end up associated with us. It was one of the things Raf had taught me to be careful about. We made it a few blocks before Inky started talking.

"So, Dante?"

"What?"

"Your name. Corazón likes it."

"So?"

Apparently he didn't get the hint from my tone. "It's unique. A family name?"

"No."

"Your mother chose it, then?"

I sighed out a white cloud and shoved my hands in my pockets. Jesus, he wasn't going to let up. It would be easier just to give in, even if I couldn't imagine what the hell he was getting out of this. "Yeah, she did. She loves—loved—books and plays. Stories and characters. For a while, when I was a kid, she wanted to be an actress. We lived in New York City, and she was always going to auditions, doing stuff with little theater groups, all kinds of stupid fucking projects that never amounted to anything."

"What happened?"

"Nothing. Maybe she sucked at it. I don't know. But she was too softhearted. It gutted her when she got rejected, sent her into a bad mood for days. For a while she got back up, tried again, but I guess you can only get smacked down so many times before you realize you're better off staying on the ground." I shook my head, remembering. "She loved it, though. Decided that if she couldn't act, she was going to write plays. We moved here because it was cheaper than New York, and she tried. At our first apartment, she had an old computer, one of those boxy things, and for a while she'd get up and sit at it for at least a few hours before lunch."

"That doesn't sound too bad."

"I liked that apartment. It had a lot of windows, and Mom had plants growing in most of them. I remember the smell of the incense she burned. It was cool for a while, but everything she wrote got rejected. Again and again. It hurt her, and she tried to cope. It was just chardonnay and weed at first…. What does this matter?"

"You must have wanted me to ask." Inky's weird eyes were wide with concern.

"Why do you think that?"

I'd started walking faster, wanting to get away from him, but he sped up and closed the distance until his shoulder pressed against mine. "It's what I do… what I am. I'll become whatever you need most. You must need to talk."

"Bullshit." But: "What's that like? You're never yourself? Only what other people want you to be?"

"Yeah. And it's like… well, it's just what I am."

"But what do you get out of it?"

Inky looked up at the cloudy sky and smiled. "So much. I get so much. For a while I get to be the center of somebody's universe. Their air, their sunshine, their sunset in the evenings. All of it. I get to make them think everything is perfect and beautiful, that the world never looked brighter. For a while, every little thing I do, the way I blink, the way I smooth down my shirt when I'm waiting for the bus, all of it is perfect in their eyes. Best thing they've ever seen. I scratch my arse and their heart swells. Haven't you ever had a girlfriend?"

"No."

"A boyfriend?"

"No."

He prodded me with his elbow. "Not even for a weekend? A night?"

"I'm not interested."

"Because you think it would interfere with you looking out for your sister?"

I was getting irritated. Well, more irritated. "Because I'm not interested. It all seems like a waste of time. Messy. What's the point of this?"

"The point, for me, is coaxing that adoration out of someone. There's a period—a honeymoon period—where someone's so infatuated you can do no wrong in their eyes. Sometimes it can last for a year, sometimes only a day or two, but during that time, people give off an energy. It's thick and sweet and golden. Better than honey. It's what sustains me."

"I'm glad I don't have to depend on anyone like that," I told him. "After a while, they're going to find something wrong with you. They'll try to change you, or they'll find somebody else who looks better."

Inky shook his silvery hair around. "You're not wrong there. It doesn't last, but I get to keep a little piece. And every one of them is unique. I wouldn't trade one of them.

"But I do need to be careful. The desires of some people, well, they could shape me into something I don't want to become. I steer well clear of those who like hurt and humiliation. So you'll understand if I stay close while we're in here. Latching on to your need for a confidant will save me from being influenced by those who like people begging in bloody heaps at their feet. There are people in this world who get off on some really fucked-up shite."

We'd stopped in front of a junk shop, one I'd seen before but never paid much attention to, its windows dirty and full of secondhand lawn mowers and power tools. It surprised me when Inky went inside and met a muscle-bound bastard in a black T-shirt.

"We gonna have a problem again, mate?"

The big guy shook his head and went to push a button. A garage-style door rolled up, exposing a lone hallway, and I followed Inky through a corridor that opened to a bar with a middle-aged woman behind it drying glasses with a cloth. There were some rooms opposite the bar, full of mismatched furniture. Behind it was a jukebox and a few more tables.

So this was the mage bar, Hex. What a shithole. Also empty. Aside from an older guy with a neatly trimmed beard and a sweater vest reading a book in a corner, this place was beat. Inky shook his head. "I guess we'll have to go downstairs."

"Why is that bad?" Damn, his tone and body language made me really miss my gun.

He wasn't normally a guy who was lost for words, and that made me nervous. "Just stay close."

I nodded as I followed him down a narrow staircase, but I wasn't going to be intimidated. I didn't care what kind of special powers these assholes had. I'd fought my way through worse.

When we reached the basement, I changed my mind. In fact, I thought I was going to puke. And it wasn't the musty smell turning my stomach.

The place was mostly empty, and it was dark except for some Christmas lights strung on the bar toward the back. Towards the middle, hundreds of candles outlined an area the size of a basketball court. Smoke billowed out from what looked like fancy metal planters, and it smelled like burnt hair—just nasty. A dozen or so people stood inside the ring, and instead of the velvet robes I'd pictured, most of them wore tight black clothes with fetishy touches like harnesses, collars, and corsets. Whatever. I grew up in Philadelphia, not exactly sheltered, so I was no stranger to the shit some people got off on. There were clubs for stuff like this around the city, but mostly the people who went to them kept to themselves, and they weren't hurting me—or, in most cases, anyone who didn't enjoy it—so I didn't think about them much. They tended to be people with more money and time than sense.

But these assholes had someone—something, I guess?—strapped to a table between them. It was hard to tell from a distance and with the shadows flickering around, but it looked like a young man with really hairy lower legs, furry almost, that ended in what I could only call hooves. A little tail poked up just above his buttcrack. And he was screaming, his voice raspy, crying out in a language I couldn't understand as the people around him smacked him with whips and burned him with wax from the candles. Worst of all, they were…. A line of guys waited behind him, even some women with strap-ons….

My right hand went to my left armpit. The only thought in my mind was that I was going to waste all these assholes. In my line of work, I'd learned to look the other way a lot of the time. But this—

No gun. I reached into the back of my pants but came up empty again. Fuck! I could smell blood, smell what they were doing, and it crawled inside me like dirty fingers pushing into my nostrils and down my throat. I gagged. I didn't even realize I'd started walking toward them until Inky's grip on the back of my coat stopped me. I jerked out of his grasp and spun around to face him. "Get your hands off me!"

His pink eyes, pale and glowy in the darkness, darted over to the gathering. "There's nothing we can do. I know it's shite, but we can't stop them. We'd just get ourselves killed."

"We can't just—" The creature choked out a few more sobs, followed by obvious begging—I didn't need to understand the words to know that. I wanted Blossom. I wanted him here, and I wanted him to kill every last one of these fuckers. I felt dizzy, and Corazón's spicy stew splashed against the back of my throat, but I managed to choke it back down as Inky took my elbow and guided me to the far side of the room opposite the bar, where he helped me lean against the wall.

Fuck. There was nothing I could do.

And these people might have my sister.

"What are you drinking?" Inky nodded toward the bar.

"I'm not old enough."

"Bollocks." He went over, spoke to the bartender and returned with a big glass.

I sipped. Rum and soda, mixed strong. It settled my stomach a little. My nerves, not so much.

"You've gotta calm down, Dante," Inky said. "Your righteous anger's wiggling in under my skin, and I don't want to be compelled to do something we'll both regret."

I almost spat my drink out. "Righteous anger? I might not be what most people consider a decent human being, but Jesus Christ!"

"I know." He put his hand between me and the wall to rub my back, and then he guided me behind the bar and toward an arched opening. "Grenade launchers? Really?"

"What?"

"I told you, I can read people's desires. You're pining for a grenade launcher. First time I've experienced that."

"I guess I am."

"You want to raze this place to the ground, stand triumphantly atop the smoldering remains."

"It would be the fucking right thing to do," I said. "When Ros is safe, and when she's grown up and doesn't need me anymore…."

"You know, when that day comes, you might discover you have some dreams of your own. Things you want for yourself, if you let go of the anger."

I shook my head as he led me down another narrow hall and into a little room with yellowed plaster walls, dark wood trim, some bookshelves, and a fireplace in the corner. How the hell did somebody let go of anger in a world like this? I couldn't imagine wanting anything except to not have to keep getting up when the world punched me in the face. All I wanted was the option to stay down for once instead of stumbling back to my feet and bracing for the next blow.

Two people sat at a table playing some kind of a game with cards I didn't recognize, several empty glasses between them. One of them, a guy who couldn't have been much older than me, looked up and smiled. "Incubus. Welcome back."

The person across from him had short hair, shaved in the back, with a few neon blue synthetic dreadlocks woven in. They wore a loose sweater that slid down to expose a slender shoulder, where I could see part of a tattoo like an ornate picture frame, and they pulled out a chair with a wink at Inky. "Have a seat."

These two seemed pretty normal, and I calmed down a little bit as I sat next to the one with the dreads and heavy sparkly eyeliner and Inky sat across from me.

The guy with the messy auburn hair took a sip from a tumbler of what smelled like whiskey. "What brings you here?"

"Actually, I hoped to run into you again," Inky said. "So are you two just business associates or friends?"

The guy smiled at the person across from him. "Very old friends. I didn't know the two of you had met."

Inky laughed. He seemed relaxed—he was either enjoying himself or doing a good job faking it. "Only briefly. Saved me from suffering some absolute shite music. I didn't get your name, though."

The person next to me stretched out their arm. I noticed several weird clunky digital watches on their wrist as they shook hands with Inky and said, "Jet. Jet Zama. You can call me JZ or Jayz, or whatever, really."

"You can call me Inky. And this is my friend Dante Mayfield."

The guy reached across to me. "Emrys Rathburn." Raf had taught me some things to look for when dealing with clients, body language and shit like that. Emrys smiled and his eyes were warm, but he was definitely sizing me up. I made eye contact and held his gaze so he knew he wasn't intimidating me. It seemed to work, because he released my hand with a small respectful dip of his head.

"Something we can do for you?" Jet asked.

Inky held up a finger to pause the conversation. "We're gonna want drinks for this." He went to the bar and came back with a beer for himself, another whiskey for Emrys, something bright blue that faded to lime green for Jet, and another rum and Coke for me. Then he told them the story of Ros's disappearance and all the places we'd looked so far. I noticed he left out any mention of Blossom.

Emrys circled the rim of his cup with his fingertip, staring into the amber depths instead of looking at us. "How did this girl and her abilities come to your attention, Inky?"

"We… I met Dante first."

Emrys wiped his finger daintily on a napkin and looked up at me. "But you never knew your sister had any magical talent. How did you happen to meet an incubus?"

"In the neighborhood," I mumbled.

"What I want to know is why you're associated with neo-Nazi human traffickers." Jet plucked the paper umbrella out of her—his? their?—drink and sucked on the end.

I didn't say anything. What I did was none of these people's business. I couldn't bring attention to Raf and his operation. I wouldn't. Raf trusted me, and he'd given me a chance when no one else would.

I wondered what Emrys and Jet saw when Inky raked his silvery hair back and pinned it behind his thick horns. He'd looked human to me before Blossom did whatever he did to my eye. Did he look human to them? Did he really look like whatever they wanted to see the most? "Look, we need to know if we can trust you," Inky said. "What guilds are you affiliated with?"

Emrys sat up a little straighter. "None. I'm a free agent and intend to stay that way. The only contact I have with any of the factions is to do occasional translations. I'm selective, but I have to make a living."

Inky nodded, seeming satisfied. He turned to Jet.

"I'm a member of Electrosensory Mirage. We're… more of a collective than a guild. And if there's something we're interested in knowing, we already know it. If we don't, chances are we don't care. If what you're trying to ask is whether we're going to run to Sekhet-Aaru or Wú Cháng with whatever you tell us, the answer is no. I can't stand any of them. Frankly, I'd like to see them gone from the face of the earth. So… what are you trying to say? How did you guys really meet?"

Inky sighed. "What we think is… it seems like Rosalind accidentally summoned something. That's what led me to her. Probably also led whoever took her."

"Summoning is difficult magic," Emrys said, "even for practiced mages. But you think a nine-year-old girl accomplished it by mistake?"

"Seems that way," Inky said.

Jet leaned their elbows on the table. "What did she summon?"

"Something… impossible."

"What?" Jet persisted.

"If you're willing to help us, you'll find out," I said. "Boy, will you find out."

"It's certainly interesting," Emrys said. "I can't deny being curious. I'd be willing to look into it. I won't promise more than that until I have a better idea of what we're dealing with."

For the next half an hour, we filled them in on what we'd learned so far.

"Mercedes-driving mages." Jet shook their head. "There's a good chance that means Sekhet-Aaru. I won't pass up a chance to stick it to them if I can. I'll take a peek. But I'm with Emrys. If it starts to get too dangerous, I can't guarantee I won't bounce too."

"I think the abandoned hair salon is a good place to start," Emrys said. "Let's meet there first thing in the morning. Whoever is responsible for this might have left something behind."

"I'll see what I can track down on the car," Jet said. "I don't care how badass they are, no mage that I know of can conjure a Mercedes. That means there'll be a trail. If it's in a computer anywhere or on CCTV, I can find it. The problem will be narrowing the search results." Jet talked fast when they got excited, and their chatter tapered off to disjointed muttering as they pulled a laptop from a bag on the floor and connected it with a wire to one of their watches.

"This is good news, right?" Inky looked at me with such a pleading expression that I took pity on him and forced a smile.

I'd only have to wait a few more hours, and I was hitting a wall. By now, not even I could pretend I could keep going without a few hours of sleep. Then, hopefully, I'd have some answers. If this turned into another dead end, I didn't know what I'd do.

Chapter Seventeen

I'd spent most of the day sanding the crown molding in the upstairs guestroom, and tomorrow I planned to start ripping up the carpet and maybe even the old tile in the attached bathroom. As soon as everything was finished, I'd move my mother in here where I could keep a closer eye on her in her advanced age. I wanted to make sure she would be happy, that everything would be the way she liked it. I'd decorated it with tropical flowers and provided curio cabinets for her collectibles. I would hire her a nurse, and she would basically have a private suite. I hated thinking of her stubbornly living alone with no one to help her as she got older, but....

After what I had seen when I'd followed Dante, I needed any distraction I could get. Every time I stopped working, the images returned and the questions quickly followed. But it had been dark for several hours now, and my stomach was protesting the fact that I hadn't eaten since breakfast. My foot was also objecting to the long day of work. I took a quick shower, slipped into a pair of sweatpants, a T-shirt, and my ankle brace, and went downstairs to the kitchen.

The first thing I did was turn on the espresso maker. Now that machine was one investment I knew I would never regret. Opening the refrigerator, I contemplated what to make for dinner. I enjoyed cooking and wished I had more opportunities to make meals. Aside from the occasional neighborhood barbecue in the summer, it just wasn't worth taking the time to turn out a nice spread. One of the pitfalls of living alone, but one I had long ago accepted. In my line of work, a family or even a partner was a liability I couldn't afford. One day soon I'd need to figure out a way to keep my mother from harm and attention, but it would be a pleasant change to have a dinner companion each night.

Eventually I decided to make a fried egg and bacon sandwich with a small salad. I took it into my study, set it on the desk, and checked my phone. No messages, which indicated no fires to put out. That wasn't unusual. I'd been scrupulous when choosing my people, and that meant they knew their jobs and I could trust them to take care of most things without me. But in this case, it also meant no news about Dante's sister.

Dante. I had to find out what he was involved with and if I needed to take steps. Though I knew it was a long shot, I opened my laptop and searched for "Magic in Philadelphia."

I shook my head. Of course I didn't believe in magic, but what else could explain what I'd seen?

As I ate, I scrolled through pages and pages of magic-supply stores and performers in the city. That led me to dozens more sites referencing the card game Magic: The Gathering. Trying some different combinations of words and terms, I sifted through lists of pagan organizations, New Age bookstores, and online retailers selling things like incense and essential oils. I finished my dinner and my coffee and hadn't found anything promising, so I went to a cabinet and poured a few fingers of bourbon into a glass before returning to my desk. After another hour of coming up empty, I remembered something Moirin had said about the dark web. It wasn't an avenue I'd ever had to explore as I had plenty of real-world contacts and preferred face-to-face meetings for a multitude of reasons. I had always assumed accessing the darknet would be difficult, possibly beyond my technical skill, but after reading a few articles and downloading an onion router, I found a series of directories, wikis, and link dumps.

Looking at it, I felt like I'd been transported back to the nineties, and it was painfully slow. Very little of what I saw was criminal in nature—mostly sites where people wanted to communicate anonymously, or those originating from places where any political statement necessitated discretion. Of course there were anarchists, UFO conspiracy theorists, pornographers, and pedophiles, and I considered searching for information on the WLF and their activities, but Moirin's contact would have already checked, and whoever they were, they were far better at this kind of thing than I was. I found a few people offering burner guns for sale or even assassinations, but based on the language, I had my doubts. Most likely these were scams that would take a potential customer's Bitcoins and run.

After a few hours slogging through the darknet, I leaned back in my chair and rubbed my eyes. They stung and felt gritty. I stood to stretch and make myself another espresso. I also toasted a piece of bread in the hopes it would prevent the coffee and alcohol from giving me heartburn. I still hadn't found anything, even among message boards full of conspiracy theories so wild no one could invent their existence. Maybe I hadn't seen what I thought I'd seen.

But no. No. I knew what I had seen as sure as I knew that if I returned to that spot in the woods, the strange misshapen tree would be there. Thinking about it, I shuddered, feeling vulnerable and alone in a way I hadn't since I'd received the news about my brother and I'd first had to face the idea that the world did not operate in the manner I'd always believed. Before returning to the study, I checked all my locks and made sure my security system was armed. When I sat down, I opened one of my desk drawers and slid the false bottom aside to reveal the Ruger SR45 I kept there. I was reassured by its presence, the feel of its angles against my fingertips.

One of the conspiracy-theory message boards was still open, and as I read, I noticed a commenter posting as H_Yardley repeatedly directing other users to a site called the Black Chamber "if you want to know what's really going on."

Having wasted most of my night, I decided I had little to lose. Between memories of what had happened in the woods and some of what I'd seen on the darknet, I didn't even want to consider sleeping. I followed the links to the page, another display of blinking green letters on a black background.

Dear Guest,

YOU ARE BEING WATCHED. USE EXTREME CAUTION!!! WHILE YOU ARE ANONYMOUS ON THE DARKNET, VARIOUS ORGANIZATIONS CAN SEE YOU ARE USING AN ONION ROUTER FOR SOMETHING. SOME OF THE ORGANIZATIONS DISCUSSED HERE MIGHT HAVE CAPABILITIES BEYOND THAT. HAVING THIS KNOWLEDGE PUTS YOU IN DANGER!!! PROCEED WITH CAUTION.

You are here because you know your life is not your own, that you are being controlled. You are here because you know you are being lied to, that the truth is being deliberately and aggressively hidden. What you do not know is how long this conspiracy has been perpetuated against you, or what has been committed in its name. If you choose to continue reading, the life you had before will be gone. You will no longer be able to ignore what is being done. You will be taking the red pill. Before proceeding, be sure you want the responsibility of this knowledge.

This writer certainly had a flair for the dramatic, though I'd noticed this wasn't unusual on many of these sites. Below his introduction was a long list of dozens of articles. I went to the first one: *Major Magical Guilds and Factions.*

Dear Guest,
BEWARE!!! DO NOT SHARE THIS INFORMATION WITH ANYONE!!! DO NOT SPEAK OF IT IF THERE IS ANY CHANCE YOU WILL BE OVERHEARD. DOING SO CAN PUT YOU IN DANGER!!!
This is the information I have been able to uncover on the major factions, but I must assume it is incomplete.

SEKHET-AARU

Some sources estimate Sekhet-Aaru has been in existence for almost two thousand years. It is impossible to dispute the level of power this guild has gathered. It is equally impossible to imagine what their ultimate goal might be, but we can be certain it will not benefit the people of this world.

The guild's name translates to Field of Reeds and is a reference to the ancient Egyptian concept of paradise or heaven. Some speculation exists that Sekhet-Aaru believes itself to be destined to bring paradise to the world. However, its methods are cutthroat. There is an abundance of evidence showing the guild's control of many multinational corporations and world governments, including the governments of the United States and many European nations. Whether this group of mages is operating with or without the knowledge of elected and appointed government officials is not clear.

In addition, there is evidence that the guild has orchestrated many pivotal world events as far back as the fall of the Roman Empire. Please see my essays detailing the clues that show their hand in over thirty historical events. Taken cumulatively, it is hard to deny that Sekhet-Aaru is fabricating wars, economic collapse, and possibly even natural disasters to further their own ends.

What are those ends? Certainly distraction is a continuing goal of the guild, and events are often organized to draw the attention of the populace away from their machinations. There is evidence that they are also staged to distribute power, granting it to some and stealing it from others, for reasons that are known only to guild members.

As far as an end game, there is some indication that the guild is moving its pieces into place for a denouement. Prophecies taken seriously by many magical practitioners indicate that a major event is imminent. They believe that magic and history move in cycles of two thousand years, and that we are two thousand years or more since the last major event—the founding of the Roman Empire by Augustus and the time when magic "broke" with mundane society. Mages were driven underground, though Sekhet-Aaru took full advantage of this to manipulate politics from behind the scenes. Some believe that the guild plans to remedy this. One theory states that the mages will orchestrate a total societal collapse that will allow them to step in as saviors and regain the place of power they feel they deserve.

Sekhet-Aaru is by far the greatest threat facing the human race. They are willing to unleash plagues and destroy entire nations of people to further their goals. More evidence can be found in my essays. For example, there is evidence the guild became aware of climate change not long after the Industrial Revolution. It is clear that the guild took control of newly emerging technology, manipulating some of it while suppressing other advances. Who knows what technology they have kept secret? It is extremely likely that Sekhet-Aaru encouraged climate change. Two phases of their plan appear to be controlling energy sources and water. The third and probably most terrifying is the rumor that they will, at an opportune time, release some sort of a magical/biological weapon that only they have a cure for.

The question we must ask is not whether Sekhet-Aaru will control every aspect of our lives. They already do. They are carefully keeping you distracted with minutiae, keeping you just content enough to not take risks, giving you just enough that you are afraid to lose it. By the time the population becomes aware of what is happening, our chances of standing against it are likely to be slim to none.

THE COUNCIL OF ANTIQUARIANS

The Antiquarians are a much more benevolent guild than Sekhet-Aaru, but their views of humanity in general are equally dismal. Rather than using knowledge to manipulate and grab power, the Antiquarians hoard magical information, believing it to be beyond the understanding of the average person.

The guild seems to have formed around the time of the break, with the goal of protecting magical manuscripts and items from destruction. With the advent of Christianity, its mission became even more critical, and as a result, the guild became much more secretive and isolated. It is impossible to find even the briefest mention of them throughout the Dark Ages and the medieval period. They remained underground until the late Renaissance at the earliest, when it is rumored that men like Leonardo Da Vinci may have reaped the benefit of some of their accrued knowledge—with or without the realization of the guild's existence. To this day they are steadfast in their mission to protect their treasure "until they are needed." It is accepted that they, too, believe some sort of epic event is coming in the near future. Until then, the world is unlikely to know the extent of the knowledge held by the Antiquarians, if we will ever know.

Though evidence shows the members of this guild to be scholarly and peaceful, if elitist, they are more than capable of using the information they control to their advantage. It is probably only this that grants them autonomy from Sekhet-Aaru, who rely on what is reported to be a massive library for their own magical endeavors.

Little more is known about the Antiquarians due to their secrecy. If they have goals or aspirations to power, we will likely not know until it is too late for us to do anything about it.

WÚ CHÁNG

This guild is truly the stuff of nightmares. Members of Wú Cháng are able to perform magic impossible for other mages. It is not surprising that even Sekhet-Aaru is afraid of Wú Cháng and is careful to keep it appeased.

The guild likely formed during the Han Dynasty in response to the consolidation of power in Imperial China and the resulting bureaucracy. Like its counterparts in Europe, the guild went underground for survival, and the timing, which coincides with the split in the Western world, is hard to ignore. Wú Cháng is somewhat more mercenary than other factions, and there is evidence that they aided in military campaigns and political power grabs, particularly during the reign of Emperor Wu of Han.

These mages are expert flesh manipulators and necromancers. Their knowledge of human anatomy rivals that of a world-class surgeon. Combined with magic, they use this information to exact horrific torture and mutilation. They are able to control growth and decay in skin, bone, and muscle. Their methods also offer them an infinite number of ways to cause death. Without even making their presence known, a member of Wú Cháng can cause a blood clot to form, facilitating heart attack or stroke. They can perforate the internal organs or cause bones to weaken and deteriorate. As a result, they often work as assassins. Other victims are left blinded, crippled, or terribly disfigured.

The guild's name translates to impermanence, though they have perverted the Buddhist tenet to give themselves permission to kill without remorse. From its founding in China, the guild has spread out and now includes people of various nationalities operating in dozens of countries. Like Sekhet-Aaru, they have become wealthy over the years and control many lucrative businesses.

These mages are known to work in pairs, mirroring the Heibai Wú Cháng (Black and White Impermanence)—two deities from Chinese mythology in charge of taking the dead to hell. For those who are interested, the names of these gruesome escorts are Xie Bi'an (White) and Fan Wujiu (Black). Interestingly, they are sometimes described as a single being, which is either benevolent or an instrument of punishment. From what is known of the guild's history, morals play little part in which of these manifestations someone is likely to encounter.

It goes without saying that if someone gets on the wrong side of this guild, they WILL DIE. There's nothing they can do to stop it. If they have plans for the event the guilds agree is coming, they are not known. Of all of the guilds, Wú Cháng is the most shrouded in tradition, superstition, and fear. I have collected several essays on bizarre injuries and medical anomalies believed to be the work of these mages, but be warned—they are very graphic and not for the faint of heart.

THE WHEEL

This is a smaller and newer faction that operates primarily in the American Southwest, Central and South America, and parts of the Caribbean. Like its European cousins, the guild formed to protect magic and mages from destruction, but in this case, it was to protect Native magic from European invaders and likely began around the time of their arrival in the New World. Since then, it has absorbed and adapted various Native traditions and is believed to have access to the forgotten magic of several civilizations. This claim can be backed up by reports of the guild's mages having mastered shape-shifting—an ability out of the reach of the other factions.

Within the last few hundred years, The Wheel bolstered its ranks with Native practitioners from other parts of the world, particularly among slaves arriving in the Americas from Africa. Currently, they welcome any mages whose beliefs align with their own, but they remain an insular community, mistrustful of outsiders and fiercely loyal to each other. Unlike the other guilds, The Wheel is active in promoting the well-being of the nonmagical members of their communities. They believe these people will be essential when the expected event comes to pass. The Wheel does not seem to have designs on global power, but it is clear that they will do whatever they must do to ensure they are never exploited again and that their traditions and way of life are preserved. Impressively, The Wheel has successfully resisted being absorbed, or later, wiped out, by Sekhet-Aaru for well over three hundred years.

The faction's name is simple out of necessity—the group formed from people speaking dozens of different languages—but it is also symbolic. Things will come full circle, or what goes around comes around. Again, the similarities between the belief that something significant is coming and the prophecies of the Mayans, Aztecs, and others is difficult to dismiss. The timelines coincide a little too closely for comfort, at least for mine.

THE ORDER OF MARIAN

This faction of feminist practitioners, who prefer to be known as witches, formed in the British Isles and spread to western Europe in an attempt to preserve local magical traditions when the Romans invaded, though there is strong evidence the Order existed prior to that time, just not secretly. The group contains both men and women. They are Luddites who believe industrialization is harmful to both the earth and the human race. Opposite to most other factions, the Order looks forward to the coming event with anticipation, because they think it will purge the world of harmful technology and usher in an era of peace and a natural paradise in an agrarian society aided by magic.

Though I should be writing this entry in the past tense. The Order of Marian disappeared in the late 1700s, and I cannot find even speculation as to why. Prior to that time, they seem to have been a force to be reckoned with, mainly because of their affinity with nature spirits, some of which were quite powerful. They were said to be able to summon the fey easily, and they were feared for this reason. My research indicates that mages have been unable to duplicate this feat in many centuries, at least. From what I have learned of the unpredictable and often violent nature of these fey, that's likely a good thing.

ELECTROSENSORY MIRAGE

The newest of the factions, this group prefers to be called a collective, and it's an apt term. Organization is loose at best, with most members operating in small cells and communicating via advanced technology. You won't find them on the darknet. Don't try. The collective seems to have little in the way of an overriding philosophy, though a strong resentment of rules and authority is common. Many members are working for individual causes like environmentalism, animal rights, or income equality.

What ties ESM together is the opinion that the future lies in a combination of advanced technology and magic. Using their unique skills, they have devised ways to merge the two to great effect. Several prominent scientists, computer programmers, and engineers are rumored to be affiliated with ESM. I haven't been able to confirm this.

If ESM sounds like a pack of unruly kids behind computers, you're partly right. But don't be fooled. These techno-mages are capable of things even skilled hackers can only do in their wildest dreams. They have resisted aggressive attempts by Sekhet-Aaru at absorption. The larger guild, along with Wú Cháng, cannot operate its businesses without automation and technology, and so far both have proved unable to devise magic similar to what is used by ESM. The collective manages to keep Sekhet-Aaru at bay by threatening their financial assets, or in some cases, wiping them out. Their knowledge of the members and operations of both of the larger guilds also gives them an insurance policy, since it can always be leaked.

Remember, these people are capable of hijacking nuclear launch codes.

And they probably know you're reading this.

It ended there, and I sat staring at the green letters on the black screen, my eyes on fire, my thoughts racing. It would be easy to dismiss what I had read as the rantings of a paranoid lunatic, if a well-spoken one. But though I was no historian, I had to acknowledge some of the parallels the author had drawn.

And then there was what I had seen in the woods. What else but magic could cause something like that? Had the two men with Dante been mages? Had they belonged to one of these groups? If they were manipulating Dante, coercing him, I would put a stop to it. Right now I wanted to believe that was what was happening. I didn't have the mental energy to consider other possibilities.

I stood and stretched. I'd been at my desk for the better part of six hours, and I was no longer a young man. I wandered over to a shelf and ran my fingers over the spines of the books, looking for something to read when I went to bed. I needed to think about this, but not tonight. I was too depleted. After some consideration, I chose Maja Haderlap's *Angel of Forgetting*. I was fluent in the Romance languages, so the German novel would tax my skills enough to keep my mind from other things. Besides, the subject matter was fitting.

If any of what the article said was true, something was going to happen, and maybe happen soon. I had no fear that people would lose their desire for the products I provided because of magic. In fact, the demand might increase. Weapons meant power, maybe the power to stand against oppression—to resist what these people had planned for the rest of us. After I got a few hours of sleep, I had to think about that. I had to get more information, and I might have to prepare.

Chapter Eighteen

Charlene was fascinated by the contents of the oddly shaped little human building, and I had to admit, I could not blame her. As much as I missed my own lands, with their rolling silvery-green hills and mutable, dusk-lit glades, where the wind and the leaves danced together like ill-fated lovers and the streams and pools were full of nymphs with lovely singing voices, at least this place was interesting. It held the strangest things: rows of chairs roofed with mushroom-like umbrellas, scissors and combs floating in brilliant blue fluid, spongy brightly colored cylinders, and lengths of mortal hair arranged in braids and colored every imaginable shade. It was quite beautiful, despite the obviously abandoned state of the small shrine, or whatever it was. A row of pegs held a few tiny jeweled clips, and these I could not resist. Some resembled butterflies, other birds and flowers, and many were further adorned with ribbons and brilliant colors of spiraled or plaited hair. I sorted through them, choosing some of the best to keep for myself. What could be the harm? The way they were designed, they had clearly been left here as offerings for my people. Besides, this place was soon to be transformed into a facility for serving up the carcasses of sheep. Hideous.

"Blossom!"

I turned toward Inky, irritated at the interruption. "Yes?"

"Care to join us?"

"Maybe in a bit." I returned my attention to the intricate little treasures, finding a particularly nice one made of bronze filigree and decorated with yellow flowers and a fall of golden locks.

"Let's just get to it without him," Dante snapped. "We're not getting any closer to finding Ros, and it's fucking freezing in this shithole."

Now this I could not permit. It would hardly be fair to leave them to muddle through their problems without the insight I could provide, and doing so would only prolong my exile. Although, when I returned to my home, I might make a greater effort to visit this realm in the future. With a longing look at the rack of clips, I went to sit down with the others, who had arranged the mushroom-topped thrones into a circle.

"Mushroom circles mark places where the barriers between worlds are thin." I waved my hand around our makeshift ring.

The one called Emrys watched me with guarded interest. He was stuffy and dull, and nothing special to look at either. His companion, Jet, however, was far more intriguing. They had a sharp edge that sparkled in the right light like a good sword, and like the most interesting mortals, part of them was somewhere else, seeing things beyond what other mortals could perceive. Inky just scowled at me like a beast I was keeping from rut, and Dante lowered his forehead into his hand.

Jet took a small black rectangle from a satchel near their feet and opened it like a book. Light and color darted across Jet's face as they looked at it, their fingers moving fast, clicking rhythmically. It surprised me to feel the vibration of magic coming from them, and it was a bizarre kind of magic, all tangled up with and dependent on mechanisms and numbers in different combinations, changing and moving with a cycle as predictable as the seasons—as malleable in the right hands. I leaned a little closer. It had been a very long time since I had experienced anything new… and yet, not new.

"So, here's where I'm at." Jet flicked their blue-streaked fringe out of their face. "I used an algorithm, enhanced with a little bit of magic, to determine the most likely make, model, and year of our black Mercedes. Then I sent my Sherlock off looking for it."

"Sherlock?" Dante asked.

Jet looked up at him and smiled. "It's a combination of a spell and a program I wrote to help find things, figure things out. Initially it will scour websites and databases for whatever I want it to find. Because it's not restricted to any particular network, it can look all over: private business records, police and other official files, CCTV, and even cell phone photographs and text messages sent by people who might not have even intentionally mentioned it. It can also adapt its code without me to bypass firewalls and security measures. But the coolest part is that it can gather and interpret the information it finds, and even make rudimentary decisions as to what to do next. Like, if it thinks it found the car we're looking for, it knows to then infiltrate the GPS records on that vehicle to find out where it's been."

"Whoa," Dante said. Though most of what Jet had said sounded like gibberish to me, he looked impressed. "And did it? Did it find the car and then get into the GPS?"

Jet winked. "Of course it did. My kung fu's the best. But that isn't all." They clicked some more with their fingers. "It was able to find the car, confirm that it was in this immediate area on the date you specified, track it to the car service it belongs to, and even tell me who was driving and what he had for lunch. Burger King, actually. At 1:13 p.m. And he was hungry. Ate two Angry Whoppers, an order of onion rings, extra Zesty Sauce, and a dutch apple pie. Ugh. That actually sounds really good."

"It sounds horrifying," I hurried to say. "The apples here are sad and tasteless, while the ones that grow at my estate are so perfect, when the juice touches your tongue, you can feel the lives of all of those who are buried in the soil that feeds the tree."

"Interesting," Emrys said.

"Whatever," Dante spat, his fingers digging into the stuffed horse he held. "Who cares? 1:13 is after Blaker gave my sister to this asshole limo driver. He tricked her into going with him by saying he was taking her to breakfast, and he kept her through the night. So that would have been morning."

Jet nodded. "The car was here from 10:05 a.m. until about twenty after."

"So?" Dante's fists were balled on the horse's plush hide, the skin stretched tight over his knuckles. "Where did they go after that?"

"That's when it gets a little weird," Jet said. "The GPS shows a bunch of nonsense: Newark; Boston; Ocean City, Maryland…. It took me a while to identify the spell someone had used to scramble it. It was good, but not ESM good…. Took even longer to negate it, but by then the real data was lost. The only way to find it at this point would be to use an equation to determine the car's possible range by using the locations it was known to have visited, traffic conditions, some stuff like that."

"Which of course you did," Emrys said. Fondly, I noted.

"Which of course I did. Once I had an area, I was able to extrapolate…."

By Nuada's silver hand, the tedium of it! I stared out the window but couldn't see much beyond the frost and grime coating the glass. The winds were lazy today, and the water in the air gathered high in the sky, scraping against the breeze with its crystalline edges like strangers brushing shoulders as they passed each other in a corridor. The earth was heavy with sleep. It slept a lot more now, its vibrancy sapped by the bad things growing inside it like lesions, the poison placed there by the mortals in their pursuit of wealth and power. It groaned in its slumber, old bones grating together, unhappy to be disturbed.

What are the humans doing, faerie friend? Charlene asked as she hopped into my lap and rubbed the top of her head along my jaw.

Talking about things that are boring and nonsensical.

Why?

Dante's sister is missing. She could be in trouble. Though I don't imagine this foolishness will get us any closer to finding her.

I remember the nice little girl. She wanted to pet me, and she had kind eyes. I will help you look for her.

That is something that might actually yield some results.

"That's several miles of territory," Inky was saying. "Dozens of buildings. Maybe hundreds. How can we check them all?"

"Charlene will help us," I told them. "She has offered."

"Who's Charlene?" Emrys asked.

"Jesus." Dante pushed his fists against his eyes. "Charlene is the cat."

Inky clicked to her, and I glowered when she scampered over, jumped onto his thighs, and climbed inside his coat to curl up. He crossed his arms over her and said to Dante, "Don't dismiss her. We wouldn't have found you and your sister without her help."

I took one of the jeweled clips from my pocket and moved it around so the green gem caught and reflected the light. "Rosalind Mayfield's magic influenced the cats. It called them to her aid whether she intended that result or not. If the girl is in danger or afraid, her magic will likely be working to bring her a rescuer as it attempted to bring me to her. Charlene, do you think you could find that thread of enchantment again?"

I am willing to try. I will ask the others to help me. We know of places. Secret places. We can hide and watch without being seen. We can see and hear many things.

I nodded. "Good. Very good."

"You can talk to her?" Jet asked. "Wow!"

"What does she say?" Emrys asked.

"She will help us, and the other cats of this human city will as well."

"In the meantime, the rest of us should get searching," Inky said with a defeated shake of his head. "We have a lot of ground to cover."

"Yeah, but some locations are more likely than others. I used a magical program to calculate—"

Dante stood. "No. That's a huge waste of time. It's obvious what we need to do."

"What?" Emrys asked, looking at Dante like he might suddenly erupt in flames.

Dante turned to Jet. "You said you know everything about this guy, the driver. The Burger King eater. Do you know where he lives?"

Jet raised their chin and crossed their arms over their chest. "I know how many days of school this guy missed in third grade. I can tell you whether he's circumcised, if you really want to know."

"I just want to know where I can find him," Dante said. "Because I'm going to go to wherever he is, and I'm going to make him tell me where he took my sister."

"What if he won't talk?" Emrys asked.

Dante smiled, but there was no joy in it. "He will. Eventually."

I hurried to stand, hurried to follow Dante as he stomped toward the door while Jet packed up their supplies—among them, I noticed, the computer Dante had found in that filthy cabin in the mountains. I was still bitter that I'd been prevented from amusing myself further with the coarse men inhabiting it. This was likely to be the most fun I would have for what could be a long time.

Gradually the others joined us in the charcoal-encrusted snow outside. "You must let Charlene go," I said to Inky.

"Look, mate, I don't think that's a good idea." He pulled his coat closed around the kitten until only her white snout and black nose poked out. "She's just a baby."

"She wanted to help. Insisted on it," I said, but he still looked stricken. I wondered if he would cry. What would that be like? "I will cast a spell of protection over her."

"Well… I mean…. Yeah, all right," he finally said, reaching into his coat to hand Charlene to me.

As I worked the magic over her, I felt a cold sensation, like blunted iron dragged over my back. When I finished the spell and looked up, Jet was watching me intently, and as they did, a blue filament bisected their left eye for less than a heartbeat before disappearing again. Our gazes met, and they offered me a grin and a wink. Of all the mortals here, Jet alone did not fear me. And wasn't that potentially interesting?

I set Charlene down and wished her good fortune. She assured me she would be back within a few evenings to tell me what she had found.

"Okay," Dante said. "Who is this guy and where is he now?"

Jet looked at their wrist, where some symbols flashed across one of several clunky bracelets they wore. "Juan Lucero. I downloaded his schedule; he should be at work now. GPS tracking says the car should be at the Logan Hotel."

"Let's go," Dante said.

"How?" Inky asked. "All of us won't fit in the truck, and that's all the way downtown."

"I don't need all of us," Dante said. "I can do it myself."

Emrys reached for Dante's shoulder but drew his hand back at the feral look on Dante's face. "I'd feel better if you would let us come. You don't know what you're walking into, and we might have to change our plans. That will be quicker and easier if we're already together, in case things don't work out with your… method."

I laughed. "They will work out. I will make this man tell us what we want to know."

"You will keep your pale, skinny arse in the car where there's not a chance of every mage in this city seeing you!" Inky shouted.

Jet slipped on a pair of dark glasses and pulled a hat with fur-lined flaps over their head. "He's right, you know. I can't imagine what the mages would do if they found out there was a faerie here. They'd go to great lengths to get their hands on you. Sekhet-Aaru in particular has been jerking off to the idea of faerie servants for the last couple hundred years. And you don't want them getting ahold of you. They're assholes. Listen, we'll take my car and follow you. The hotel only has valet parking, so if we can't find a spot close by, we'll meet you at the main entrance." Surprisingly, Jet reached out and took my hand. "You should go someplace safe."

"We'll drop you off at Corazón's house," Inky said.

"No! I will not sit idle while the rest of you go off and have fun without me."

"You will if you want to get home," Inky said, and unfortunately, I couldn't argue. This world was dotted with diversions, pretty things scattered amongst all the detritus, but I certainly did not want to stay here forever. I'd perish of boredom.

I GROANED as I watched the sleek men and women in their snug business suits hurrying along the downtown sidewalks. Despite the cold, the long, slender legs of the women taunted me, their muscles displayed in just the right way by their high heels. Their desires washed over me as each one passed us: Mocha-chip Frappuccino, the guy in the mailroom with the ginger goatee, the girl in accounting with the gap in her teeth, the UPS driver with the great set of tits.... *I want a three-way. I want to experiment with sensual bondage. I just want someone to do the laundry so I can stay in bed and eat Oreos and read....* For a second, each one influenced me as I tried to latch on, tried to be exactly what each person wanted. I could've done it too. Done it so fucking well. Damn, these stuffed-shirt types were always into the wildest shit. *I wish my girlfriend would stick a carrot up my ass.... I read about something called electrostimulation....* As every new person came close enough to affect me, I decided he or she was the best thing I'd ever seen, with the best fantasies, the best needs to shape me into the best me. Until the next one happened by. It was excruciating, like each of them took a little chunk of me with them. An endless damned buffet behind bulletproof glass.

"You gonna be all right, man?" Dante asked, leaning against one of the columns that supported the stone pergola in front of the posh hotel's entrance.

"I don't know," I told him. I couldn't see any reason to bullshit him. "I'm used to being what people want. Without that to guide me, I lack definition, and I feel scattered and pulled in every direction. I need to be with somebody so I know what to be."

"Just be what you want."

"What I want is to be what someone wants me to be. I need that."

"You're hurting my fucking head, Inky."

A middle-aged woman in a Burberry tweed coat gave Dante a foul look, but I didn't think he noticed and I knew he didn't care. I supposed I could be what he needed for a while, let him shape me. But I'd had a taste of that back when we'd talked to that Blaker twat, and it was honestly fucking scary. Dante was angry, and not just angry because his sister was missing—he had a hard-on for the whole damned world. He hated everything, and at nineteen, he was already tired of life. He was strata upon strata of broken glass, ice, and ashes all packed tight but still ready to crumble. I didn't want that, didn't want to remember what that felt like in fifty or a hundred years.

Too bad I already would. Funny thing was, all I wanted was to show him life could be good, wonderful even. I wanted him to have something to look forward to for once, to want something for himself and bloody get it.

And where the hell did that come from? Who wanted me to want that? Not Dante. None of the people around us. But the desire had to come from somewhere.

I was saved from thinking on it too much by Emrys and Jet finally showing up.

"Parking is a nightmare in this city." Emrys shook his head apologetically and pushed his hands into the pockets of his brown wool coat. They must've had a bit of a walk, because the cold had nipped his nose and cheeks red.

"Especially on the weekends." Jet didn't seem to mind the weather. They wore something between a kilt and a skirt, with a row of plastic buckles up the side, over a pair of leggings printed with stars and planets, but above their canvas trainers, their ankles were bare. Their blue-and-black striped hoodie didn't look very warm either.

"Right." Dante nodded once. "Where do we find this asshole?"

A couple coming out of the hotel sneered at his language, and he seemed to realize our merry little band of fuckups was in serious danger of being asked to leave, because he canted his head toward the walkway. Beside us, a Jaguar pulled up to the curb, and a man handed his keys to one of the valets. Emrys pointed after the vehicle with his chin. "The parking garage is as good a place as any to start looking for our driver."

"Yeah, but there's two guys hanging out by the entrance," Dante noted. "I doubt they'll just let us walk in. Can one of you… I don't know. Do a spell or something?"

Jet grinned, slipped off their sunglasses, and stashed them in their pocket. "This situation calls for a different kind of magic, I think. Leave it to me. Just hang here and try not to look too suspicious."

Jet walked over to the two guys, one black, one white, both younger and looking bored as hell. Jet pulled something from their pocket and set it between their lips. Even from where I stood, I could see it wasn't an ordinary cigarette. Even though marijuana had been decriminalized within city limits, Jet was still taking a risk. I tensed, waiting to see if we would need to beat a hasty retreat.

"Either of you got a light?" Jet asked.

The two guys looked at each other, and a minute or two passed before one of them pulled out a plastic lighter. Jet lit up and exhaled a luxuriant—and very fragrant—stream of smoke. "You know, if there's a place around here out of sight, you guys could join me. I don't like getting high by myself. Make the workday pass a little quicker."

Without hesitation, the guy on the right nodded and tilted his head. The three of them turned a corner and disappeared into the dark recesses of the garage.

"Come on, we're in," Emrys said.

With the help of the license plate number Jet had provided, and what Emrys now had pulled up on the screen of his phone, we found the Mercedes after about ten minutes of searching. A guy in a black suit stood nearby, smoking a cigarette.

Dante practically lunged when he saw the man, and I barely managed to stick my arm out in time to stop him. "Look, let me talk to him. There's no need to beat the shite out of the poor bastard first thing. It'll only draw attention."

"Yeah, okay," he muttered. "But I'm going to find out what happened to Ros one way or another."

"Let's hope it won't come to that," Emrys said as we walked over.

"Juan Lucero?" I asked. The gangly ginger bloke didn't look like a Juan Lucero, but you could never tell.

He dropped his cigarette and ground it out with a polished black shoe. "No. Joey Trent. Can I help you with something?"

"Maybe." I met his eyes, pawed around for his desires. One thing was crystal clear—this guy was straight as an arrow. I could go pretty far to fulfill fantasies, but growing a set of tits and a fanny—or even the illusion of them—was beyond my abilities. So much for playing that card. Unfortunately, it was pretty much the only one I had up my sleeve, and I stood there gaping, trying to think of something to say.

Emrys extended his hand to Joey. "I'm a friend of Juan's, in town for the weekend. I was hoping we could get together before I go back to Newark. A lot of us around the old neighborhood miss him. Everybody wants to know how he's doing. I thought he was working today?"

Of course, that story didn't explain how we would've known how to find the car Juan drove, but Joey didn't seem to notice, and he smiled. "He was supposed to be, but he's been off sick the last few days."

"All right, man." Emrys patted Joey's shoulder. "I'll try him on his cell. Thanks, buddy. Take it easy."

"Hey, you too, man," Joey said as we walked away.

"Fuck," Dante hissed.

"I guess we'll be calling on this guy at home," I said. "Do we know where that is?"

Emrys held up his phone. "Of course. I have all the information Jet found out. How do you think I concocted that story? Let's go back out front and wait for Jet, and then we can go to Juan's apartment."

"I'm picking up Blossom first," Dante said, surprising me. He always seemed tense around the faerie.

"Why?"

"Because I'm sick of standing around holding my dick!" he snapped. "Blossom can make this guy talk, and if someone's ass needs kicked, Blossom can do that too. And he won't pussy out if shit has to get messy. No offense to either of you, but I want him at my back."

Bloody hell. I had a bad feeling about this.

Chapter Nineteen

I GUESS driving rich assholes around and looking the other way when they do awful shit pays pretty well, because Juan's building was nice—brick with wood trim, in a quiet neighborhood not too far from Center City. It even had a private entrance on the ground floor. It pissed me off that he got to live like this after what he had done to my sister and who knows how many others. Unfortunately for him, he was going to find out how I felt pretty soon. I would have preferred to go in alone or just with Blossom, but it seemed like that wasn't going to happen. All four of them stood on the sidewalk while I knocked and rang the bell again and again.

After it looked like the guy wasn't going to come to the door, Jet wiggled in front of me and did something to the security panel. As soon as they opened the door, I recognized the smell.

"Shit," Jet said. "Let's look around, but be quiet and don't touch anything with your bare hands. This'll be a crime scene eventually, and we don't want to leave any prints."

It was a typical guy's apartment—leather couch, a big-screen TV, and a couple of game systems. A little messy, but not too bad, like Juan had been busy and would straighten up on his day off, a pizza box on the coffee table and a couple of beer bottles by the sink. A few dirty clothes here and there. We found Juan in the bedroom, under a navy blue comforter, the remote near his hand.

Emrys pulled the sleeve of his coat over his hand, picked up an umbrella that had been leaning in the corner, and pulled the blankets back. Juan was wearing a pair of gray boxer shorts. He was pale, bloated, and blotchy, and he stank—a lot of people don't realize that someone shits and pisses themself when they die—but I didn't see any marks on him.

"It almost looks like he went peacefully in his sleep," Emrys said.

Jet looked spooked as they came to stand beside Emrys, and I saw them take hold of Emrys's hand. "Probably a massive heart attack, maybe a stroke."

That didn't make any sense to me. "This guy doesn't look like he could be older than thirty."

"Yeah," Jet said. "Look, let's get out of here."

"But we haven't found anything out!" I said.

"I want to leave." Jet was shaky, and Emrys looked a little pale too. Maybe it was the first time they had ever seen a dead body. "Come on. Now! We need to get out of here!"

Jet was shouting, and the worst possible thing that could happen was for us to be found in here with this dead guy. If they threw my ass in jail, there would be no one to look for Ros.

Back at Corazón's house, everybody settled down. Except for me, I guess. I was sick of coming up empty-handed again and again, tired of being jerked around, and I paced between the heaps of junk in the living room while the others sat around the table in the kitchen. Corazón thought we were all her family, nieces and nephews and cousins, here for some kind of a party. She'd put on music and was frying some fritters made of smashed-up plantains. Spicy-scented chicken sizzled in a dutch oven, but I didn't have any appetite. I needed to be doing something. At least I could get some answers.

Even though I was upset, I wasn't going to go up to a bunch of people sitting down to a meal and start shouting at them. It wasn't any of their fault, and no matter how shitty I felt, I had to remember that. My phone vibrated in my pocket, and I looked down to see another text message from Raf:

Call me. Please.

I sighed because I really didn't have time for him. I didn't want to lose my job—I needed that money to take care of my sister—but that wouldn't matter if I didn't get her back. Honestly, I was still kind of pissed that he hadn't tried to help me. I took a deep breath before I spoke so everybody wouldn't think I was some kind of psycho prick.

"Hey, Jet, could I talk to you in the living room for a minute?"

Emrys gave me a look that was a little curious and a little defensive, but he didn't say anything. Jet put down the handheld game system they were playing and stood up. Inky came too.

We squeezed onto the sofa together, and Jet looked around the room. "So. This is a lot of stuff. Quite a collection."

"Blossom loves this stuff," Inky said, shaking his head. "Thinks this place is fucking Disneyland or something."

"Look," I told them, "I'm not trying to be a dick or anything, but can we not talk about Corazón's knickknacks?"

"Okay, Dante." Inky's tone was placating, like the tone cops used to talk to a guy with dynamite strapped to his chest. It should have irritated me, but it didn't. "What do you want to talk about?"

I turned to Jet. "You seemed really freaked out at Juan's place. First time you see a dead guy?"

Jet shook their head. "I wish it was."

It hadn't been an especially gory scene. No blood, even. "The smell?" I asked.

"The people who were probably responsible," Jet said. "Do you know much about the mage guilds, Dante?"

"Not really."

"Okay." Jet shook their head. "I've never tried to explain this to anybody who doesn't know."

"Just try," I urged.

"Yeah. Okay, so you know I'm a member of a group called Electrosensory Mirage. We think that the future for mages is going to be in finding ways to combine magic with technology and science. Emrys is what's called a rogue mage. He doesn't have any affiliations. He can do what he wants without answering to anybody, but it's also dangerous for him because a lot of the guilds feel threatened by rogues. They either try to recruit them, or—

"Anyway, there's a guild called Wú Cháng. They specialize in altering flesh, and they can do some really nasty things to a person. From a young age, they start learning all about the body and its systems, which means they know every conceivable way to kill someone. Like today, poor Juan…. They could've used a spell to pinch shut one of the arteries around his heart or burst a blood vessel in his brain. They don't even have to touch him to do it. They don't even have to be that close. They might have been outside on the sidewalk when they killed him, and for all anyone will be able to tell, he died of natural causes. I guess he was lucky that at least it was quick. They could've given him cancer or a slow internal bleed."

I shuddered. How could something like that be possible? "And you think these are the people who took my sister?"

Jet looked at me with pursed lips, like they were deciding how much to tell me. "The truth is, maybe. If they did, it'll be to train her as an assassin. The other possibility is that they're working for one of the other guilds. They're mercenary, and they might have been hired to get rid of Juan so he couldn't tell anybody what he knew. If that's the case, my money would be on Sekhet-Aaru.

"Either way, if they find out we're poking into this, they could come after us."

I reached into my pocket and felt the smooth metal of my gun. It was a good little gun, but I wished I had my Colt back—or that Raf had let me have something equivalent when I'd asked. If it would even help in this situation. "Is there anything we can do?"

"I wish there was more," Jet said. "I have some precautions in place—mostly ways to detect if magic is nearby. I put some alarm systems up to keep Emrys safe, and I've updated them when I could. They're actually pretty effective, and the other guilds haven't found a way to bypass them yet, if they even know about them."

"And if we decide magic is nearby?" Inky asked.

Jet leaned their elbows on their knees and dropped their head. I took the hint, and we sat there in silence before we went back to the kitchen.

After a dinner that was so damn delicious I actually found myself enjoying it and eating until I was stuffed, Corazón went into her bedroom to watch TV, and we did our best to clear her table. Jet got out a couple of laptops and pads, along with some other shit that I had no idea what it was for. They took a few minutes to connect stuff and adjust wires. "So, without Juan's information, we're back to square one. That means searching building by building."

Jet hit some keys and a map of part of the city—mostly the downtown area—projected onto the tabletop. I blinked. I'd only ever seen things like that in sci-fi movies. Blossom's eyes widened, and he spread his long fingers over the grid. He wiggled them, and some hills and trees—also made of light—sprung up. Even some birds circled around, flickering in and out of existence. The colors sparkled in his eyes.

"I'm going to have to slap your hand," Jet threatened with a grin.

"You wouldn't dare!" he whispered.

Jet didn't answer, and the two of them looked at each other for a few seconds before Jet hit some more keys. This time a series of red dots appeared over the map—dozens of them. "These are the locations that have at least a 50 percent likelihood of being one of Juan's destinations. I've eliminated restaurants, convenience stores, things like that."

"How many are left?" Emrys asked.

"Thirty-seven."

Inky blew out a long breath. "Bloody hell. This is going to take forever. Especially if some of those buildings contain multiple flats."

"They do." Jet shook their head. "And we'll have to somehow check every one of those apartments. Getting inside alone will take time. I know some tricks, but still."

My eyes stung, and I felt like I was going to hurl my insides out. Every second that went by without me finding Ros was time somebody could use to take her farther away from me. She could already be in Mexico… maybe farther. I got up and hurried through the living room and out the door. I was going to lose it—I couldn't stop it from happening anymore—and I didn't want to do it in front of an audience.

Outside it was cold, especially without my coat, and the sky was clear the way it only was on the bitterest winter nights. I looked up at the stars and they blurred when I couldn't hold the tears back. I wanted to scream, to pull the mailbox out of the ground and use it like a club to smash everything around me. But it wouldn't do any good. Nothing would do any fucking good. I covered my face with my hands and cried like I hadn't cried since I was five years old.

But then I caught my breath. I wouldn't do it. I wouldn't give up on Ros, because I was the only goddamn person she had in this world, and she deserved a chance. It wasn't her fault that she was stuck with only me to see that it happened, but until I couldn't drag myself up off the pavement, I was going to keep trying.

The door creaked open and closed quietly, and I hurried to wipe my snot and tears away on the sleeve of my sweatshirt.

"You all right?" Inky asked.

I didn't turn to face him. "I just… I needed some air."

"Perfectly understandable. It was getting a little stuffy in that kitchen. I was sweating myself."

Just what I wanted him to say. He was good, and I had to remind myself that he didn't really care, that it was just the way nature had made him, the same as a cat's instinct to chase a mouse. "So much of this doesn't make any sense. Like Jet and Emrys. Why are they helping us? What are they getting out of it? Because they can't be doing it for nothing. That doesn't happen."

"I understand why you don't trust us," said a gentle voice. "I don't think I would feel differently in your shoes."

I hadn't realized Emrys had come outside with Inky, but I wasn't going to take back what I said. It was still true. I turned and looked at him. "Why, then?"

"Believe it or not, I try to be a good person. Being decent and being a mage aren't contradictory, though I can see why you might look at it that way. You've had a hell of an introduction to our world. But I like to think I'm the kind of man who helps a little girl when she needs it.

"As for Jet, well, Jet can't resist a puzzle, and Jet also kind of likes showing off. But mostly, Jet hates Wú Cháng and Sekhet-Aaru. They're both trying to take control of ESM, because whether they want to admit it or not, ESM probably is the way of the future. So if Jet sees a chance to stick it to them, they will. Jet's also here because I'm here."

"More than friends?" I asked.

Emrys smiled. "Much more. True soul mates is the way I would describe it. Though even that feels insufficient."

"Huh," Inky said. "I wouldn't have guessed that, and I can usually tell."

"My relationship with Jet isn't typical. It isn't a physical relationship, because I don't have any desire for that kind of thing. Jet gets what they need elsewhere. None of that means we don't love each other." Emrys put his hand on my arm. "Believe me when I say I know what it means to love someone so much you would die to protect them."

"I didn't mean to pry," Inky said softly.

"It's okay," Emrys said. "It's not a secret or anything I'm ashamed to admit. Just the opposite, in fact. But let's get back inside. It's cold out here, and we still have work to do."

Amazingly, I felt a little better. When we sat back down at the table, Jet put a steaming mug of coffee in front of me, and I curled my frozen hands around it. Then, staring at the red dots on the map, I made a decision. "We can't search all of these by ourselves. We need help."

"We should enlist the aid of the cats!" Blossom said cheerily. "They can search quickly and quietly, and they have the numbers."

The cat thing still weirded me out, but at this point I couldn't say no, so I nodded at Blossom. "There might be something else we… something I can do," I told the others. "I might be able to get some of the people I work with to help us. They'll be good at this type of thing."

"The gunrunners?" Jet asked.

"How do you…? Never mind. But yeah, them. Some of my boss's associates might be willing to lend a hand."

Emrys shook his head. "A whole other group of people exposed to our secrets. I don't know if I like that. It's not just dangerous for us, but for them. If Wú Cháng or Sekhet-Aaru think these people pose a threat, they won't hesitate to eliminate them."

I snorted. "Assholes might have their hands full."

"I still think it's a bad idea," he said.

"Do you have a better one?"

"Actually, I do. It isn't something I like doing, but—"

"Em, no."

He lifted a hand, and Jet fell quiet.

"But in this case, I don't think we have another option." He held one hand a few inches above the map. "I devised my own kind of magic. I don't practice it very much, and I make most of my living by translating magical texts, but it's actually quite effective. It involves probability."

If there was one thing I'd hated in school, it was math, and I sure as hell didn't know how it was going to help. My doubt must've shown, because Emrys smiled. The son of a bitch was really hard not to like. Then he continued.

"Right now, there's a basically equal probability of these thirty-seven locations being the one where we'll either find your sister or find something to lead us to her. With this magic, I can improve those odds. Not only can I perform an enchantment to help us see the probability better, I can do a spell to improve our probability of success. As it stands, our probability of finding what we're looking for by tomorrow is around 4 to 5 percent."

Blossom clapped. "Ingenious! What are you waiting for? Do the magic and make our probability of success 100 percent!"

"I don't know if I can do that," Emrys said. "It's extremely difficult to achieve a full 100 percent probability, and besides…."

"What?" I asked. "Just get it as high as you can."

He shook his head. "It doesn't come for free. I-I don't entirely understand it, and I've yet to work out a way to predict…. Say a man is driving home from work somewhere in the city. If he's careful, his probability of making it home safely is likely over 99 percent. However, by increasing one probability, I alter others. That man's chances of reaching his home without a fatal car accident might drop to 38, 39 percent. Imagine: a child with a good probability of recovering from an illness; a burning candle with high odds of being blown out before it burns down a building; an airplane with an almost certain chance of landing without incident. Any of these probabilities could be affected, and I have no way of knowing which. Any freak accident that happens in the city over the next week could easily be my fault.

"And the higher I try to increase our probability of success, the more I will potentially lower someone else's."

Blossom arched an eyebrow. "Of course. Everything is a bargain."

"But I see little choice except to boost our odds somewhat." Emrys nodded once, and it seemed like a response to an argument he was having with himself. "Otherwise this might be doomed before we even get started."

We all sat in silence while he went to the kitchen sink, washed his hands, and dried them slowly, finger by finger, on a tea towel. He circled around the table twice, behind those of us who were sitting down. I started to feel weird, like I was supposed to be somewhere else, had to get there even though I didn't know where it was. Corazón's kitchen with all its crappy knickknacks seemed wrong, like it shouldn't exist, like it had just appeared in front of me. I had a nagging feeling of not knowing how I got there, and then a sense that here might not be real—like it could change into something completely different if I even blinked. I expected it to change. I wanted it to change, but at the same time, I was scared shitless it was going to. Just when I thought I was going to change, when I started to consider that the things I remembered about my life might've been dreams or my imagination, the air kind of… shivered, and Emrys sat back down.

Almost instantly, I felt normal again. Something occurred to me. "That magic. Could you increase your probability of winning the lottery? Or of finding a bag of money?"

Emrys chuckled, sounding a little tired. "I suppose I could try, but I don't even want to imagine the price I would have to pay for doing something like that. Now, let's see if my efforts have gained us anything."

"Let me refresh this." Jet pushed some buttons, and the little red dots on their map danced around, appearing and reappearing for a few seconds before they seemed to make up their mind. This time there were only two of them.

Inky whistled through his teeth. "That's cut our work down to size."

Jet nibbled their lower lip as they squinted at the dots. "We should get a couple of hours of sleep and then go. If we split into two groups, we can search both locations at once."

"Blossom should stay behind," Inky said. "It's too dangerous to let these goddamn mages learn of his presence. Er, present company excluded."

The faerie opened his mouth, probably to argue, but Jet beat him to it. "Nope, if I'm going where it looks like I'm going, then he's coming with me." They pointed to one of the dots on the map. "This import-export business in Chinatown is almost definitely a front for Wú Cháng. Even though they scare the shit out of me, I'm the best person for the job. Emrys is a rogue; him going is out of the question. Besides, I'm Asian, so I'll stand out less. I can probably even convince them ESM is interested in their, uh… services. But I'm not going in there without all the firepower I can get at my back. And that means Blossom."

The smug look the faerie gave Inky reminded me of a kid my sister's age.

"The rest of us should gather information and plan our part of the mission," Emrys said.

I guessed I would be the muscle for our group. I wished somehow I could talk to Raf, get him to give me some better weapons—but without explaining why I needed them.

When my phone hummed with a text from Raf seconds later, I thought about Emrys's weird probability thing, and a chill ran up my back.

Dante, I insist you call me. It's important.

I rubbed my forehead. Whatever Emrys had done left me with a dull headache and a low throb in my temples. Standing up, I excused myself. I might as well get it over with. If there was even a chance Raf had found some information about Ros, I couldn't afford to let it go.

I put on my coat, went to stand on the stoop, and called him.

"Dante, I was worried about you. Where have you been?"

"Just looking into some leads about what might've happened to Ros," I told him.

"And have you found anything?"

I considered, and it didn't take me long to decide I didn't want to try to explain all of this. He probably wouldn't believe it anyway, and he'd likely think I'd lost my fucking mind. "Not really."

"Well, you're supposed to go on deliveries with Carl in the morning."

Damn, I'd forgotten. I went along for protection—not that Carl usually needed it. It was easy work—and easy money—but I didn't want to put off looking for Ros. Not now that we might actually have a chance. "Look, I can't do it. Can you find somebody else?"

I braced myself for one of the lectures about responsibility and loyalty that were worse than if he'd just screamed and sworn at me, but he said, "Sure. I understand. You've got a lot on your mind. But I would like to meet with you. To replace the item you lost."

My Colt! That was fucking perfect, and I might need it if we got into trouble wherever we were going. I hadn't expected him to offer after I'd been blowing him off the past couple of days, and I wondered if it was more of that probability stuff at work. It would certainly help my chances of success. "Yeah. Yeah, that would be great. Let's meet tomorrow. Is six too early?"

No matter what Emrys had said, if there was a downside to this magic, I couldn't see it.

Chapter Twenty

"What's it like where you come from?" the mortal called Jet asked me as we rode in their small turquoise carriage. I finally had my chance to witness the tall towers of glass up close, or at least to observe their walls reflecting the somber striations of the predawn sky as we traveled past. At this proximity, they were not as impressive as I had imagined they would be—just human buildings cobbled together from stone and ore with little artistry and less originality. Utilitarian, like all things the mortals favored. It should not have disappointed me as much as it did.

"It is not like any one thing." I felt suddenly quite wistful. "My lands alone are so vast that they encompass deserts of shimmering golden sands, forests where the trees are wider around than these structures. Their branches twist together in patterns like the finest lace, and the ivy that covers their trunks shines like cut gems. Then there are other woods where the trees are gray and their branches and leaves droop like a stream of steadily falling tears. They are full of whispers, of memories. Those places are shrouded in mist, and some places are so thick with bracken that the light never touches the ground. Dark things live there.

"And then there are meadows where the light shines all the time, day and night, in soft golden shafts. The colors of the flowers are so bright they would hurt your eyes and plant in your mind thoughts of the earliest days of your life, those hours before you forgot how to see magic. And they dance with the wind, and together with crystal clear brooks, they sing such songs that if you ever heard them, you would spend the rest of your days trying to remember the melody." I sighed. "And I have estates. Thirteen of them."

"You sound like you miss it."

"Of course. There is always entertainment, balls, dancing. Performances. Tell me. Do you hunt?"

"Hunt?" Jet laughed. "I play first-person shooters, if that counts."

"I don't know if it does," I said, perplexed. "It is great fun. You should try it."

"You'd take me to your lands?"

"Of course!"

"Why?" Jet looked away from the road for a moment to study me with eyes lined in sparkling kohl. A streak of light like a shooting star raced across the left one. "I mean, why me?"

It surprised me that they did not know, but then mortals were blind to so much. I honestly didn't understand how they managed to stumble through their brief lives, but I tried to remember to be patient. "You are a special kind of human. You stand with one foot in one world and the other someplace else. You see different things with one eye than the other."

After a sharp intake of breath, Jet said, very softly, "I suppose that's true."

"Then will you come? After this plodding little drama has played itself out?"

"I don't know. I couldn't leave Emrys."

"Emrys?" Could they be serious? "That dull boy with his dull brown hair? What does he have to keep you here compared with what I can offer? The wonders I could show you?"

Jet shook their head. "Emrys is not as dull as you think. He makes me better. Maybe you aren't seeing with both eyes."

"I always see everything." I crossed my arms over my chest. "And since I have been in this world, I have yet to see anything out of the ordinary."

"Well, maybe you haven't been keeping the right company." Jet winked. "I could show you some things."

"Indeed?" This prospect intrigued me, as Jet held knowledge of things not familiar to me. What was the magic I felt in the strings of numerals? There was a language to it, as sure as the voice of the clouds scraping across the sky, but I did not understand, and I wanted to. I might encounter something new after all.

"Yeah, and maybe I will, you know, after this. Assuming we're alive and not blind, crippled, or riddled with lesions or cancer…." Jet shuddered. "You know what these mages can do, right? They can manipulate your flesh in almost any way they can imagine—turn your blood to dust, stop your heart, make your bones too brittle to stand…."

I laughed. I did not mean to mock Jet's distress, but I could not help it. "How do you know I have any of those things? How do you know I'm not made up of wild air and the light on the sea and the dreams the poets can't quite remember upon waking? I am not afraid of these mortals."

Jet arched a brow. "Well, that's nice for you. Maybe I'll get lucky too."

After that, we sat in silence except for the music coming from a little device attached to our conveyance. Finally Jet guided the carriage into a vacant lot and got out to hand some slips of paper to a man in a booth. Then they got back in the carriage and turned to me. "You need to disguise what you are. If they know you're a faerie when we walk in there, we won't be walking out. You can do that, right? The glamour?"

"Yes, though mortals like Corazón can see through it. And Dante. I took the cowl away from his left eye."

"Then we'll just have to hope they still have the cowl. Make yourself look like you belong here."

I peered out the glass, which was quickly becoming covered with an etching of frost, for an example of the kinds of mortals who lived in this area, but aside from the attendant—too old and fat for me to ever consider emulating—I found none of them on the street, the early hour and chill in the air likely persuading them to enjoy the warmth of their beds a little longer. "Who belongs here?"

"Well, it's Chinatown."

"So I should make myself look like you?"

"I'm Japanese. But close enough, I guess. Better than nothing. Though not too much like me. It'll be weird if we seem like twins."

"You're giving me very little to work with," I complained. "Why don't I just make myself invisible? I can make it so I'm not seen at all."

"That probably works on average people, but a lot of mages can sense energy. I don't care if you're made of sea-foam and unicorn farts, you have a life force. If these people detect a life force and don't see a person emitting it, they're going to get suspicious. That'll be bad."

"Then I'll need some kind of template."

"Here." Jet picked up the small rectangle that had been providing our music and dragged their finger across it. Then they turned to me and showed me an image of a very handsome young man in a dark suit. "Can you do that?"

I did as I was asked and looked to my companion for approval.

Jet nodded. "Okay. Just follow my lead and keep quiet. Don't use any magic unless there's no other option; it'll only draw attention to us and maybe give us away. And if there's no other option, nothing fancy. Just get us the hell out of there."

I bristled at this mortal telling me what to do, assuming they knew better than I did, but curiosity proved more compelling, and I followed Jet through the snowy streets for over a quarter of an hour. We passed beneath an ornate archway and into a compact and colorful neighborhood full of shops and eateries. I assumed one of these would be our destination, but Jet led me beyond them, to an area of plainer buildings and down an alleyway that dead-ended at a stone wall. Finally we stopped in front of a set of glass doors with the words Yan Luo Imports written in red paint edged with gold. I wondered how in the world those people who wanted to patronize the establishment would ever find it.

Inside was dark, the only illumination provided by domed lights set high among the metal rafters of the ceiling. Subtle scents of cedar and sandalwood drifted on the otherwise stale air, and shelves held statues and sets of dishes, their gilt edges glittering softly. I reached out to trace a finger along the back of a ceramic dragon.

"Don't take anything," Jet hissed, leaning in.

"I wasn't." I frowned. In truth, the objects sparkled so beautifully they were hard to resist.

"Uh-huh." Jet continued past the long rows of metal shelves and through a set of doors at the back of the building. Beyond them, a man opened wooden crates with a metal bar. He looked up from his task and grunted to acknowledge us.

"Nǐ hǎo," Jet said. "Máfan nǐ?"

The man stood and brushed his palms on his trousers, his suspicious expression lessened by the sound of his native tongue. "Nǐ hǎo ma?"

"Xièxiè. Wǒ jiào Zama Jet. Wǒ zài zhǎo lǎobǎn. Actually—" Jet sighed and shook their head. "Nǐ huì shuō Yīngyǔ ma?"

"I speak English," the man said.

"Oh good," Jet said. "My Mandarin is pretty rusty."

"Is there something I can do for you?" The man was guarded if not outright impatient. I watched his hand move to clutch the iron rod he'd leaned against the wall even though his eyes never left my companion.

"I do wish to buy something," Jet said. "But I don't think I can get it here. Maybe what I need is somewhere else in the building?"

"That depends what it is you need," the man answered.

"Impermanence."

The two of them stood staring at each other for several moments until I felt sure the man would refuse. But then he nodded once and opened another set of doors. "This way," he said. "Cōngmáng!"

We followed him through another door and into a storage room where boxes and crates filled all the available space, with only narrow trails between them. The next room was more of the same, but the third was empty save for a huge silk tapestry depicting a compelling scene—mortals skinned alive by all manner of interesting creatures—hanging on the back wall. Our host pulled it aside to reveal yet another small door. He turned to Jet and smiled. "As long as you are Wūshī, the door will open."

"Okay." Jet put their hand on the brass handle and closed their eyes. I waited as they released a little wisp of magic into the mechanism sealing the door, and then it was swung open.

"You will need to go down to the third level," our guide told us. "From there, follow the main walkway straight back until you see a red door. I would suggest you do not stray from the path."

"Very good," Jet answered. "Thanks for your help. Xièxiè."

The man harrumphed, and we stepped into the darkness.

By the time we descended the first stair, every particle of light had disappeared, and the blackness enveloped us until Jet produced a beam of bluish light from one of the bracelets they wore. It allowed us to find the next stairwell and then the next. Finally we reached a thick metal door marked with a trio of horizontal lines that increased in length at the bottom.

Three.

Beyond it was a massive warehouse with ceilings so high they were lost in shadow. Shelves reached dozens of feet above us, all of them filled to the brim with wooden crates. Larger statues and vases sat on the floor around them, fantastical creations in ivory, jade, and terra-cotta. The path we were to take was clearly marked with thick yellow tape stuck to the smooth concrete floor, but more than that, it was easy to follow the current of magic flowing beneath our feet. It was cold and bitter, and it smelled of death—old death, dusty and stale, long after the scent of rotten fruit had faded.

We reached another archway, intricately carved and supported by tall stone pillars. Beneath it, two lacquered red doors lined with gilded studs were set into the smooth rock of the foundation... though I sensed much more beneath our feet, and I was not eager to explore anything farther than necessary. Jet stopped in front of the doors and drew a deep breath before looking over their shoulder at me. "Ready?"

I did not like the idea of being trapped, of being cut off from the air and the sky, surrounded by metals that numbed my senses and dulled my powers, but as we had no choice, it made little sense to complain. "Let's go."

What we found inside reminded me of a temple, and perhaps that had been the intention of the mortals who had constructed it. The floors were made of stone polished to the sheen of glass, and red-and-gold silk covered the walls. A few benches of intricately carved teak sat at the edges of the long corridor, and two guardians—each of them three times our height and carved from stone and embellished with gems and metallic paint—stood watch on either side of three steps that led to a dais. I could not imagine how the mortals had transported such heavy objects here— certainly not by way of the narrow and winding stairs we had taken—and I needed little more proof of their power. Both statues wore tall hats that added several feet to their height, and both had ghostly white faces, their onyx eyes lined in crimson. One wore a patterned black *hanfu* and held a thick silver chain. Ebony hair flowed down his back, and his red tongue lolled out. The other was just the opposite: ivory-robed, ivory-haired, and holding a fan. Passing beneath them made me feel uncertain—as if I was in the presence of beings whose power might rival my own. Their magic pressed down on me like water, making movement and breath an effort. Now that was an unfamiliar sensation, one as intriguing as it was terrifying.

On the platform, a long table sat atop a fancy rug. Though there was room along its benches for probably a dozen diners, only the chairs at the head and foot were occupied, and nothing but a dish of pomegranates sat between a woman in a dark pantsuit with her hair in a severe bun and a man in a white faux-fur jacket with wispy curls almost as light as my own hair.

I waited a few feet behind Jet as they pressed their palms down to their sides and bowed low, a gesture that exuded both anxiety and instinct. Though it pained me to prostrate myself before these mortals, I mirrored the movement. I had to seem as though I was one of them— meek and servile.

The woman steepled her fingers on the table in front of her. "Where do your loyalties lie?"

"With the future," Jet answered, straightening.

"And what do you imagine the future holds?" The man leaned forward and rested the side of his face in one cupped hand.

"Cooperation," Jet said, their voice clear and strong in vast space. I was almost proud of their bravery. "Cooperation between old and new."

"This interests us." The woman dipped her head. "Speak your request."

"It is only an inquiry at this point," Jet said. "My associates are curious about the price of what you can offer."

"And who is it that needs to learn of the impermanence of all things?" The man raked his fingers through his limp curls.

"There's someone posting things to the internet, things we would rather he not post there. ESM disables them, but they find a way around everything we try. We would like it to end. Permanently."

"Nothing is permanent," the woman said.

"Of course. But a solution…. What would something like that… entail?"

"For your people, we will accept nothing less than a trade," the man said with an unctuous smile.

"What kind of trade? The people who sent me to you will want specifics."

"A service of equal value," the woman answered. "We all have our strengths, and as you said yourself, cooperation is the future. Do you agree? If so, the contract can be drawn up. We can begin work on your problem."

Jet held up their hands. "I'm just the messenger here. I'll have to deliver your terms to the people who sent me, but I have a few more questions."

"Go on," the woman drawled.

"Well, my friends, they want me to ask if… if it always has to be the, uh, the most extreme solution."

"Say what you mean." The man leaned forward, stretching lanky arms out in front of him. When his wrists extended beyond the cuffs of his coat, I noticed colorful tattoos, similar to the artwork around us, completely covered his skin. "There is no danger of us being overheard. That is impossible here."

"Okay." Jet bowed their head slightly. "Would you be able to maybe kidnap this person? Deliver them somewhere. You know, so we could talk to them?"

"This work is actually more difficult," the woman said. "It creates problems. Loose ends that need to be tied off."

"Right. Like getting rid of any witnesses. Or so I would imagine," Jet hurried to add.

The woman sat a little straighter, and I feared my companion had pushed too far. It was eerily silent in the underground room, without even the whisper of the wind. Time felt frozen until the woman finally spoke in a soft, even voice. "Yes. People often see things they should not see, things they do not understand. We take care of these problems, but we are not quick to be the cause of them."

"So, uh, theoretically, if someone else did the kidnapping, you'd come in after and clean up?"

"Every situation is unique," the woman said. "Because every life is unique. People rarely share the same fate. Tell your friends a simple solution is usually best."

Jet nodded. "I will relay that. I don't doubt they'll be amenable."

"They had better be." The man's pale eyes glittered in a way I didn't like. "We do not appreciate having our time wasted."

"That won't happen." Jet was shaking, their hands curled into tight balls. "I-I'll just go. Deliver the message."

"Then go," the woman said, her voice like the wind through brittle grass.

"I… I just…. Would you mind?" Jet walked to the wall and ran their hands over the elaborate depictions of suffering. "I just wanted to see them up close. The artistry is so remarkable."

I tensed, imagining my offense if someone had touched those treasures I most adored, and I prepared to take us away from this place. I was not finished with Jet, and I wanted to experience the wonders they had promised to show me.

Surprisingly, the man grinned. "We agree. They are exquisite."

"Xièxiè." Jet bowed again. "Thank you for hearing me, and for allowing me to be close to this beauty. I am humbled by your kindness and hospitality."

"We are always pleased by a visit from your guild," the woman said. "We will anticipate another soon. And hopefully, a mutually beneficial partnership. This is something we have desired for some time."

Jet bowed a third time, and I followed suit. As soon as we exited the temple area and reemerged into the warehouse, I had to jog to keep up with Jet as they rushed to vacate the shop. They did not even stop to say a word to me until we had distanced ourselves from the importer by over two streets.

Jet collapsed onto a bench in a small park, and I sat down beside them. "That all seemed fairly pointless," I complained. "A waste of time."

"Oh, I don't think so." Jet laughed and pressed some nubs on one of the bracelets they wore. "Look."

I leaned in to watch the tiny pictures moving across the surface of the device. They were magnificent, as real as life. I saw the man in the white coat and the woman in the dark suit, still seated at the table.

"How is this possible?" I asked.

Jet winked. "I put a very small, almost microscopic, camera and transmitter on the wall. I used a simple spell to mask it. I don't think there's any way they could detect it, not with magical or conventional means. Besides, these people are predictable; most people are. They won't expect us to even try, so they won't be looking for it."

"Can others access this information?"

Jet shook their head. "Closed circuit." They took the rectangular device from a pocket and held it up. "Everything comes directly to me, and I've made sure to encrypt it so it can't be intercepted in transit. It's all stored in here. Nowhere else. I also have a program running to isolate anything relevant and file it for me so we don't have to sift through hours of footage. And now that I have a foot in the door, it's even possible I'll be able to plant some false data into their systems. You know, mess with them if nothing else. No matter what it looked like with the statues and tapestries, they have to use computers and cell phones the same as anyone else. That means they're vulnerable."

"This magic is useful," I admitted. "But what if that machine is lost or stolen?"

"Heh. The odds of that are astronomical, and the odds that they could bypass my security measures are even smaller. Nobody outside of ESM could do it, that's for sure. Besides, I'm constantly backing up anything relevant."

"How?"

"It would be hard to explain, and pretty boring, I'm afraid."

We sat quietly as snowflakes spiraled lazily down, landing on the heads and shoulders of the people trudging past us, too wrapped up in the mundane details of their lives to even look our way.

"Hey, you up for a bit of a walk?" Jet eventually asked, resting a hand on my knee. "I know something I think you'd like to see."

SANDWICHED BETWEEN two ordinary buildings was a place that seemed cobbled together from bits of magic, as if some extraordinary mortal had plucked snippets of wishes and dreams from the ether and jigsawed them into depictions of such beauty that they took my breath away. With Jet following, I wandered the labyrinthine corridors, running my fingers over metallic tiles, bits of ceramic, and even pieces of mugs and plates. One wall was made entirely of blue and green bottles held together by mortar, and other bottles hung down like a chandelier. These I could not help loving, their cobalt color, the way they caught and bent the wintery sunlight, the sound the air made as it skipped along their open mouths… the happiness and wonderment stored within them, aging like wine, gaining in potency.

The ground I stood upon was adorned with patterns, bits of stories written on clay, pictures of eyes, lips, animals. There were flowerpots, spoked metal wheels, fountains…. People had left things: dolls' heads, small sculptures, bits of metal. Coins. "Magical," I whispered, stopping to rest my palm against a column covered in swirling prismatic designs. "To transform these objects in such a way…. It is almost as if we have wandered into a dream or a spell, as if we are no longer in the same realm."

"I thought you'd like it," Jet said, sitting down on the edge of an ornate metal chair. The wall beside it read *Slowly but Surely*, and the figure of a prone woman built entirely of tiny squares stretched out above, the words *Essence of Existence* meandering along her torso, a crack bisecting her face, and a sun-colored square framing her head.

"Who created this? A mage, surely. Certainly someone with the blood of my people. To see things in this way is beyond the abilities of an ordinary mortal."

Jet took a clear pouch from their pocket and began eating what looked like pastel worms coated in white powder. "That's kind of an arrogant way to look at it. You shouldn't underestimate us."

I crossed my arms over my chest. "Most mortals have no vision. They are basically blind."

"But not all." Jet shoved a wad of the worms into their mouth and chewed. "What I think is, most people's thoughts follow a similar pattern: they associate things with other things in the same way. Linear, I guess. But some people can make the associations other people miss, and they put things together in ways that would never occur to most." They gestured to an archway a short distance from us. "I could show you more. Something even better."

"Even better." When I was freed from the girl's summons, I was going to find the mortal who had constructed this and take them to my lands to build something similar for me—but bigger, better. A whole city constructed in this manner. I wondered what else I might find to keep and store away. I should start collecting items, average things mortals treasured: a lucky coin, a broken bit of a mother's earring, a sugar spoon that recalled tea and biscuits with a beloved aunt. Those things, in the hands of this artist, would combine to create something with a resonance more profound than I could even imagine. All that stored emotion interacting, overlapping…. I scratched at the stiff collar around my neck. "But can I take off the glamour?"

"What, does it itch?" Jet chuckled.

"It is tiresome. Glamour can be amusing, but it is also a lie, and lies are only entertaining for a time. After a while it becomes a burden to remember the details."

"Huh." Jet stood and brushed some snow off their snug trousers. "It probably doesn't say anything good about me that I completely understand that."

"So?"

Jet hooked their elbow with mine and led me toward the place where this magnificent little world intersected with the much larger, much duller one. I wondered if the mortals crossing that threshold appreciated their escape from the mundane. To enter this place was to be an animal let out of a cage for a precious free gambol. "Leave it on just a little longer. Just until we get where we're going."

"Where is that?" I asked.

"You'll see."

Chapter Twenty-One

Emrys used the GPS on his phone to guide us to a posh suburb: all big yards, pseudocolonial houses, and streets wide and clear of cars due to the attached garages. Dante suggested we park several blocks away so our piece-of-shite truck wouldn't attract attention, and I trusted him to know what he was talking about. He was the criminal in our little band, after all.

I was bloody sick of the winter, the wet and the snow. What I wanted was a beach, some sunshine. Normally it would've been easy enough to maneuver myself into a situation where I'd be able to enjoy both… and probably a lot more. As we walked and the cold numbed my face and stung the edges of my ears, something peculiar happened. I was thinking it would be lovely to find myself a rich cougar and convince her we needed a Caribbean cruise when I remembered I couldn't soak up her energy even if I did. The desperation for it had gone, that crazy, obsessive hunger just a dull ache in my gut now, but I was sad. What was the point of going on if I could never taste that again, that spicy-sweet perfection of someone else's absolute adoration? It was like I could only ever eat plain oatmeal—for the rest of my life. And my life was a damned long time. It was as if all the color drained out of the world and I stood in a grainy black-and-white photograph.

But then I turned to Dante, and he was so bloody bright. His warm golden skin clashed hard against the gray of the sky and leafless oak trees, and his brown eyes were rich, saturated—all the color sucked out of everything else concentrated there. The scant light gleamed off the leather of his coat, and his worn hoodie looked as soft and lush as velvet. The cold had drawn a dusky rose to the surface of his cheeks, where a downy coating of whiskers lined his jaw. The shadows his eyelashes cast. The chapped skin at the edge of his lower lip.

And I knew. I didn't want to leave him. He wasn't going to have sex with me—I felt that as sure as I felt the cold water seeping into my canvas trainers—but I wanted to stay with him, see that good things happened for him, see that he was happy. But what was making me want it? It didn't make sense. I wanted what others wanted me to want, and this kid sure as fuck didn't want me hanging about like a nursemaid. But damned if that wasn't exactly what I yearned to do.

Even if it meant trudging through this frigid slush with my bollocks trying to retreat into my belly, instead of finding someone wealthy and horny to whisk me off to the Bahamas.

Blossom's chicanery must've sent me round the bend.

Emrys interrupted my self-assessment. "Because of whatever spell was used to keep anyone from tracking the car, Jet couldn't get us an exact address—said they might not have been able to even without the spell, since it depends where the driver parked. But they narrowed it down to a two-block radius." He looked down at his screen. "Which means we have eleven houses to check."

I shook my head. "Bloody hell. This could take forever. How are we even going to get inside?"

"This is a wealthy area," Emrys said. "These houses will have security. It won't be a simple matter of breaking in a back door, I'm afraid."

Dante stared off down the street, his hands in his coat pockets. Then, like a cat who'd seen something move, he took off like a shot. After a quick glance at Emrys, who seemed as lost as me, I jogged after him.

Someone had left a Valentine's Day wreath on a tripod in their lawn near the walk. Typical bored rich person project, likely something inspired by a guest appearance on a morning show, it featured uneven strands of pink and white tulle, plastic roses, and faux baby's breath. Nestled among the fabric and foliage, some papier-mâché cherubs plucked harps and blew gold-painted trumpets. They'd been outfitted in glittery tutus for modesty, and wings formed from iridescent cloth and wire stood out from their backs. Dante crouched and traced a finger along one figure's tangled chenille hair.

"These remind me of the dolls Ros makes. She's really brilliant. I wish I had paid more attention to the stories she made up for each of them. King Oberon and Ariel and Cobweb…. I always just pretended to listen. There was always so much else to do."

Emrys knelt down next to Dante. "When I was in school, my class did a production of *A Midsummer Night's Dream*. I only had a small part, though, one of the faeries."

"My sister loved reading about the faeries. She loved my mom's old books, the plays about the sylphs and the enchanted forests. She's so much smarter than me. I can still barely understand that stuff."

Emrys stood and spoke in a voice so stiff that I understood why he was given a smaller part. "Over hill, over dale, thorough bush, thorough brier, over park, over pale, thorough flood, thorough fire…. Over hill… over dale. Over dale…. Thorough brier, over dale…. Thorough brier, over dale…." He shook his head and pinched the bridge of his nose. "I can't seem to stop saying that. I…. Thorough brier, over dale. Thorough brier, over dale. I don't know what's wrong with me. I feel so compelled. Thorough brier, over dale."

Dante got to his feet and backed away from Emrys. "What the hell, man? You been into Jet's stash?"

"No. I rarely smoke marijuana. I…. Thorough brier, over dale."

"This isn't some kind of fucking joke!" Dante shouted.

"Wait." I hurried to get between them because Dante looked livid and Emrys seemed an oar short to starboard. "I've seen something like this happen before. Is there…." I spotted it. One house sat on a lot surrounded by hedge roses—briers. Leaving Dante and Emrys to bicker on the path, I went up to the big house's porch and inspected the three letterboxes by the door: *1: Singh, S. 2: Dale, R. 3: Temporary.*

I looked over my shoulder and called, "He lives on the third floor."

Dante sprinted up the walk. "How the hell do you know that?"

"Look." I pointed to the labels. "Over Dale. And we came through the briers already."

"This…." He scratched the back of his head. "If this is Ros trying to help us, why would she be so cryptic? Why not just tell us where she is?"

Why indeed. "Blossom tried to explain it to me. He thinks she's not doing it on purpose, that the magic is adapting to her wishes without her direction." I shook my head as I looked at the fancy door with the patterned glass panels. "It's hard to believe, but this is almost exactly how we found our way to you in the first place. Disjointed pieces that came together, made something we could follow."

Emrys nodded. "I can't say I've ever seen anything like this, but it makes sense in an odd way. Your sister seems to have the ability to control magic, but she's never learned how to direct it. Her emotions and associations are acting on the bits of magic that are always present, and they are manifesting accordingly. She likely doesn't know she could be clearer if she tried. You said she loves these plays, especially the ones about forests and faeries. If she's scared and thinking about them to comfort herself, it's likely influencing the magic." He put a hand on Dante's shoulder. "But there's one definite positive here. She's alive. Otherwise I doubt this would be happening."

For a few minutes Dante stood staring at the calla lilies etched into the door's glass. I felt the moment when he made a decision, like the step off the edge of a bridge, irrevocable. He opened the door and entered a large foyer with parquet floors and a staircase on either side that curved up to a landing. A tasteful faux Tiffany lamp dangled from the high ceiling, scattering shards of colored light across the hardwood. Dante went to the intercom and mashed the third button with his finger several times in rapid succession. We waited, and when there was no answer, he stabbed at it again. I wanted to ask what he would say if he got a response, but his desperation was making him reckless. Dangerous.

Well, more dangerous.

He must've pressed that button fifty times before Emrys said, "Nobody's at home, it seems."

"Fuck." Dante kicked the bottle-green wall and left a dent in the plaster. Without acknowledging us, he hurried back outside and around to the back of the building, to a tarmac lot with six spaces marked off and a pair of big plastic dumpsters. There was also another small porch where a snow shovel leaned next to a steel door, and a fire escape that wound up to a small balcony on the third floor. As soon as Dante looked up, I knew what he was thinking, and I didn't like it.

"We can't," I said.

"Why not? What if she's in there?"

"Look, mate. This is a whole different world from your neighborhood. If someone sees us, the cops will come. They'll come fast. People here won't just look the other way. If we're arrested, whoever has your sister will get spooked and take her someplace else. We'll be back where we started. And if she isn't in there, we need to talk to the person who lives in that flat, find out what they know. It'll be harder if we frighten them off."

"I agree," Emrys said. "Anything this person knows isn't in a phone or a computer. Otherwise Jet would have found it. We need to figure out a way to speak to them."

"And how the hell are we going to do that from out here?"

"Let's watch the place," Emrys said. "Give me some time to think. If I don't come up with anything, we should at least wait until it gets dark to increase our chances of getting in undetected." He looked over his shoulder at a copse of trees near the end of the lot. "I'll stay here. You two go around front and keep an eye on the entryway. Send a text if anything happens, and I'll do the same."

"Two hours," Dante said, "and then I'm going in there if I have to blow a hole in the wall to do it."

We found a good hiding place in a kids' playset made up to look like the Victorian houses around it. It stood across the street in a wide patch of lawn between two homes, and from the layers of snow and ice, I guessed it hadn't been used in a while. Dante leapt from the walkway to the wooden stairs—I assumed to avoid leaving tracks—and I did the same. The turret room at the top of the slide offered plenty of room for us to sit and wait; it even had curved benches built in, though within minutes, my bum was soaked and going numb. I wondered if I should try to comfort Dante, talk him down. If he would want that. But when I tried to get a sense of his desires, I found his tunnel vision had only focused like a beam of light through a magnifying glass, the point aimed squarely at a bay window on the third floor of the house. I decided to stay quiet.

After a while I zoned out, left with nothing to do but watch the subtle change of light as afternoon wore on toward evening, note the small changes in the shadows the bare branches cast on the snow. When Dante's phone vibrated, it was so obtrusive that I flinched.

"Emrys said a guy in a blue Lexus just pulled in." Dante angled so he could have a better view through the arched opening, and I did the same.

The guy who came around the side of the building and went in the front door was pretty unremarkable—tan overcoat, navy suit, brown briefcase. Short brown hair with a biscuit-sized bald patch in the back. I was too far off to get a real sense of what he wanted, but I could feel an urgency thrumming through his slightly portly frame. He was excited about something. But then, it could be something as simple as some leftover takeaway he knew he had waiting in the fridge. I waited to see what Dante would do, but he stayed frozen in what had to be an uncomfortable half crouch, staring at the door the man had gone through.

Before long, the fancy streetlamps flickered to soft amber life, and with them came tiny shadows on silent feet. The cats converged on the house, melting into the darkness cast by bushes and trees until no one who hadn't seen them arrive would know they were there—even though I saw a dozen before I stopped counting.

"Good sign," I whispered to Dante.

Before he could answer, his phone buzzed again. His face looked ghostly in the blue light from the screen, the shadows deep around his eyes. "Emrys said a car just pulled into the alley and stopped a few houses down. Dropped someone off. A guy. He's heading our way. I think we should stop him, see what he's doing."

"All right."

Following Dante's lead, I crossed the street and pressed my body against the side of the house, beyond the light spilling from the big windows on the first floor. Something brushed my calf, and I looked down into a pair of luminous eyes. Joy and love warmed my chest, and I began to reach down, but Dante elbowed me hard in the ribs. Even in the shadows, I couldn't miss his murderous look. "I'll come back for you," I promised the big black cat purring hard at my feet.

"Shut the fuck up," Dante hissed out between his teeth.

I held a hand up in surrender just as a slender guy came around the corner. I thought hustler right away from the combination of his hip-swinging gait and the guarded way he held his spine straight and bunched his shoulders. When he stepped into the light, I saw professionally highlighted hair, foundation-smooth skin, and subtly glossed lips.

Dante stepped in front of the guy, blocking his path and getting right in his face. "Who the hell are you?"

"Whoa, buddy." The guy tried to step back, but Dante mirrored him, keeping their chests flush. "What the hell?"

"I asked who you are and what you're doing here," Dante said.

"I'm visiting a friend. What's it to you?"

"Bullshit. You're sneaking around, and I want to know why."

"Look, it's none of your business. Just get the fuck out of my face, man."

It was the wrong answer. Dante grabbed a handful of the guy's silk shirt, spun him, slammed his back against the house, and pressed his forearm across the guy's throat. He made wet choking sounds, and blotchy red showed through his makeup.

Dante leaned in until his lips almost touched the guy's sideburns. "You look, asshole. I don't have a problem with you, and I don't want your money, but if you don't tell me the truth, I'm gonna kick your ass."

I could see the second the guy realized it wasn't posturing on Dante's part, like somebody flicked a switch behind his eyes. He nodded as best he could with Dante's arm across his throat, and Dante let up a little bit.

"I work for an escort service, Gold Standard. The guy on the third floor, Mr. Schneider, is a regular client. He usually asks for Jamie, but he's on vacation. So I'm here. That's all. Making a living, man. Same as anybody."

When Dante looked at me, his slightly touched, toothy smile would've given Blossom a run for his money. I took a step back, but I knew what he was thinking, and I couldn't say it was a bad plan. He asked the guy a few more questions and then he reached into the pocket of his tight trousers and pulled out his wallet. "Good. Now get the hell out of here. I'm just gonna keep your driver's license in case you decide to open your mouth about what happened tonight. Anybody asks you, the guy changed his mind. Say anything different and I'll find you. We have an understanding?"

"Y-yeah."

Dante let the guy go and handed him back his wallet. He had too much dignity to turn and run right away, but as soon as he reached the parking lot, I could hear his heeled dress shoes pounding the tarmac.

I shoved my hands in my pockets and shook my head. "Guess that's my cue, then."

"Is that a problem? I thought you liked this stuff. I thought you'd welcome the opportunity. If not, I can go up and make the guy talk. My methods might be a little more direct, but—"

"No, no. It isn't that. I'll do it. I'll…. Dante, I'll do it for you."

Chapter Twenty-Two

WHAT THE hell had I been thinking, saying that to Dante? I raked my fingers through my hair even though the guy wouldn't see it as I stared at the hole Dante had kicked in the wall. He didn't want that, didn't want a connection between us, and I bloody well knew it. *I* had wanted to say that to him, wanted him to know. Needed him to know, for myself, and that wasn't supposed to happen. Scared the shite out of me, truth told. I preferred having a set of instructions to follow, the desires of others to guide me. My own….

I put it out of my mind, popped a few mints in my mouth, and pressed the button on the intercom.

"Yes?"

I had to sound peppy, like I was at least pretending to be glad to be there. "Hi, Mr. Schneider? My name is…." Fuck! Should've prepared something. I looked around frantically until I noticed a print hanging on the wall. *Water Lilies*. "My name is Claude. I'm from Gold Standard."

"Oh! I'm looking forward to meeting you. Just go up to the landing and then take the stairs on the left. There's a locked security door at the top, but I'll let you in."

I did as I was asked, and the guy from earlier greeted me in some pajama pants and a T-shirt. He smelled freshly showered with a soft hint of some expensive cologne. He looked me up and down and smiled.

Good a start as any.

As I followed him into a tiny alcove where an umbrella stand and some muddy trainers sat on the terra-cotta tiles, I could already feel his desires molding me. I was a little on the small side, in good shape but not stocky, more of a dancer's build. Mr. Schneider liked having the advantage, being physically superior. I could run with that, sure. I didn't mind getting tossed about a bit now and then. Not at all.

Beyond the alcove was a more normal wooden door, and past that, his apartment. It was nice if a little clinical—all earthy masculine tones from the leather sectional to the plaid throw pillows. From the gas fireplace to the wet bar on one end of the living room to the open-plan kitchen and its exposed brick, it all looked like a picture out of a magazine. I had the feeling of being in a showroom, not someplace a person actually lived. Even the knickknacks on the mantel and bookshelves seemed chosen by a designer, rather than personal things with any meaning behind them.

Everything for appearance, like my host. He was one of those gift boxes in a department store window, covered in expensive paper and perfect ribbons, but empty on the inside. He was also something of a vacuum, his need to fill that hollow place tugging me toward him. He needed what I had to offer, needed it desperately, and that felt damned good.

"Let me take your coat."

I slipped it off and handed it to him, and he hung it in a narrow closet in the hall. Then he went to the bar and took two tumblers from underneath it. "Can I offer you a drink?"

"Whiskey's my poison." My voice came out higher than I expected, lilting and filled with innuendo. Mr. Schneider seemed to like it; his grin took on a feral edge. "But not bourbon. Scotch or Irish, if you have it."

"Good man." He winked. "I have Macallan or Bushmills. Nothing terribly exotic, I'm afraid, but they're both decent." He watched me expectantly as I sauntered up to the bar and leaned one hip against it.

"Bushmills is great. You've got good taste. I like that." I brushed my fingers across the back of his hand as he slid my drink over. "Seems like fewer and fewer guys these days know how to appreciate the finer things."

He tapped the rim of his glass against mine. "Well, to mutual appreciation."

He had nice eyes, the soft blue-gray of an old chamois shirt. A little vapid, maybe, but no malice. No sadism. He liked impressing me, liked knowing more than me. I could use that.

"Mmm." I sipped my drink. "So this one's Irish, right? What's the difference?"

He talked for a while about stuff I already knew: barley, distillation, aging, casks. I put my elbow on the bar, leaned in, and rested a cheek against my palm. I got the distinct feeling that most people didn't pay much attention when Mr. Schneider talked, and it was ramping him up that I did. I could feel that special light and energy spilling off him like heat from a flame, taste it in the air, smoky and leathery and dirty, like the whiskey.

He refilled our glasses and picked them up. "Let's move to the sofa and I'll get a fire going. Some cold spell we're having, isn't it? How about some music?"

"Sure, Mr. Schneider. I like everything. Whatever's on the radio."

He chuckled. "Please, call me Brandt. And we're not going to settle for any of that studio-manufactured stuff. I'll teach you a little bit about the classics."

"I'd like that," I said, standing between the coffee table and the chaise longue end of the couch.

"I hope you're not nervous," Brandt said as he fiddled with an iPhone hooked into a set of speakers.

Of course I wasn't; this was what I did—and liked—best. That was why I knew it turned him on that I was a little unsure, and I milked it, saying, "The truth is, I'm a little new to this."

"You mean working for the escort service?" He sat down, took my hand, and guided me to take a seat beside him.

"Uh, all of it, actually. I haven't had many—" I gulped and lowered my face so my positively cherubic blond curls hid—but not completely—my blush. "—many lovers."

Brandt pinched my chin and angled my head up. He brushed the hair out of my face. Smiling, he ran his thumb along my lower lip. "That's okay. I'll show you what to do. I'd be happy to."

"I'd like that too." If I could show this guy a good enough time, he'd be putty in my hands. After the best fuck of his life, he'd probably answer any questions I asked.

Guess I'd give it to him.

Not a problem.

WE HAD a nice time. Brandt was versatile, it turned out, and he had a lot of stamina. We went twice and then sixty-nined on the rug by the fireplace for a while, but we both needed time to recover. Well, I didn't, but proving that wouldn't help my cause, especially not with this guy. He liked flattery, and I laid it on thick. Yes, I needed some information if he had it, but I also fucking loved satisfying people, making their dreams come true. I'm just wired that way.

I reached up and pulled a blanket off the couch, tucking it around us. Brandt was shining like a lighthouse, absolutely infatuated with me. Some of it was even sticking, though it was fish-food flakes when there was lobster and filet mignon right within my reach. I couldn't have it, thanks to whatever Blossom had done. Still, a snack was better than nothing, and I expected the supply would keep coming strong for at least a few weeks, maybe longer.

I should've been perfectly content.

But I couldn't stop thinking about Dante out there in the cold, his laser-pointer stare on the window just above us. He was counting on me, and for maybe the first time in my existence, that meant something to me.

I made a show of looking around. "This is an amazing apartment. It looks like a picture out of a book. You must have a good job. I bet you're an important guy."

He beamed. "I have a lot of influence. In fact…. Well, you probably wouldn't believe me if I told you."

I already knew he was Sekhet-Aaru; I'd seen a gold money clip with their crossed-reed insignia on the counter in the bathroom. "Sounds serious. Are you, like, part of the government?"

He paused, probably considering how much to tell me. I was banking on his desire to impress me winning out over whatever secret oaths he'd taken, and I wasn't disappointed. "People only think the government runs everything. But there's a, I guess you'd call it a secret society of people who wield the real power, and they control the government. Several governments, in fact."

I giggled. "Come on. You're messing with me. That's completely bonkers."

"I know how it must sound—paranoid, nuts. But… I am one of these people, one of a very few who knows how the world really works… knows the real mysteries of power."

Once again, he proceeded to tell me a lot of things I already knew. He had one part correct—if I hadn't already known this shite was true, I never would've believed it. Nobody would, and that worked in their favor. Now that I had him in a talkative mood, I had to figure out a way to ask about Rosalind, one that wouldn't be too obvious, because as insecure and needy as Brandt might be, the man wasn't a fool.

He gathered me onto his chest and crossed his arms over my back, speaking into my hair. "Do you think I'm crazy?"

"It's all kind of… James Bond," I said, tracing my fingers down his arm. Beneath his layer of padding, Brandt had a good amount of muscle. "Do you… these people do that kind of secret-agent stuff?"

"What kind of stuff?"

"I don't know. It sounds like you can operate outside the law. Can you kidnap people?"

He stiffened beneath me. Damn. I'd taken it too far. It wasn't in my nature to be deceptive, wasn't anything I'd ever had to do. "Why would we do that?"

"Right," I said, shifting so I could trace my thumb around his nipple. "Even secret societies can't pull off that kind of thing, not without getting caught. Nobody's that important."

"Oh, we could if we wanted to."

"You're just teasing me now," I challenged. I sat up and yawned, reaching for my shirt that was draped over the arm of the couch.

Nails scraped lightly down my back. "I'll pay double if you stay the night."

"I don't know. I feel like you're making fun of me."

"No." He stood and went into the kitchen to draw water from the refrigerator door. "Jesus, no. It's just that I'm not supposed to talk about it. But I… I have done something like that. Recently."

This was it! I had to play this just right. I went to stand behind him and wrapped my arms around his waist. "What, personally? That's kind of exciting. I don't think I've ever met a man who could get away with kidnapping someone. Other people… they'd be too scared. They wouldn't know how to do it." I trailed my hand down his belly and grazed the semi he was sporting. "Can you tell me?"

"Will you stay the night?"

I laughed, making sure the hot, wet air puffed against his bare shoulder. "Depends how good of a story it is."

"Well, I'm afraid I wouldn't really call it kidnapping. More of a rescue. There was this little girl, and she was living in deplorable conditions. A drug addict for a mother, a vicious criminal for a brother…."

By the time he finished a tale that made him sound like a knight in shining armor, we'd migrated back to the sofa with some pita chips, vegetables, and hummus he'd taken from the fridge.

"What happened to the little girl?" I asked. "Is she all right?"

"Oh, of course she is. We aren't the kind of people who would harm a child."

Sure, just the poor bastard driving the car…. "Where is she?"

"She's with our organization. One of our high-ranking members is going to raise her, give her a chance at a good life. She'll have real power, and—and you look like you don't believe me. Again."

I wiped some hummus off the corner of his mouth with my finger. "I'm trying to keep an open mind."

"What if I could show you?"

"How?"

"There's a party tomorrow night. People from my organization, from all over the world, will be there. It's a sort of meeting we hold every year. I was actually planning to ask you anyway. Have you ever been to the Poconos?"

'Course I had. "No! It's pretty fancy, isn't it?"

"You will be in awe." He kissed the tip of my nose. "So you'll come? I'll pay, of course. And if you have a friend you can bring along, it'll mean a nice tip for both of you. Maybe Jamie?"

"Hmm. I know someone you might like even better. Do you like Asian guys?"

"If they're as hot as you."

"If I'm going to a fancy party tomorrow, I should go. I'll need to get ready."

He groaned and tugged me over so I was straddling his lap. "Can't you stay just a little longer?"

Aw, hell. One more couldn't hurt.

Afterwards, I found Dante sitting on the back porch steps, leaning his head on a post, asleep. Two cats curled in his lap, and six or seven others huddled around him like they were trying to keep him warm. Brilliant little creatures. It broke my heart a little to see Charlene wasn't among them, and I hoped she was all right. I knew it had been a bad idea to send her off on her own.

But I had good news. So good, I took a risk and touched Dante's cheek to wake him. He flinched and opened his eyes, and I couldn't help my wide grin.

"I did it, mate. I found her."

He got to his feet, cats scattering. "Let's go."

I shushed him. "I've already got a plan to get us to where she is. Where's Emrys?"

"Jet picked him up. Said they were going to a hotel. Couldn't take the cold, I guess. He texted me the address and room number."

"But you stayed?"

"Didn't want to lose you," he muttered.

"Let's go," I said. "I might as well fill everybody in at once."

"But Ros! We should go to her now."

I shook my head. "No. We're going to need to prepare."

Chapter Twenty-Three

"WHAT'S THE lad doing now, turning tricks? Selling his arse?"

For some reason Moirin's observation made me angry, and I wanted to shout at her, ask her how she could even suggest something like that. But after I realized stress and exhaustion were warring against my better judgment, I had to admit her assessment made at least some sense.

As we'd waited in a nondescript sedan, black and high-end enough to look like it belonged in this neighborhood, we'd seen Dante and another man enter the big house on the cul-de-sac called Greenbrier. I hadn't gotten a good look at the other man when he entered through the front door, while Dante, presumably, used the back entrance. But I had seen him clearly when the two of them came around the side of the building: small, well-dressed, not exactly effeminate but prettier than average.

They walked up the block together, and Moirin waited until they made it a few hundred yards from our location before she started the engine, leaving the headlights dark. Three and a half blocks away, Dante and the blond man got into the same dilapidated pickup I'd seen in the mountains.

Moirin accelerated to keep up with them as they pulled onto the quiet street, but I held up a hand. "Don't let them know we're following them. Remember, that was the whole reason we put the tracking device on the new gun I gave Dante. We can use it to find them if we have to."

She snorted. "In case you've forgotten, I've done this kind of thing a time or two before, my fine friend. And as I haven't been asking the questions I should, the kinds of questions it would be prudent for me to ask in a situation such as this, I'd think you'd be shutting up and thanking me. Besides, it was my contact what whipped up that little bauble—and it didn't come cheap."

"You're right," I conceded. "I do appreciate your help. And your discretion."

"If it turns out the boy's a snitch, I'll gut him meself."

"I've assured you that isn't the case. I would have taken care of it if it was."

"Aye, and I trust you. Wouldn't be here if I didn't."

"There's no one I would rather have by my side," I told her. "We've been through a lot together, and neither of us would be where we are today without the other."

She chuckled. "And people say it's the Irish who have the gilded tongues. But you're right, and if there's some… boon to be had at the end of all this, I trust you to be sharing."

"If we play this right, the benefits could be beyond anything we've ever imagined."

My phone rang, and I reached into my pocket to answer it, because no matter how difficult it was for me to relinquish control, I did trust Moirin. "Devereux."

"Evening, boss. Just checking in about that job you might need doing."

Amazingly, I had almost forgotten. Ghost guns from Puerto Rico, those assembled by craftsmen in hidden workshops in the jungle, untraceable and often superior to what manufacturers offered, were one of our most lucrative and sought-after products. They were the future, and one day I hoped to set up workshops here. But until that became possible, I had to smuggle them in. They came by shipping crate to the Delaware River Port Authority, and retrieving them and overseeing them loaded into a tractor trailer was one of the few tasks I liked to supervise personally. I'd bribed the necessary officials; that wasn't the problem. Hijacking was always a threat, especially with the issues we'd been having with the White Liberation Front. But like Moirin, Devereux was trustworthy. He had far less to gain by betraying me than by remaining loyal. I rarely let my emotions reign over logic, but something deep inside me needed to know what was going on with Dante. "You have a good crew?"

His deep, rich laughter echoed in my ears. "You even need to ask? We have the best. We will get it done, and that I guarantee."

"All right, then. Be cautious. We might be being watched."

"Bien sûr. You know it, boss."

"Très bien. Call me when it's done."

"That I will do. You enjoy your evening, now."

I disconnected the call as we pulled up to the downtown Philadelphia Hotel Palomar. I turned to Moirin. "Are you sure?"

"GPS leads here," she answered. "Posh place."

"It is."

"Valet parking in a private garage," she said. "What do you want to do?"

Money wasn't a problem, and I'd taken care to make sure the car couldn't be connected with me. "Let's park. The bar is still open. We'll go there."

"Long as you buy me a drink."

I loved the Palomar, a fully restored art deco building enhanced with local art, and normally I would be absorbed in noticing details I'd missed on other visits, but tonight I had too much on my mind, and I had to focus to follow Moirin to the restaurant and bar. She ordered a Harp and some snacks—a platter of mussels and the deviled crabs. I nodded to the bartender and said I would have the same.

In addition to the hotel's guests, lots of locals came to Square 1682 for dinner. I'd done so myself, and I liked their take on classic dishes. Tonight I wasn't hungry. Between worrying about my shipping container and imagining what Dante could possibly be doing in the guestroom of an expensive hotel, I knew I was in for a long night of acid reflux.

With that thought in mind, I pushed my beer back at the bartender when she set it on a napkin. "I apologize, but I've changed my mind. I think I'd rather have a merlot."

"No problem," she said with a smile. "Anything else I can get for you?"

"No, thanks." I picked up a slice of baguette and nibbled on the edge, hoping it would soak up some of the acid churning in my stomach. Unfortunately, it couldn't remedy the real source of my distress: the dark thoughts worming their way into my mind. I wasn't normally one to be maudlin, but I couldn't shake the feeling of foreboding, and it led me to imagine every possible disaster that could befall me. I could only remember one other time in my life when I'd experienced such dread— the night the man came to our door to tell us my brother had been killed in the line of duty. That was the first time my world had collapsed; the day in the woods had been the second.

I took another sip of my wine, but it was bitter. I was being foolish. I was not a clairvoyant; I didn't even believe in such things. At least I hadn't before.

Just when I thought my night couldn't get more stressful, my phone chirped with a call from Devereux… on FaceTime. That was unusual to say the least, and I hurried out of the bar and through the lobby as I answered. As soon as I made it through the gilded glass doors of the entryway, I ducked around the side of the tall, narrow building. My blood seemed to stop flowing and turn thick and gritty in my veins when I looked down at my screen.

Instead of Devereux, a white man with a shaved head stared back at me. He had a black bandana tied around the lower part of his face, but it didn't cover the faded swastika tattooed over his left temple. From the crinkle of his eyes, I knew he was smiling.

"Well, well, well. If it ain't the bean-eating asshole who thought he was too good to do business with us. I bet you've changed your mind now. Ain't that right, Pedro?"

"How did you get this phone?" I forced my tone to remain calm and neutral, even though my racing blood was loud in my ears, spattering silver dots across my vision and engorging my fingers as I clutched my phone.

The big Nazi laughed. "We got lots of things that used to belong to you, ese." With a grainy black-and-white blur, he panned to a snowy patch of asphalt where Devereux and Louie sat back-to-back, hands bound behind them, faces bloodied and swollen, heads hanging.

I didn't even want to think about what had become of the rest of their crew as another smear shifted the view to what I knew was my shipping container—my guns. Men with their faces concealed stood in a circle around it while a forklift hoisted it onto a flatbed that was decidedly not mine.

"That's right, asshole. We got your boys, we got your guns, and best of all, we got the location of your warehouse."

"What warehouse? What are you talking about?" I certainly didn't keep my merchandise in a single location.

The Nazi narrowed his eyes. "Too late to play stupid now. We have connections. Powerful allies. And we know all about Gardegris Towers. We're taking it away from you too. Power back in the hands of the white man, where it fucking belongs. Your time's done, motherfucker. You and all the rest like you. Blood and soil."

My grip tightened on the phone as the Nazi's face came back into view. I had been too lenient with these *hijos de la gran puta*—a mistake I would remedy as soon as possible. I had underestimated them, and I was as angry with myself as I was about what had happened. "Sigue con tu vaina, lambe bolsa. I'm coming for you, and I'm going to kill every Nazi mamaguevo in the tristate area."

He started to say something, but I had heard all I needed. I threw the phone onto the sidewalk and crushed it with my heel. It was compromised, and I had others.

For a moment I closed my eyes. I could not remember the last time I had been so angry that my fists shook. Growing up, I'd hated being the smart one, the schemer, the one who could think his way out of any situation. Academia—everything from languages and mathematics to art—came easily to me, but I would have traded it all to be more like my brother Ramon: healthy, strong, and charming. I'd hated the club foot that prevented me from playing sports or following my brother into the Army. But over the years, I had come to terms with my gifts, grown to realize I was the lucky one, because what I had been given would not fade, like speed or strength, with time. No, the blade I wielded had only grown sharper with use.

I needed my mind—its unique way of coming at a problem—now more than ever. But I also needed muscle, and that meant calling in favors.

As soon as I'd collected myself enough to accomplish it, I went back inside the hotel and found Moirin still at the bar, a group of admiring men—and women—standing in a crescent around her stool. She smiled and batted her eyes at a few of them, but as soon as she saw me, she forgot them all in her haste to join me near the entrance. I must not have gathered my composure as much as I'd thought.

"What is it? What's happened?" She clutched my arm, and I laid my hand over hers to lead her into the empty lobby, to a secluded corner where we wouldn't be overheard. Then I hurried to provide a summary of what had happened outside, what I'd learned.

A deep crimson stained her cheeks. "Fecking maggot-arsed hoors. They're dead."

I nodded. "They're headed to a place called Gardegris Towers. Damn. I should've looked it up before I disposed of my phone."

Moirin already had hers out. "It's a historical property in Milford. Belonged to some Frenchman, a conservationist who made a fortune on hybrid plants. Established a school... friends with prominent occultists of the day... available for weddings.... They think this is where we're keeping an arsenal? That doesn't make a damn bit of sense."

"Sense or not, that's where they're going, and they have Devereux and Louie. They could be bringing the latest shipment as well. We need to be there."

"If they volunteered the information, we'd be fools not to think trap," she said.

"I know. That's why I need you to call in every favor I'm owed. Talk to your people; talk to everyone who holds me in high regard. Gather them. Have them meet us at Gardegris Towers, and tell them to come armed for a fight. This ends tonight. I'm not letting these Nazi scum gain another inch of ground. Not one."

She narrowed her eyes and smiled. "Aye, now you're talking my language. I'll be there with all of Hell behind me, ready to kick some arse. What about Dante?"

I shook my head. "Forget him. I'm not sure if he can be trusted, and we can't afford to take chances. Those pendejos learned the location of my shipment somehow…. They said they had allies."

"I meant what I said before, Raphael. I know you've always favored the lad—"

"I know. It will be dealt with." I leaned in and kissed her cheek. "This first. I want an army at that estate, Moirin."

"You'll have it. Where will you be?"

"I have something I need to take care of… in case I don't make it back."

Chapter Twenty-Four

"ALL I'M saying, love, is 'I'm gonna shag you hard on the sink and then fix you a drink' is not 'Stairway to Heaven.'"

We'd been sitting in this expensive hotel suite while Inky and Jet argued and Emrys quietly flipped through the TV channels. I was trying my best to be patient, to be satisfied that we'd be getting my sister back soon, but I felt like they were being dismissive, talking about this bullshit without a care in the world, and it was starting to annoy me. But I'd been on edge ever since Jet showed up without Blossom and told us he'd wandered off. Sure, it sounded like something he'd do, and I couldn't even pretend I was surprised, but I didn't like the idea of walking into whatever we'd be walking into without him at my back. He was the strongest of us all.

"I'm not disagreeing with you." Jet packed a fat, greasy bud into a blue glass pipe and held it close to their face like they were examining a diamond. "I just don't think you can claim nothing of merit is being produced now, like the last decade or so has been an anomaly and creative achievement is abnormally stunted. Yeah, a lot of music sucks. But a lot of it sucked in the seventies, and I'm sure plenty of it sucked in Mozart's time, but we never heard about it because it didn't last. Because it sucked."

"Maybe, maybe not," Inky said. "Truth is, these things can be cyclical. They called the Dark Ages that for a reason. It could be the timing thing. Maybe as we get closer to whatever's going to happen, human energy is moving elsewhere."

"It's hard to deny that intellectualism is vilified at the moment," Emrys offered. "And things have only gone downhill since the 2016 election. Being ignorant and believing falsehoods is almost a badge of honor now. Not a fertile environment for artistic excellence."

I thought about that, about what Raf had said about the climate encouraging people like those fucking Nazis. It pissed me off. I clenched my fists. There wasn't a damned thing I could do, and that just pissed me off more. All my life I'd been standing at the bottom of a hill, too busy dodging the shit that rolled down it to think about climbing up a few feet. These guys were the first people who might understand that, but I still wasn't comfortable trying to explain and risking getting labeled a whiny pussy.

"Don't think Sekhet-Aaru isn't doing this on purpose," Jet said as they lifted the swirly glass pipe to their lips. "Uneducated people are easier to control, and so are divided people. Encourage tribalism and you effectively distract the populace from how bad you're screwing them, even while you weaken their ability to stand together to stop you. But still… people are resisting. Artists. They might not be the ones getting rich doing it, but are they ever?" Jet was just about to spark up when there was a knock at the door.

"Ooh, I bet that's room service!" They jumped out of their overstuffed chair and went to the door, then came back with a cart covered in food under shiny silver domes—and half a dozen bottles of that expensive champagne with the orange labels, Veuve Clicquot. I recognized it from the dinner parties Raf threw sometimes, and I knew it cost a lot. I said as much.

Jet winked at me as they popped a cork and uncovered a plate of fresh strawberries and fancy little cakes. "Courtesy of the American Family Association, so drink up." They filled several glasses and handed one to me before sitting back down. Their eyes never left me. "You're cute."

I almost dumped my wine on my crotch. "What—me?"

Jet laughed, but it wasn't mocking. "Yeah. You straight? Gay? What do you like?"

I can't say the attention made me uncomfortable, but it was tiring… like being pestered by a salesperson when you had no interest in what they were selling. "I'm not down. Sorry."

Jet shrugged. "Figured I'd offer. Man, I know I wouldn't turn down a chance to burn off some tension." They hit the bowl, held it, and then sighed out a stream of smoke before offering the pipe to the room.

Inky reached over to take it, a funny glimmer in his eye as he watched Jet. "You, uh… you in need of a shag, then?"

"I'd kill for one," Jet said. "You?"

His eyes lit up like somebody handed him a winning lottery ticket, but almost as quickly, the light went out. "I've had this spooky feeling, like I'm a piece in a puzzle I can't see, a fucking marble rolling down a track…. I'd love something to distract myself for an hour or two, but—" He glanced at Emrys. "I don't want to step on anybody's toes here."

Emrys chuckled. "You think I claim any measure of control over Jet? No. I have no desire to restrict anyone's freedom. By all means."

Inky coughed out the smoke he'd inhaled. "You sure, mate?"

"Absolutely. Have a good time."

That lottery-winning smile was back as Inky looked over at Jet. "Yeah?"

Jet stood up and brushed some weed crumbs off their thighs. "Oh yeah." They gestured toward the door to one of the bedrooms, and Inky followed.

"Just so you know, I can do a lot to fulfill your fantasies, but I can't spring a set of tits or anything."

"That's okay," Jet answered. "I like it all. Cock, pussy, whatever. I know my way around whatever you're packing."

"That's good to hear, 'cause I've got a big fucking cock—"

"That's great, but you have to know how to use it too."

"Bloody hell. You kidding me right now?"

Jet laughed. "Actually I am. But by all means, keep feeling like you have something to prove. In fact, how about a peek at what you're working with? I wouldn't mind doing a—"

Thankfully, the door shut, and a second later, Daft Punk's "Get Lucky" drowned out whatever else they were saying. I let out a breath and took a sip of wine. Across the coffee table, Emrys was smoking leisurely and flipping through the channels again. Finally he stopped on some fantasy movie with elves and dragons. I guess he didn't see enough of that kind of shit in his day-to-day life.

Before long I heard the telltale bang of the headboard against the wall. Somebody squealed; I couldn't tell who. I looked over at Emrys. "So... this is super fucking awkward."

He blew out a line of smoke, and it drifted up to the ceiling to join the cloud that had formed. How they weren't throwing us the hell out of this place, I had no clue. "Is it?"

I tipped my head toward the bedroom door. "You don't think so?"

"Hmm." He leaned forward to poke through the foods under the shiny domes. "I guess I'm used to it. Jet has a healthy libido, especially when they're stressed. There are worse coping mechanisms."

"Right." I nodded, remembering what he had said outside Corazón's house. "And you don't like to fuck."

"Do you find that unusual?"

"No, actually…. I, uh, I always thought it was just me. Everybody I know, the people I work with, it's like their whole damn world revolves around getting ass. Like it's the ultimate prize. I never got it. The lengths they'll go to…. Backstabbing friends, lying, even killing. It's like, they let it have so much power over their lives."

"Ever done it?" Emrys asked.

I shook my head and stabbed a fork into one of the small, round steaks he'd discovered. "You?"

He nodded as he chewed a mushroom. "I've had sex with Jet."

"Is it, like… fun? Is it everything everybody makes it out to be?"

"It's pleasant. It feels good. But then again, so does a foot massage. Now will I let the pursuit of a foot massage sway my every decision? No. I agree with you about people giving it too much power. It can be like watching animals in heat.

"And I don't understand the claims of intimacy. For me, with Jet, talking, sharing experiences and communicating on a deep level, is intimate. Rubbing genitals together is just that. Almost silly. I've never been able to understand how it demonstrates love or devotion. Jet says I'm wired differently than most people."

"Yeah?" I leaned in. I couldn't help it; I had never met anyone who understood. Usually when I expressed indifference about sex, people either thought I was lying or that one day something would kick in and I'd be chasing down ass like my life depended on it, like they did. "Have you always felt that way?"

He nodded. "Where I grew up, it was isolated. Rustic. We didn't have the internet, and we only got a few TV channels. I had no idea how obsessive people were about sex until I left home. I just assumed everyone was like me. The concept of structuring your life around it, sacrificing so much to secure it… I couldn't understand. I still don't, not really. People will stay in miserable relationships, pretend to be what they're not. Rearrange not just their lives but their entire personality. Jet says I'm missing the connection most people have that ties an appreciation of beauty to the desire to put my genitals against the person I find beautiful."

"Yeah, I know what you mean. I guess I'm missing that connection too. I see girls I think are good-looking, even a guy sometimes, but it all shorts out somewhere between my head and my dick."

"So you've never been curious?"

My cheeks heated, and I took a deep swallow of champagne.

"I don't mean to make you uncomfortable," Emrys said. "I know in our culture for a man not to have had sex is perceived as some sort of a failing, but I assure you, I don't see it that way. Still, you don't have to answer."

What he said made me feel better. It was the truth. Moirin and Devereux and the others made fun of people for not being able to get laid, called them losers and other nasty shit. It had always been hard for me to fake a smile and nod along. It felt good to admit "I haven't had sex. I don't want to. It all seems... kind of messy. Like more trouble than it's worth. I haven't told many people, and when I have, they think I was molested or some shit."

Emrys chuckled. "Isn't that ridiculous. I've heard the same. That and pity... people who feel sorry for me because I'm 'missing out.'"

I'd heard that too. "Shit. I always thought there was something wrong with me. Truth is, sometimes I think... I feel...."

"Superior?" Emrys asked. "Because you're above its influence?"

I nodded. "The shit I've seen people do just for some ass.... It's like watching addicts."

"Well, anything you need has power over you, and I understand the temptation to feel that way," he said. "But we should always endeavor to respect everyone's differences. Jet has helped me to understand a great deal, though they, unlike most, attach very little sentiment to the act. But in the end, we're all beholden to something."

Things in the bedroom were heating up—and getting really loud. Despite the enlightening conversation we'd just had, I still didn't want to hear the play-by-play. I stood up and went to get my coat from the closet by the door. "I'm going to go check on my mom in case shit goes bad tomorrow. Make sure she has a week or so's worth of food in the house."

It surprised me when Emrys also stood. The guy was still a mystery to me, and I wasn't sure I believed his story about helping us out of the goodness of his heart, but I liked him, and I liked being around him, especially now. So I didn't refuse when it was obvious he wanted to come with me.

WE HIT up a grocery store, where I bought bread, peanut butter, canned soup, and some frozen dinners—shit that wouldn't go bad. It was also the most preparation Mom would put in before she decided it was easier to go without. When we got there, I carried the three plastic bags into our apartment with Emrys quietly following. It was cold and dark inside, and it smelled like piss and BO.

I flicked on the light. The coffee table shards still covered the floor, and Mom was passed out on the couch clutching a bottle of vodka. I left the food on the kitchen counter and shoved the past-due electric bill into my coat pocket. If I didn't die up in the Poconos, I guessed I'd pay it. But one thing was for sure: I wasn't coming back here, and I wasn't bringing Ros back here. I didn't know if Raf's offer of the apartment still stood—shit, I didn't even know if he would want me working for him anymore after how badly I'd flaked lately—but I would figure out something. No more of this.

No more.

"Dante? Are you all right?" Emrys laid his hand on my shoulder, and surprisingly, I didn't want to tear his arm off.

"Shit, I…. Yeah. Sometimes I feel like crap for letting my sister grow up in this dump. Like I should've done better."

"I'm sure you did the best you could," he said quietly. I guess he didn't realize an atomic bomb wouldn't wake my mom when she was drunk and coming down off glass.

But he was right. "I did. I do. I… I don't know. It just isn't fair to her. Fucking dumb luck. She could've been born into a different family, had a big house, nice clothes, gone to a private school. But to the rest of the world, my sister is worthless. They see her and… and she's nothing." I ground my teeth to keep from yelling even as tears stung my eyes. "All because of this tweaker bitch. She had her chance, and she wasted it. But I can't… I can't just walk away and let her die. She's my mom. I should, though." I turned to him. "I should walk. Shouldn't I?"

His eyes were shiny and big. "I can't answer that for you. I'm sorry."

I shrugged his hand off even though I knew he didn't deserve it and I was being a complete dick. I ran my fingers through my hair and pulled on the strands above my temples. In this light, Mom almost looked the way I remembered her from when I was a kid—when she would take me to the park, or we would make a stage out of an old cardboard box and put on a puppet show. She wasn't an evil person. She was just weak—soft in a hard, sharp world. I'd figured out pretty quickly that this world chewed up soft people, and I'd realized I couldn't be one. I had to cut away everything soft, like Mom hadn't been able to. Should she be left to die for that weakness? "I'll never get anywhere if I keep taking care of her. She's grown. Is it okay to walk away?"

I didn't expect Emrys to answer, and he didn't. I looked away from my mom, and I did what I usually did. I prioritized. I couldn't worry about this now. Not yet. "Let's get the hell out of here," I said to Emrys, forcing a smile in the hope that he'd know I wasn't pissed at him—or ungrateful. "We have a lot to do to get ready for tomorrow, and even if we do everything right, odds are we aren't walking away from this one."

"The probability is… not in our favor, but—"

"But what?"

"I sense some outside influence on the probability, like something is constantly rearranging the odds and elements toward… some outcome. But before I can even begin to analyze it, it changes, like the original probability is straining to reassert itself, almost in a tug-of-war. I've never experienced anything like it. It's… vast, so faceted, with so many pieces, I cannot even begin to imagine what they're trying to form. When it all comes together, though, I suspect the results will really be something."

"Great." I wished I had a hell of a lot more guns. I wished Blossom was with me. I wished I had never heard of any of this shit, let alone gotten tangled up in it. But I had been wishing for things as long as I could remember, and never once had it done a damn bit of good. I suspected it would get me just as much now, if not less.

Chapter Twenty-Five

THE EVER-CHANGING display of lights and symbols surrounding me almost distracted me from fantasizing about the thousands of forms of suffering I planned to inflict on Jet Zama. If they feared the machinations of the assassins we had visited together, then the most trifling example of what I had in store would likely make their little mortal heart seize up in terror. And rarely had I anticipated something as much as seeing the moment the realization of what they had done struck terror into their eyes, like a bolt of lightning hitting the ground and scorching everything around it. Possibly they would fall down dead as surely as if my description were more than a metaphor.

And I couldn't have that—not until I spent several decades showing them the folly of leading me to this dank little room and imprisoning me between the glossy squares covering the walls.

The insolence to assume they could deceive me—one of the fey! And yet they had, and with greater ease than I cared to admit. It had taken only the promise of seeing further wonders, of experiencing something novel after so long. Following the brilliant display at the mosaic garden, I had believed it. I had been eager, excited to ride in Jet's small carriage and follow the duplicitous mortal into the old block building and down the stairs into the darkness.

Then I had approached a table covered in peeling green paint—the same one where I now sat—to examine an orchid made from filaments of light growing out of a tiny silver square. The flower bloomed gloriously before slowly starting to die and curl in on itself and disappear before the process began again. In the few heartbeats I spent enthralled, Jet flicked a switch, and the dozens of squares surrounding the table crackled to life.

The spells were potent. Colored writing, glowing in the gloom and representing dozens of human languages, crawled across the screens, encircling me with binding enchantments that were not only varied but seemed to change of their own accord, rearranging their elements and the combinations of languages, phrasing, and symbolism almost as soon as I started to understand the magic's working. If I had not been its victim, I might have admired a charm so intricate. Yet without fully understanding how it was done, I somehow knew the components and the possible combinations would extrapolate, project themselves into new magics without the caster's intent. They had a life of their own, a dreaming intelligence behind the flashing neon characters. I also knew that the possible combinations were nigh on infinite—certainly enough to keep me here for many, many years.

Worst of all, I could see freedom just beyond my grasp in the form of a thick cord plugged into the wall at the base of the steps we'd descended to reach this cursed place. I knew that dislodging it would steal the energy from the screens, and the writing scrawling across them would fade as instantly as a dream upon waking. And I could've reached that cord in a dozen strides, if not for the electric spells containing me.

Hours passed as I suffered that cruelest of all tortures to my kind—boredom. I crossed my arms on the table and let my head fall against them, visions of the torment I would inflict playing like a pantomime behind my eyes. Beyond the chilly walls made of pitted stone blocks, I could feel the sky bid farewell to the sun, the last of the rosy golden light receding to make way for the crystalline night. How I wanted to be beneath the jewellike dome as the moon rose and the stars began to sparkle one by one.

What would become of me if I were forced to remain here? I thought it quite possible I would lose my mind.

I don't how much time passed before a sound on the stairs caught my attention, but night held full dominion, making the electronic magic even starker against the blackness, as if the colored symbols had been carved into the darkness, their glow allowed to pulse and bleed through. Beyond the shifting washes of pigment, something glimmered, something small and low to the ground—twin pinpoints of light focused on me with unwavering intent.

And behind them, a familiar awareness.

I leapt to my feet, sending the leprotic metal chair clattering. I approached the ring of light corralling me, the arcane energy digging into me with white-hot tines as soon as I got within a few steps of the screens. Still, I was able to crouch down and look through a cleft in the squares.

When I reached out my hand, Charlene trotted easily over the barrier, unaffected by magic that had not been meant to contain her, and hopped up on my folded knee.

As she rubbed her head beneath my chin, Charlene said, *You have brought me on quite a hunt. For a while, you disappeared from the eyes of the cats, and we could not even find your scent. It took me much cleverness to track you to this place. It is a bad place.*

It is, I agreed. *I would very much like to leave it, and now that you are here, you can help me to escape.*

What must I do?

Remove that cord from the wall and the magic containing me will lose the source of its power. I pointed.

I stood to watch as Charlene scampered over and closed her teeth around the thick gray cord. At first I feared she would not have the strength to yank it free, but I shouldn't have underestimated her. Finally, with a growl, she dislodged the thing, and the light and color on the screens disappeared faster than I could blink. I knelt again, and when I stretched out my arm, Charlene ran along it to seat herself upon my shoulder. Together, we ascended the stone steps covered in moldy blue carpet and stepped out into a night scented with burning chemicals and the possibility of icy rain. I remembered the painted words and pictures that decorated the metal door Jet had led me through as well as the building's block exterior. Yet I was not familiar with this part of the city, and my time sequestered in that dank cellar had dulled my recollection of the routes we had taken to reach it. I decided quickly it would be easiest to enlist the help of a mortal.

As I walked the quiet thoroughfares, I noticed many mortals living in the space between the gaudily decorated buildings. They were dirty, and stacks of refuse surrounded the small pressed-paper dwellings where most of them took shelter. Quite a few of them noticed our passing—they possessed the ability to see worlds beyond their own—yet I did not think they would be of use to us. We needed a human in possession of a carriage.

A few blocks away, two women in coarse black gowns and head coverings were handing out boxed meals from the back of a modest conveyance. They held one out to me when I approached. Clearly they did not have the power to see through the cowls over their eyes, the misconceptions they labored beneath as effective as a heavy blindfold.

I waved away the brown box that stank of overcooked broccoli and fish. "I will require transport." I jutted my chin toward their carriage. "We must leave at once, and leave that foul-smelling food behind. I don't wish to breathe its stench whilst I travel."

Lacking the will to resist—the inherent servility part of the reason I selected them—they did as I instructed, and Charlene and I made ourselves as comfortable as possible in the rear compartment of the vehicle. A ghastly sculpture of a strung-up corpse swayed to and fro as the women navigated the pitted streets. Seeing the gaunt body, twisted with agony, returned my thoughts to Jet Zama, and I was thus able to allow my imagination to entertain me until we reached a section in the north of Philadelphia that seemed familiar. I remembered the names of some of the streets near Dante's home—Diamond and Emerald—but it took much circling, backtracking, and searching before our erstwhile chauffeurs stopped their carriage in front of his building. I waved the women off and went inside, where I found only Dante's mother snoring in a stinking heap. I was sorely tempted to put her out of her misery, but escaping the suffocating odor of the place was far more pressing.

I must find Jet Zama, I said to Charlene, *and after that, hopefully my incubus. I don't imagine they would have returned to Corazón's house, but we should make our way there regardless. I should like to see that the woman is getting by without me to keep her company. She is likely forlorn, and I should reassure her that we will be returning soon.*

I like her, Charlene agreed. *And I am hungry.*

Excellent. It is only a short distance away.

When we reached the walkway in front of Corazón's home, I was interested to see we were not alone. Another vehicle sat next to the curb, and a man in a dark coat made his way toward the porch, picking his way slowly over the ice and walking with a slight limp. I easily traversed the surface of the snow and intercepted him just as he raised his fist to knock. I touched his shoulder, and he turned to me, mouth slightly agape. He was an unassuming man, handsome in an elegant, understated way, and with a current of something sharp and bright pulsing behind his deep brown eyes, like sunlight through colored glass.

"I… know you." He removed his spectacles and rubbed them on the sleeve of his dark wool coat. "I'm sure I've seen you before. Who are you, and what are you doing here?"

"I am here to visit a dear friend," I told him. "Why are you here?"

He squinted as if he wanted to resist telling me, but of course that was impossible. "This is my mother's home. She's elderly and suffers from dementia. I'm checking on her, making sure…."

"Go on." I fluttered my hand around.

"M-making sure none of my enemies have come here to harm her."

I tapped my finger against my chin, watching as pieces to a puzzle slotted into place and some sort of a picture began to form. Before I knew what it was trying to depict, more pieces would need fitted into place, but at least a few things were clear—in the disjointed way of the mosaic garden. "Corazón is your mother. So you must be… you must be Raphael, not Ramon. The scholar, not the soldier."

"That's… right." His eyes cut into me like diamonds. "And you… you know Dante. You were with him in the forest. You killed the big Nazi…. Killed him with your plants."

I couldn't resist a smile, a clap, and a small hop at the shiver he attempted to quell. "Oh, I am glad you got to see that. Too fine a bit of magic to go unappreciated."

"Magic…." He pinched the bridge of his nose with the hand that wasn't holding his glasses. "I read about it. The mages and their guilds. You're one of them? A mage?"

"Ugh. Of course not!" I leaned toward Charlene as she chewed on a strand of my hair, delighted by the way her purr grew louder when she opened her mouth for a nip.

"Then what—"

I waved my hand again. "This is not important. And you need not worry about Corazón's safety. I have enchanted this place so no one wishing her harm can enter here. If they try, they will spend the rest of their lives wandering through the worst nightmare they've ever had, trapped inside their mind until they die of starvation." I exhaled and considered the glittery, frozen cloud that issued from my lips. "Or exposure, I suppose. What I want to know is where I can find Jet Zama."

"I don't know that person," Raphael said.

"They would be a friend of Dante," I explained. "Quite striking. Japanese, with blue hair."

He nodded. "I think I have seen them."

"Tell me where to find them."

"I'm not sure, but Dante was at the Hotel Palomar… I don't know if he still is. I have to speak with Moirin. She's tracking him. But before I can do that, I need to go home and pick up another burner phone."

"Very well. I shall come with you. We will need to secure a meal for my friend Charlene when we reach your domicile."

"I… find I cannot say no. But you should know that it might not be safe where I'm going. I have enemies."

I raised my leg and pointed my toe, stretching my ankle and calf. "Perhaps we can help each other out. I might even be mildly entertaining. Though not for your enemies, or mine, I expect."

Chapter Twenty-Six

So when I say I've had very few bedmates as enthusiastic and creative as Jet, it carries a little more weight than when most say it. And I mean every word. What a fuck. I felt melted—fucking bone-liquefied—as I lay on the sodden sheets drinking champagne straight from the bottle. Every time I moved, something different hurt, and bloody hell, I'd barely noticed not being able to feed while we were shagging. Now, with the TV blaring K-pop videos and pop rocks still exploding behind my eyes, I realized I'd done this because I wanted to, for fun, not sustenance. I didn't think that'd ever happened to me before—a choice based on something other than survival—and it was an icy splash on my warm and well-chafed testicles.

I still needed a hefty dose of that mortal glowy stuff, but I didn't feel like I was going to shake apart without it.

Maybe if Blossom had really gone, the effects of what he had done would start to wear off. Hell, maybe they already had. I was certainly feeling sated. What I needed now was some Mexican takeout to go with this wine, a long shower, and a day of sleep in a bed cleaner than this one.

But my phone bouncing across the nightstand with an incoming text told me I wasn't going to get it.

It was Brandt. *How about breakfast tomorrow?*

Thought the party was tomorrow night, I responded. *Need time to get ready.*

Bring a tux. I'll get you a room here at Gardegris Towers. You can get ready there. And we can have some fun beforehand ;)

Shit. No way would Dante be up for any fun with Brandt. I had to think of a way out of this.

Horny cunt didn't give me a chance. *Claude? Not changing your mind? If so, I will call the agency for a replacement.*

Course not. Looking forward to it. I'll meet you tomorrow a.m.? What the fuck else could I say?

;) Great. Sending directions to the house. Wait until you see this place. You need transportation?

No, I'll drive myself. See you soon ;) Can't wait to get back on that big dick of yours!

Jet came back into the room, soaking wet and wearing nothing but a grin. Their smile fell away when they saw me. "What?"

I raked my sweaty hair back. "Bloke what invited me to the party's insisting I be there for breakfast. Me and Dante. Couldn't figure a way out of it without him calling in for another boy and ruining the whole thing, so I agreed. Dante's going to shit his knickers. He'll kill me if I put him in that situation."

Jet pursed their lips. "Dunno. I think he'd suck a dick if it meant saving his sister."

That thought… Dante on his knees… it was wrong. "Well, I don't want him to, all right? Would you put Emrys in that situation?"

Jet held up their hands in surrender. "All right, all right. So tell the guy Dante is running late and he'll be along later. He might be disappointed at first, but as soon as you get down to it, he'll be fine. I'll be there, and I can make sure he can't call the agency, or anyone else."

I nodded, feeling better. "Yeah, it's not exactly hopeless. Don't suppose you can help me get hold of a couple of tuxes?"

They turned and bent at the waist to rummage through their discarded clothes, giving me a good view of the Nikola Tesla tattoo in its ornate frame that covered the left side of their upper back, *Electric Jesus* written in swirly script beneath. They came up with one of their many cell phones. "If you're willing to pay, you get hold of anything you want. And the National Policy Institute's footing the bill, so no need to be frugal. I'd go D&G, personally." The tossed me the phone, where some suits were displayed on the screen. "Pick something out and I'll go get it. I have an errand I need to run before we head up to the Poconos anyway."

THE SUN was just coming up as we left Philadelphia, heading north on I-476. Emrys drove and Jet rode shotgun, while me and Dante sat in the back seat. No one was talking much, and I'm sure we all had our own reasons for that. Jet had expressed being nervous around so many powerful mages, and though I sensed there was more to it than that, I didn't press. Truth be told, I just wanted to get this over with. I wasn't overly fond of posh mages either, but mostly I wanted Dante to get out from under the stress he'd been subjected to constantly for almost a week. I wanted him to hug his sister… smile.

Fuck me, I just wanted him to be all right.

And to that end, I'd do my part. It hadn't escaped me that with Blossom gone, nothing compelled me to help. Nothing to stop me walking away. Well, not nothing. Something was keeping me here, something that wasn't hunger or even the desire for a shag—a barbed hook lodged in my sternum that ached when I pulled against it. It was something probably best looked at later, though I couldn't help but wonder what I would do, whose company I would keep, if my baser needs no longer drove me.

It took a little under three hours to reach the Rodeway Inn about five miles from Gardegris. There, we dropped Emrys and Dante off, and me and Jet continued on to the castle—and I don't use that term lightly.

It was a French-style chateau made from local fieldstone and trimmed in ivory scrollwork and Wedgwood blue shutters. The whole thing was the size of a city block—maybe bigger. Four round towers stood at the corners—each one of them as wide around as a decent-sized house—topped with steep, pointed slate roofs, all of them adorned with little bay windows. A huge balcony edged with a stone railing stretched the length of the front, where it overlooked an enormous tiered fountain with a life-sized sphinx crouched on top. Even sitting in the car in front of the entrance, I could see outbuildings and gazebos dotting the massive European-style gardens on either side.

I half expected to hear a strain of harpsichord music on the breeze and maybe tumble across some powdered-white birds in tall wigs. Truth be told, it didn't feel that long ago that I'd walked among—and bedded—people dusted with ceruse and draped in brocade. Had some good times back then and wouldn't have wept to be back in a time with no bleeding faeries and only guns that barely worked at ten paces. Instead, I spotted some blokes in black trousers and white shirts milling about under the portico. Valets. I was surprised when Jet pulled up and parked. I'd expected to be dropped off, but it seemed Jet planned to stay. They took a large military-style black bag from the back seat and shouldered it as if the contents were especially valuable and fragile. Electronics, probably. I didn't get a chance to ask before we were directed inside and told to check in with the concierge.

I gave the cute girl behind the desk a bullshit story and dropped Brandt's name. After a quick phone call—presumably to his room—she gave me the location on the third floor and told us to go on ahead.

Again, Jet came with me, and as we climbed the curved stair that would take us to the balcony overlooking the massive entryway with its half a dozen fireplaces, white marble floors, stags' heads dotting the walls, and a crystal chandelier the size of a swimming pool, I whispered over my shoulder, "Not planning to stand in for Dante, are you?"

Jet snorted delicately. "No. I just needed a way in. I have some work to do."

I dragged my palm along the cool carved stone railing as we made our way toward a library with powder-blue velvet furniture and pale wooden shelves reaching the ceiling. "Yeah? What sort of work?"

Jet shrugged. "I just need to set some things up for later. You know, with the phones and computers. Even if we don't end up needing it tonight, I'm sure I can collect credit card numbers, contact info, shit like that. And spy. I'm going to sneak around a bit, see if I can hide some surveillance equipment. Gotta keep up with these assholes if we're going to have a chance of stopping them. I need to know what they're planning."

I nodded. As much as all that made sense, I didn't like it—and I didn't know why. "Don't they have tech-mages of their own to detect that shite?"

"Sure, but they don't have me." Jet winked a glitter-encrusted eye and stood on tiptoe to kiss me on the cheek. "Keep your head down tonight." Jet's eyes were serious now, maybe even scared. "Get the little girl and then get the hell away from here. Don't wait. Not for anything."

"That's got me worried, love. Something I should know?"

Jet shook their head. "Only that these people are filth. They're cruel and arrogant and selfish, and they place no value on anybody but themselves. They should be wiped out. It would be better than they deserve. And I like you. I like Dante too. I don't want anything to happen to you, but—I just want you to get away from here as soon as you can."

Jet's desires were zinging and bouncing all over the place like a sparkly rubber ball from a vending machine, ricocheting off the silk-papered walls and leaded-glass windows faster than I could close my hand around. Righteous anger, kind of like Dante's, with the same scent of gunpowder and plastic; a longing for freedom that tasted like ozone as it whisked past my lips; something I could only call a love of chaos, and it was sweaty flesh under vinyl, overheated electronics, stale smoke, old booze, flashes of color like a dozen storms overlapping, trance music, bursts of fat neon kanji, Molly, paint splattered on cement blocks— random, but not. There was a pattern to it all if you looked closely, an elegant equation written in eyeliner and twisted wires and the angles of interlocked limbs. Perhaps Jet's greatest desire was staring at it until the mechanisms humming beneath the surface took shape—

And then it was gone, replaced by an overwhelming desire for me to be all right, for us to see each other again. Bloody hell. I curled a hand around Jet's smooth cheek and kissed their forehead. I wanted to see them again too, and not for feeding. It was just something I wanted. And as we stood there in a shaft of silvery light from the ten-foot window, ensconced in the scents of leather and old pages, I knew I had changed. It was fucking terrifying.

Suddenly I wanted to go shag Brandt rotten so I didn't have to examine this too closely. "I'd better get on."

"Dante will be taking a cab here this evening. Me and Emrys will be… around."

"All right. I'll see you soon, then."

"Right." Jet soon disappeared amongst the stacks of books, and when I could no longer hear their boots squeaking against the polished wood floor, I turned to continue on to Brandt's room, wishing I had said more, but not knowing what.

EMRYS SAID I looked good in the suit Jet had delivered, but I felt like a tool. He also said the hotel where I was getting ready was a rattrap, but compared to our apartment, it was the lap of luxury—clean sheets, hot water, TV, and a heater that worked. So I guessed we weren't going to see eye to eye on everything. But we had a lot in common, more than most, I guess.

"Stop tugging at it." Emrys brushed my hand away from the cummerbund.

I scowled into the chipped bathroom mirror. "What the hell is the point of this stupid thing anyway?"

He shrugged. "Tradition, I suppose. Just something that's expected."

"Yeah, I'm not so great with doing what's expected."

When Emrys looked over, I couldn't quite read his expression. "Yes, no kidding. I suspect that's another way in which we are alike. Tell me how you came by your… skills."

I grunted out a laugh. "You mean shooting shit and beating people's asses?"

When he nodded, I went on. "You saw where I live. You have to be able to handle yourself just to walk down the street. Add to that a tweaker for a mom who sold it when she had to, and school was no Princess cruise either. Shit, by ten or eleven, most of the boys in my classes had joined up."

Emrys arched a thick reddish eyebrow. "Joined up?"

"With one of the gangs."

"But not you," he noted.

I ran some water on my hand and tried to squash down a point of hair that kept sticking up. "It would have gone easier on me if I had. It puts people at your back, and nobody fucks with you. But…. It's hard to explain. I didn't want to owe anybody. I didn't want anybody saying I got what I had 'cause of them. And I just didn't want to be controlled." I shook my head and watched a glob of shaving cream slip toward the drain in the sink. "Wasn't a bargain I wanted to make."

Emrys surprised me by saying, "Smart. It's quite similar with the guilds. I know my life would be easier, not to mention safer, if I became a member. And some of them, like ESM, aren't actually terrible. But there's a sacrifice of individuality there that for some isn't a bad thing. Perhaps it's even positive, being a part of something. But I don't want to be a part of anything. I've tried to explain it to Jet, who doesn't understand why I won't put the pin on my lapel and be ESM in name only. They say ESM won't restrict my freedom, that they'll only ask for some work now and then, that my life won't be much different. But that's not really the point. I can't make Jet understand, but I'm betting you do."

"Yeah."

We spent the rest of the time it took me to get ready in silence. Then we went back into the main room to wait for the Uber that Emrys ordered. I eyed my gun lying on the stand between the beds. I knew without asking that I couldn't carry it, but somebody might as well.

I handed it to Emrys. "Know how to use a gun?"

"Midwestern farmer's boy, remember?" he said as he put it into his coat pocket.

"There's some extra ammo in my jacket." I jutted my chin toward the leather coat hanging from the doorknob. "Can't hurt."

As much as I wanted him to tell me it wouldn't be needed, I sure as hell didn't expect him to. And I wasn't wrong.

CHAPTER TWENTY-SEVEN

AFTER STOPPING at my home for weapons and supplies, we drove to the Poconos. I left the vehicle hidden on what was likely an old logging road and changed into military-issue cold-weather gear designed to camouflage me in the snowy woods, including a thermal hood that covered everything but my eyes, and, of course, a Kevlar vest. Then I armed myself and prepared for the trek of several miles. It would exacerbate the pain already shooting up my leg, but it was necessary. I needed every advantage I could get; I couldn't relinquish the element of surprise over some discomfort.

Finding a defensible position from which to observe Gardegris Towers presented its own challenge, as the terrain was flat for probably a mile in every direction. I finally decided to position myself in a fairly thick copse of hemlock trees maybe nine hundred yards from the front entrance.

I spread out a piece of white plastic to keep me dry, watched all the while by my unsettling new companion, the cat still perched on his shoulder. It hadn't taken me long to discern his assistance was far from guaranteed. Trying to ignore him, I located some thick branches and piled them up as a prop for the two sniper rifles I'd selected: Dakota T-76 Longbows that fired .338 Lapua Magnum rounds. They'd allow me to thin the enemy's ranks considerably—but only if I stayed hidden. I spread a second tarp and began covering it with evergreen fronds, snow, dirt, and clumps of frozen leaves.

"What are you doing?" Blossom asked, standing with his arms crossed, apparently uncaring if he was seen. I was afraid to reprimand him.

"I've explained. People are coming here to hurt me, a lot of them and with a lot of weapons. I need to get entrenched so I can kill as many as possible before I'm discovered."

"It's odd." He took a few steps toward me, his pointed-toed boots not breaking the icy crust over the snow. "Mortal thugs, who have nothing whatsoever to do with mages, who probably aren't even aware of the existence of mages, coming to a gathering of so many mages."

"Mages?" I asked. "No, they're coming here because they believe I'm using this place to stockpile weapons."

"It hardly changes the fact that there's an intense amount of magical energy building here. I sense dozens of magic users. So I have to wonder: Why the convergence? Can it possibly be coincidence? A question I asked myself recently, I might add. What could bring all of this together, anticipate all the variables?"

His speech—his very presence—gave me a headache, and not figuratively. A dull pain pulsed behind my eyes, and it worsened the longer I looked directly at him. His appearance felt like a filament, an image projected over something else without quite concealing it. When I caught a glimpse of him from the corner of my eye, I saw... something else. "What did you... conclude?"

"Conclude? Oh. Nothing. My incubus thought it was the girl. The girl." He shook his head, pale hair swinging back and forth, releasing a smell like crushed leaves, like summer. Out of nowhere, he bounced on his toes and chuckled. "Well, this proves me right! It wasn't the girl after all; it couldn't have been. If the force that brought those pieces together is the same as the one collecting these pieces—and one must assume it is, as the likelihood of two such forces is even more ludicrous—then clearly the girl is not responsible! Because the girl is not here! Ha-ha!" He twirled around on the ball of one foot, the cat mewling and holding on for dear life.

The only chance I had of making it out of this mess alive was to focus on what I could control and understand. Agonizing over the implications of the rest would only distract me. I turned back to my rifles and used a scope to get a better idea of the lay of the land.

Blossom watched me for maybe ten more minutes before releasing a theatrical sigh. "Well, if I stay here, I shall perish of boredom. And it is not as though Jet Zama will approach such an obvious danger."

That comment got under my skin even though I shouldn't have let it. "Obvious? This person you're looking for will never know I'm here."

"Hmph. You either underestimate them or overestimate yourself. But it doesn't matter to me. Come, Charlene. We shall execute our own reconnaissance. The trees will have seen much. They have little else to do as they doze through the dark part of the year."

When I turned from my scope to say something to him—I don't know what—he was already gone, and with no trail left to indicate his passing.

I tried to be glad of his absence, but I couldn't quite get his words out of my mind. I'd convinced him to accompany me in hopes of procuring his aid, but I'd soon realized he was too fickle to rely on. Yet he firmly believed this person, Jet Zama, could be nearby. Dante had been with Jet Zama. Could Dante be here? For what possible reason?

I pulled out the phone Moirin had given me, the one her mysterious technologically adept friend had rigged up to track the device planted in Dante's gun. Swiping my fingers over the screen, I slowly magnified the map, homing in on the blinking red teardrop.

It was only a few miles from my location.

Dante was here, but why? My first thought was deceit. Had he come with the skinheads who'd hijacked my shipment? Why? Maybe they did have his sister and were using her against him. Or maybe he'd come ahead of Moirin to help me. If he needed power, why had he split from Blossom?

Would I have to kill him? The possibilities troubled me to the point I almost became impatient for the battle to begin, even with the knowledge that I might never leave this little patch of woods.

By evening, dozens of people in formalwear had arrived for some sort of event. Their cars and clothing told me they were wealthy, but they seemed normal enough. Another check of my map showed Dante was here—on the property. By his speed, he was likely on foot and moving through the trees, about half a mile from my position. My palms grew clammy inside my gloves. He could know I was here. He could be trying to take *me* by surprise, put a bullet in the back of my head before I even saw him.

It would be the last thing he ever attempted. My rifles wouldn't be ideal for a quick, close-range kill, but I'd anticipated that possibility, and I patted the Sig Sauer P200 Hunter in its holster at my hip. Dante was incredibly skilled, a prodigy, but that couldn't compete with my years of experience. If one of us would be left to rot on this ostentatious property, I would make sure it wasn't me.

Chapter Twenty-Eight

Emrys had asked our driver to drop him off at the end of the mansion's long driveway, and he'd quickly disappeared into the trees on the outskirts of the property. As soon as I got to the entrance and found Inky waiting with his client or whatever-the-fuck, I wished I could've done the same.

This guy Brandt was exactly the kind of prick I hated most. An entitled bastard who thought having some money made him special. Better than me. He probably never worked a day for it either. Probably fucked people over—drove people out of their homes or jacked up the prices of their prescriptions. The way he was smiling at me, looking me up and down, made me want to yank his guts out with my bare hands. I was nobody's goddamn merchandise.

When Inky leaned down to kiss my cheek, he whispered, "Calm down, mate. You're scowling. Going to give yourself away."

I forced a slow breath out between my clenched teeth. Right. Play along. I could do this. I had to. For Ros. And I did. I smiled and put my hand on the douchebag's arm when he held it out to me. At least I had the satisfaction of seeing Inky, with his bigass horns and long silver-white hair, as he really was and knowing this tool couldn't.

When we got inside, I noticed something else about the way I could see now. In the huge main room, probably about a hundred people milled around—all guys in tuxes and women in shiny dresses. Most of them looked the way I would expect, but some of them had this weird glow—an outline of colored light mostly around the head and shoulders, sometimes over the face, almost like a veil. For most of them it was faint and I had to concentrate to notice it at all. But for a few, it was bright enough that I squinted. I don't know how I knew, but I just knew that colored light meant the person was a mage. Weird. I hadn't seen anything like it with Emrys or Jet.

Not all of the guests were human either. There was a tall woman with grayish green skin and limbs that seemed to have three joints too many sort of… gliding around, dragging limp, zigzaggy legs behind her, twisted arms up by her chest. What looked like moldy, oily Saran wrap covered her, and now and then a black tongue would dart out and kind of… taste that colored light. I didn't know what it was, but I was near pissing myself watching.

Then there was a—I don't know if it was male or female; it had pretty feminine facial features but was lanky like a guy—creature with mottled metallic skin and some kind of feathers for hair. The lady it followed wore a gold-and-black sequin dress in a similar pattern—kind of like couples wearing matching T-shirts. But I didn't want to think about that too much, so I turned my attention back to Inky and this Brandt asshole, who'd moved next to a table of little appetizers next to the wall.

"It's still early," Brandt was saying. "Most of the important guests haven't arrived yet. In a few hours, they'll open up all these conference rooms"—he waved his hand to indicate the big sets of double doors around us—"and there will be speeches on various topics. After that, dinner will be served in the hall at the back of the chateau, and then the real fun begins."

"Wow." Inky's eyes were crazy wide as he fawned over this dick. "That's really something. All of this is so incredible. Isn't it, Dan?"

It wasn't until he elbowed me in the ribs that I realized he meant me. "Right." I pictured kicking Brandt in the nuts as hard as I could and then kneeing him in his smug face when he doubled over, blood and teeth falling on the floor, which allowed me to flash a pretty sincere smile his way.

This sucked. I thought I'd be able to treat this like any other job—watch and listen for anything out of the ordinary, get what I needed, get out. But how the hell could I do that when there was no ordinary? I could barely keep track of which way was up.

But an even bigger part knew that if I failed, no one else would come for Ros or care what happened to her.

Fuck that.

I got through the next hour or so by imagining shooting the people I'd seen in the basement of that mage bar. I bet plenty of these assholes did the same or worse to entertain themselves in their spare time. Every time Brandt spoke to me, I pictured myself walking up behind one of them and pressing the barrel of my gun to the back of their head. I thought about the sound it would make, what the blood and brains that spewed out would look like in the candlelight. A .45 leaves an impressive exit wound. I predicted how the bodies might fall—forward, off to the side, sort of slumped over on themselves, legs twisted underneath. I guess it was enough to keep me looking reasonably happy, because Brandt kept winking at me and Inky didn't jab me in the ribs again.

More people were arriving, and though I knew jack shit about tuxedos and ball gowns, even I could tell the ones the newer people wore were better, more expensive. It was in the fit, the way the light hit the material. It was in the way the people carried themselves: confident, carefree, looking at everyone else like we all smelled a little like shit but they were generous enough to allow us in their presence and even smile now and then. These people were used to getting their way in every situation, used to having their asses kissed.

Just the kind of pretentious fucks I hated.

The crowd split into two groups to watch the new arrivals like they were a parade. We were toward the back, farthest from the mansion's front door, and in the middle of the group, which meant I couldn't see very well.

I was afraid I would miss my sister being brought in.

I shouldn't have been.

"Bloody cunting impossible," I whispered before I caught myself.

It was like looking into the sun. My eyes watered, blurring the party into a mosaic of metallic hues, stinging my retinas. I grabbed hold of Dante's shoulder so I wouldn't lose him. He was squinting and looking away while Brandt—and everyone else, from what I could tell with my limited perception—looked on, oblivious. Hard to believe not one mage in here possessed true sight, but there we were, cringing back from the gold ball of energy moving up the aisle.

No ebb and flow of power anymore, then. She'd come into her own, and come into it like a supernova.

In the center, as if floating, was a little girl in a pale yellow dress, chestnut ringlets held back by a dainty gem-dotted band.

I hurried to get around Dante and shield him from Ros's eyes because I didn't know if she'd cry out if she saw him. She did that and we'd be fucked. No, I had to keep her from seeing him until we could get her on her own. Slowly I guided him toward the back of the throng as Ros's escort—an older black man so gorgeous he made my nipples tingle, wearing a suit that like as not cost as much as everybody else's combined—took her hand and led her toward one of the tables where artful little desserts were arranged on three-tiered silver stands. He smiled gently, and as they passed, I noted his desires were kind: shortbread dipped in milk tea, corgis snuffling in front of a fire, the smell of the city after a summer rain. And he wanted to make Ros happy, to sit her on his lap and read from *The Wind in the Willows*, putting on different funny voices for each character.

It wasn't what I had expected.

The light… well, it became bearable. I can't rightly say it dimmed, but maybe I got used to it. I looked over my shoulder and caught Dante's gaze. Then I canted my head toward the back of the room. We needed to talk, and I didn't trust in Dante's ability to go along with whatever story I fed Brandt. Better to just sneak off for a bit.

Brandt had plenty of shiny things to distract him, and we made our way to a long hall that must've led to a food prep area, judging by the staff coming and going with carts and trays.

I backed Dante against the wall and pinned him there with my larger body, my hands at his hips. He stiffened, and I leaned in and whispered into his ear. "Don't get the wrong idea, mate. We need to talk, and I don't want to be overheard—or disturbed."

Some of the tension dropped from his shoulders and spine. "Yeah. What's the plan? Do you have one?"

"I don't know if you can call it a plan. In case you haven't figured it out yet, love, none of this is my forte. Best I can come up with is you wait here, and I'll go out there and find some way to lure your sister to this hall. There's a kitchen at the end of it, and that likely means a door to the outside—servants' entrance, for deliveries and shite. It's simplistic, but it's all I've got."

"No, simple is good," Dante breathed against my face. "Less that can go wrong. But why you instead of me? Ros has seen you before too. She could give you away."

I moved my hand up to give his shoulder what I hoped was a reassuring pat. It was hard to maneuver around a bloke whose desires read as machine-gun fire and wet ash. "I just… I just think my chances might be better. More experience handling these pompous twats is all."

He let out a resigned breath. "Right. And I'm no good at being what people want. I only know how to be me."

I pulled back so I could see his face. "You've mastered the harder of the two, mate. Listen, I know this is hard for you, trusting people. But I'll do this, Dante. I've got your back."

For what felt like forever, he stared up at me, eyes glistening and lips pressed thin. Finally he whispered, "I know."

With those two words, he broke something loose inside me, deep in my guts, and I wanted to kiss him so fucking bad—even though he didn't desire me and I would get no benefit. But I wanted it just the same, and I didn't want to stop wanting. Still, I stepped back from him and smoothed my hands down my jacket. "It'll like as not take me a bit, if you want to try to scope out our escape route."

He nodded once. "Good idea."

"Yeah." I adjusted my bow tie even though it didn't matter how I really looked. People would see the projection of Brandt's desires, and they'd see even that through the colored lens of their own. I didn't need to prepare.

But in my long life, I'd never needed to accomplish a goal, put myself out, or take any kind of a risk. I was lazy, I indulged, and I abandoned things when they stopped being fun or fruitful. I'd never imagined being guided by anything but my own whims or the pleasure of my partners. Now, goddammit, I'd made a promise, and I intended to keep it even if it meant bringing this whole place down.

Chapter Twenty-Nine

There.

Headlights coming around the bend in the road. The sounds of engines. Dozens of vehicles. That was Moirin and my army. Somehow, miraculously, they'd made it here ahead of the skinheads who had abducted my people and stolen my product. That gave us the advantage. I needed to speak with Moirin as soon as possible, tell her where I wanted everyone positioned. As I dug for the burner phone, I caught sight of the red dot connected to the tracking device on Dante's gun.

According to the red teardrop, he was right behind me, less than twenty feet away.

Rapa tu mai!

I closed my hand around the Sig Sauer, ready to use it. He might ruin everything. In dealing with him, I might lose the only advantage that would allow me or any of my people to leave this place alive.

My only chance was to dispose of him as quickly as possible.

I held the pistol and waited for the slightest shift in the shadows behind me, the faintest crunch of snow or leaves, all the while keeping one eye on the red teardrop that inched slowly closer.

There.

After hours of small talk and schmoozing, kissing arses, I managed to find Ros alone, picking at a tray of charcuterie not far from the hall where Dante waited. I wound my way through the crowd until I stood a few feet behind her.

She put her little hands with their little french-manicured nails flat on the table's white cloth and spoke without looking back at me. "I remember you. I remember your horns. You brought your cat Charlene to my house."

Had to admit, that caught me off guard for a moment, but I hurried to snap myself out of it. "That's right, love. I'm a friend of your brother.

He's been very worried about you. Been looking everywhere trying to find you."

"Is he here? Dante?"

"Yeah, he's round the corner, waiting for me to take you to him."

"What if you're lying?"

It wasn't what I'd expected her to say, that was for damn sure. I didn't quite know how to respond. For reasons that are probably obvious, my powers don't really work on kids, and the way she spoke, monotone and flat, without giving me the benefit of seeing her face— Well, I didn't know what she could be thinking. All I could think to say was "I'm not."

"Mr. Mengiste, the man I was with, is very rich and very smart. He lives in London, but he said he met my mother in New York City. That she never told him she was pregnant, and when he found out, he looked everywhere to find me. He wants me to come live with him, and he says I'll be happy there."

Bugger me, now that she mentioned it, I could see the resemblance, and it explained what I'd felt coming off the guy. "And is that what you want? To live with him in London?"

"I-I don't know. He's a nice man. He said he only wants me to have a better life. I don't like it when Mom is always sick, throwing up and sleeping all the time. And sometimes she gets mad for no reason and yells at me. Dante can't always be there. He has to go to work. But… but I love Dante." Her little hand shook as she brushed it over the iridescent fabric of her dress. "I love Dante, but being with my… my dad, I feel like a queen from a story." She finally turned to look up at me, and her wide brown eyes were glistening with tears. "Is it selfish to like the books and the dresses, the big bathtub with flowers in the water?"

I couldn't answer with my heart jammed up in my throat.

Turned out, I never got the chance.

First thing I noticed was the lights outside the ballroom windows, and then the shift in people's moods—relaxed and happy to curious, apprehensive.

And then fucking scared when bullets hit those big windows and glass shot into the room, raining over everyone. People screamed. They backed away.

One of the bullets must've hit a wall sconce, because it flickered, followed by a shower of sparks and a burnt plastic smell. By then I could feel magic, feel the mages letting it build. It danced over my skin, and my hair stood on end. The noise from the gunshots echoed in my skull, and while I could see people's mouths moving, see them pointing, giving and following orders, their voices were sludgy and slow, like a song played on melted vinyl.

Another round of gunfire. People dropped to their knees and protected their heads with their arms. Ros was crying, though not hysterically; her eyes were wet and swollen, and her lips trembled, but she'd either learned or inherited some of her brother's pragmatism. I scooped her small body up and hugged her to my chest, turning my back to the front of the chateau to put myself between her and whatever hell was breaking loose outside.

Just in time too.

The staccato patter of bullets sounded again, and then the chandelier came down. Shards of crystal flew everywhere, embedding in flesh as well as the old-fashioned horsehair plaster walls. A quick glance over my shoulder told me at least half a dozen people had been underneath it, and their blood pooled around the debris. Others were down too, and everywhere I looked, I saw more blood. Smelled and tasted the metallic tang. Heard cries and sobs.

Hunching my shoulders over Ros's head, I sprinted down the corridor leading to the kitchen and ran for the servants' entrance like I'd never run before.

I had to get her the hell out of here, get her as far from this place as I could.

If I could make it into the woods, we might not be seen by whatever fucking army seemed intent on bringing this whole place down. If we stayed to the trees, we might be able to put a mile or two between us and this….

Just then, that was all I cared about.

THERE, CHARLENE said. *I smell them.*

Sure enough, I detected movement in the shadows beneath some elderberry stalks, a streak of darkness moving past a big bay window. Jet was bent almost in half, shooting from place to place along the building's exterior as if with a specific destination in mind.

Beams of light from dozens of conveyances cut through the brittle darkness, reflecting off the metallic strand Jet stretched from one block of a malleable white substance to the next, which they carefully secured where one of the central towers abutted the front of the building. For a few moments I watched them work with great intent and concentration, though I sensed no magic being performed. I stretched and curled my fingers, eager to sink them into Jet's flesh and hear their screams, but I waited until the moment would be perfect. I didn't want to waste it.

The thunderous cacophony of a large machine shook the ground upon which I stood, and I heard Jet draw in a sharp breath. Still crouched and taking advantage of the shadows cast by the rosebushes, they turned in the direction of the sound. When Jet's eyes fell on me and Charlene, they seemed compelled to stand.

"No!" Jet's fists shook around the devices and spool of wire they held. "What are you doing here? You can't be here!"

I smiled until I could feel the night air against my gums at Jet's agitation. My retribution would be a thing of beauty. But just as I lifted my hand to begin, a series of rapid pops shattered the pregnant quiet. The window behind Jet crumbled, raining glass into the building. Eyes wide, Jet reached up to wipe the blood from their cheek with the back of their hand. Screams came from inside. From the lawn at the front of the chateau, shouting and more explosions erupted. I was irritated by this distraction to the vengeance I had so anticipated, but before I could think of how to vent my frustration, projectiles hit the wall close to where I stood, producing small clouds of powdered stone. Jet got to their feet and launched themself at me. My back hit the ground hard, frozen soil and thorny fronds digging into my skin. Charlene had leapt from my shoulder and now stood a little way off, growling low in her throat.

I closed my hand around the back of Jet's neck, ready to throw them aside and continue as I had planned. But then they spoke, lips moving against the edge of my ear.

"I know you'd like to kill me, and I also know you won't believe me if I tell you I only wanted to protect you, that you really have no idea what these people will do if they get ahold of you. But it doesn't matter. I have something I know you can't resist in motion here."

"Get off me." I pushed Jet to the side before standing, and then I offered them a hand. I suppose I was following an instinct that rarely led me astray, or that told me I was about to witness something… singular. As Jet got to their feet, I scooped Charlene up and held her inside my elbow. She began to purr, and I waved my fingers to shield Jet and myself from what was becoming quite the gathering on the front lawn. Jet watched me with the eyes of a cornered animal, and as I watched them back, pieces slotted into place, a picture slowly forming. "You did this. You somehow caused all of these forces to converge here. It wasn't an act of fate."

Their smile was self-satisfied, as well it might be. "No fate, and not even very much magic. When Dante handed me that computer he took from the Nazis, it was a cakewalk to infiltrate all of their systems. These guys are assholes, sure, but they're only a small part of a much larger picture. They're working for Sekhet-Aaru, the mage guild gathered here tonight. Over the last few years, me and the rest of ESM, along with some unaffiliated hackers and anarchists, have discovered a lot of Sekhet-Aaru's plans. It would take a while to explain, and I sincerely doubt you care, so I'll just say they want to bring this world to the brink of annihilation, and they're closer than we had any idea. Inciting racial violence is a big part of their end game.

"When Inky and Dante learned about this gathering, I knew I couldn't pass up the opportunity." Jet gestured to the crystalline brick affixed to the building. "There's this hot Irish lady I do tech work for sometimes, and she has some friends who are geniuses with explosives. She needed a pretty complex bit of tracking done recently, so I agreed to it, in exchange for enough C-4 to turn this place into a crater."

I tapped my fingertips together and grinned. Was it any wonder? Jet had manipulated the situation like a master, and not even I had had any idea. My admiration was not even grudging, and I seriously considered forgetting the unfortunate situation in that dank little room.

"Why lure these lumbering oafs?" I pointed to the bald men spilling out of the corrugated metal rectangle.

Jet winked. "They're not the only ones I lured. Are we safe?"

"As a babe in its mother's arms," I said.

Jet picked up the spool of wire and the devices they'd held when they'd tackled me to the ground, then kissed Charlene between the ears, hooked their arm through mine, and led me toward the fountain at the front of the house. "Then let's watch the show."

Chapter Thirty

There.

There was the road that would take me away from here. I didn't belong here—I was a thug from North Philly, and I didn't have it in me to be anything else. But my sister wasn't. She fit in with these people. She had been smiling, swaying to the music, enjoying the fancy food. And she had looked so fucking pretty in the kind of dress I'd never be able to give her. What right did I have to take her away from all of that? And where would I even take her?

As I jogged around the mansion, heading for the large fountain out front, a shitload of headlights suddenly blinded me. All kinds of cars and trucks and vans were gunning it up the driveway and kicking up gravel as they hit the brakes.

What the fuck?

Survival instinct kicked in, and I pressed my back against the building where I wouldn't be seen but could still see what was happening out front.

The vehicles lined up to the left and right of the fountain, six on one side, eight on the other. Then people started getting out, armed like they were headed into a war zone, assault rifles gripped tight, faces covered by masks and bodies by bulletproof vests. They started taking up positions, some of them using the vehicles for cover while others fanned out, hiding among the bunches of trees or disappearing into the shadows beyond the lights of the house. My heart was hammering, and sweat ran into my eyes even though it was fucking freezing out here. But all I could do for now was watch.

I heard a familiar female voice shouting orders in a language I sort of recognized but didn't understand. It was Moirin, all in black, crouched in the back of one of those long contractor-style vans, telling her people what to do as she handed out guns, grenades, and even what looked like sticks of dynamite. Opposite her, two black men I didn't know were laying spike strips across the driveway.

What the hell could these people be doing here? At this weirdass mage party? And why?

I didn't have much time to think about it before a tractor trailer hauling a flatbed with a shipping container strapped to it came barreling up the road like a bat out of hell. It slammed to a stop and jackknifed, the bed sliding into place parallel to the building. As soon as it did, Nazis started pouring out of the container, and they hit the ground shooting. I heard glass break, and all I could do was hit the dirt.

The only thing on my mind was my sister and getting her out of here. I used my elbows to pull myself along as the WLF sprayed the house and the line of vehicles in front of it with bullets, and Moirin and the others who had apparently come here expecting them returned fire.

As soon as I felt like I wouldn't make myself an easy target, I stood and ran for the back entrance.

THE CRUNCH of snow told me Dante was about to make his move, and none too soon. Moirin and the others were losing ground fast due to the sheer numbers the WLF had gathered. I drew my pistol, rolled to my back, and fired three shots into the silhouette looming over me from a distance of less than ten feet.

A strange sensation overtook me, one I could only explain as a feeling of occupying several different realities—complete with all their variables—at once. When it passed, leaving me wondering if I'd somehow stumbled into a dream, the corpse I expected wasn't lying in front of me. Instead, a young man who wasn't Dante but rather one of the people who'd been with him at the hotel took a step toward me and pressed the barrel of his own gun to my forehead.

"Who are you?" His voice was gentle but remarkably clear considering the chaos a few hundred yards away. "What are you doing here?"

I couldn't see any sense in lying, and I knew I had to talk fast. "You're a friend of Dante's. He works for me. Perhaps he's told you about it. I am an arms dealer, and yesterday, these neo-Nazis hijacked one of my shipments and kidnapped some of my associates. They contacted me. They believe this place is some sort of a bunker, a warehouse where I store my merchandise. I can't imagine what led them to believe it—"

He shook his head. "Jet."

"Excuse me?"

"Nothing." He lowered his weapon. "I don't think you have any idea what you've stepped in here. You should leave this place."

I turned away from him in time to see a big man—one of Moirin's or part of the Polish gang I sold to—take a bullet to the back of the head, blood and brains pouring down his chest from what had once been his face. Again, I positioned myself behind the Longbows and waited. The Nazis were well entrenched behind the truck and shipping container, but as soon as one of them showed his face, I would only need a second—

"You're the one who should get out of here," I said to the young man without taking my eye away from my scope. "This is going to be a bloodbath."

"I-I have to find my friends," he stammered, the reality of what was happening probably sinking in at last. "Jet and Inky. Dante and his sister. Oh God. The little girl!"

Rosalind was here? Apparently so was Dante—and not just his gun, which this man now carried. It was out of character in the extreme for Dante to surrender his weapon, and his having done so could not bode well. It also meant he had no means of defending himself. What a nightmare. I had only a split second to hope they might find their way to their unusual cat-loving friend before I noticed a trio of men creeping out from behind the truck, brandishing my beautiful handcrafted Puerto Rican weapons and advancing on the spot where some of Devereux's associates had positioned themselves. I had no doubt that if not for me, they might take my allies by surprise. I got the leader's head in my crosshairs and squeezed the trigger. His head disintegrated in a red spray. I moved to the next man.

One. Two, three, and done. No one was near enough to gauge my position, so I would get at least a few more shots in. I needed to make them count.

STANDING BESIDE Jet and watching the mortals hurl molten projectiles at one another was entertaining for a brief few moments, but their attacks had no real originality. No creativity. The explosions and blooms of flame produced by the factions closest to the chateau were impressive, but it would simply be a series of repeated maneuvers until either one side or the other retreated or everyone was dead. I yawned and turned to Jet. "You mentioned the arrival of others?"

They grinned. "It should be any minute now."

True to Jet's prediction, it was not long before another carriage—this one sleek, shining, and bloodred—turned onto the lane encircling the mansion. It stopped behind the large vehicle towing the metal box, and the silence following was so stark and sudden compared to the previous chaos, my hearing grew instantly acute; I could hear soft sobs inside the building as well as the confused whispers from those who cowered, weapons clutched, near where we now stood—on the steps leading to the chateau's front doors.

"Why have they ceased battling?" I asked Jet.

"I don't think it's by choice. More likely a physiological reaction. Muscle atrophy, fatigue resulting from a drop in blood pressure, paralysis—could be one of a hundred things, really."

Now that I knew to look for it, I could taste a ferrous sort of magic on the air, something old and steeped in blood. When I saw the pale man and his striking companion wandering slowly up the lawn, her in her sharp suit and perfectly styled hair, him in his furs, I understood the source.

And I understood what else Jet had put in place when we had first met these two far beneath the city. "But why?"

"Even if I blow this place up, I'd be foolish to think it'd be the end of Sekhet-Aaru. This little side project they've got going with the Nazis isn't only unknown to plenty within their own organization, but a total secret to their allies in the other guilds. I want Wú Cháng to see the kind of people they're working with, the kind of lowlife racist pigs at least a portion of Sekhet-Aaru is. It's gotta at least instill doubt, maybe cause a rift, right?"

"It seems a reasonable strategy."

"I knew you'd see it my way. I… also might've led them to believe that they'd happened upon some emails between high-ranking members of Sekhet-Aaru detailing how they would bring Wú Cháng under their heel, how they didn't deserve a place in Sekhet-Aaru's new world order because most of them are Asian. But I clinched it by going after the one thing Wú Cháng really values: their money. I made some easily traceable—but large—transfers from one of their import businesses to a PAC known to be controlled by Sekhet-Aaru. One with close ties to well-known white supremacists."

"Clever." The way Jet's mind worked fascinated me. I'd never met a mortal quite like them.

"Really, I figured, if nothing else, I could blow up a couple of these creepy bastards too. It would've been a feather in my cap; these jerks are nigh-impossible to kill. I… kind of can't believe they only sent a pair."

"Should I kill them now?" I asked. "While they're not expecting it?"

Jet shook their head. "Let's see what they'll do. I doubt I'll ever get a chance to tap into their organization again, and they'll have updated their security by now. It'd be ideal for them to take word of Sekhet-Aaru's ties to the Nazis back to the rest of their people, and a war between the two guilds, even a cold one, will save me a lot of work. I can concentrate on taking out some of the really awful research they're doing while they kill each other's soldiers. I couldn't have done it without you, by the way." They kissed the apple of my cheek.

"I still have not decided to let you live," I reminded them.

"Well then at least let me bask in what I've done here. This was a lot of effort, a lot of risk."

The man and woman passed us and stopped halfway up the stone staircase.

The man reached into the pocket of his fluffy coat, withdrew a small gold case, and lit a clove-scented cigarette. The smoke curlicued up to mingle with the wavering sulfurous sheet the mortal weapons left hanging about the building and grounds. He breathed in some of the sweet smoke and exhaled theatrically, basking in the imposed attention of everyone else. "Well, well, well," he said, pale lips drawing back to reveal long white teeth. "This is quite some gathering. An interesting collection of… individuals. We have questions. You."

He pointed, and a man in a brown leather jacket and black beanie looked around as if surprised he had been chosen. No one else had regained the ability to move. For a few moments, only the smoke curtaining the estate moved, nudged to and fro by the breeze, supplemented by the puffs of frozen breath supplied by the captive audience. Then the man screamed, and the woman in her sharp suit said, "Those stomach cramps you feel are only the smallest sample of what I can do to you. Now, unless you want me to pull your innards apart and leave you to die slowly as your bleeding intestines leech away your vigor and bloat your body, step forward and answer our questions."

Unsurprisingly, the man came a little shakily to the base of the stairs, his beefy arms still entwined about his torso.

What happened next was much more unexpected: a soft swish, and two projectiles struck the woman, one landing almost perfectly between her eyes and tearing away the back of her skull upon its exit, the other slicing across the side of her neck and drawing a spectacular font of blood. Her ruined head lolled to the side like a flower too heavy for its stalk, and the body dropped amidst a cloud of snow.

My erstwhile chauffeur had chosen a fortuitous target, and I couldn't help a grin. This would certainly affect the situation in unexpected ways.

The man in white screamed "No!" and flung himself over the body of his companion. With their famed anatomical prowess, these mages could likely pry the doomed from death's rigid grasp, but in this case, there was nothing left to save. At the height of my power, I could've chased the essence of life—what mortals call the soul—through the in-between realms, but there was nowhere to return it, not with the vessel so irreparably damaged. And homing it elsewhere…. Well, that was a specialty not even I possessed, and one not without serious disadvantages.

The man seemed to come to the same conclusion, and as the combatants, newly freed from the spell, took up their arms and joined the fray again, he also entered the battle. The first man he reached dropped to his knees and clutched his chest, shortly to expire, judging from the blood frothing from his mouth.

The gunfire resumed, and soon bodies littered the lawn and blood stained the snow. From inside the chateau, mages ran forth, spoiling for a fight, though they did not seem to understand what had happened or who they faced, or even why. They looked silly and lost as they cast their gazes about, crumpled in on themselves in their shimmering garments as the cold ran its brittle nails over their skin.

I had only one concern now. The girl was here, and I had to reach her before she was spirited off somewhere else, forcing me to spend another moon seeking her out.

Besides, much to my regret, I had made a bargain to keep her and Dante safe, and I always fulfilled my oaths.

I secured Charlene inside my coat and touched Jet's elbow. The orchestration of this mildly entertaining spectacle had eased my ire toward them. Killing them now would be like smashing a graceful iridescent vase. "Come."

"Where?" Jet asked.

"Inside. I must find Dante and his sister and see them safely away from here."

Jet shook their head. "Emrys was supposed to be watching from the woods. He's still out here somewhere. I can't leave him behind. Besides—" They glanced over their shoulder at the building. "—I have unfinished business. Don't hang there. Inside, I mean."

"I won't be able to spare the energy to keep you under my protection if we separate."

"I know. I can take care of myself." They pressed the tips of their cold fingers to my cheek and met my eyes. "You need to do the same. I really did lock you in that cellar to keep you away from these people. I know things, and they have plans for your kind. Getting ahold of you would give them a huge advantage, and I can't let that happen." They smiled, but it was forced, artificial. "Besides, I kind of like you. Go."

I hurried to follow their advice. Not that their speech had frightened me. That would be outlandish. Avoiding the mages inside could only expedite my quest. I'd go around the chateau and search for another entrance.

CHAPTER THIRTY-ONE

I STUCK to the shadows as I made my way to the back of the house. Some kind of crazy shit was going on out front. First it got dead quiet and stayed that way for probably five minutes, and then the shooting started back up, worse than before. I didn't know what was happening, and I didn't care. I couldn't. I had to get Ros and get her away from here. People were dying, and the cops would be coming. Even out here in the woods, I was surprised they hadn't shown up already.

I hoped Moirin and everybody else would make it out of this, but I'd have to think about it later. They were grown, and my sister was only a little girl.

The back of the place was like a different world compared to the shit going down out front. Here it was still and quiet, the snow sparkling. I panted out white clouds as I climbed the steps to the kitchen entrance, and just as I reached the door, it flew open. I jumped back, fumbling by my hip for a weapon that wasn't there. Fuck it. I'd use my fists if I had to. I was fighting my way to Ros if it was the last thing I did.

But I recognized the figure that stepped into the orangish light, and relief flooded me. When I saw what Inky had hugged to his chest, I couldn't stop my tears. I couldn't even stop a sob as I pressed my forehead to Ros's and curled my hand around her little face. She was crying too, her fists wrapped around my lapels as she said my name. Her hair smelled the way it always did, and a few things hit me as I buried my face in her springy curls. One, I hadn't expected to get her back. On some level, I'd prepared myself to never see her again, never touch her. That made me a piece of shit. Two, Inky did this. I owed this all to him, and I didn't know quite how to process being able to trust someone to that extent.

But it would have to wait.

"We have to get out of here," I said. "Now."

"Can we get to one of the cars out front?" Inky asked.

"No way. It's a war zone out there. We're on foot." I slid out of the tux jacket and wrapped it around Ros. Then I looked out over the grounds. There were some hedges, gazebos, shit like that, then what looked like an orchard. Beyond it, the woods. As much of a city boy as I'd always been, I wanted to make it into those trees where we would have some cover and a place to hide.

"Here's the plan," I said. "We make for the woods. Then we can try to find the road from there. There's a lot of open space between here and there, though, and we're going to stick out like a sore thumb against the snow. We skirt the edges as much as we can, and we move fast."

Inky nodded, looking more serious than I'd ever seen him. "Let's go."

To the left stood some tall bushes, and we stuck close to them, running as fast as we could in dress shoes, bent almost in half to keep low. It was slippery as hell, and I hated having my back to all those guns. Keeping Inky in front of me, I pressed for that orchard, and when we got to the rows of what looked like apple trees, I took Ros from him, and we spent a few minutes catching our breath. So far it didn't seem like anyone had tailed us, but a blind idiot could follow our tracks, and I didn't want to take any chances.

We kept running, and my luck ran out and I fell once, tearing my pants and ripping up my leg. But I kept Ros from getting hurt, and with the adrenaline, it just felt kind of warm and throbby. I was still moving, which meant nothing was broken, and the woods were getting closer. Damn orchards had to stretch for two miles, and at the end was a steep slope I hadn't seen from the house. I had to swing Ros around piggyback so I could free my hands to grab for rocks and roots to help me make it up. I didn't notice until I got to the top that I'd fucked up my knees even more than I had the first time and there was blood running down both my legs.

Inky was panting, holding his ribs. "Fuck me, we made it. Oh shite. Sorry."

I waved him off. Ros had heard worse. "Come on." Once we made it a few dozen feet in and some evergreens provided shelter and shadow, I felt safe to lean against a trunk.

We'd made it. "Are you okay, baby?" I asked Ros. "You didn't get hurt when I fell?"

"I'm okay. Just cold. I want to go home."

"Me too," I said, holding her close. Almost the second I felt safe, the pain in my beat-up legs started to make itself known, and I wasn't sure I could keep walking. I actually wanted to lie down for a while, even here in the snow. But that wasn't an option.

Inky put a hand on my shoulder. "You all right, mate?"

I wasn't, but saying so might scare Ros. "We need to find a way out of here. Do you have a phone?"

He shook his head. "Lost it fighting my way out of there. Our best bet is to get to the road. If we're lucky, someone will pick us up. If we're not, we'll have to make our way back to the motel. At least from there we can get an Uber. Listen, why don't you relax here and I'll take a look around, see if I can get an idea which way we need to go?"

"Yeah." It was all I could manage.

He disappeared into the trees, and I brushed some snow off a log so I could sit down. Ros cuddled against me, and I closed my eyes, just for a minute.

When I opened them again, Inky was tapping my shoulder, smiling down at us. "Could be worse. I found a dirt track close by, and it looks pretty well traveled. Looked open at the end, and I'm betting it joins up to the road."

"What are we waiting for?" I got to my feet and my aching knees almost gave out, but I made myself stay upright. This damn nightmare was finally almost over, and that room back at the Rodeway Inn sounded more heavenly than any castle.

"I can walk myself," Ros said, and her sassy tone made me smile. She didn't like being treated like a baby, even now.

I looked at her dainty little shoes and shook my head. "Maybe when we get to the main road, where your feet won't get wet. Okay?"

"Yeah, okay."

I felt the scabs that had formed while I was sitting break open when I started to walk, the fresh blood warm against my chilled skin. I tried to ignore it. In a few hours at most, I'd be tucked in a motel bed with Ros, watching TV and eating candy from the vending machine. Inky would be in the other bed, and that made me feel good too. It was enough to keep me taking one step and then another.

BLEEDING WOODS again. Fuck me. But it could've been worse. At least we'd made it out of there mostly in one piece, though Dante was clearly in pain even if he was too proud to admit it. At least he didn't argue when I offered to take Ros. I hoisted her up onto my shoulders, and she giggled when she grabbed hold of my horns. Shouldn't have surprised me that she could see them back at the chateau—or that they hadn't fazed her. Kids were adaptable like that.

Luckily I was right about the dirt track, and after walking it a quarter mile or so, we reached the tarmac. I looked left and right. In one direction the road sloped down some, though that meant fuck all to me. I had no idea where we were or what direction we needed to go. I looked to Dante.

"Downhill," he said.

I couldn't think of a reason to argue, and we walked another twenty minutes or so. Up ahead was a sharp curve, and I hoped we might find something—anything—when we rounded it.

I have to remember to be careful what I wish for.

Dante froze as soon as the white van came into view, and he jerked his head toward the brush on the side of the road. As quietly as we could, we edged that way, but it was already too late.

The half dozen guys who'd been leaning against the van smoking spotted us before we could escape back into the woods. One of them pointed with the assault rifle hanging from his shoulder, and the rest came running. Ros muffled a squeal, and Dante widened his stance, hissing out, "Take her and go. I'll hold them off."

I didn't get the chance to tell him how bloody ridiculous that was because before I could take a step, two of the skinheads had circled around behind us. The barrel of a rifle jabbed me in the back.

"Don't move."

"You. Hands up," a lanky guy with a buzz cut and some scruff said to Dante.

"Hey, I recognize this little fuck," said a guy with a gnarled beard and a gut like a beach ball jutting out between his suspenders. "He works for that wetback gunrunner. I think he took out some of our guys when we tried to get a hold of that first shipment." He spat on the ground.

"What do we do with them?" asked a blond guy who might've been good-looking if he wasn't a fucking Nazi.

"We have to stay here so we can call the rest of our guys if we see a hint of the cops," said the guy with the gut. "We can tie 'em up and throw 'em in the van until we get out of here."

"Fuck that," said an older guy with a bunch of prison-style tattoos and what looked like a burn scar covering most of the left side of his face. His eyelid looked melted shut. I shuddered. "Put the little bitch in the van. She's worth money. Take the other two into the woods and shoot them."

The lanky guy pulled Ros off me, and she started sobbing. With a hoarse cry of pure pain, Dante lunged, but the blond caught him in the jaw with the butt of his gun, and he sprawled out on his back. Before he could get up, the guy had his boot on Dante's throat. He looked down at Dante and said, "Hold still, boy. You and your friend here are getting a bullet in the head for the Aryan blood you spilled. Ain't nothing you can do about it. But if you use some common sense and stop being a horse's ass, I won't do it in front of the girl."

Dante nodded once, and then the pudgy fucker was hauling him up and marching us down an embankment and into a copse of old oak trees. The only chance we had, as far as I could see, was Ros's magic. But she didn't seem to have control, and besides, her spells took time to play out. We were royally fucked.

The big guy shoved Dante forward, and he stumbled. "On your knees."

One of them poked me with a gun again, and hands closed around my shoulders and forced me down. The snow soaked my trousers instantly, and something beneath it scraped my legs. The cold metal dug into my hair while the older Nazi pressed a revolver to the back of Dante's head. I closed my eyes because I didn't want the last thing I saw in this world to be him dying.

CHAPTER THIRTY-TWO

PRIMAL FEAR had compelled me to take my shot with the sniper rifle when the woman in the black suit had paralyzed everyone. My companion said something about us being beyond the range of the spell, but whether it was genuine or the power of suggestion, I could feel the atrophy creeping into my muscles, and I reacted.

In doing so, I gave away our position as well as the thrall that held everyone still. I could already see a group of skinheads cautiously advancing on us, and I wouldn't have been surprised if others were attempting to flank us from the other side. I looked up at the young man. "We can't stay here. We have a better chance of survival if we watch each other's backs."

"Agreed."

I handed him one of the Longbows. They weren't the best choice at close range, but I had no intention of leaving them here so they could be looted and used against us. Besides, they might still be useful. This young man at least knew how to handle a weapon.

A couple hundred yards away, some people from Devereux's crew took cover behind a crescent formed by three SUVs. Their position was not only closest to us, but also to the road away from the chateau and the semi holding my guns. I shook my head. Why would they bring that truck here? Then it occurred to me: they thought they would need it to transport the arsenal they believed I had stored here. I jutted my chin toward Devereux's men. "Those are my friends. Make for them. I'll cover you, and when you reach the vehicle, cover me while I run."

He nodded once and sprinted without hesitation. It wasn't long before the three Nazis noticed him, but I targeted the one in the center and blew his head off from two hundred yards, leaving nothing from his shoulders up. I knew some of these white supremacists came from military backgrounds, but apparently not this group, because instead of reacting, they stood frozen by what they'd seen. I made a split-second decision, and instead of aiming for the next man's head, I put one bullet in his thigh, another in his gut. He screamed and flew back, a trickle of blood steaming where it hit the ground. My instinct proved right, and his companion dropped to assist him. I knew there was no honor in this, no creed. These men moved in packs like animals, and all their courage and bravado came from numbers. Despite their claims of superiority, the uninjured man was afraid to face me one-on-one. It was typical of his kind.

Sparing a quick glance back to Devereux's crew, I saw my new friend had reached the others and now stretched across the hood of a black Escalade, his eye pressed to the rifle's scope. I hoped the sense of decency I felt from him was genuine, because I had little choice except to trust him. Devereux's people wouldn't recognize me in my gear, and I hadn't shared my name. I ran.

Every time my bad foot made contact with the ground, pain shot up my leg. I'd exerted myself and spent too much time in the cold. Within a few steps I was hobbling, an easy target. As much as I pushed myself, I couldn't go any faster.

Something streaked across my back, and I barely bit back a scream at the intense burn. Acrid smoke from my smoldering parka stung my nose, and I realized what had hit me wasn't a bullet; it was something on fire, something small but burning hot enough to penetrate the layers I wore and blister my flesh. It had come from the direction of the house. A group had gathered on the staircase, though I couldn't see them well through the smog. Another volley of burning projectiles shot from the assembly, coming straight for me. I ducked and covered my head, trying to keep moving as best as I could.

I heard the soft whisk of a silenced shot, followed by a feminine shriek. I couldn't look to see if my new associate had hit his target. Even if he hadn't, the people on the staircase would scatter; they'd seek cover. Anyone would. It was instinct. It might give me a few minutes to get to safety.

I felt heat across my back again as a larger fireball sailed over me, probably missing me by mere inches. I heard it hit metal—one of the vehicles. When the Escalade caught fire, I could no longer deny that this was no ordinary flame. It had to be… somehow enhanced. As much as I didn't even want to think the word *magic*, I'd never been one to deny something just because I found it inconvenient or frightening.

The people who'd been using the vehicles as cover fled, and I joined them as quickly as I could, prioritizing the threat of an explosion and pushing hard for the empty lawn behind the SUVs, alongside the road leading off the property. Adrenaline lent me enough of a burst to break the crust of that stretch of snow just before the Escalade went up with a deafening boom, shooting flames, shrapnel, and sparks into the dark sky and singeing my back. I smelled hair burning as I flopped over in the snow, trying to soothe the blisters across my shoulders and along the back of my skull.

I'd managed to hold on to my rifle.

My eyes burned and gushed as a watery silhouette approached me. I could just make out the brown coat and striped scarf… and the extended hand. I grasped it and let myself be pulled to my feet, trying to breathe through the ensuing dizziness. The chemical air pinched my lungs when I drew it deep, and I coughed up ash.

With my head ringing like the inside of a church bell, I forced myself forward, still clutching the young man's hand. The flames would spread to the other vehicles, and I needed to get clear of them before it happened… get to some cover if possible. My vision was still obstructed, but about a hundred yards away was a little hillock with a statue on top—a faun playing a syrinx, I saw as we got closer—and surrounded by some sort of ornamental bushes. The mound stood only about four feet high, but it would be better than nothing. My companion seemed to feel the same, and we rounded the slope just as the other two SUVs erupted, one seconds after the other, filling the air with oily smoke.

I dropped to my knees. The pain in my foot nearly brought tears to my eyes. My coat hung in strips, exposing my back to the frigid air. When I ran my hand over the back of my head, crinkled, burned hair fell out in clumps. I looked around at a dozen or so black men and a few women. Doing some quick calculations, I thought fifteen people divided by three cars meant most of them had made it to safety, even with the minor wounds most displayed, probably from shrapnel. I hoped so.

"What now?" one man asked.

"We get the fuck out of here," said a woman with close-cropped curls. "This has gone to shit. Nothing more we can do."

Most of the others murmured their assent, until someone asked the obvious question. "How? Walk back to Philadelphia?"

"My name is Raphael Guzman," I said, surprised at the clarity of my voice when my throat felt scabbed over. "Some of you know me or have heard of me. I'm here for my guns, and I'm here for Louie and Devereux, if they're still alive." I pointed with my gun. "That semi might hold both.

Either way, it can get us away from here. We need to fight our way to it and kill the Nazis defending it. It's the only way we're getting out of here."

Some of them nodded, but one man said, "There's dozens of those motherfuckers, and who knows how many more inside those containers. They'll pick us off one by one."

The young man who'd helped me shielded his eyes and jutted his round chin toward the truck. "Look. They're concentrating on what's in front of them—the people on the steps of the house and the ones off to the left, attacking from those trucks and vans. They might have a few guys guarding their goods, but they can't spare more than that. There's a chance they don't know we survived the explosions, at least not all of us. If we sneak up from behind, we can catch them by surprise."

I was impressed. This young man was sharp, he thought like a soldier, and he didn't let the chaos around him cloud his mind. But the others didn't look as pleased; they looked skeptical, maybe mistrustful.

"And just who the hell are you, white boy?" asked one of the women.

"My name is Emrys Rathburn, and more than that…. Well, it would take a long time to tell. Suffice it to say if these Nazis are your enemies, then I'm on your side."

"How do we know that? You could be one of them, leading us into a trap."

"No," I said. "Emrys has my trust, and his point is a good one. We should go now, before we lose the element of surprise." Something exploded, and a white pickup truck shot into the air and then landed on its side with a screech and a crunch. "We should go now, while the Irish are keeping them busy. Who has long-range weapons?"

They held up their guns, and most of them were armed for power, not distance: high-caliber revolvers, sawed-off shotguns, half a dozen Desert Eagles they'd almost certainly bought from me. In addition to the Smith & Wesson Magnum holstered by her hip, a woman with long braids pulled up into a bun held a stunning .338 Lapua. I nodded to it. "Are you accurate with that weapon?"

"Bitch, I could circumcise you from half a mile with this beauty." She kissed the top of the scope.

"Excellent. You, me, and Emrys will start. We'll take out as many as we can while the others circle around and flank them from the left. We'll also serve to draw their attention. Now with this wind and the poor visibility, we're in for a challenge. Emrys, can you do this?"

His pink tongue slid out to wet chapped lips. His distress was plain on his face as he met my gaze. "There's… there's no other choice, is there? No choice but to kill them. Shoot them in their backs."

I could see that while intelligent, he had a gentle heart. I put a hand on his shoulder. "It's them or us."

A moment passed, and then his pretty features hardened and he looked like a completely different man. "Then it's them. Jet's out there somewhere. You can count on me."

"Let's do it."

The three of us positioned ourselves as best we could in a less-than-ideal location, and the rest, crouched low, moved left. Anyone watching would see their dark clothing against the snow from a mile away, but it didn't seem like any of the Nazis were watching their back—an amateurish mistake.

I tried to get one of them in my crosshairs, but my scope seemed smeared with something. I used the cuff of my jacket to wipe it, but the smudges remained, and I realized my vision was still suffering from the toxic cloud in the air. No matter. I knew what I had to do, and as I pressed my eye to the scope, I let the world beyond that tunnel disappear. The sounds of the battle receded until I heard only the slosh of my own pulse in my head. I selected a target, got him in my sights, and squeezed the trigger. I moved to the next: one, two, three. At the periphery of my vision, another man fell even as the Nazis regrouped, splitting up so some of them could face us while the rest tried to defend the truck against Moirin's people. I swiveled where I crouched in the snow so I could concentrate on the Nazis fast approaching our position, and I took down another man with two bullets to the chest.

Just as I prepared to find another target, the rest of our group clashed with the Nazis, and Emrys's plan succeeded. They were caught by surprise, and our people thinned them quickly from the left, carpeting the Nazis with fire to great effect. A few of our enemies were able to return fire, and I thought I saw some of the Nazis go down through the stinging membrane coating my eyes, but within minutes it was over, and ten or more Nazis littered the ground, their blood melting the snow. I knew dozens of other white supremacists were entrenched around the lawn, but we'd managed to gain the truck—the guns. It was a victory, and I clawed through my pain to get to my feet and join the others, Emrys and the woman following.

I shook my head sadly as I passed three young men who'd fallen, trying to assuage myself with the thought they had plenty of company, and I would be sending them more. The fragile neutrality I'd nurtured for so long could not go on. I needed to fight these people.

Since the others had already positioned themselves behind the semi, I hoisted myself onto the bed, opened the latch, and entered the shipping container. Dozens of wooden crates sat in neat stacks against the walls, carefully secured with heavy nylon straps. They held tens of millions of dollars' worth of handcrafted untraceable firearms, but my attention zeroed in on the three men lying between them, and I limped over and crouched down.

Devereux's hands had been duct-taped behind his back, and he lay on his side, both eyes swollen, lips split, and hair matted to his forehead. When I touched his shoulder, he groaned, "Raf? Merde. Didn't… didn't think… we'd be getting out of this one. I can't say why they didn't kill me. Maybe thought you'd pay to get me back. Or having me would lure you here to be killed. You must have worked some kind of a miracle."

Miracles of a sort had been involved, but I would explain it later. I took a combat knife from my belt and freed his hands, saying, "Try not to move. I'm sure you have some broken bones."

I checked the others. Louie was alive but unconscious, and I couldn't wake him. The other young man, whom I didn't recognize, was dead.

"We need to get Louie to a doctor," Devereux wheezed.

I nodded. "We all need to get out of here. It's a bloodbath out there, and we can't let the authorities get these guns. Not after what they cost. Look after him. You're safest in here for now."

I could get everyone into the container, and its thick metal walls would do much to shield them from gunfire, but first I had to alert Moirin and her people. If we ran and left them, they would either be slaughtered by the remainder of the Nazis, subjected to who-knew-what kind of attack from the people in the chateau, or arrested.

I needed a way to signal them, and it wasn't as if she would answer her phone. As I stumbled toward the square of light at the end of the container, I rubbed at the pain blossoming behind my temples. I couldn't figure out what to do, how to save my people and my merchandise.

It was hard to believe that as a boy, my fondest dream had been to fight battles like this for a living.

Chapter Thirty-Three

WHEN I dropped from the bed of the truck, Emrys was waiting for me, staring down at a small phone and looking broken.

"Any word from your friend?" I asked.

He shook his head. "I tried texting them but didn't get a reply. Which I guess isn't a big surprise considering—" He waved his hand at the disaster around us.

"I have a similar problem." I wouldn't deny that I needed his help, needed his quick thinking to help me figure a way out of this. "We have to get out of here before the authorities arrive, which I can't believe they haven't already, but I need to get word to my associates there—" I pointed to the battered huddle of vehicles on the opposite side of the drive and closest to the house, being used as a base by Moirin and the others. Between us and them lay bodies from both sides and pockets of Nazis who showed no sign of surrender or retreat. "We need to get all those people into the container and get out of here."

I pulled a small pair of binoculars from a pocket in my pants, but my vision still hadn't recovered. I passed them to Emrys, still hoping he might have an idea. "See anything?"

"It looks like—" With a gasp, he dropped the binoculars and pulled his pistol—Dante's gun—as he ran. I recovered them, brushed away the fouled snow, and squinted to watch the wavering shapes.

Emrys's friend Jet had run to Moirin, and they stood talking, Jet gesturing wildly with his—her?—hands and Moirin shouting over her shoulder. The pale man in the outlandish fur coat stalked toward Jet's back, while Emrys ran hard in that direction, somehow managing to avoid taking a bullet even though every Nazi still breathing fired on him. With the exception of a few men, the people attending the party had retreated inside, most likely to take shelter in a cellar and wait for the authorities.

Emrys shouted. Jet looked over their shoulder and held their hand up to the man in white. Whatever they said to attempt to placate him, the way they waved their hands around at the destruction to try to impart something, failed. Even from my position, I could see anger and hate in his posture, the way he moved. Jet cowered, curling their shoulders forward and retreating a few steps, though I noticed no weapon.

The man in white lifted his hand just as an especially brazen Nazi emerged from behind the white pickup, his AR-15 pointed at Jet. Moirin lunged, tackling Jet to the ground, while whatever the man in white had aimed at Jet seemed to strike Emrys. He stopped running midstride and nearly doubled over. A second later the Nazi's fire hit the man in white, and blood bloomed like poppies down his left arm. He ran for the stone stairs, and in the ensuing crossfire, I lost sight of him.

Emrys recovered, and his mouth moved rapidly. Moirin nodded and yelled something to her people. A moment later a man handed her a bundle of dynamite sticks. She lit it, lobbed it where the remaining Nazis had congregated, and then ran hard in the opposite direction, following her people. They headed for the woods where I'd been concealed and then looped back around to cross the road farther from the house and make for the semi.

I scrambled to climb into the cab and made it just as the detonation of that dynamite seemed to tear the earth apart. Clumps of frozen soil, shards of metal, and human flesh so mangled that no body parts could be recognized slammed the side of the truck and splattered the windshield. I used the wipers just as Moirin hopped onto the seat next to me, grinning from ear to ear.

"Now that's what I call an evening's entertainment, love."

"None of the vehicles can be traced to us?"

"This isn't my first dance," she said. "You'll be wanting to get a move on, lad."

I did as she said, turning the semi as sharply as I dared and gunning it hard, tearing up gravel as the engine revved and I made for the road. As we hit the asphalt, I breathed a sigh of relief. "I can't believe it's over."

"That's not the last of the fun," Moirin said. "In fact, the best might be yet to come."

Before I could ask her what she meant, an explosion that made everything we'd been doing seem like children firing slingshots tore the night in half with a chasm of orange and a thunderhead of smoke.

I SMELL Dante's blood, Charlene said, again perched upon my shoulder. Sure enough, I soon found the trail: two deep sets of footprints sprinkled with dark blots and smears. It seemed they'd escaped through the orchard and into the forest, where they made their way back to the road.

They are in danger, Charlene said. *The boy and the girl.*

"Yes, I sense that too, through the bargain I made with Dante. We must hurry."

ALL I could think of as the barrel of the gun bit into the back of my head was what was going to happen to my sister. I pictured it all in sickening detail, and even with death seconds away, I tried to figure out a way to save her. I had to do something.

Then there was a bang, the familiar scent of a gun firing, followed by the muffled sound of a body hitting the snow. I couldn't look. What good would come of it? It would all be over soon, and there wasn't a damn thing I could do. I hung my head as tears and snot dripped down my face, and I bit my lip until I tasted blood.

Bang. Bang.

I took me a second to realize that while everything still hurt, I wasn't dead. I hadn't been shot, though I'd pissed myself a little. Slowly, completely disoriented, I opened my eyes and looked over at Inky, who was staring at the puke that steamed between his knees. Next to him, the fatass skinhead lay facedown, two holes in his back and half of his head gone, brains spilling out.

Behind me, the lanky guy with the five-o'clock shadow shoved his gun into a shoulder holster and said, "On your feet."

"What the fuck is going on?" I asked, my voice high and trembling.

"My name is Special Agent Merrick Alden, with the Federal Bureau of Investigation. Just keep your hands where I can see them and keep quiet."

"My sister!"

"She's safe. I've been undercover in a joint operation with the ATF to investigate both human trafficking and the huge influx of illegal firearms to this area over the last five years."

"Shit, you… you saved us?"

"I don't know about that, Mr. Mayfield. You must realize you're in a lot of trouble—you and the man you work for, Mr. Guzman."

"Fuck me," Inky muttered. "You're taking us in?"

"Any minute now, agents posing as neo-Nazis will be calling to tell our friends up there at the van that the police are on their way. My ATF associate will convince them to leave without us."

"And take my sister with them?"

"It was the only way to save your life," Agent Alden said. "We'll recover her as soon as you two are safely in custody—along with Mr. Guzman. We know he's using this property to stockpile weapons."

I barely heard what he was saying about Raf's guns. All I knew was they were planning to let these Nazi pigs take my sister, and I didn't buy the shit about recovering her later. She wasn't going through any more. I wasn't going to let it happen.

Then I remembered the fat fuck had been planning to shoot us…. He had a gun. I looked around without being obvious, and I saw it at the base of an old tree where it must've flown from his hand. It was about eight feet from where I knelt. I'd only have one chance. I launched myself forward, closed my hand around the grip, rolled to my back, and pointed the gun at Agent Alden. If this motherfucker knew as much about me as it seemed, he'd know I was faster than him. "I'm getting my sister, and if you want to stop me, you'll have to kill me." Which I knew he couldn't do. He needed me for his case.

I hoped. And I tried not to think about the dead Nazi whose gun I held.

Keeping my attention locked on him, my eyes glued to his, I walked backwards through the trees, trying to feel my way with my feet so I wouldn't land on my ass and lose whatever advantage I might have.

The agent was jabbering on, using a calm tone to try to talk me down. "Dante, I'm on your side here. You'll only be putting your sister in danger by going back up there. The Nazis have to believe you're dead. After you testify, we can get both of you into witness protection. You can start a new life, and so can she."

I ignored him, and when the ground got too steep for me to keep backing up, I turned and ran. When I got back to the van, the blond guy was leaning against the hood looking at a cell phone. I stopped a few feet from him and said, "Your asshole friends down there are dead, and I want my sister or you're next."

His eyes got wide, and he slowly lifted his hands to chest level, fingers spread. "Agent Alden is dead?" he hissed out.

Fuck. This must be the ATF guy. "Put that pistol on the ground slow and kick it over to me."

"You don't know what you're doing. You—"

"Do it!"

"All right, all right."

"And don't fuck with me. I'm not stupid."

At that, he snorted, but he laid his pistol down gently and nudged it over to me with the toe of his boot. Without taking my eyes off him, I crouched down to pick it up and took off the safety. With my left hand, I held it ready to fire while I kept my piece trained on him. "Tell your Nazi friend to bring my sister out."

Doing the last thing I expected, he cocked his head at me. "Or what?"

"As far as he knows, you're one of them," I said. "White race brotherhood and all that bullshit. Don't you think he values your life?"

He heaved out a sigh and shook his head. "You don't know these people."

"My sister."

He glanced over his shoulder and then back at me, but before he could say anything else, the side door on the van screeched open, and the greasy bastard with the beard stepped out—a pistol pressed to my sister's head.

"Dante!" Ros looked pale, and she was shivering. Or trembling. I couldn't be sure. But she held her head up and wouldn't give the bastard the satisfaction of crying. That made me proud.

I pointed one gun at the ATF guy, the other at the Nazi. Nobody moved, their breath freezing as it hit the air. We were at a standstill, and everybody here knew it.

Behind me, branches snapped and boots crunched through snow as Inky and Agent Alden followed me up the hill. Not that it made a damn bit of difference.

The old Nazi flicked his eyes in their direction. "Where's Big Pete?"

"Big Pete's dead," Agent Alden said.

"This little piece of shit again?" the Nazi said, jutting his chin toward me. I wished I could've taken credit for it.

Agent Alden said nothing. Again, we were stuck standing there staring at each other because nobody could make a move without somebody else popping a cap in them or somebody they cared about.

I'd never been anywhere so quiet. Aside from our breathing, it was like a void. I could even be sure time was still moving.

The ring of a phone was so shrill, so loud, that I flinched, like the sound would cause an avalanche or something.

The blond ATF guy still stood with his hands raised, and when he met my eyes, I knew he wanted to convey something. "I'm going to reach in my jeans pocket and answer that," he said. "If I don't update our people, they'll come to check up on us."

I nodded once. "Do it slow."

He pressed the phone to his ear. "Yes? Bad timing. No. No, I understand." He put the phone back in his pocket and looked at the bearded Nazi. "The rest of our team is withdrawing from the mansion. The authorities have been notified."

"Do they still have the guns?" the Nazi asked.

"I don't know, but we need to get out of here. Now. The police are on their way. They'll be blocking off every road in and out of the area."

The Nazi shook his head and spat on the ground. "I can't walk away from this, man. Not after the Aryan blood this little asshole has spilled. I can't let him leave here alive."

"Pass the girl to me," the ATF agent said.

"You know, I think I'll do her too. Let the kid watch. It's not like the world needs another mongrel kid that nobody wants. It's only—"

His face twisted into a grimace, but he didn't seem able to open his mouth… or move at all. The ATF guy's eyes darted back and forth, and he muttered, "What the hell is going on here?"

I noticed a familiar scent, something like freshly mown grass, and Blossom stepped into the circle we'd formed and up to my sister. He pinched her chin between his thumb and finger, angled her face up toward his, and looked at her for a long time, oblivious to the rest of us. "It was you. Astounding."

"I didn't do anything wrong," Ros said in a small, scared voice.

"No… well, I'm sure you didn't do it on purpose. How could you? I can scarcely fathom how you did it at all. You have quite a talent. A gift. Oh! And Charlene is happy to see you again."

"Hi, Charlene." All I could see was Blossom's back, but I imagined my sister reaching up to pet the kitten. "Are you the angel I prayed for?"

Blossom snorted. "Praying does not work."

"Well you're here." Already, the attitude had snuck back into Ros's tone.

I worried Blossom might get angry, but he threw his head back, laughed, and patted Ros on the head. "You and I are going to have a lovely time together. But first, it seems there's a small matter to take care of. My lady?" He bowed with a flourish and held out his hand. Ros took it, and Blossom led her away from the big Nazi. "Would you care to do the honors?"

She looked up at him, confused, and he fluttered his free hand around. "Well, never mind. Tell me, Rosalind. Which do you like better, birds or flowers?"

Her face scrunched up in thought before she said "Flowers" with a decisive nod.

"Excellent choice." He crouched down next to her and draped his long fingers over her shoulder.

A hoarse scream and some spit tore out of the Nazi's mouth. Little green shoots pushed their way through his T-shirt one by one, until dozens of them grew out of his chest in tight spirals and a pool of blood melted the snow around his feet. He hacked up a glob of something wet and red as the tendrils thickened and sunflowers, poppies, daisies, and a bunch of other shit I couldn't name bloomed. Something cracked, and a brown vine shot out of his wrist, his hand hanging limp and useless as the vine wound its way up his arm, squeezing, tearing off strips of his leather coat and then strips of skin and meat before it wrapped around his throat.

He fell to his knees, moaning, sobbing, and trying to beg. Everyone else, even Ros, stood quietly watching. His flesh fell off in chunks, and flower petals fell with it. I could see the rungs of his ribs, his exposed guts writhing around. His head shot back, face to the sky, and a thin silvery tree shot out of his mouth. Lacy pink flowers pushed their way through the blood and bits of organs on the branches. A red rose the size of a baseball sprung out of each eye socket, and the Nazi twitched for half a minute before he went still.

Blossom walked over, plucked one of the roses, and tucked it behind Ros's ear.

I thought I was going to puke. "Fuck," I said.

He waved me off. "Don't overreact, Dante. I checked for thorns first."

"Can we please just get the bloody fuck away from here?" Inky's voice sounded as close to shattering as the Nazi's skull.

"What about these others?" Blossom asked.

"They're not bad men," Ros said.

Maybe not, but they wanted to throw my ass in jail. Raf too. "Can you just… leave them like this? Keep them from moving until we can get away? We can take the van."

Blossom scratched Charlene's head absently. "Of course, though it would be easier to extend the effect if the one who summoned me here releases me."

"How do I do it?" Ros asked.

He knelt down to her level, looked her in the eye, smiled, and rested a hand on her shoulder. His demeanor was… weird, almost paternal. "You can see, yes? Yes, of course you can. Look closely. Some ropes are binding us together, ropes of light. They're green and gold, sparkling."

Ros gasped. "I do see them. They're pretty."

"They are." Blossom nodded. "But you must sever them. Each and every one. Only then will we both be free."

Ros's face settled into a determined expression I knew well. "I understand. I wish you could stay and keep me and Dante safe. How do I do it?"

"Pull your magic out of the strands and back into you. When you've done that, I'll be able to extricate my own essence. Without either of us to sustain them, the bonds will grow brittle, and you will be able to break them."

"I'll try." She closed her eyes, and for ten minutes or more, we all stood watching as she scrunched up her face and sweat beaded across her forehead. She panted and her hands curled and uncurled.

Blossom watched closely, his face unreadable.

Finally Ros grunted and staggered back a step. "That's… the last of them."

Blossom rolled his shoulders back and shook out his hair. "Ah. Much better. And Rosalind, I believe you'll find that you won't need anyone keeping you safe for much longer."

"But for now she does," Inky said. "We all do. Let's get the hell away from here before something else happens."

I shoved both guns in my pockets, took Ros's hand, and we got into the van. I was afraid to relax, afraid to believe this might finally be the end.

But what else could come at us now?

Chapter Thirty-Four

WE DITCHED the van about a mile from the motel and walked the rest of the way. Dante and Ros walked hand in hand, and Charlene rode on Blossom's shoulder. I couldn't help but wonder why he was still with us, after he'd had his knickers in such a twist about being stuck here and even conscripted me to help him get loose. Come to think of it, his release meant I was free as well, didn't it? I had what I'd wanted most since stumbling into this mess, and somehow it didn't seem that important—nowhere near as important as making sure Dante and Ros were safe and finding out what had happened to Jet and Emrys.

Still, after I saw to that, I intended to gorge myself.

I sat on the bed feeding Charlene bits of beef jerky from the vending machine. A couple of hours after we made it back to the motel, someone knocked on the door. I started to get up, but Dante held up his hand and picked up the gun he'd set on the night table. Then he opened the door a crack without releasing the chain, and after a few moments, his rigid posture relaxed. Jet, Emrys, an older man in tattered military gear, and a dead-gorgeous woman with short hair came into the room. Jet threw their arms around my neck and kissed me before flopping onto the bed. Emrys sat next to Jet, and the woman leaned against the wall. The man who must've been Raphael stared at Dante. "Hello, Rosalind."

Ros looked sleepy, but she managed to wave. She clutched the stuffed horse Dante had hauled around so religiously.

"Raf," Dante said. "What the hell are you doing here?"

"I'm not sure I know," he answered.

They both nodded, an obviously unspoken agreement to worry about it later, figure things out when they weren't so bloody exhausted they didn't even know their own names.

"Well," Raf said. "I have a shipment to protect and friends in the hospital. I should head back to the city. Would you like me to take you and Rosalind along? You can both spend the night at my house. You'll be safe there."

Jet sat up. "No, they won't."

"What do you mean?" Dante asked.

Jet shook their head. "Look, don't ask me to explain everything right now, because I need about a gallon of Red Bull first, but I did some checking in the last few hours while your boss dropped off the truck and got your guys to the hospital. Sekhet-Aaru knows about your sister, and they know what she can do. They know everything about you, and they're not going to stop until they get her back."

"I won't let that happen," Raf said. "I'm going to fight these people, oppose their agenda. I can no longer reconcile the kind of man I've always imagined myself and sitting by while Nazis prey on children and those… those others manipulate and control us from behind a curtain. I plan to stand against them. I have enough weapons to outfit a small army."

"That's a start," Jet said. "But you're going to need more than guns or even bodies to hold them. You need hearts and minds behind those weapons. You need to know what you're up against."

"Maybe you can help me with that," Raf said.

"This gorgeous creature's been helping us all along," the short-haired woman—Moirin?—said. "Who do you think does all my tech work? And is a mighty fine one for an evening's company." She winked.

I dragged my hand across my eyes. "Bleeding shite, how much more convoluted can this all get?"

"Never mind that," Dante said. "Jet, what are you saying? We need to get out of the city? The state?"

"I don't know if that will be enough," Emrys said gently.

"What? Then what?" Dante's voice rose, cracked. He looked down at the gun in his hand, and I could see on his face the moment he knew it couldn't keep them safe. Poor, poor man.

"This is the most powerful organization on the planet," Jet said. "Maybe in history. I dealt them a blow tonight, but we'd be stupid to think they're gone. These people… they're everywhere."

Dante's eyes were wide. "Are you saying there's nowhere we can go? Nowhere safe? Doesn't anyone know?"

"I do," Blossom said, and fuck me, he almost sounded compassionate. "I know a place Rosalind will be safe. It is also a place where she can learn to use her gifts."

"Where?" Dante asked.

"Come." Blossom stood and walked into the motel's parking lot, which was empty except for a white SUV. The snow was unbroken, pure and glistening. Looking at it, I could scarcely believe everything that happened a few miles from here. Above the bare branches and the peaks of the evergreens around us, a virginal pink crept into the sky. Blossom walked to the end of the gravel patch and stood between a pair of snow-covered wooden picnic tables. He moved his hands in graceful loops, and a warm golden light spilled from the center of a copse of trees.

As we all stood staring, a woman emerged. She took a few steps out of the clearing and looked about with the cool disregard almost exclusive to royalty, though she wore a simple green linen dress overtop of an equally unassuming white chemise. She had delicate features, more freckles than I'd ever seen, and hair so red it made the rest of the world look like a faded photograph. It was arranged elaborately in ropes and braids.

Blossom walked up to the woman, and I expected one or the other to bow, though I couldn't begin to guess which one. Finally she spoke. "I did not expect to see you again so soon."

"Apparently a great deal of time has passed in the mortal world," Blossom said.

"My people have not been as oblivious to the goings on here as yours," she said.

"So you know why I've invited you here?"

She smiled, and when she looked at Ros, her seafoam eyes glowed as bright as her hair. Desire like I'd never felt rolled off her like a scent. Such *want*. "Yes."

"And you'll take her?"

"Wait." Dante stepped forward. "What the hell is going on here?"

"Dante, this is my friend Niamh. In the past, both of us have done favors for the other, made bargains. In order to fulfill the bargain I made to you, I must ask her to take Rosalind."

"Take her where?"

Niamh knelt down to Ros's eye level. "I live on a beautiful island hidden from the rest of the world. It's full of lovely forests, fields of wildflowers, and lakes and streams as pure and clear as crystal. There are white harts, wild horses, animals of all kinds living free. And all the people there are good and kind, and they have magic, just like you. We can keep you hidden from the bad people, and we can teach you. It'll be just like going away to school."

Ros looked over her shoulder at Dante, who had tears running down his face even though he was smiling.

"We call our island Avalon after the island of legend, and it's a world all on its own, where there is no pollution, no hunger, no greed, and no one tries to hurt each other. I'm part of a group called the Order of Marian, and you can be a part of our group too. Our family."

"I don't want to leave my brother."

Dante broke then and dropped to his knees to embrace his sister and cry softly. All I wanted in that moment was to ease his pain, but I knew I couldn't just as surely as I knew what he was going to say: "It's okay, baby. It sounds nice, like the forest of Arden, and you'll be safe there. I… I want what's best for you. It's all I've ever wanted."

"I know. I love you, Dante." They were both crying as they pressed their foreheads together.

He pressed the stuffed horse to her chest. "Don't forget about Touchstone."

As Dante stood up, swiping his nose with the back of his arm, Blossom said, "If I might be permitted, I have a gift for you, Rosalind." He took the toy and set it on the ground.

The stuffed horse stretched and shifted until in its place stood a perfectly proportioned pony the color of cotton candy, with a mane like spun gold and hooves like pearls. She had sunshine-yellow eyes and long, spindly legs. Prettiest little thing I ever saw, and she gave off a scent like vanilla and lavender. When Ros reached out a hand, the pony knelt down so the girl could climb onto her back.

Niamh gasped. "That is no trifle."

"I swore an oath to keep the girl from harm," Blossom said. "Besides, I like her."

"So I see," Niamh said. "Well, lass, are you ready to see your new home, meet the rest of the Order?"

Ros nodded and smiled. I had to hand it to the faerie twat; the pretty new pet did a lot to take Ros's mind off the severity of her situation. As anyone would, she touched her pony's neat little ears and spun-floss mane, clearly enamored. Niamh put a hand on Blossom's elbow. "Old friend, I suspect we'll see each other again sooner rather than later."

"Do you know something I don't?" he asked.

She met his eyes and smiled. "Do you not hear what the winds and the waves are whispering? The way their voices grow more insistent by the day? The fate of the world will soon be decided. Me and my people have been waiting for this time. You should make yourself ready as well."

Then the two of them walked back into the trees. The golden light faded, leaving the world feeling sadder and colder than before, and they were gone.

"Gone," Dante whispered. "All that, and I lost her anyway. At least she'll be happy, I hope."

"What about you?" Jet asked. "Sekhet-Aaru will try to go through you to get to Ros. You know, you could come with us. Me and Emrys, and—" They turned to me.

"If you'll have me," I said.

"Heh. Stay hydrated, big guy. You could come with me, Emrys, and Inky. Help us fight those assholes."

"I thought I wouldn't be safe," Dante said.

"You won't," Emrys said. "But I imagine you're used to that. As a rogue mage, I'm not safe from the guilds either, but I can tell you it's better not to be alone. We watch each other's backs, and you can trust us."

Jet pointed to their eye. "I have a little bit of an insurance policy. It's probably not enough to keep them from coming after your sister, but… I wear a contact lens that allows me access to certain ESM networks. It also allows me to record… and upload. I got some footage of the fight, evidence of people using magic, and it's currently being safely bounced around a grid of protected servers all over the world. It might be enough to keep them off your back, at least once they learn Ros is gone. I'll do what I can."

As I watched him, I hoped he'd say yes. I could feel his desire for a place to belong, a sense of purpose now that Ros had gone. Maybe with friendship, his anger and despair would fade in time. He might not want sex, but I felt sure I could be what he wanted, give him a reason to look forward to life for once. "Yeah, mate," I said. "I'd like that."

Before he could answer, Blossom bent, scooped Charlene—who'd apparently escaped when we'd left the door to the room open—onto his shoulder, and said, "And I offer an alternative."

"What?" Dante asked.

"Come with me. We'll fight the mages together—not with plots and secrets and machines, but with my magic and your proficiency with those weapons. We will make them pay, and no one will be able to stop us."

"Dante…," Raf said.

But I saw the glint in Dante's eye, and I remembered how he'd felt in the basement of Hex, that righteous anger. It was the only way he knew how to define himself, especially now that he'd lost his sister, and it burned in him like a sun. I knew I'd lost him even before he nodded to Blossom and whispered, "Yeah."

Blossom clapped and pirouetted on the ball of one foot. Charlene yowled.

"What you're planning is no life for a cat," I said, surprised how petulant I sounded. Fuck me, but I didn't want to lose Dante… not to the faerie twat, and not to the rage that was going to leave him a cinder. But I'd done all I could. Maybe he just needed to work it out of his system.

Blossom heaved a dramatic sigh and rolled his eyes. "Oh all right." He handed Charlene to me, and I situated her inside the tuxedo jacket I still wore. "But if anything happens to my good friend, you'll have me to deal with."

"No empty threat, that," I grumbled. "Now piss off if you're going. Dante… take care of yourself. And, uh, look us up sometime."

He actually met my eyes and smiled, making my innards feel warm. "You might want to stay away from that shithole mage bar for a while, though."

They turned to go, and Jet called out, "Hey, when do I get one of those horses?"

Blossom waved without looking back, and Moirin said, "JZ, my love, if you're looking for something to ride…."

When I turned toward Moirin, she was giving me the up and down without even trying to hide it. Funny thing was, I could feel the spark coming off her, that sweet golden energy so thick I could taste it, but her desires weren't coaxing me into any specific shape or molding my personality to her whims. Oh sure, I'd do the things she liked, Jet too, but I'd do them because I wanted to. Because dammit, I was me. More me than I'd ever been before. I'd become something completely different, maybe unique in the world.

It didn't scare me.

More and more, I liked the idea of looking like me, getting turned on by what turned me on, being annoyed by my own issues. Best of all, I had a feeling I could bring some fantasies to life without altering myself, and for the first time, I'd stick around after the honeymoon came to an end. It would take more work than I was used to, more compromise, but to have people who valued me just the way I was? People who cared about me, would fight for me, after the shine dulled?

Bloody hell, that's the stuff dreams are made of, isn't it?

AUGUST LI plays every game as a mage. He thinks the closest thing to magic outside of games and fantasy is to bring things into existence from nothing, which he does in words and images. As a proud trans man, he hopes to bring diversity and representation to all those who want to see themselves in the art and stories they enjoy. He's a perfectionist, travel enthusiast, and caffeine addict.

Gus makes his home on the coast of South Carolina, where he spends his days in search of merpeople, friendly cats, and interesting pieces of driftwood. He collects ball-jointed dolls, tattoos, and languages. He believes in faeries and thinks they're terrifying… but still wants to meet one.

Ash and Echoes
Book One of the
Blessed Epoch
August Li

Blessed Epoch: Book One

For the past few years Yarroway L'Estrella has lived in exile, gathering arcane power. But that power came at a price, and he carries the scars to prove it. Now he must do his duty: his uncle, the king, needs him to escort Prince Garith to his wedding, a union that will create an alliance between the two strongest countries in the known world. But Yarrow isn't the prince's only guard.

A whole company of knights is assigned to the mission, and Yarrow's not sure he trusts their leader.

Knight Duncan Purefroy isn't sure he trusts Yarrow either, but after a bizarre occurrence during their travels, they have no choice but to work together—especially since the incident also reveals a disturbing secret, one that might threaten the entire kingdom.

The precarious alliance is strained further when a third member joins the cause for reasons of his own—reasons that may not be in the best interests of the prince or the kingdom. With enemies at every turn, no one left to trust, and the dark power within Yarrow pulling dangerously away from his control, the fragile bond the three of them have built may be all that stands between them and destruction.

www.dsppublications.com

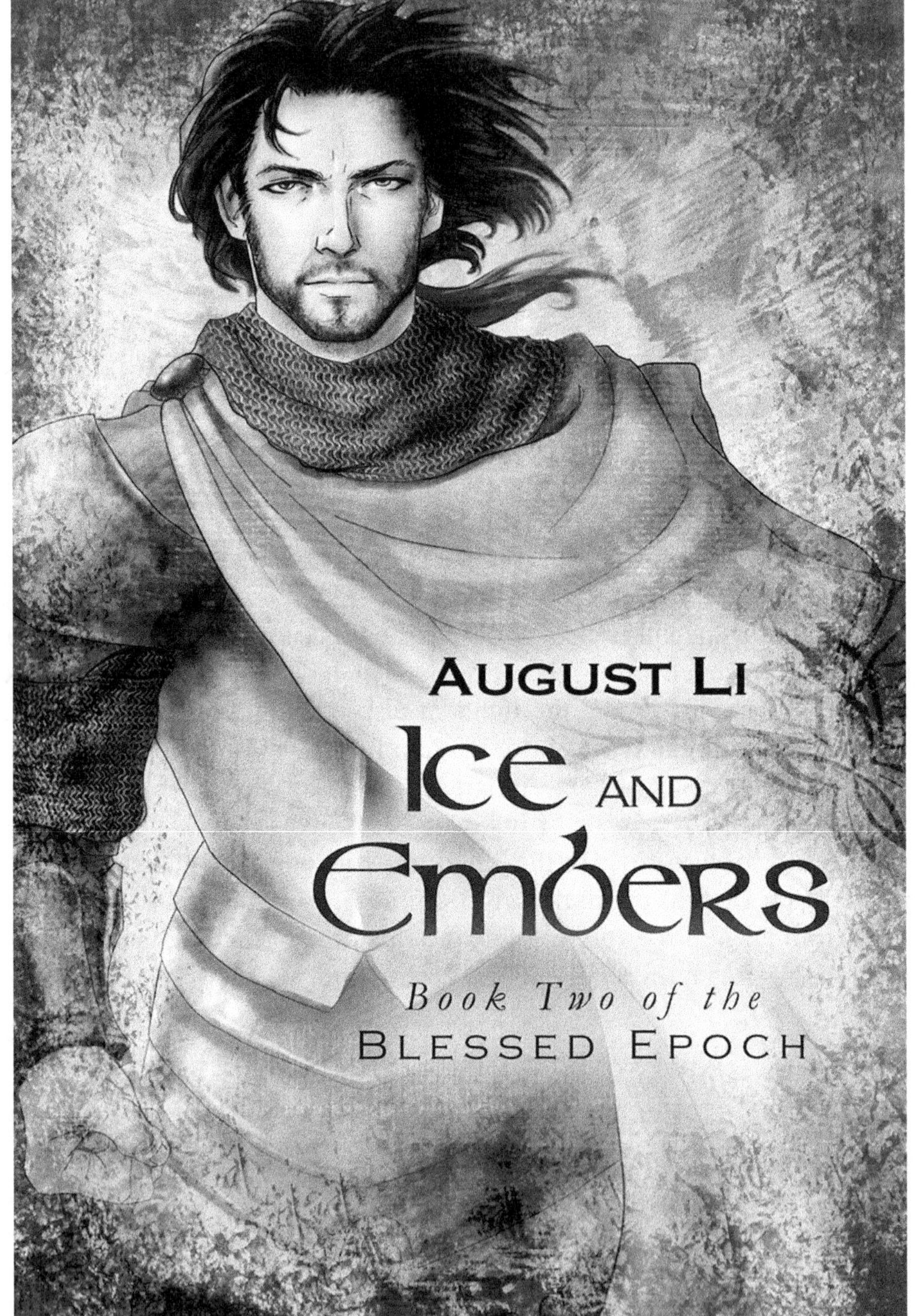
August Li
Ice and Embers
Book Two of the
Blessed Epoch

Blessed Epoch: Book Two

Despite their disparate natures, Yarrow, Duncan, and Sasha united against overwhelming odds to save Prince Garith's life. Now Garith is king and the three friends may be facing their undoing.

Distraught over Yarrow's departure to find the cure to his magical affliction, Duncan struggles with his new role as Bairn of Windwake, a realm left bankrupt and in turmoil by his predecessor. Many of Duncan's vassals conspire against him, and Sasha's unorthodox solutions to Duncan's problem have earned them the contempt of Garith's nobles.

When word reaches Duncan and Sasha that Yarrow is in danger, they want nothing more than to rush to his aid. But Duncan's absence could tip Windwake into the hands of his enemies. In addition, a near-mythic order of assassins wants Sasha dead. Without Yarrow, Duncan and Sasha can't take the fight to the assassins. They are stuck, entangled in a political world they don't understand. But finding Yarrow may cause more problems, and with his court divided, King Garith must strike a balance between supporting his friends and assuaging the nobles who want Duncan punished—and Sasha executed.

www.dsppublications.com

Iron and Ether
Book Three of the
Blessed Epoch
August Li

Blessed Epoch: Book Three

Sasha was born to, and has always defined himself by, the secret assassins' Order of the Crimson Scythe. He chose the love of Yarrow L'Estrella and Duncan Purefroy over his duty to his clan, forfeiting his last mission and allowing Prince Garith to live. Now, the order—previously Sasha's family—has branded him a traitor. He's marked, and that means the brethren of the Crimson Scythe won't stop until Sasha is dead.

Garith's twin kingdoms balance on the brink of war, and all three men have reasons to help the king, whether loyalty, duty, the interests of their own lands, or gold in their pockets. Still, Yarrow and Duncan are willing to abandon their reasons to seek out and destroy the assassins' order to keep Sasha safe. But Sasha isn't sure that's what he wants. Loyalties are strained by both foreign invaders and conspirators in their midst. It's hard to know which side to choose with threats piling up from every direction and war looming, inevitable, on the horizon. Their world teeters on the precipice of change, and Sasha, Duncan, and Yarrow can only hope the links they've forged will hold if Garith's kingdom is torn apart.

www.dsppublications.com

Cairn and Covenant
Book Four of the
Blessed Epoch
August Li

Blessed Epoch: Book Four

An assassin's unexpected mercy granted Octavian Rose his life and freed him from his father's control, but it left him with little more than the clothes on his back and the determination not to waste his chance at a life of his choosing.

As Octavian sets out to make a name for himself, he refuses to compromise his ideals for money or status—a decision tested as he works his way up the ranks as a mercenary fighter and novice mage. Along the way he forges friendships, takes lovers, and makes bitter enemies, all while striving for the power he feels he deserves and can wield fairly.

With the advent of the Blessed Epoch and the discovery of new cultures, the world is changing. Octavian's decisions will affect not only those closest to him but will have profound worldwide consequences that he cannot begin to imagine. For twenty years, Octavian does what he must, and his choices bring him brilliant victories alongside crushing losses. Time and again, he must choose between what is right for all and what is beneficial to him, while hoping for the wisdom to tell the difference.

FREE Short—*A Lesson and a Favor*

Eight years before meeting Yarrow and Duncan in *Ash and Echoes*, the man now known as Sasha lived and breathed for a single purpose: to kill for gold and the glory of his cult and dark god without emotion or hesitation. In this lost tale of Sasha's early career, he's dispatched on a difficult mission—one with a surprise in store for him.

FREE Short—*Archer's Regret*

Sylvain Damasca has seen and done it all since walking away from his wealthy family and the promise of a future title. He's had more men, money, and adventure than he can count—including a part in the founding of Rosecairn—but he's restless, and no amount of gold, wine, or casual companionship can scratch his itch. It might be time to deal with the one thing he left unfinished, if he can find the courage to face the only man who ever got underneath his skin.

www.dsppublications.com

Calling
and Cull
Book Five of the
BLESSED EPOCH
AUGUST LI

Blessed Epoch: Book Five

Whose hand will orchestrate the change in the world?

The decade-long war with Johmatra is over, but peace hangs by a thread in Garith's kingdom. Yarrow, isolated in his island realm, refuses to abide by the treaty or to follow the dictates of the priestesses. Others—Octavian Rose among them—are uneasy with the growing military power of the temples, and the mage island of Espero remains a tenuous ally. Garith knows his people cannot weather another conflict and that infighting will leave their lands vulnerable to further invasion. The arrival of a Johmatran ambassador with his own agenda calls everyone's loyalties into question.

Sides will be chosen, and the consequences of those choices will have repercussions no one can foresee. Even among the turmoil, Yarrow is determined to have his vengeance against the thirteen goddesses and heal the world's magic. But how far will he go, and what lines is he willing to cross? As unlikely alliances are forged and enemies are revealed, Prince Thane seems to be the key to forgotten knowledge that will shape the future—and some will do whatever it takes to control him.

www.dsppublications.com

STUDIES IN DEMONOLOGY
ROGUE
IN THE
MAKING
TJ NICHOLS

Studies in Demonology: Book Two

The blood sacrifices have brought rain to Demonside, but across the void, the Warlock College of Vinland is still storing and gathering magic, heedless of the warnings of the international magical community. The underground is full of warlocks who disagree with the college, but do they care about wizards and demons or only about snatching power?

With a foot in each world, Angus is no longer sure whom he can trust. The demons don't trust humans, and even though he is learning more magic, he will never be one of them. He is human and only tolerated. Some demons would be happy to slit his throat. It's only because his demon is powerful in his own right that Angus is alive.

Saka only has a year to prove that Angus's people can change and that the magic taken will be rebalanced, but the demons want action. His affection for Angus is clouding his judgment and weakening his position in the tribe. Time is running out, and he must make a choice.

www.dsppublications.com

Choose your Lane to love!

Readers love the Little Goddess series by AMY LANE

Vulnerable

"What can I say about Amy's writing that I haven't already said? Not much. She's fantastic, I love everything she writes."

—Love Bytes

Wounded

"There is much darkness in this book, but there are rays of light as well. I look forward to furthering this series."

—Prism Book Alliance

Bound

"I loved this book. That's actually all I have to say. I loved it and it left me reeling."

—Gay Book Reviews

Rampant

"I think *Rampant, Vol 1* is my favourite book in the series."

—Prism Book Alliance

By AMY LANE

The Green's Hill Novellas

LITTLE GODDESS
Vulnerable
Wounded, Vol. 1
Wounded, Vol. 2
Bound, Vol. 1
Bound, Vol. 2
Rampant, Vol. 1
Rampant, Vol. 2
Quickening, Vol. 1
Quickening, Vol. 2

Published by DSP PUBLICATIONS
www.dsppublications.com